D1187281

The Man Who Would Be God

The Man Who

HAAKON CHEVALIER

Would Be God

G. P. Putnam's Sons   *New York*

For Carol

Though this novel confessedly has its point of departure in reality, it is a work of the imagination, and elements that have been borrowed from reality have been so transformed that any resemblance to actual persons or events is unintentional and fortuitous.

PART I: *Suspect*

For 'tis the sport to have the enginer
Hoist with his own petar.

HAMLET, III, iv

Chapter 1

EVER since that August day when she had met Sebastian for the first time, Tanya had had the feeling that she was walking on clouds. Not all the time. In fact, it was only a part of her, one side of . . . Anyway, everything connected directly with Sebastian was somehow not quite real—was, not less than real, nor more than real, but *other*.

She had gone to bed with him that very night without even having any idea who he was. She had been swept by a wave of emotion. Never would she forget what she had lived through that day: the extreme nervousness with which she had looked forward to making her first political speech before a large audience, heightened by her sense of the importance of the issue of peace at that grave hour of the world's history; the purely physical shock she had received when the first tomato had hit her; and then the dreadful panic that had seized her as she had sensed the savage awakening of the mob spirit.

Some thread of consciousness and responsibility had broken at that point, and what had happened subsequently had registered only in a twilight zone of her awareness: her arrest, her being hustled off, with Maggie Garnett and Hal Norberg and the others, pushed into the Black Maria, taken to the jail and booked. She was still dazed when, several hours later, she met Sebastian, whom Professor Garnett had introduced simply by saying, "My young colleague here has been kind enough to . . ."

It was only the next morning, awakening in a strange bed and finding him beside her, still asleep, that she had looked at him appraisingly, and that the realization had come over her as she studied his features relaxed in sleep, had come over her slowly, accompanied by a tingling in the back of her neck and up her scalp, and by a hardening of her nipples, that this man lying naked and vulnerable beside her was somehow molded of a different substance, was of a finer clay than the other men she had known.

She could not explain it, but she knew it with absolute certainty. He was not handsome, and his body was tortured. Looking at his face, which even in the repose of sleep had great expressiveness, and something of the eagerness and tenseness that she remembered from the night before, she found her imagination carried out of this century, out of this hemisphere.

She remembered the appeasing tumult of their first embrace —the need, the sureness, the tenderness—and how the image of a white swan had hovered over it. Leda? Lohengrin? The tactile memory of soft swanny down, of whiteness, of light and a river and floating, floating above a lurking primitive fear, a kind of sacred awe induced by the unfathomable and the immeasurable.

She was swept off her feet as completely as if she had been a giddy girl without any experience or even any knowledge of the facts of life. For weeks she had been as if benumbed, in a state of bliss bordering on what she imagined it must be like to be drugged by opium. Everything that had filled her life up to then became suddenly unimportant. She hardly ever saw her parents, to whom she was usually so close, she neglected her work for the party and missed her unit meetings for weeks on end. She even frequently cut her music classes, though her playing had suddenly taken on a new depth, and she kept up her practicing as assiduously as ever.

That first phase of intoxication did not last too long. She had of course known from the beginning that they belonged to different worlds. But there was all the unfamiliar ground to explore. He exerted a strange fascination over her, as she was sure he did over everyone else. He felt music as few people she knew did. He even was very tolerant of her political convictions, often attending political meetings and parties with her, contributing overgenerously when funds were solicited, and showed a certain interest in the problems that absorbed her. And yet the more she was with him the clearer it became that they were poles apart. It was not only that he was rich while she was poor, that he belonged to the world of privilege while she belonged to the workaday world. It was something more fundamental: she belonged to the earth, to the people who labored and struggled, he belonged to some more exalted sphere, accessible only to a very few.

When she woke up one day to discover that she was pregnant (it must have happened that first time), she suddenly realized that she must make a decision, especially as a new element had begun to creep into her feelings for Sebastian: she was falling in love with him. She often wondered what would have happened if Sebastian had not taken it into his head to buy her that piano. It had in any case changed the course of their lives. Every time she played it she was reminded of that day, and it was the one thing that she had never told him. She had come to him fully intending to bid him a last farewell. While he was away at Harvard she made up her mind to end her affair with him and, without telling him anything, to have an abortion. He lived in a world that was alien to her. Despite his tenderness, despite her love, there was something in him that frightened her. And then the piano appeared. The gesture itself infuriated her. It was perhaps for this very reason—she couldn't be sure—that she had changed her mind and decided to tell him.

When he insisted on their getting married and her keeping the baby, she completely broke down. Despite her misgivings she was unable to say no. Perhaps, then, he really loved her? If so, it was all right.

They took a ride all the way across the state border one weekend to get married—there was no point, Sebastian said, in advertising the fact that she was over two months pregnant.

And everything seemed to belie the anxiety that she had felt from the beginning. Sebastian was very sweet to her parents—both Russians. He bought her a car, an extravagant one, and she had to learn to drive. And they at once began looking for a house. Sebastian explained that the baby had to have a lot of air and space, a garden to play in. After inspecting dozens of places they settled on an old-fashioned, rambling one-story house that she immediately fell in love with. It had belonged to an artist and was partly furnished, and had a large garden around it. They moved in in March, and the baby was born in May. They named him Eugene, but from the first day they called him Gino.

Most reassuring of all was the way Sebastian had developed politically. This she was convinced was by no means, or was only indirectly, her doing. He suddenly became aware of the contemporary world, for the first time began to read the newspapers, to listen to the radio, to explore contemporary history and politics and economics. In an unbelievably short time he learned what it had taken her years to learn. He digested and remembered everything, and his insight and his imagination shed light on the multiple problems that were constantly arising. He joined and became active in the Teachers' Union, and then became involved in one group after another—committees for Spain, civil liberties, labor defense, Soviet-American friendship, the Chinese people, academic freedom. . . .

Shortly after the New Year, Bill Parrish came to them for a serious talk. Sebastian had already been approached by Bruce Patterson and Professor Cummings independently, and had decided to join the party. To her amazement Bill refused to let him actually become a party member. Sebastian would meet with the unit regularly, and in every way act as though he were a bona fide member, and the other members would so regard him; but he would pay no dues—he could make his own financial arrangements with the party, but outside the unit. Sebastian fought the idea vehemently, before he finally and reluctantly yielded.

"Why do you have to relegate me to the role of an *als ob?*" he grumbled.

Bill gave him a long look.

"A time may come," Bill said at last, "when it may prove to be of great advantage—for yourself, but possibly also for us— to know that you never were in fact a member."

"All right," Sebastian said then. "But no one is going to prevent me from regarding myself in my own mind and conscience as a communist."

"The way you feel inside," Bill replied, "is the only thing that really matters."

Also to her amazement, Bill was very insistent that *she* resign from the party immediately. She could work in broad front organizations, he said, but should keep out of fractions. Perhaps later . . . Sebastian would go into a closed unit that was to be kept small. When it got beyond a certain size it would split into two separate units. Bill himself would be the contact man for the district headquarters. When he was away one of the younger and less conspicuous members of the group would keep in touch with the organizer in charge of the closed units.

The upshot of it was that she was no longer a party member, but that Sebastian to all intents and purposes was. She was suddenly an outsider, while he was in. She had passed the torch on to him.

The reason for this abrupt reversal was, as Bill paradoxically explained it, that Sebastian had to be protected. The fact of his having married a communist would of course cause something of a stir, but was excusable in him, since he would be presumed not even to know what a communist was—but excusable only provided she detached herself immediately from her former affiliations. If Sebastian gradually became interested in progressive causes, his prestige would then carry its full weight. As for her, she was to retire to the relative obscurity of being a professor's wife, except that she should concentrate on her music and establish herself as a concert pianist.

All of which hurt her pride no little. She wanted to be out there fighting, side by side with her husband, for security, justice and peace. But Bill told her not to worry, that as Sebastian's wife she would be worth ten militant party members, and that in any case she should regard her retirement as only temporary and strategic. They could say what they liked, it was hard getting used to.

By the time the baby came in May they were well settled in

their new house. Sebastian was busy with his teaching and research, but at all hours of the day and night there were calls
upon him for help and advice from members of this, that or
the other committee. There were meetings several times a
week, there were letters, statements to the press, leaflets, mani-
festoes, protests to be drafted or edited. Every mail brought a
sheaf of newspapers, ranging from *The New York Times* to the
Daily Worker, periodicals, pamphlets, urgent pleas from one
cause or another. The house was constantly buzzing with graduate students deep in nuclear physics or engrossed in some political issue. Tanya developed a passion for gardening. She
practiced her music assiduously and was planning to give several concerts in the fall. On top of which they often had company for dinner, or went out for dinner, to movies, the theatre,
concerts, lectures. The days and weeks and months were too
short to hold everything that had to fit into them.

It was a full life—full enough, it seemed to her, especially
after Gino was born and began to do something besides eat and
sleep, to make a dozen people happy. And most of the time she
surely *was* happy. Yet often a strange mood would come over
her, and she would wonder. What was that vague sense of
menace that she felt hanging over her—over her, and Sebastian, and now Gino?

There were times when the life she had known before she
met Sebastian seemed so remote that she would even wonder
if she was still the same person. Her childhood memories were
framed by the small, dark, cluttered apartments that had been
her successive homes in town, and, before that, in New York
and Chicago. Her father, Fyodor Krylenko, who had come to
New York as the representative of a St. Petersburg food export-
ing firm, had become a book dealer. Her mother, Anna, who
was of an aristocratic Moscow family, was the daughter of a
diplomat who had committed suicide while on post in Washington, leaving his widow and daughter with a small annuity.
Tanya's parents had met in New York at a Russian Easter
party. All her early memories were dominated by Russia,
which she had never seen, built up for her by her parents' rem-

iniscences, by fairy tales and folk songs and all the Russian writers from Pushkin to Chekhov. Her father remained to this day a devotee of Tolstoi and Kropotkin, though he continued, without sharing the views of the new regime, to read avidly everything that came out of Russia.

Try as she would she found it impossible to *feel* what she had felt before she had met Sebastian. What had it been like, living with her parents in town in the small apartment back of the bookshop through the years of the depression and after: the affection and the gaiety (as well as the explosive quarrels) that often made them forget the chronically meager income; going to school, practicing four to six hours a day, giving occasional piano lessons? Or later, when she had taken a room of her own, with kitchenette, and had sung and played in night clubs, and had her first serious love affairs? Or still later, when she had gone to college, her first amateur concerts, the days and nights she went hungry, her brief career as a model in a life class (cut short because, as the art instructor explained, she "would have been perfect for Praxiteles, but was catastrophic for a class of wolf cubs who couldn't take their eyes off her long enough to look at the paper they were supposed to be drawing on")?

What could she recapture of the wonderful winter and spring with Bill Parrish, just before he went off to fight in Spain? Or of the two following years when partly in order to make his absence bearable she had plunged into agitational work for the party, concentrated study of her music, and many casual but comforting affairs, while waiting for Bill to come back?

And that was when she had met Sebastian.

Those years had been stormy and passionate and difficult, a time of searching, full of worries and uncertainties, but full also of the ideals, the slogans, the demands, the indignations of the party, of the warmth of comradeship, so full that it had whirled past like a moment; and when Bill came back, with wounds of the body but with faith and love unscathed, she found herself with child and committed to marrying a professor whom his colleagues looked up to as a towering giant in the most abstruse of scientific fields.

Was it the revelation of love that had drawn the screen between the present and the past? Ever since her first affair, at sixteen, when she had been rudely taken, and immediately after abandoned, by a clarinet player on whom she had had a terrible crush, she had made it a rule to blot out the past tense of love. Had she had five lovers or fifty? It did not matter. What mattered was that she had loved, and truly loved, and that this had been good; though love had always been a secondary thing: second to her ideals, second to her music. Her lovers had all been musicians or left-wingers, and quite often both. Her deepest attachment had been to Bill, leader of men, hero of Spain, whom she cherished still as a dear friend.

No. What Sebastian had brought her was the revelation of Sebastian. It had been so overwhelming that it had utterly changed her, changed the world, changed her relation to it, altered the weight and the sense and the flavor of all things for her.

Mark and Eve Ampter had been among the first to call after she had come home from the hospital, to have a look at the new citizen.

Tanya classified the people who formed her new entourage into three loose categories: A, her parents and a very few old family friends; B, Sebastian's and her left-wing friends, old and new (most of them old to her, all new to him); and C, Sebastian's friends, students, and university and scientific colleagues. The Ampters, while they partly fitted into categories B and C, were really in a category of their own. Tanya liked them both and felt quite at home with them. But it was really Sebastian who had struck up the acquaintance, and it always impressed her as a somewhat odd association to have taken hold.

There seemed offhand to be nothing about Mark to predispose Sebastian to single him out for attention, and perhaps one could merely fall back on the generalization that the basis of friendships was irrational and dictated by chance.

But Tanya could not get over the feeling that there was something more. There must be some secret attraction, perhaps some challenge in Mark's personality of which Sebastian himself might not even be aware, that served as a stimulus. Mark was intelligent, attractive, likable. But he certainly did not have a highly original mind, there did not seem to be any mysterious depths to probe in him. Perhaps, though, there was something else.

Meanwhile Mark was becoming more and more interested in progressive ideas. He had joined the Teachers' Union, he was active in several organizations, making speeches, doing committee work. He was obviously crazy about Sebastian, and Tanya had a hunch that it was largely because of Sebastian that he was being drawn into the left-wing movement. And perhaps that was secretly the reason why Sebastian was in turn drawn to him.

In Eve, whom she liked immensely, she had begun to sense lately an unaccountable reticence. From time to time when Sebastian and Mark were off to some meeting, Eve would come to the house to play four-hand piano pieces. But she would never talk about herself. She always had to be urged to come. And while she impressed one as an extremely natural sort of person, she often seemed ill at ease, especially when she was with Mark.

But this was not a time when the private life, whatever its satisfactions or its problems, allowed one to forget the world's troubles. Sebastian's growing concern with political problems was a measure of the aggravation of the international situation. The surrender of Madrid, the dissolution of the Czech republic, Italy's invasion of Albania, and then the announcement of a military and political alliance between Germany and Italy, were all signs pointing in one direction. In Manchukuo a border fight had broken out between Japanese and Soviet Mongol troops.

"We're headed for war," Sebastian kept repeating gloomily.

And at the same time new developments in his own special field were absorbing him more and more. He had to fly east for a scientific conference shortly after the baby was born. And again in July. But this time he took Tanya along, "for a piece of our overdue honeymoon"; and she spent several days visiting the New York World's Fair, while Sebastian and a dozen colleagues met in a classroom with a big blackboard, to discuss the mysterious atom.

It was only in August that they finally got away for a real vacation of several weeks. They went, taking Gino and a nurse along, up into the mountains of Wyoming. There Tanya met a quite new and different Sebastian: woodsman, hunter and nature lover. He was as much at home in the wilds as in a laboratory or drawing room. It was now just about a year since they had met, and when she thought about all that had happened to her, the change that had come into her life, she sometimes had to pinch herself to make sure she was not dreaming.

They breathed the wonderful mountain air, took long hikes, hunted and fished, swam in mountain lakes, ate ravenously, became tanned and healthy, and observed a pact that they had made not to look at a newspaper or listen to a radio or think about the problems of the world.

The mail that had accumulated by the time they got back in September, with all the newspapers and periodicals, filled several cartons. But what awaited them besides, when they got home, was the news of the Soviet-German pact and of the outbreak of war in Europe.

They had hardly entered the door in the early afternoon, carrying Gino and his things, when the telephone began to ring. It had probably been ringing constantly all those weeks. That evening more than twenty of Sebastian's students, as if in response to a secret signal—for no one had invited them— gathered at the house.

The talk lasted late into the night. Sebastian listened. The others had to fill in the picture for him of what had happened in the past weeks. They told him of the panic that the Soviet-German pact had caused among the Left, of the wild scramble for cover that the fellow-travelers were making, the frantic rush to dissociate themselves from the Soviet Union and from the native communist growth, and of all the breast-beating and recantation. All over the country, as Hitler marched into Poland, as the war in Europe spread, as the communists in France were being attacked and denounced as traitors, writers and publications whose attitude toward Russia had ranged from friendly tolerance to enthusiasm right up through the summer now suddenly discovered, each in his own way, but with a curious uniformity of pattern, that communism was a sinister conspiracy and that the Soviet Union was a totalitarian state in every way as reprehensible as Nazi Germany. Hundreds of party members, and even old and trusted leaders, were daily jumping off the train of history that Lenin had spoken of, panic-stricken by the unforeseen turn it had taken. The *Daily Worker* stuttered bravely, but made no sense.

Everyone had talked himself out, and in the ensuing silence, as the bottle of whisky was being passed around, all those young faces turned expectantly to Sebastian. He sat slouched in a big square armchair, exhausted after the long drive, looking as though he were miles away. Then he seemed to come to, straightened in his chair and reached for his pipe, but without trying to light it. He looked at the expectant faces. At last he spoke.

"Even in the worst situation," he said in a low voice, "there is a right move, and there are many wrong ones. Since the Western powers violated their pledge to Czechoslovakia in Munich, Russia's situation has been dangerously exposed. This is surely the right move. Because it's the one move that can foil the plot of a united attack on the Soviet Union by Germany and a coalition of Western nations—France and England, with American support. Beyond any question, the blueprint for this attack has top priority in the strategic plans of all the general staffs. The pact is not an alliance with Germany. It is a quarantining of Germany against any combination with the West. The whole foreign policy of the West since the World War has been directed to grooming crusaders for an anticommunist war. And now by one brilliant move Soviet diplomacy relegates the whole plot to the rubbish heap."

Sebastian paused and shook his head, and a sly grin passed over his face. "This is going to be beastly to explain," he said.

And after this there were many other sessions, with other students and with various colleagues, lasting far into the night.

One day Sebastian said to Tanya, "Don't you think Mark is ripe for joining the party?"

He had brought Mark's name up before the other members of his unit. They all knew him. They approved the suggestion, and it was agreed that Sebastian, since he knew him best, should feel him out—not actually to ask him to join (he must not expose himself), but to estimate his reliability.

"I would guess so," Tanya said. "But how are you going to go about gauging his reliability?"

"That's what I've been wondering." The question had not arisen for the other members.

"And yet," he said, "why shouldn't the same question arise for everyone? Discretion of course is one thing: some people are temperamentally so constituted that they can keep things to themselves without any effort, while others are perpetually spilling over. And there is conventional honesty. I think both qualities are fairly easy to determine. But reliability: that is a question of how a person will react under pressure, when subjected to extreme imperatives—to danger—to threats—to torture. How can one know anyone well enough to know how he will behave under circumstances of that kind? Perhaps it's something one can know even about oneself only when one is put to the test."

The question suddenly assumed a gravity she had not originally seen in it. It was true. Whom could you really trust? Could you even trust yourself, to the ultimate point?

"Well," said Sebastian, "let's have the two of them up for dinner some time next week. We've seen quite a lot of them, and got to know them a bit. But we've never looked at them and thought about them with this in mind. Let's just have an evening, and see how we feel about it."

For some reason she had been in the mood for a special evening, and she had gone to some trouble to prepare for it. The garden was lovely at this season, just when summer was turning into autumn, and many of the plants that she herself had put in were now blooming—late zinnias, early chrysanthemums, white and purple asters, roses and delphiniums. She had filled the house with flowers and made a large bouquet for Eve to take home.

Gino that evening had his first puréed carrots, which he took to like a little man, so that it was in a way an occasion for him too. Sebastian was just going through a little ritual play with him before he was to be put to bed, when the telephone rang —it never stopped ringing!—and Tanya picked him up while Sebastian went to answer, and waited for him to be finished so he could kiss Gino good night. She stayed within earshot just long enough to make sure it wasn't the Ampters begging off. She gathered that it was Sebastian's chairman, Professor Maynard Reed. As she walked off, carrying Gino in her arms, down the length of the living room toward the tall window overlooking the garden, she heard Sebastian's voice saying something about Einstein having written a letter to the President.

That other world, the world of science in which Sebastian was so much at home, would always be foreign to her, and it was partly this that gave him a quality of strangeness for her. She had wanted to learn something about it, and Sebastian had tried, in the beginning, to teach her some of the fundamentals. She had in fact learned quite a bit, particularly about how atomic science had developed from John Dalton down to the present, and become somewhat familiar with many of the terms that she heard Sebastian use when he "talked shop" with his science colleagues or his students.

She remembered the first time he had ever spoken to her

about science—it was the day he had given her the piano, the day that had changed so many things for her, and for him as well. She remembered his excitement, speaking of the discoveries that had revolutionized his field in the last forty years.

"I wish I could convey to you," he had said, trying to bring it down to terms she could understand, "something of the sense of dedication that animates those of us who are working in this field—and I don't mean only the top people, like Heisenberg, Dirac, Oppenheimer, Hahn or Enrico Fermi, but our students as well. We all have the awareness that we are on the threshold of one of the greatest adventures in the history of mankind. . . ."

That last phrase, particularly, had recurred to her again and again. And she had tried to make some sense of the infinitely complex things that went on inside the atom. But when they began talking about the wave and particle properties of matter, Planck's constant, Heisenberg's uncertainty principle, Shroedinger's wave equation and the whole field of quantum theory, her mind simply went blank.

Holding the baby in her arms, looking at him and trying fully to digest the fact that this was Sebastian's son, that Sebastian had engendered this tiny creature who had to be fed and washed and have his diapers changed, that same sense of strangeness that she so often had when she thought of Sebastian came over her again.

But why do I feel this way? she wondered.

The Leda myth reverted to her mind, and in turn brought up another image from way back in her childhood. She could not immediately place it, and then it came to her: it was in a fairy tale . . . one of Andersen's she was quite sure . . . Swans . . . *The Wild Swans*. What Tanya particularly remembered was that at the climax of the story the little princess had finished all the tunics, except one sleeve of the last and smallest one . . . The image of the little prince with one white swan's wing had haunted her whole childhood, and she thought of it now in connection with Gino. She had to glance at him to reassure herself that he had two perfectly good arms.

"You've seen the news?" Mark asked, almost before he and Eve had got inside the door.

Having just got Gino to bed and listened to Sebastian telling him impossible stories about creatures that never existed, Tanya was still a little up in the clouds, and did not at once understand.

Sebastian said, "You mean about Russia invading Poland?"

"Yes."

Sebastian managed to dodge the question. He mixed martinis, and the conversation, starting with a discussion of a Tibetan painting of his done on *tang-ka* that hung on the wall, moved to Chinese painting and Oriental art in general, to the Japanese invasion of China, to imperialist war; and by the time they went in to dinner had settled on American foreign policy.

Eve accompanied Tanya out into the kitchen to help her bring things to the table. Tanya had had a definite impression this time when Eve and Mark had appeared at the door, that there was some kind of strain between them. She would have liked to sound her out tactfully, but Eve was a girl who had herself well in hand, and she did not respond to Tanya's invitation to confidence.

Her reserve did break down, however, when Tanya opened the refrigerator and brought out a huge covered bowl.

"What's that?" Eve asked.

"It's our first course," said Tanya, removing the lid. The bowl was filled with caviar.

"Oh, my sainted aunt!" Eve exclaimed.

Caviar had been for Tanya all her life not so much a coveted luxury as an expensive necessity that one must periodically, by whatever desperate expedients, somehow manage to afford. Sebastian had taught her how really to enjoy it. It was very simple. You had to know it and understand it, of course, to begin with. And then the important thing was to eat a lot of it, without any fillers on the side. Just a little lemon juice, "to raise the flavor one octave," as Sebastian put it, with a floor of black bread under it and a crystal canopy of vodka over it.

That and nothing else. It made an excellent first course, exactly fulfilling Sebastian's ideal of luxurious simplicity.

The caviar and vodka diverted the conversation from diplomatic to gastronomical channels. To everyone's amazement, they managed to empty the bowl of caviar as well as the bottle of vodka.

Mark jumped up when Tanya called for a strong man to bring in the next course, the *pièce de résistance*, which was served in the big copper casserole that it was cooked in. It was a special dish of Tanya's, with split lobster tails in their shells, quartered chickens, okra, wild mushrooms, onions, herbs and saffron.

"If everyone could eat food like this every day," said Mark, "there would be no wars, no social problems, no economic problems . . ."

". . . And we should have to talk about other things," said Sebastian.

There was a bright little glint in his eye as he lifted his glass of 1923 Vosne-Romanée, and Tanya knew that her dinner was a success.

As the conversation moved lightly through the rest of the dinner—from salad to Marxism to cheese to the French economy to dessert to Tom Anderson's political views to coffee and brandy in the living room, with many topics in between—Tanya kept glancing at Mark and Eve and thinking about them in the light of the question of Mark's reliability.

"Would you feel like playing a little?" Sebastian asked her, as they were sitting relaxed in the living room.

"Yes, do, please!" said Eve.

She was practicing these days Beethoven's Fourth Piano Concerto, the G-major one, for a concert she was going to give with the W.P.A. orchestra in October. She knew the whole piece thoroughly by now, though there were many passages she needed to practice further, and she could roam at will over its beckoning fields of harmony, exploring its riches along bypaths of variations, giving free rein to her bent for improvisation.

She sat down to the piano—*her* piano. She played the muted opening notes of the first, the allegro, movement, which are scored for the piano alone—a B chord, first sustained, then repeated in four quarter notes that establish the rhythmic pattern of the first theme, followed by a slow, faltering upward movement which is taken up, with more force, by the orchestra before it bursts into the triumphant clarion call of the second theme.

Music, which had always been a dominant passion with her, had acquired an even deeper meaning for her since she had known Sebastian. For him it was not, as for her, a creative medium, a discipline, a realm of symbols and meanings to be explored and conquered, but a haven. Not, however, just a safe place to escape to when the pressures of life became too great, but a world whose laws and categories were self-contained and into which nothing foreign to it need enter. He did not become passive and immerse himself in music as in a soothing bath, like so many so-called music lovers. His mind continued to work actively even here. He had an apparently spontaneous grasp of musical structure, and when he listened even to a large orchestra he actually heard *all* the voices, both individually and in their harmonic relationships. He could analyze and reconstruct a whole symphony in all its essentials after a single hearing.

But music for him was play and not a means of ordering experience. It was a realm of freedom, perhaps the only realm in which he could escape the oppressive consciousness of his superior powers and the loneliness it condemned him to. He had never told her this, of course, but she sensed it. What she, on the other hand, had always looked for in her music was a cherished solitude, a sense of her own identity defined not in relation to other people but in terms of her own oneness and wholeness. Now, in this magic realm, without ceasing to find herself, sovereign and inviolate, she also found Sebastian—but a different Sebastian: not the Sebastian of the dizzy heights, of the swift, unerring mind, of the strong will, but a Sebastian stripped of everything but his sentient, receptive humanity. Her music, she now knew, was for him not just a pleasure or stimulus or change of climate: it was a need.

As the bonds of the evening loosened, and the Ampters prepared to go home, Tanya again became aware of the strain between the two of them—as though both felt a reluctance to leave the company of others and to find themselves alone with each other again.

Sebastian pressed on Mark a last drink of brandy as a stirrup cup.

"Only enough to hold me," Mark said, "while you answer that question we began with."

"You mean the Polish business." Sebastian squeezed his lower lip thoughtfully between his thumb and forefinger. "Suppose you answer that one yourself."

Mark wanted to dodge it, but Sebastian insisted.

"What if a group of your students were to ask you why Russia invaded Poland? What would you tell them?"

Mark scratched his head and made a visible effort to order his ideas. "Well," he said at last, "I'd have to begin, I guess, by going into the reasons for the German-Soviet Pact . . ." and he gave, in his own way, substantially the same analysis that Tanya had heard Sebastian expound.

Sebastian nodded agreement. "That seems to me just about right. And I'm afraid practically no one will believe it." A light danced in his eyes which made him look very young. "But that's no reason why one shouldn't say it!"

"But what about us?" said Mark. He finished his drink and put down his glass. "When do you think we'll be dragged into the war?"

Sebastian shook his head. "There's only one thing I'm sure of. We'll stay out as long as the pact remains in effect. That may not be too long. In any case, there's a lot of misery ahead."

After the Ampters had left, Tanya let herself sink back on the down cushions of the sofa, and the warmth of Sebastian's nearness hovered over her. She was very tired, as she often was these days. She kicked off her shoes, and Sebastian poured a

little more of the oil-smooth cognac into her snifter. The doctor said her fatigue was an aftermath of having the baby, but
it wasn't only that. It was everything—all the things that had
happened, the new life, the new responsibilities. But at least,
as far as the great big problems were concerned—wages, social
justice, civil liberties, racial equality, and the issue of war and
peace—she had passed a part, the larger part, of the burden
over to Sebastian. He was so much clearer, so much more effective, than she was. She had loved the old days, of course,
when she had been active on her own, but now she was being
carried along in Sebastian's wake, the way made smooth for
her—though he always turned to her for advice, and never
made a decision without consulting her.

Sebastian was sitting in the armchair opposite the sofa, his
legs stretched out and his feet crossed, toying with his pipe.
Had he come to any conclusions, she wondered, about Mark's
reliability?

"By the way," she said, "did you notice anything about Eve?"

"Eve? . . . She was a little nervous, wasn't she?"

"Yes. I think there's something between them. She holds
something against him."

"Oh?"

"What do you think?"

"I don't know."

"I mean, would it make any difference?"

"About his joining our group? That would depend." He
fell silent. "I don't think it can be anything serious."

"No, I'm sure not."

"They both seem very well-balanced. And essentially well-
adjusted."

"Eve takes no interest in things political."

"Yes, we've gone into that."

"But is it indifference? Or is it a form of protest?"

"I don't know. It's probably not fundamental."

"Probably not."

She turned her head to face him. "But taking him into your
group is serious."

"Yes."

"You *trust* him?" It was a statement, rather than a question. "Yes."

He considered it for a moment. "You see, trust and trustworthiness—like all moral terms, they're terribly tricky. It isn't the most suspicious people who're the least often fooled, nor the most trustworthy who are the most often trusted."

He got up and began to pace.

"We live in a time of suspicion, unfortunately. And suspicion is cumulative, and breeds fear and intolerance. I think that this is the sign of sickness, this lack of trust in people, and it leads to the denial of freedom, to the suppression of ideas, to arbitrary government and regimentation. This is what we are fighting, this is what we *must* fight, or it will destroy us. And this is why we must trust one another."

Stretched out on the sofa, luxuriously able to wiggle her toes within the sheath of her silk stockings, feeling the delicious sweet sharpness of the brandy invading her, Tanya was enjoying a sense of curious detachment. She was floating on a kind of misty plateau from which she could contemplate everything with serenity.

"I sometimes wonder about you and Mark," she said. Her own voice sounded a little odd to her. "Actually, you have very little in common."

Sebastian was nodding and smiling, and it occurred to her that his face now had a peculiarly Jewish cast.

"Yes," he said. "I've wondered about that myself." He was standing before her, looking down at her. "There is so much we do not know," he said slowly. "We are given a little time—all too short a time—to learn more than can ever be learned: man's relation to the universe, man's relation to man, and man's relation to himself. I have a sneaking suspicion that those of us who seem to the world at large to be the most disinterested—I mean scientists, concerned with matter and motion and so on, things that seem to have nothing to do with themselves as anatomical entities composed of bones and flesh and the rest—are actually as much concerned with that third category of problem as with anything else: I mean with man's relation to himself."

He broke away from the position he had been standing in for several minutes, and sat down in the armchair opposite her.

"I suppose," he said, "that if I were to be absolutely honest, I should have to say that the thing that draws me to Mark is that he reflects me in a way I like to see myself in." He thought for a moment. "He gives me the feeling that he likes me precisely for reasons which I should most like to be liked for —and which," he added with a malicious smile, "I should probably like myself for if I had happened to be somebody else."

A question that had often prodded her came back to her.

"Doesn't the fact that Mark isn't a scientist, and can therefore not communicate with you in an area that is so important to you, rather limit the range of the feelings you can have for him?"

He shook his head. "We really don't know ourselves, of course. But to the extent that we do, I think a parallel professional interest is a complicating factor." He looked up, an enigmatic expression on his face. "Like sex."

But she would not let the talk become too subtle, or range too far afield.

"That means, I take it, that you're in favor of Mark's joining your group."

He nodded gravely. "I think he'll be fine."

Chapter 2

MARK had said to himself in those first months, This is a job. There is this to be done. I must take such and such steps. . . .

He was by nature methodical and energetic; he was professionally ambitious; and what was more, he was challenged by this assignment—it was "big," and he had been given a great responsibility.

It was a busy time for him, because in actual fact he was holding down two jobs, and he couldn't neglect either of them, even though the university job was only a cover. As it had worked out, it was the university job that necessarily took up most of his time since it was geared to a daily routine and was something he could not allow to pile up. And it embraced three activities, each of which could have been a full-time job: teaching, attending courses, and doing research for a Ph.D. thesis. Besides which, he was a married man and the head of a family.

All had gone relatively smoothly during the months following his interview with the Chief. He had concentrated on his university work. He had taken a full schedule of courses, and striven to make himself at home in the field of economics and to become acquainted with the various members of his department. He had had to do an enormous amount of reading. He had got along well with Anderson, who would occasionally invite him and Eve over to his house for an evening, and he was exploring the possibilities of a thesis subject that might grow out of a study of the steel industry since the turn of the century that he was making in connection with his professor's seminar on corporate structure. Teaching was a completely novel experience for him, and he found it richly rewarding.

Because his investigation of Sebastian Bloch was a long-term project, he was able to pursue it without having a feeling that he was under pressure. He joined the Teachers' Union, where he regularly ran into Bloch and most of his left-wing entourage.

He had regarded the Teachers' Union initially merely as a breeding ground for subversive activities. Its meetings were the occasion for stormy debates on every national and international issue, the local almost invariably taking a radical position, and the main activities seemed to revolve around protests, pleas, resolutions and fund raising, and were concerned with strikers, jailed labor leaders, antilabor laws and matters even more remote from the teaching profession. And at these monthly meetings and in the committees that he was invited to join he was able to gather plenty of material for the reports that he was sending in more or less regularly to the Chief's office.

But there was another side to the Teachers' Union's activity, and as he came to know it better he was bound to recognize that it absorbed more of its members' attention than he had realized in the beginning. A great part of their energies went to recruiting membership among the schools and colleges, and they were basically concerned with educational problems. Mark was giving more and more thought to teaching as a profession, and he had to recognize that there was nothing really subversive about the union's slogan, "Democracy in Education —Education in Democracy." The cause the union fought for —more and better schools, more and better teachers, higher standards of scholarship, greater independence for the teaching profession and recognition of its high dignity—was a cause that made sense to him. He had the same conflicting feeling about it that he had about Bloch himself. Bloch was a communist, and therefore subversive. But exactly what did it mean, to be subversive?

For a time after his last conference with the Chief, Mark had been able to keep all disturbing ideas in the background. "Compartmentalize" was a word the Chief often used. He stressed the importance of keeping separate things in separate compartments. And for months Mark had tried rigidly to compartmentalize. There was his family life; there was his professional life; and there was the academic life that served as a cover. There was the investigation of Sebastian Bloch, and the duty that went with it, of reporting Bloch's movements and activities. And there was Sebastian Bloch the human being. How easy it would be, he thought, to fall under the sway of that magnetic personality! But he knew he must not, and he fought it.

When in May, after the Blochs had had their baby, Mark and Eve had gone to call on them, it was the first time Mark had seen Mrs. Bloch since he and Eve had had cocktails with the Blochs in their apartment last November. It was also the first time he had seen the new house in broad daylight, though Eve had been there several times in the afternoon to play the piano and had been impressed by how grand the place was. To make the occasion even more memorable, this was the time they had all agreed to call one another by their first names.

It was when he began to think of him as Sebastian rather than as Dr. Bloch that Mark, for the first time since the Chief had tried to straighten him out, had become prey to serious qualms about his assignment. Sebastian was coming to regard him more and more as a friend. How could he go on, under the cloak of friendship, building up a file that could someday do him incalculable harm? Yet this was what he had contracted to do, what he was being paid to do, and what it was his duty to do. The Chief had put his trust in him. He couldn't let him down.

It had been purely by chance that the existence of Sebastian Bloch had come to the attention of the security service in the first place. Mark had then been on the force for two years. An attractive Russian girl, Tanya Krylenko, a night-club entertainer who was a Communist Party member and under routine observation, had been followed to Sebastian Bloch's apartment; and after that, Bloch had been spotted with the girl at a number of left-wing gatherings.

It was the first time since his initial interview, when he had been taken on the force, that Mark had sat down in the Chief's office. Normally the Chief would stand up when you came in, and start walking slowly toward the door as he talked, and when he and you reached the door the business had been transacted. But not this time.

Occupying the same gray leather armchair, in exactly the same place as on his first interview, Mark had had the illusion of experiencing those two moments of time simultaneously. The morning rays of the same late September sun had been caught by the curved steel slats of the gray Venetian blinds screening the south and east windows, and were diffused in this shadowless gray office room; the gray walls, the gray linoleum floor with its plain gray carpet, the gray steel desk, all had the same bareness, and he had been conscious of the same indefinable aseptic odor. And behind that desk, devoid now as then of an ash tray, the same J. W. Gregg who at forty-two as at forty gave the impression that he was made of stuff impervious to the corroding tooth of time. The same silver-gray hair, the same steel-gray eyes, the same handsome, square-cut face on which thought, laughter, pain, sorrow, had left no trace.

The moment of illusion had passed. The Chief had pulled out a folder from the left top drawer of his desk and thumbed through its contents.

"Let's see," he had said, without looking up. "You left the University in 'thirty-five . . . Two years in law school . . . You never got your law degree . . ." The angle of his head had shifted almost imperceptibly and he had looked at Mark. "Ever think of going back?"

"No, sir. That is . . ."

"I know. Your father's accident. And then your marriage. But practical considerations apart, have you ever contemplated going back?"

"Well, naturally I've thought about it, but—"

Mark had been puzzled. The Chief was not given to asking idle questions.

"I like my job," Mark had said. "And I know I can't do both."

The Chief had looked at him. There was no expression in the small steely eyes, but from the slight muscular contraction around their inner corners Mark had recognized what was meant to be a look of measured approval.

"You're a good man, Ampter. Your record is one hundred per cent."

The Chief had let the sheet of paper he was holding drop back on the pile of documents in the folder. He had looked at Mark squarely.

"But we're thinking of sending you back to school."

He had not given Mark time to sort out his reactions or put them into words.

"Up to now," he had continued, "all the cases you've handled have involved federal crimes. The thing we have in mind is an assignment of a quite different kind. It's a far tougher one than any you've ever tackled."

He had paused, to let this sink in.

Mark had desperately wanted a cigarette, but it was an unwritten law that no one smoked in the Chief's office. The Chief had reached into a drawer and brought out a big square ash tray of heavy glass and placed it on the edge of the table closest to Mark.

"Go right ahead," he had said.

Mark had been flabbergasted. "Sure you don't mind, sir?"

"Not a bit."

With the first drag of smoke Mark's self-possession had returned.

"I'm at your orders, sir."

The Chief had leaned back in his swivel chair and folded his hands, fingers interlaced.

"This isn't that kind of assignment, Ampter. I can't order you to take it on. The decision has to be entirely yours." He had laid his hands flat on his desk. "In fact, if you were to take this on, the first thing I would have to do would be to ask you to hand me your letter of resignation."

Mark's left hand, holding the cigarette, had frozen a few inches from his lips.

"All right, now let me tell you about it."

The Chief pulled open the shallow center drawer of his desk and took out a large file card.

"Does the name Sebastian Bloch mean anything to you?"

"Not a thing, sir."

He reached over and took the card that the Chief handed
him, and glanced at the meager data on it.

"Sebastian Bloch," he said.

A professor of physics at the University. Very young for a
full professor. Mark made the calculation from the birth date:
only thirty-two. Born in Philadelphia. Private school; University of Chicago; Europe; Collège de France in Paris; Kaiser
Wilhelm Physical Institute in Berlin; Cambridge . . . Mark
noted that all the items concerned the man's academic career.
There were no other entries except, at the bottom of the card,
several names. In the upper left-hand corner was a small
blurred photograph, a copy of a passport picture, obviously
taken when the subject was considerably younger.

Mark examined the photograph for a moment. It was in
fact the face of a youth of barely twenty. Something about it,
despite the fact that the values of the face were distorted as in
any passport photograph, struck Mark as uncommon, yet he
could not put his finger on it. It was a lean, angular face, whose
bone structure, for all the youthful softness of the contours, already suggested something akin to austerity. The hair (one
could not tell from the picture whether it was light or dark)
looked fine and straight, and was brushed down over the forehead, where it made an untidy shadow. The nose was long, thin
and asymmetrical, and the ears large, but close to the skull.
The mouth was only a faint line of shadow in the picture, and
the chin was similarly hard to make out. The wide eyes looked
dreamy. So far as the features composed at all—and perhaps
this was only the effect of the poor, smudged likeness—they
conveyed a disconcerting impression of guilelessness combined
with unflinching assurance.

Was it this man, Mark wondered, who was demanding that
whoever worked for him should resign? He looked up at the
Chief and put the card back on the desk.

"How does he come into the picture, sir?" he asked.

"He doesn't come into it," said the Chief. "He *is* the picture."

Mark said nothing. He had handled important cases before: fraud, trade violations, blackmail, labor disputes, kidnaping, murder. But he realized that this business was of quite a different order.

"Let me give you a little background," said the Chief.

He leaned forward in his chair, facing Mark, hands clasped between his knees.

"You read the papers. You see the way things are moving, abroad. One of these days Germany and Russia are going to be at each other's throats, and it may not be a long way off. When that happens, we're going to be pulled in, sure as shooting. As a matter of fact the thinking in Washington is that we can't live with either communism or fascism. Sooner or later we may have to destroy both. We could of course let Hitler and Stalin fight it out first, and then take on the winner. But that's been ruled out. It's too risky. There's always the danger of their joining forces. So we'll have to get into it. However things stack up, what we have to look forward to for the foreseeable future is trouble. So we're starting to get ready for it—quietly, but from the ground up. And that's where you come in."

A long ash had formed on Mark's cigarette. He cautiously conveyed it to the glass receptacle and crushed out the stub.

"Modern wars," the Chief continued, "call for all-out mobilization of manpower and resources; but, perhaps even more importantly, for the mobilization of brain power. They are fought on the ground, at sea, and in the air. But they may be won or lost in the blueprint rooms and in the laboratories. It used to be the brains of statesmen and the military that counted. They still count, of course. But now—and get this, Ampter—it's the longhairs who may turn the trick."

Mark's attention snagged on the word "longhairs." Somehow he would not have expected it from the Chief. He uncrossed and recrossed his legs and reached into his pocket for another cigarette.

"This," the Chief went on, "creates a wholly new problem. Statesmen are trained in the game of international politics, and the military in the game of war. But these science fellows know nothing about either. And some of them have some pretty wild-eyed notions. The problem is how to keep them in line."

"How do you mean, sir?"

"I mean politically—and in other ways. These are valuable men. Indispensable, in fact. But because of that, anything they do or say, or even think— You see what I mean. What it comes down to is security."

The Chief reached for the Bloch file card where Mark had left it on the desk, and without looking at it held it upright, resting on the blotter, bracing it with his fingertips.

"So much for the generalities. We'll have to go into all this in detail when the time comes. But now let me tell you about this Sebastian Bloch. In the first place, as you see, we have practically no checked data on him. What we have here"—he reached again into the middle drawer, and pulled out a thin folder—"is mostly in the realm of hearsay, though some of it is pretty reliable. It's at least something to start with."

He let the folder drop to the desk, joined his hands and leaned toward Mark.

"This man—" he said, and paused. "Let me put it this way: we have reason to believe this man possesses the best set of scientific brains in the country—maybe in the world, we don't know. Several things about him are rather special, apart from his brilliance. For one thing"—he pointed to the papers before him—"he's said to have what they call a universal mind. He doesn't limit himself to one specialty like most scientists, but seems to be completely at home in the whole realm of science, and in the arts as well. Another thing: he seems to have little or no personal ambition. He's published quite a bit, of course, under his own name, highly technical stuff . . ." He referred to the papers in the pile. "Mathematical theory, quantum mechanics, spectrum analysis . . . But the story is that most of the important contributions he has made have been ideas passed on to colleagues and students, or work done in collaboration, for which he has never claimed credit. The result is that no one knows the exact extent of his contribution to recent developments, but everyone agrees that it's immense."

He paused for a moment, and then went on: "There's one last thing. Doesn't seem to make too much sense, but these reports harp on it. It's—how shall I say?—well, here: why don't I read you . . ."

He thumbed through the pile of papers.

"Let's take this one. Quote: 'Any account of the man, even a cursory one, would be incomplete without the mention of a quality which strikes all who approach him, and which for want of a better term I will call his "spirituality." It is an indefinable quality, and can perhaps most helpfully be likened to a kind of invisible light that radiates from his presence. He exerts a charm that few can resist, gives off a warmth that communicates itself to those around him. If he were not the hard-headed scientist that he is, and if we were living in an age of faith, one would be tempted to regard him as touched with saintliness. This exceptionally gifted young man, I am deeply convinced, will conquer new worlds, not only in the realm of matter but of the spirit.' Unquote."

The Chief looked up. "That was written by a man who is a hardheaded scientist himself—an electronics engineer, and one of the country's top production administrators."

The Chief rose, pushed back his chair, and walked slowly around his desk, his head sunk between his shoulders, his hands deep in his trouser pockets. Mark followed his movements as though he were watching the mechanism of his own thinking processes working at a knotty problem. The Chief stopped just in front of him.

"All this, as you well realize, has nothing directly to do with why we are interested in Sebastian Bloch, though it explains the degree of our interest. The reason we come into the picture is this—" He looked at Mark sharply. "There's a Mr. Hyde to this Dr. Jekyll. It looks as if our young scientist isn't one hundred per cent saint. He's been traveling lately in pretty bad company . . ."

The Chief told briefly about the Russian girl being followed to Bloch's apartment, and about Bloch being seen with her at left-wing meetings.

". . . To put it bluntly, Ampter," said the Chief, "we suspect Sebastian Bloch is a communist, or something pretty damn close to it."

Mark had had occasion many times, in the weeks that followed, to wonder whether his decision had been ill-considered, even foolish. The Chief had urged him to take his time, but Mark had said, without hesitation: "I've already made up my mind. I'll take on the assignment." But what had he in fact taken on?

The time had been too much absorbed by immediate things to allow him to give his full attention to that problem. He was off the office payroll. He was getting an expense account. A promotion and a raise that went with the assignment were being credited to him—"*if* you come back," the Chief had added, with a dead look in his eye. Mark had been game. He hadn't even consulted Eve. But—what had he in fact taken on?

The first problem had been to establish a status for himself in the University community. He had originally planned to go back to Law School. But it became obvious that if he were to enroll as a law student with the hope of lasting more than one semester he would have to devote his full time to it, and this was out of the question. After a good deal of shopping around, he decided that economics was his best bet. His two years of law would be a great asset. He could be working for a Doctor's degree, and he could make his candidacy last as long as he wanted to. And as luck would have it, he even got an appointment as a teaching assistant. It was a perfect cover.

Eve had been difficult.

"I don't get it," she had kept saying, when he had tried to explain to her about the assignment.

The trouble had been that he wasn't too clear about it himself. Or rather, no—that wasn't quite true. He had been very clear about the exalted function of the police, secret or otherwise. The maintenance of law and order. But more than that: the function of the police was as much positive as it was negative—more so, in fact. It was like medicine. Preventive medicine—crime prevention. The American home, the American way of life, American institutions. The policeman should not be a forbidding figure of a stern, punishing man with a stick and a gun, the terror of evildoers. Much more, he should be a reassuring symbol of peace and orderliness to upright citizens, the protector of the weak, the guide, the helping hand. He was a safeguard, a guarantee, a positive force.

But—well, Mark's present assignment was altogether different from any he had ever handled before; and the man he was after this time was not an embezzler, a forger, a kidnaper, but —a scientist.

Eve kept asking awkward questions. "What has he done?"

In the three years of their marriage they had not had a serious quarrel. Now he could feel the air becoming charged.

The question as to how he was to meet this Sebastian Bloch and work up an acquaintance had of course been uppermost in his mind from the beginning. But there had been too many practical matters to attend to at first, and weeks had passed without his ever getting a glimpse of him. However, the assignment was a long-term one, and he could afford to move slowly. Above all he had to be careful to make no false step. And meanwhile there had been plenty of preliminary work to keep him busy. Since he was investigating Bloch, he would also have to investigate all Bloch's contacts. The office had supplied him with a certain amount of material to start with: individuals, organizations, activities. He had kept his eyes open, got around, met people, taken his bearings.

The first time he had laid eyes on the man who was his quarry he had totally failed to realize who he was until afterwards; a fact that still rankled with him, months later. The occasion had been his first luncheon at the Faculty Club, which he had immediately joined on receiving the invitation to membership automatically sent out to all teaching appointees. In the crowded dining room, among three or four hundred colleagues, young and old, with the buzz of talk and the clatter of dishes all around, he had for some reason noticed this man crossing the room. There was nothing really remarkable about his looks—nothing, at least, that he had been aware of at the time. But later he had realized that this was because of a mysterious quality in the man that made you immediately accept him on an equal footing, as though he were an ordinary mortal like yourself, whereas you really knew that he belonged to a different order of beings: a legendary character, perhaps a hero of classic tragedy. But this, Mark knew, was absurd, and whenever subsequently such a notion had crept into his mind he had severely dismissed it.

The man had blond hair, thick, short and rather unkempt, of an indeterminate shade, dark eyes, a lean face that at first glance looked suffering and haunted, but at second glance brooding and benign. He was of medium height and thin, and his way of moving suggested a slight physical deformity, an irregularity that wasn't a limp or a twist of the body but was nevertheless perceptible, perhaps a trace of some spinal ailment—and Mark had told himself at first that it was this that had attracted his attention.

A couple of minutes later he had seen the man cross the room again in the opposite direction, escorting a much older, stocky, gray-haired man whom he seemed to envelop in a warm aura of welcoming and deferential attentions. Some distinguished visiting professor, no doubt. Mark had noticed the two settle at a small table at the far end of the room, and all through luncheon he had found himself again and again watching that distant figure. Not once had it occurred to him that the man might be Sebastian Bloch.

He had seen him again on several occasions. Each time he had been aware of a peculiar attraction, an indefinable fascination which the man seemed to exert not only on Mark but on the people around him. Sometimes in a crowd, for instance, Mark would feel an irresistible impulse to turn his head and look in a certain direction, and he would see that it was Bloch. He soon discovered that what made him turn his head was not any mysterious telepathic force, but simply the fact that a special look came into people's faces in Bloch's presence, and he had come unconsciously to recognize it before he realized what it was linked with.

Getting back into the academic routine after an absence of two years and undertaking a teaching assignment for the first time had constituted a major challenge, and Mark had found himself working harder, for longer hours, than he had ever done before. The professor under whose guidance he was to do his graduate work had turned out to be something of a slave driver. But as he had got to know him better, he had come to like him more and more.

Thomas Anderson was youngish, dynamic, caustic in manner, a fighter and a rebel. In his seminar on Corporate Structure, the third volume of Karl Marx's *Capital* was on the required reading list.

"I'm assuming," Anderson had announced at the first meeting of the seminar, "that you've all read the first two volumes. If not, you don't belong here."

Mark's study of Marx's work had been limited to the rapid perusal, at the investigators' training school in Chicago, of extracts from the *Communist Manifesto,* and other, mainly polemical writings, wrapped in a body of commentary that necessarily had a certain slant. But the seminar was a requirement for the doctorate, and in any case Mark felt that if he attempted to dodge it he would be shirking his duty. Here was an exceptional opportunity, which the service could not usually offer its operatives, of getting a thorough grounding in the basic principles and the philosophy that he had been called upon to combat.

He had told Anderson that he had read the volumes, though a long time ago, and that he would immediately reread them. For weeks he had sat up night after night, after a hard day's work, trying to cover at least thirty pages at a sitting, wrestling with data, concepts and a point of view so alien that in large areas he could only mechanically register the matter dealt with.

As he got to know Anderson better he began to wonder about his political views. Certainly he was a left-winger. And he claimed to be a more than casual friend of Sebastian Bloch's. Perhaps Mark would be able to meet Bloch through him.

One day in December Tom Anderson had said to him, "Going to the Spanish Bazaar Festival next Friday?"

"I hadn't planned to," said Mark, "I didn't know about it."

"It's a big shindig that's being put on by the Spanish Refugee Committee. A good cause. And you might enjoy it."

When Anderson mentioned that Sebastian Bloch was sure to be there, Mark decided he must attend the party.

The place was crowded, and Mark and Eve had had to edge their way in slowly. In the middle of the big entrance hallway Mark found himself pushed up against a stunning blond girl in a very low-cut candy-pink taffeta evening dress. He let his eyes drop from the dream-face with its big blue eyes, rested them for a fleeting moment on the dazzling exposed area of her bosom, then followed the long slender movement of her bare arms from her satin-smooth shoulders, just a few inches away, down to the tray she was holding, trimmed with yellow, red and purple ribbon, and piled with gardenias.

"Don't you want to buy a gardenia for your wife and help the boys who're fighting in Spain?" she asked with an enchanting smile.

"Why—yes, of course!" He felt flustered, and the purity of those large blue eyes made him uncomfortable.

"It's one dollar," the flower girl said enticingly.

"No, don't . . ." Eve signaled to him. But just then a handsome Spanish-looking youth appeared from nowhere. With a ceremoniousness that he seemed to have invented for just this occasion he selected a gardenia and pinned it on Eve's bosom. Mark forked out a dollar bill.

The congestion eased a little as they reached the main corridor that led to the court which, like the entrance hall, was decorated with streamers and flags of the Spanish Loyalists. This was the Independent School of Arts and Crafts, and the students had done posters for the occasion—caricatures of Franco, Hitler and Mussolini, pious portraits of Negrin and Miaja, scenes of bombed cities, ragged women defending their children with guns and bayonets, slogans in Spanish. Mark was astounded to see the formula *¡No pasaran!* still being used. When will they wake up? he wondered.

The question applied also to all these people. What did they think they were accomplishing? Because of his new assignment, and despite the pressure of the last couple of months, he had been reading the papers with a sharper eye to the foreign and political news than he ever had. This was particularly necessary because he no longer had the regular briefing at headquarters to depend upon.

Only a fool could fail to decipher the handwriting on the wall: Franco had won the war in Spain. He had marched to the sea, cutting the Red forces in two. Even though his drive on the Ebro was being slowed up, the Loyalists were bound to collapse within a matter of weeks, especially now that non-intervention was actually going into effect. The fact that Franco had just sent 10,000 Italian troops home told the whole story.

He caught himself looking furtively at the gardenia on the lapel of Eve's black tailored suit. It reminded him that he had bought it partly out of a confused sense of guilt; the attraction he had felt for that girl was tangled up in a funny way with the whole crazy pattern of his relation to Eve, though it had nothing directly to do with it. But its happening this evening, on this occasion, seemed to point up the irony of the fact that every time it looked as if the two of them were at last going to have smooth sailing, some kind of storm seemed to blow up.

Eve had never been happy about his being in the agency, though she had gradually become reconciled to it. Now this new assignment had stirred her again to revolt. It had led, after the family Thanksgiving dinner the other night, to their first serious quarrel. "I just don't like the assignment you've taken on," she had exploded. "I hate it, and I don't want to have anything to do with it!" Her outburst had been so unexpected, and had outraged him so deeply that he had lost his temper. ("That was the only good thing about it," she had sobbed later. "You don't lose your temper often enough.") They had made up, but neither had convinced the other. He had had to more or less bully her into coming along tonight. He had a feeling that if he was to carry through this assignment successfully he would need her moral support.

In the wide corridor they were able to walk side by side, and he glanced at her out of the corner of his eye. She was exactly his idea of a woman—almost as tall as himself, well-built, with bold strutting breasts, a slim waist and long well-shaped legs. She looked good in clothes and she looked even better out of them. With her wavy blond hair, her big blue eyes and her flashing smile, she was the kind of girl men turned around and looked at, and whenever he took her out he felt proudly possessive. It was funny now, though, to have Eve along on what after all was a professional assignment. But as a matter of fact, everything that he did from now on, his days and nights, every moment, were a part of that assignment. And she, and even two-year-old Jimmy, were a part of it.

Later, after they had slowly worked their way toward the center of the immense flagstoned court with its high glass roof, everything seemed to be easier. There were arcades on four sides under which booths had been set up, decorated with bunting in the Spanish colors—red, yellow and purple—offering a variety of wares and attractions. In the center a bar in the form of a great circular counter around an oasis of tall greenery had been rigged up and on its periphery the greatest concentration of people was gathered. Somewhere an orchestra was playing Spanish-sounding music.

"Let's get a drink," Mark said. Attractive young girls in long evening dresses circulated in the crowd selling tickets that could be exchanged for drinks—a technical evasion of the liquor-license law.

Mark recognized quite a few people in the crowd, which was a surprisingly "respectable" one. He could not get over the number of people who seemed to have thought it worth their while to come and attend what was after all a kind of political demonstration. There were even, here and there, a few men in tuxedos. He introduced Eve to the Andersons whom she had not yet met, and Eve and Helen immediately went into a huddle on the care and feeding of children. Anderson, who was talking to Professor Lindsay, a colleague in the Economics department, took Mark by the arm, and the three moved over to the bar and ordered drinks.

As they were talking, Mark's eyes were caught by a face at the opposite side of the circular bar, appearing in profile through a break in the greenery. The young man, no doubt a student, was looking at something, or more probably at someone, and it was the look rather than the face that arrested Mark's attention. It was a look of unconscious, self-effacing intentness, a look of surrender, but illuminated by the object of its contemplation, that Mark could only liken to one of worship. And then suddenly, as the broad back of a bartender beyond the leaves screened off the face, Mark realized with absolute certainty that it was Sebastian Bloch whom the student had been looking at. He passed his hand across his forehead, on which he felt little beads of sweat.

He went back to Eve. "Let's take a look around," he said.

A lot of people had obviously gone to a lot of trouble to put on this show. Women had baked cakes and cookies, made jams and jellies and candies, sewn, knitted, embroidered, made toys, exercised treasures of ingenuity and skill in turning out a variety of wares that seemed to be selling at a brisk rate in the dozens of gaily decorated little booths. People's attics, basements, closets and libraries had been ransacked for books and periodicals and objects of all kinds that had been discarded but nevertheless had value. Eve saw a brass coal scuttle that she said would be just right to keep next to the fireplace, and since the three dollars asked did not seem an excessive price, they bought it.

The money raised by the bazaar, it was explained, would go to "bring our boys back from Spain." The International Brigades in Spain were in fact being evacuated under League of Nations supervision, and the various pro-Loyalist committees in the States were taking charge of getting the members of the Abraham Lincoln Brigade and other groups of American fighters shipped home.

As they made the round of the booths Mark watched the people and listened to the talk, which was mostly of war and peace. Beneath the prevailing cheerful mood people spoke of the news in worried tones. Hugh Wilson, the American ambassador to Germany, had just arrived in Washington, called back to report on antisemitism and other problems. The Jewish persecutions and confiscations were continuing. In France a general strike was being called to protest the Daladier and Reynaud decrees. In China the Japanese, having taken Canton and Hankow, were continuing to advance. One small group was discussing unemployment at home. The figures mentioned were between eleven to thirteen million.

Mark was particularly on the alert for individuals who were, or should be, on his list. So far he had spotted Max Baum, the regional Communist Party secretary, Daisy Radcliffe, the twenty-three-year-old party organizer and glamour girl, May Barnett, the gray-haired sweet-old-lady fifth grade teacher who was an undercover party member, and Jane Middleton, the daughter of the dean of the Law School, a sculptress, who was the official contact for the closed units of the party.

"Look over there," Mark whispered to Eve. "That's Leo Vorontov, the C.P. treasurer for the district, and—"

"I don't care," said Eve coldly. "I don't want to know about it."

Mark felt himself go tight inside, but he said nothing.

They were now two-thirds of the way around the court, and at the other side of the circular bar. A casual glance told Mark that Sebastian Bloch was exactly where he had guessed him to be. On the fringe of the circle gathered around Bloch he saw Bill Parrish, the party's hatchet man sent out by New York headquarters, who had fought and been wounded in Spain and who was a former lover of Tanya Krylenko's.

Mark looked at Eve. "How about another drink?"

"Why not?"

They headed toward the bar.

"By the way," said Mark in his most casual manner, "you see that fellow over there in front of the—"

"You're so subtle," Eve broke in. "I've been watching him for the last half hour. He's your problem child." She did not give Mark time to catch his breath before she added, "I don't like him."

Mark ordered two highballs. Inwardly he was boiling.

Eve turned toward him where they stood at the bar, pressing her body against his.

"Look, darling," she said. "I don't intend to make things complicated for you. I know you need me to tag along with you on social occasions on this job. I'll be a good sport and I'll tag along, honest I will, and I won't disgrace you." She stroked his cheek with her free hand, having put her coal scuttle down on the paving. "But just don't ask my opinion about anything or anybody."

This was certainly no moment to start an argument. He heard a woman's voice behind him say something about "that stunning-looking girl there with the black hair wearing all the orchids," just as he was looking at the girl who he decided must be Tanya Krylenko. And she *was* wearing orchids, and she *was* stunning-looking.

"No," he heard another woman's voice say, "they just got married." Mark checked back in his memory. Yes, it was nine days ago, according to his information. They had got married out of the state, quite privately. The woman behind him must be someone in the know.

Some twenty people, in small scattered groups, formed a quiet little island amid the noisy, seething throng surrounding them. As Mark steered Eve toward the edge of it he heard unfamiliar language.

"The stability of the resonance level," one young fellow was saying, "has to be understood in terms of the approximate conservation law for isotopic spin."

His friend, a short Jew with thick glasses, scratched his disheveled head. "Yah," he said, twisting his face into a grimace. "Otherwise, how to explain the how-shall-I-say absence of long-range alphas in the dominant *s* capture reaction?"

Bloch, in an adjoining group, had just concluded what seemed to be a rather long and careful statement that he had made with evident relish but that was quite inaudible to Mark five feet away. Now he immediately turned to the two whom Mark had overheard but whom it did not seem possible that Bloch could have heard while he was talking. He smiled at them and shook his head slowly.

"It might," he said almost apologetically, "be a good idea to investigate the yields of long-range alpha particles and gamma rays in the range about 250 kilovolts."

Someone at Mark's elbow wheezed and made embarrassed sounds, and Mark turned and recognized Fritz Leutner, a research assistant in physics who was regarded as one of Bloch's most brilliant students and associates.

"They're t-talking a-b-b-bout the gamma radiation you g-get when you b-b-bombard b-boron with p-p-p-protons," he said.

Suddenly something happened that caused the several little huddles to dissolve, and without Mark's being aware of any-one much shifting his position there seemed to be a kind of circle, and in the center of it stood the flower girl in the candy-pink taffeta gown. There was something so fresh and natural and appealing about her that without any noticeable effort she had become the center of attention.

One man immediately came forward and bought a gardenia for his partner, and a second one followed suit. Then there was a pause. Attention was so riveted on the blond girl that when her gaze swept rapidly over the group in search of a possible third customer all eyes followed hers. Caught first by the big spray of green-and-white orchids that Tanya Krylenko was wearing on her black silk dress, they traveled from one woman's dress front to the next, to find each adorned with a gardenia, until they alighted simultaneously on the stiffly tailored bosom of a severe-looking middle-aged woman. Then all eyes, synchronized with the flower girl's, made a sideways leap to the man beside the woman, obviously her husband. He was a short, square, thick-set man in his early sixties, with bristling gray hair, small eyes that lurked behind thick glasses, a stubborn mouth. Most of the people by this time had bought one or more objects which they were carrying, as Eve was her coal scuttle, but the gray-haired man and his wife were empty-handed.

Then after an embarrassed pause Sebastian Bloch stepped forward. The moment he moved, Mark felt the release of tension—felt it in himself, but also in the group.

It all happened very simply.

Bloch (with his slight, almost imperceptible oddness of movement that Mark by this time was used to) stepped forward into the center of the circle where the girl was, and with a gentle nod toward her as if asking her permission picked out a gardenia from the basket, with a certain studied care, and turned to the middle-aged woman.

Mark was now observing very sharply, and with a fascination that was in part consciously professional but at the same time involved other levels he followed what was happening. He felt a complete identification with Bloch in his predicament.

Bowing slightly to the woman as he held up the flower, Bloch said, "May I have the pleasure—"

But before Bloch could complete what one sensed from the first words would be an immaculately polite little speech which might conceal a shaft of malice directed at the woman's husband, the old man took a step forward and put out his hand stiffly and ludicrously in front of his wife's torso.

Mark immediately sensed that Bloch was in trouble. Almost as if he were prompting him, Fritz Leutner, who was still standing pressed against him, breathed heavily and whispered, "P-p-professor de Rivas . . . He's the chairman of the Sp-p-panish department and the head of the local p-p-p-pro-Franco g-group."

"Mrs. de Rivas," said the undersized man, with a strong foreign accent, delivering each syllable deftly and sharply, "does not gwelcome this attention . . ."

He paused for a moment, and the silence seemed to Mark to be leaden and oppressive.

"Especially . . ." Professor de Rivas continued, and pointedly turned his sharp little eyes on Bloch's bride, "especially gwen it comes from—"

"Oh, Dr. de Rivas!"

Mark's sudden shout instantly drew the startled attention of the whole group, and he barged breathlessly into the open circle as if he had been hurrying for some distance, continuing to talk as he went.

"Excuse me, I've been looking for you," he said, approaching the elderly couple.

He had noticed that the woman had betrayed extreme embarrassment when her husband had started making a scene, and he was counting on her to help him carry through the Boy Scout act that he had improvised on the spur of the moment.

". . . There's an urgent telephone call for you, I'm sorry if I'm interrupting anything, but I think you'd better hurry . . ."

"Come quickly, Juan, it must be your mother," said Mrs. de Rivas, instantly seizing her husband's arm and dragging him toward Mark, who turned and led the way through the crowd which parted to let them pass. The professor, red in the face and perspiring, was making little explosive chugging noises, but his wife looked at Mark with an expression of vast relief.

"That was very clever of you, young man," she said, when they were completely clear of the group. "I don't know how I can thank you . . ."

"Gwere is the telephone?" her husband puffed.

"There is no telephone, my dear. You will never understand anything. All there is is that this very nice and clever young man has saved us from a most embarrassing situation."

She turned to Mark.

"You must excuse my husband," she said. "He isn't quite as

bad as he seems. The trouble with him is that like all Spaniards he is a fanatic. He should stick to philology and leave politics alone. Fanatics at whichever extreme are equally bad. Don't you ever become a fanatic, young man," she said, looking at him severely.

She held her hand out and up in a regal way.

"Good night, young man, I don't even know your name. And thank you again. Do come and call on us, you and your charming wife. Yes, I noticed her. She has a lot of good sense, you listen to her. Say good night, Juan."

The professor, his face a deep purple, seemed close to the bursting point. The only sounds he could utter were, "Pt-pt-pt . . ."

Eve had greeted him with a mock-dramatic cry of "My hero!" as he reappeared. He was immediately surrounded amid loud congratulations, and introductions were made all round.

He had had an odd feeling when he shook Sebastian Bloch's hand for the first time. It was a large, bony hand—not the slender, graceful one he had expected. A shadow of misgiving had fallen over him. He had never before shaken hands with a man he had been out to "get." Now he was out to get Bloch. And here he was shaking hands with him. He was playing a Judas role.

But he was allowed no time for introspection as he was plied with questions from all directions. Sebastian Bloch cut the discussion short. "I think this place is much too noisy. And besides, we've probably done our duty here for tonight. Why don't you all come to our place for a nightcap?"

Half an hour later Mark and Eve had found themselves in a big, chilly barn of a room on the top of a commercial building.

"This is an odd place for a professor to live," Eve had remarked, as they had puffed up the three long flights of stairs around the shaft of a freight elevator.

"He's an odd professor," Mark had replied.

One long wall of the room was all glass, and draughts blew

in through the joints. A fire was burning in the tiny fireplace in the middle of the opposite wall, but it could not possibly heat the huge room. In spite of the elegant grand piano that occupied one corner, the place gave an impression of bareness and austerity.

But they were immediately plunged into the animated spirit of the gathering. Mark saw at a glance that including Eve and himself there were twelve people all together. Bloch poured stiff drinks of whisky—instinctively Mark noticed that it was Jack Daniel's Sour-Mash—in tall five-and-ten-cent-store glasses.

They all wanted to know exactly what had happened when Mark had gone off escorting the de Rivases toward the non-existent telephone call. His rendering of Mrs. de Rivas's little speech and of the professor's inarticulate parting sounds caused general hilarity.

"But whatever made him show up at the affair tonight?" he asked, when he had finished his account. Professor Cummings, the Latin professor, who was already on his list, had just explained to him a moment before that de Rivas, who was the chairman of the Spanish department and the wealthy author of the Spanish grammar most widely used in the country's schools, was also the chairman of the so-called Citizens' Liberty Committee, which supported Franco and was backed by most of the rich and influential people in the community.

"The answer to that," said Tom Anderson, "would involve an analysis of the fascist mentality."

"Oh, I don't think that's necessary," Bill Parrish broke in. (Mark made a mental note of the fact that he was listening for the first time to one of the country's top party functionaries.) "All you have to do is look at him. He's a man with a chip on his shoulder. He's dyspeptic, he likes to make himself miserable. His committee could never put on an affair like this. They have a lot of money, but they have no people. We've got the people."

After a few more exchanges Fritz Leutner's wife Hannah brought the conversation around to de Rivas's wife.

"And do you know what?" she said excitedly. "On her way out she slipped one of our girls a five-dollar bill. 'For Spain.' Anonymously, of course."

Hannah Leutner was small and birdlike. She was not really pretty, but because of the way she handled herself she was as attractive as if she were.

"That's one of the reasons," she went on, after explaining about Mrs. de Rivas's background—New England—and her independent spirit, "that I get such a kick out of working on these parties. Something unexpected and wonderful like this almost invariably seems to happen."

Mark was enjoying the conviviality. He felt strangely at home in this group. But at the same time he was not forgetting his purpose in being here. However, he knew the importance of not trying to force things. Already he had been unbelievably lucky. He finished his glass. This was wonderful whisky. Here he was right in the heart of enemy territory, after just a first skirmish. Yet he could feel no elation.

"Let me fill your glass." It was Bloch himself, who had an unobtrusive way of anticipating the wishes of the people about him.

The talk was turning into a post-mortem of the party.

"We'd taken in over three thousand dollars by the time we left," Hannah Leutner announced. Mark gathered that she was mainly responsible for the organization of the party.

As he looked at one after another of the people, it struck him that this was a quite extraordinary group. All of them communists probably, except the Andersons and perhaps Cummings.

He wondered for a moment if Bloch was possibly naïve. Could it be his wife who, perhaps without his being aware of it, carefully selected their "friends" among party comrades and sympathizers? Certainly Parrish was her contribution to this group. But Bruce Patterson and Fritz Leutner were both students of Bloch's, and Patterson at least was an avowed and outspoken communist, who often addressed student rallies in the name of the party. He exuded intelligence and untidiness. His hair, his necktie, his limbs, seemed at every moment to be flying off in different directions. He was obviously Jewish and good-looking in a devil-may-care way. Great reserves of strength showed in the lines of his face, and his sparkling green eyes seemed to be perpetually leaping with the same agility as his mind. His wife Genia was a social worker, and an active party member like her husband according to Mark's records. Professor Albert Cummings was a tall and bouncy gent in his middle or late fifties, wearing a neatly trimmed graying beard above which his pale eyes had a look of almost childish innocence. He was a very eminent professor of Latin, and high in the councils of the University. But he was also active in the Teachers' Union and was often to be seen at left-wing parties.

The talk about the party led to the war in Spain, and the mood changed to one of gravity. Many unspoken questions hovered over the discussion of the desperate situation of the beleaguered young republic, split into two islands by Franco's march to the sea. Was there any hope? Had all the sacrifices and suffering been in vain?

Sebastian Bloch stood near the piano, and most of the others sat on the odds and ends of chairs scattered about the room. There was suddenly a silence as though a secret signal had been given, and everyone looked at Bloch who had been listening to the talk, but had said nothing. Mark could feel that they were all looking to him to express something that they obscurely felt and that needed to be voiced.

Bloch nodded his head ever so slightly. There was a faint smile on his lips, but it was a smile of sorrow.

"Yes," he said, almost inaudibly. Then, a little more distinctly, but in a voice that was still low: "Perhaps I should say a word."

As he listened, Mark became aware that Bloch's voice, his manner of speaking, was casting a curious spell over him that he struggled to resist. Never had he heard the authority of a personality asserted so powerfully by such gentle means.

"For two and a half years the Spanish Republic has fought desperately for its existence. It's been a losing fight, and now it is almost the end. The civil war has involved a terrible loss of life, and untold suffering. In just a few weeks Franco will be master of all Spain. It will be an important victory for fascism. It will be a disastrous defeat for democracy. It means that there will certainly be a general war."

What Bloch was saying was both so unfamiliar to Mark and so persuasive that he felt utterly disorientated at the same time that his mind was categorically rejecting it all. This was false doctrine. Bloch excoriated the democratic governments that were paving the way to incalculable disasters for themselves by cynically throwing the Spanish people to the wolves of fascism; he paid a tribute to the heroism of the Spanish people.

"They have lost," he said. "But we can't say that they've fought and died in vain. They gave their lives to preserve a certain value of which they were the incarnation—a reckless courage, a tragic sense of life, a pride, a magnificence, a dream of grandeur—and they died because those who give lip service to such values betrayed them. By their betrayal the Western so-called democracies have proved that they are powerless and unworthy to defend those values, which are the values of a humane and creative, a true, culture. Those who fought in Spain on the loyalist side have assured the continuity of that culture, have consecrated it by their death, and we shall take it up tomorrow where they have left it." He shook his head. "The people pay," he said sadly, "the people suffer, the people die. They lose every battle—except the last."

The last sentence was spoken with such ringing conviction that even Mark was stirred. He had been gazing at Mrs. Bloch during the latter part of the speech. She had been watching her husband with rapt attention, and it was the first time Mark had had a chance to study her face at leisure. She was beautiful, but so uniquely so that he could compare her to no other woman he had ever seen. She had a broad, shiningly smooth, rounded forehead framed in a pure, etched line by the wavy mass of dark, fine hair, and her elongated eyes, surprisingly blue, like lapis lazuli, slanted imperceptibly upward above her sharp cheekbones. Her delicate, slightly upturned nose gave her a disarming, appealing look, and her mouth with its even rows of small teeth had a contagious expressiveness.

She came up to him shortly afterwards, when the general conversation had started up again and then broken into fragments.

"This is all pretty new to you, isn't it?" she said to him, looking at him with a candor in those blue eyes that made him feel exposed and vulnerable.

He panicked for a moment. Was she one of those people with a special gift of insight who could see through every ruse and disguise? He had to think quickly.

"I'm afraid so," he said. "All my life I've lived in a kind of vacuum, and now suddenly I discover reality."

On the spur of the moment it seemed the best line to take.

"I'm not surprised it shows," he added, "though I hope it isn't as obvious to everyone as it is to you. I can't tell you how impressed I am by your husband!"

She smiled warmly. "I'm so glad to hear you say that. He's quite a wonderful man."

Mark had the feeling that she was looking at him with something like admiration.

"But you've made an impression on him, too, you know," she said. "He doesn't often take to a new person as he seems to have taken to you."

The several conversational groups formed and dissolved. Leutner and Patterson had begun talking physics and had gone off to a table in the corner of the room to work with pencil and paper. Cummings and Hannah Leutner had just sat down and were joined by Anderson and Parrish. Mark found himself standing alone with Sebastian Bloch in the middle of the room.

An unexpected sound suddenly rose above the murmur of voices. It was a succession of musical notes, sharp, precise and ordered, which both stirred up a turmoil of mixed emotions and imposed upon the moment, by their pattern and their assured yet ambiguous beckoning to the memory, a sense of coherence and continuity.

Mark glanced back in the direction of the piano. As he had guessed, Tanya Bloch was playing. But Eve was sitting beside her on the wide piano bench, watching the keyboard. They had found a bond in common.

Bloch was smiling, both looking at Mark and looking through him. Mark did not recognize the piece, but it was the kind of music that he sometimes felt had been secretly stored, since the beginning of time, within himself, awaiting only a moment like this to be released by the magic of a musical instrument. It was a strong and happy music, the notes rising and plunging and executing intricate movements around a theme that kept composing and decomposing, elusively. It became linked, as he listened, with the face of Sebastian Bloch, as though there were some necessary connection between them. And for the first time Mark saw it as not merely a face, a set of features to be recognized, but as the expressive register of a personality. Looking at it he was conscious of two startlingly distinct impressions. One was an impression, conveyed by a tender, brooding look in the eyes and by the expectantly half-parted lips, of absolute candor, of warmth, almost of excessive eagerness for friendship and even affection. The other impression was a little uncanny and indefinable. In attempting to grasp it, he found himself falling back on concepts that he knew did not make sense but that had their origin in his adolescent attempts, through religion and legend and daydreaming, at grappling with the problems of death and immortality. It was the face, he found himself thinking, trying at the same time not to go outside the realm of the rational, almost of one who had been *beyond—on the other side*—and had come back.

The piece ended, and the voices in the room rose again.

Bloch began to question Mark about himself, about his reaction to the Spanish party, about his plans; but his questions were very discreet, asked, Mark almost had the feeling, rather out of politeness than out of inquisitiveness, although at the same time they conveyed a genuine interest proffered as a fund available for him to draw on at any future time.

When Bloch hinted that he was curious to know what had

prompted him to come to the Spanish party this evening, Mark replied, "To tell the truth, I went to the party because of you."

Bloch was obviously intrigued, and Mark reminded himself again that if the most successful deception most closely approximated the truth, nothing was so deceptive as truth itself.

"Because of me?" said Bloch.

"Well, as you probably know, Tom Anderson is a great admirer of yours. He's talked about you so much that I was curious to see you, and when he told me you would be at the party I decided that was my opportunity."

Bloch smiled warmly. "And it turned out also to be mine."

But as a host Bloch could not give his exclusive attention to any one individual or group.

Mark had been stealing a glance at Eve, from time to time, to get an idea of how she was reacting to these people, and particularly to Bloch, but she had a gift for concealing what she thought and felt behind that good-looking face of hers. He was about to go over and join her and Tanya Bloch when he heard Hannah Leutner, in the group over by the couch, mention the name of Hal Norberg. She was saying that she hoped the party for the Norberg Defense Fund would be half as successful as tonight's Spanish party had been. Bill Parrish assured her that because it involved a local issue, and a straight labor one at that, it was bound to be even more successful.

Mark went over and joined the group. This was a subject he happened to know something about. Norberg was the labor leader whose deportation hearing was opening in a few weeks. He was accused of having lied under oath in testifying, in connection with his application for citizenship, that he had never belonged to a subversive organization. Mark's office had built the case against the Norwegian troublemaker whose electrical workers were spearheading the industrial union drive that threatened to overrun the state.

These people here were claiming that Norberg was being framed. Surprisingly enough it was Professor Cummings who despite his air of timid respectability spoke most fervently in Norberg's support.

"As chairman of the Norberg Defense Committee," said Cummings, in his best lecture manner, "it has been my privilege to observe him at very close range. I must say he has impressed me deeply."

Mark checked his memory of the facts. This was a heaven-sent opportunity of seeing how much respect these people had for the truth. He put in:

"What a man may have written or said as long as fifteen years ago shouldn't automatically be used against him. When he filled out his first papers in 1923 he may have acted in perfectly good faith."

"Of course he did!" exclaimed Genia Patterson who acted as part-time volunteer secretary for the Norberg Defense Committee. "They're trying to deport him now on the ground that in filling out those papers he withheld the fact of former membership in a subversive organization and so was guilty of attempting to obtain citizenship by fraud. The whole thing is a frame-up. He never did belong to any such organization."

"I haven't followed the case too closely," Mark said cautiously. "But isn't there a membership card in the evidence proving that he was a member of the Communist Party?"

"It's a photostatic copy and not an original," Cummings said. "And so it isn't acceptable as evidence. That's one thing. But apart from that, the name on the card has nothing to do with his name. Either it's a fake or it's someone else's card."

Mark at this point became aware of Bloch's presence on the outer edge of the group.

"If I understand correctly," Mark said, "the name on the card would be Norberg's party name at that time—1921 or 1922, I believe. And that is attested to by two witnesses who were members of the same unit in Stockholm."

"Have you ever been in Stockholm?"

Mark was startled—by the question itself, but even more by the voice, which was Bloch's, but which had a colorlessness, an utter absence of any emphasis that nevertheless suggested a hard purposefulness.

"Why, no—"

Bloch smiled. "It's a lovely town, full of memories of Gus-
tavus Adolphus, Christina and Charles XII. But you see: Hal
Norberg, though he's done a lot of traveling, has never been
in Stockholm either."

"What about those two witnesses?"

"Informers," said Bloch, his lids drooping beneath arched
eyebrows, "paid to testify as they were told."

Mark had to face the fact that he knew less about the case
than he had thought. Bloch was grossly misinformed, certainly;
but Mark could not prove it, and even if he could it would be
foolish to argue further. He had no choice but to run for cover.

"Well, there you are," he said with a good-natured smile.
"You read the papers and you think you have the facts, and half
the time the truth is just the opposite of what they have made
you believe."

This was taken very well—so well, in fact, that a little later
as last drinks were being passed around before the party broke
up, Professor Cummings took occasion to speak to Mark. Mark
had noticed the old man eying him appraisingly for some
minutes.

"You know," said Professor Cummings, carefully examin-
ing the fingernails of his right hand, "I think the best way to
get at the truth about a person or a situation is—well, to approach them directly and see them and know them for yourself."

He scrutinized his nails intently, while Mark was prey to an
odd feeling—that of a man with a mask being advised to put
on a mask. Professor Cummings lifted his eyes from his fingernails without moving his head.

"We need another good man on the Norberg Defense Committee," he said. "If you have a little extra time and could see
your way clear . . . it would help us . . ."

His eyes had dropped to his fingernails again, but when he
raised them once more his face had a look of seriousness.

". . . and I think you might find it very instructive."

Mark, without appearing too eager, reckoned he could find
time to work on the committee, and acted properly grateful.

The party broke up shortly after this, and Bloch saw everyone to the door with much old-fashioned courtesy. Mark had wanted to leave early, but Eve got involved in a discussion with Tanya on piano compositions for four hands, and somehow they were the last to make their departure.

"Perhaps the two of you could come over some afternoon soon," Bloch suggested, as they were moving toward the door. "We could have a talk. We've hardly had a chance to get acquainted this evening."

As Mark took Bloch's hand he had a curious feeling that the warmth of the other's grasp was more generous than the occasion warranted. He had never had any personal dealings with ecclesiastics, but he could imagine one of those kindly parish priests one read about, showing just such tender solicitude toward one who so far as he knew was merely a casual guest.

A few weeks after the Spanish party, Mark had sent a message to the Chief urgently requesting an appointment. The immediate response had come in the form of instructions to be at a solitary spot in the country, at three o'clock the following afternoon.

It was a cold late-February day from which all the life seemed to have been squeezed out. A low mist hung over the surface of a lake, partly blotting out the opposite shore, blurring a screen of trees and some low hills. The grass and shrubbery had a leaden hue, and the lake itself was a dull sheet of gray immobility. There were no signs of human habitation— the State College buildings were a mile or two beyond those hills. There was no one in sight, and their two cars, standing some distance apart by the edge of a golf links, had the peculiarly desolate look of mechanical contraptions that had been abandoned.

"I had to see you, sir," Mark burst out, the moment they met. "But I didn't want to put you out . . ." He ran his fingers through his hair. "If I had had any idea . . ."

He looked around at the deserted scene: the lake, the mist, the line of trees, the golf links dripping with precipitation.

"Is all this secrecy really necessary?" he said. "Couldn't we have met in some less out-of-the-way place?"

The Chief was on the point of lashing out with a reprimand, but he realized at once that the question betrayed a subtle change of perspective. Thus he said casually, "I admit a lot of the precautions we take are unnecessary. But you know our rule. And we feel a war coming on. Our most conservative experts say it will hit Europe before the end of summer. There's too much at stake in this case for us to take any chances. It's being conducted completely outside routine channels. No one, not even the top chief, knows you're the agent. There's no record of your connection with the case—or mine either, for that matter. Your reports for the time being are seen by no one but myself. That's our end of it. As far as you're concerned, you're moving into a situation in which more and more you are going to be surrounded by people among whom there are bound to be one or more foreign agents. All of which amounts to saying that we should be as careful as we can without impairing the effectiveness of our work."

They walked on in silence. Mark's face was somber.

"The fact is, sir," he said finally, with obvious reluctance, "that I'm not very happy about the job."

"Suppose you tell me about it." The Chief tried to put a suggestion of warmth into his voice.

Mark hesitated. "The thing is . . . I don't seem to be able to believe in it . . . I don't *feel* it . . ."

He looked at the Chief.

"When I was on the trail of an embezzler, or a counterfeiter, I knew what I was doing. I knew what I was after. And I felt good about it. But this—"

"I know," the Chief broke in. "I warned you about that."

Mark gave a nervous little shrug.

"I wouldn't be talking this way, sir, as you know, if I was throwing up the sponge. But I'm worried. I'm trying to think this through."

The Chief wanted just a little more to go on. "Suppose you try to define the problem a little more precisely."

They were now about a third of the way around the lake. Their steps reverberated on a board walk that led to a boat landing. Everything was stowed away and locked up for the winter, but around the small floating pier several swans with gracefully curving necks glided silently.

Mark said, "It would be the same problem if it were anybody else, of course. Fundamentally the same, I mean." He was feeling his way. "But it seems special because of him. It's a matter of degree, I guess. If it's wrong to do it to anyone, it's that much wronger to do it to him."

"Wrong?" the Chief could not help asking.

"Yes. It feels wrong." They were back on the asphalt walk. "Every time I see him I feel as if I'm . . ."

He stopped and turned to the Chief with an almost pleading look.

The Chief put his hand on Mark's shoulder, a gesture quite foreign to him.

"Listen, Ampter," he said. "Let me tell you something. The very fact that you feel the way you do—that you *can* feel this way—is the reason you're the man to do this job, and the reason I picked you."

He withdrew his hand and began walking again. It was too cold to stand still. Ampter lit his first cigarette.

"You know," the Chief went on, "all this is a matter of perspective."

Mark was about to say something, but the Chief raised his hand.

"Yes, I know. Bloch is not a criminal."

They walked on for several moments in silence.

"Bloch is not a criminal," he repeated. "But there's one thing you mustn't forget. Stepping in after a crime has been committed is only part of our job, and the less important part. Our biggest job is to prevent crime. Now I don't need to give you any lectures on this subject. You know that there is one kind of crime that is more dangerous than all the common-law crimes put together, and that is political crime: crimes against the State. Anything that threatens the security of the State, that

weakens or contributes to weaken the authority of the Government, anything that partakes of the nature of a conspiracy to
undermine or subvert or overthrow the Government, comes
under that category."

Mark had listened attentively. He looked thoughtful. But
the Chief could tell that he had not hit the mark.

"Listen," he said. "What I'm trying to say is this. This is a
political case, not a criminal case. There are going to be more
and more political cases from now on. This is your first, and it's
a tough one. There's never been one like it; it's unique. But as
I told you in the beginning, if you want to pull out, now or any
time . . ."

"But I never . . ."

The Chief cut him off. "Just keep it in mind."

The path had taken them into a small wood, away from the
lake, to avoid the broken shoreline, and now again swung back
to follow the water's edge. They were just about opposite the
point where they had parked their cars. The mist had settled,
to form a low sheet that hung over the water detaching it from
the land.

The Chief sensed that so far he had made little headway in
overcoming the reticence, or resistance, that he had noticed in
Ampter the moment they had met. Or perhaps rather it was a
deep bafflement. Ampter had lost none of his fighting spirit, of
that boyish enthusiasm which some of the fellows on the force
kidded him about. But he had hit a snag. He was stuck.

The Chief had felt it coming on through the reports, without paying too much attention to it at first. He understood it
now. Ampter was overwhelmed by Bloch's personality. In the
presence of that towering intellect, Ampter, who up to now in
a professional capacity had had to cope only with the criminal
mind, felt completely out of his depth.

Sebastian Bloch. More and more the Chief found himself
visualizing him—that strange, arresting face with the brooding,
compassionate and at the same time cruel eyes, the subtle, infinitely persuasive mouth. . . . Someday, he knew, they would
meet face to face. By then he hoped at least partly to have

solved the enigma of the man, to have penetrated to that secret area where the fatal weakness, or the unavowable vice, which every man had somewhere in his make-up, was hidden. But between now and then he had to depend wholly on a fallible agent. Mark Ampter would have to be his eyes and ears, and to a certain extent the interpreter of the things seen and heard. And at the present moment Ampter was so unnerved by the aura of glamour and legend that surrounded the person under his surveillance that he was unable to make effective use of his tools of observation, and the Chief himself had to make the more or less obvious deductions from certain data submitted. It was essential and urgent to whip Ampter back into shape and get him to give his best efforts to the case.

"Our job," said the Chief after a long silence, "is to prevent trouble. Trouble for everybody, including your friend." He looked at Mark meaningfully. "The point is that you simply have to play a double game."

He had Mark's whole attention now, as though Mark sensed that they were coming to the heart of the discussion.

"You see," he pursued, "there are different ways of looking at the double game. As a matter of fact, even the most ordinary individual in everyday life plays not one but several roles. A man is one person to his mother, a different person to his wife, a still different one to his business associates, and so on. Where the double game goes off is when a man is in the pay of two conflicting parties and double-crosses both."

(All this is terribly elementary, the Chief was saying to himself as he spoke. But he was conscious of the privileged nature of Ampter's scruples.)

"What you have to remember," he continued, "is this: you're not out to convict a man, but to get information. This information can just as easily work for him as against him. What you're doing, in other words, is essentially a work of protection."

"Protection?" Ampter's interrogation seemed directed less to the Chief than to himself, and the Chief took it as a sign that his mind was exploring a new vein of ideas.

"Yes. First of all you're protecting the Government, by keeping it informed as to possible danger in a vital area. And you're also protecting Bloch, by making available to us everything that is in his favor."

Mark considered this for a moment.

"Yes," he said. "I can see what you mean. As a matter of fact I've been toying for some weeks with an idea somewhat along that line . . ."

He hesitated, and the Chief thought he detected a trace of embarrassment.

"It may sound a little farfetched . . . but my idea is this: this man is far too intelligent and well-balanced, much too— too human, and kind, and tolerant to—well, to get mixed up with this communist business, except by a fluke. The fluke in this case is the fact that he happened to fall in love with a girl who happened to be a communist. The way I see it, he can't continue to be carried away indefinitely by these ideas. He'll wake up sooner or later. This ties in in a way with what you were saying about protecting him. What I was thinking . . ."

He came to a stop to light another cigarette, turning his back to the wind. There was a twinkle in his eye as he looked up at the Chief again.

"Instead of letting him convert me to his way of thinking, why don't I try to convert him to mine?"

Instantly the Chief was on the alert, but he made his voice colorless: "Is he trying to convert you?"

"Well, no, not exactly. In fact he isn't altogether converted himself. But the people who surround him—"

"Wait a minute—" The Chief saw his opening. "You say he isn't altogether converted," he said casually.

"As far as I know."

The Chief could tell his guards were up. "What about that unit?"

"Which unit?"

"I know you haven't mentioned it in your reports. I assumed it was because you were preparing a special separate report on it. I'll be very interested."

Mark made no reply. The Chief decided that this time he

was not going to help him out. He counted twelve steps before Mark spoke.

"You're one up on me . . ." The voice was controlled, but the Chief detected hurt pride in it. Mark looked at him dejectedly. "I guess I haven't been much help to you."

"On the contrary. It's all in your reports." He had anticipated Ampter's astonishment. "The necessary elements, I mean."

"But how could you gather from anything I wrote . . . ?"

The Chief smiled good-naturedly. "It's a matter of interpreting the evidence."

"You mean you've got nothing else to go on?"

"It's enough." He was enjoying Ampter's discomfiture, but he had no wish to overdo it. "Mind you, it's only a hunch, and I could be wrong. But you know how important hunches are in our work. No, I think when you go back there if you follow it up you'll find there's a nice little closed unit that's built up around Bloch himself. In it you are likely to find Professor Cummings and Patterson and Leutner. I imagine Parrish is the contact man for the party." He looked at Ampter. "You think you can work your way into that unit?"

Mark made a grimace—the kind a man might make at the sight of a sheer mountain wall that he is being asked to scale.

"I can try."

He scratched his head.

"But I still wonder . . . It somehow doesn't seem possible. It's only a few months since he became at all interested. Surely he wouldn't already be a full-fledged member!"

"How long do you think it takes a man of his intelligence and will power to follow an idea through? You yourself told me about his reading all three volumes of *Das Kapital,* in the original, over a long weekend."

"I haven't been able to check that."

"It doesn't matter. That kind of a story is always substantially true."

Mark walked on, absorbed in thought. Then after a few mo-

ments he said, "Would you say Anderson—my econ prof—was
a member of that unit?"

"No." The Chief had to reflect for a moment to explain to
himself why he was so positive. "No, he has a different smell.
He isn't one of the elect."

He felt a smile swell his cheek muscles as he was struck by
an association of ideas.

"You know how it is: a boy and a girl. You've known one or
both of them for some time, and they start going together. You
don't think anything about it. And then all of a sudden, one
day, maybe after a long time, you see them together, and—you
can't put your finger on it, but they look different; and you
know they've gone to bed together. Well, it's the same way with
people who get religion, or who join the Communist Party.
Something comes over them: a kind of light shines in their
eyes, their voices have a special inflection."

"But you've never seen Anderson, or heard him talk."

The Chief smiled. "You write a damned good report, you
know."

The Chief's executive mind began working. "Keep a close
tab on him just the same, and put it all down. You never can
tell. An occasion may arise when we'll want to come out and
accuse him of being a member. That'll make him play ball
with us. He'll be very useful."

"Oh."

The tone of the lone syllable told the Chief his last remark
had been a mistake.

Mark went on: "That reminds me. Another thing that's been
bothering me . . . those two witnesses in the Norberg trial.
Whoever brought them into the picture and cooked up the idea
of using them to prove Norberg a communist wasn't very
bright."

The Chief found himself wondering, Does he know it was
my idea?—but he realized immediately that Ampter could
have no such suspicion. Because I'm sacrosanct, he observed to
himself wryly.

"It caused me a lot of trouble," Mark continued. "I had seen quite a bit of material on the case in the office. I thought those two witnesses, as well as a lot of the other evidence that turned out to be false, were on the level. On the principle that a man is innocent until he's proved guilty, I agreed to work on the Norberg Defense Committee, all in a spirit of fair play. I was going to show up the other people on the committee as naïve idealists, and in particular I was anxious to impress Bloch. Well, you can imagine what a fool I looked when the defense proved that those witnesses were paid to give false testimony and that Norberg's membership card was a forgery. And also how I felt at the victory celebration after Norberg had been cleared, when he came and shook hands with all the members of the committee and I had to hear myself being thanked for contributing to his vindication."

The Chief had his own reasons for being furious at the decision of the Immigration Board clearing Hal Norberg of all charges in the deportation hearing. But this was not his immediate concern. Ampter puzzled him, and for once he was a little uncertain how to handle one of his men.

He took refuge for the moment in a tangent.

"I wouldn't worry too much about that aspect of it," he said. "As a matter of fact, because of the way you've played it, and the way it turned out, you're in an even better position now than you were. They're convinced of your sincerity. Now you're really in."

"Yes, that's all right . . ."

The tone of Ampter's answers indicated that he was conscientiously weighing everything the Chief said, but was at the same time stubbornly testing some ideas of his own.

"But I was thinking of something else," he said. "This sort of thing—I mean this business of producing false testimony and forged documents in the attempt to deport a labor leader —makes matters all the more difficult, and hurts our cause. Bloch has become friendly with Norberg. He admires him tremendously, and now of course he's more sold on him than ever.

Needless to say, all this only confirms him in his ideas about our police methods and justice."

He looked at the Chief with a disarming earnestness.

"How are we going to defend our way of thinking, when facts themselves begin to argue against us?"

The Chief passed his right hand across his brow, and only as he did so became conscious of the gesture. He had so disciplined himself to eliminate involuntary movements that he was momentarily unnerved. He noticed that they had walked a considerable distance, the wind had begun to rise and was against them now, and the weather had darkened. Big wispy bales of wet-soaked fog blew over them.

Ever since the intuition had come to him that what peculiarly qualified Mark Ampter for this off-the-beat assignment was the very "softness" that he had noted down in his file after the first interview he had had with him, the Chief had felt divided. The problem was no longer the simple one of giving orders or advice, of asserting authority or exercising persuasion. In a sense he was no longer dealing with Mark Ampter, but through him with Sebastian Bloch. And, for the time being at least, he had to see Bloch through Ampter's eyes. Behind everything Ampter said, behind all his actions, the Chief was now aware of the personality, the mind, of Sebastian Bloch.

The idea and the plan had originally come from above, but he had taken over the project as his own. And in his conception it was no longer a pure and simple long-term operation of gathering data within the scope of a loosely defined intelligence program. It was something that challenged him in a direct, personal way, a need to know what fever, what consuming fire, burned at the core of that baffling temperament. Everything else, including the formal purpose of the investigation, was becoming increasingly subordinate to this.

But the immediate fact was Ampter's confusion, and Ampter's last question still echoed in his mind: How are we going to defend our way of thinking, when facts themselves begin to argue against us?

"Speaking of facts," he said, as they headed back toward the cars, "have you any idea what Bloch's activities in the scientific field are these days?"

The question seemed to have a calming effect.

Mark looked up. "None whatsoever," he said. "But I hear a lot of shoptalk. Needless to say, I don't understand it any too well. There's a terrific amount of excitement among the physicists these days, and I really don't see why. It all has to do with what goes on inside the atom."

"Something new they've discovered?"

"As I understand it, they're discovering new things practically every day. Bloch was at an important meeting at George Washington University some weeks ago where a sensational new experiment was announced. Leutner tried to tell me about it the other day. It has to do with converting matter into energy, according to a theory of Einstein's. Something that struck me, by the way, is that so many of these people are foreigners. The experiment was made in Germany, and it was a woman— who had to get out because she was Jewish—who had the idea they are all worked up over. Lise Meitner. One of the top men in the field, Niels Bohr, who has just come to this country, is a Dane, and another is an Italian, a Nobel Prize winner, named Fermi, who ran away from Mussolini . . ."

Mark went on to summarize what he had picked up about the new development. Though he had little scientific training, he had a good memory, and he seemed to have some idea of what the excitement was about. It had to do with the possibility of using atoms as a source of energy, and he went on to tell about uranium splitting up into barium and krypton and giving off neutrons, and about the problem of separating the uranium isotopes . . .

But the Chief found his attention wandering. Slow and fast neutrons, the packing factor, the conversion of neutrons into protons by the emission of beta rays . . . it sounded like one of those mare's-nests the scientists were periodically coming up with. And this at a time when the agencies of government were trimming their sails in anticipation of serious international trouble!

Chapter 3

SEBASTIAN BLOCH's eye had fastened on Professor Maynard Reed's right elbow as it rested on the shiny surface of his desk, a proper and prudent pivot for the restrained gestures the Physics department chairman made when he spoke.

"C-14 with phosphoric acid," Maynard repeated, after a pause. "You really believe it might lead somewhere? I didn't think we should wholly rule out the possibility of finding a radioactive isotope of oxygen or nitrogen, though. But perhaps you're right. I'll talk to Weber."

His voice had an emasculated timbre upon which, even at its most cordial, was superimposed a note of petulance. Although it was not this that stamped him as a refined avatar of Back Bay aristocracy, it was the vehicle by which the awareness was conveyed.

However, it was not to discuss the two years of wasted research, which were the direct fruit of his own stubbornness, that Maynard had called Sebastian Bloch in to his office. And he knew that Sebastian knew it. But he was too much of a Christian gentleman to challenge any action of his younger colleague without first calling attention to some signal failing of his own.

He put away the Weber file and picked up a sheet of paper that lay on his desk in front of him. A sharp slice of sunlight slanting in through the tall windows behind him reached just far enough to give a dazzling accent to his thick shock of white hair, wiry as a youngster's, at the same time casting his face into deep shadow.

"What I really wanted to talk to you about, though, is this letter here."

Sebastian knew without being told that it was his letter recommending Bruce Patterson for a post at Northern Plains University to set up a center for theoretical physics studies. He had dictated it yesterday and left the typed original and copy after signing it in the wire basket marked *Departmental Business* for Maynard's secretary to pick up.

"Our recommendations," Maynard continued, "are in effect departmental recommendations." He was visibly embarrassed. "We should try as far as possible, don't you think, to have recommendations on which we can all agree."

It was while dictating the letter that the implications of what he was doing had suddenly struck Sebastian. A year ago he would have done exactly the same thing: he would have recommended Bruce Patterson, or someone like him, because he was the best man for the job, and he would have recommended him even though he knew he was a communist. But now his whole perspective had changed. He was no longer a disinterested spectator. He had lost an "innocence" that had attached to all his words. And now these words—the same, perhaps, that he might have used then—had acquired an altogether different weight.

"Is there objection to him?"

Maynard hesitated. "Objection perhaps is not the word. Patterson is very able, I quite recognize that. As far as scholarship is concerned he is certainly well qualified. But as you know, scholarship, while important, is not the only criterion to be considered. And we must keep in mind that this is an exceptionally responsible post that is to be filled. For this reason, character—reliability—is just about as important as technical competence."

Sebastian's mind flashed back over what he knew of Bruce's history: a life of self-sacrifice amounting almost to heroism, devoted since the age of twelve to bringing up two younger sisters and a brother, after his parents had lost their lives in a tenement fire in the Bronx; through heartbreaking difficulties and hardships he had developed into a self-possessed, gentle, compassionate human being, the soul of honor, able, dedicated and fearless, and had in addition achieved an exceptionally brilliant record in his work.

"So far as character is concerned," Sebastian said, "I have always regarded him as above reproach."

Maynard looked at him rather peculiarly.

"Did you know when you wrote this recommendation that Patterson was a communist?"

"Oh yes. He's never made a secret of it."

"Oh?"

Maynard was silent for a moment.

"I didn't know myself until—until just recently," he said.

Sebastian registered interest.

"Yes, as a matter of fact . . ."

Maynard was speaking with reluctance.

"The president . . . He gave me a list . . . Issued to all department chairmen . . . Patterson's name is on it."

"What kind of list?"

"Well, you know . . . Since this pesky war in Europe . . . And especially since the Nazi-Soviet Pact . . ."

His face betrayed mingled regret and helplessness.

"It's a list of officers and students to be watched, I understand."

"Who is going to watch them? And how?"

"That's a manner of speaking. As far as we are concerned, it simply means that we should be particularly careful in these cases about new appointments, promotions, honors—and, of course, about recommendations for posts outside the University."

"Is this official?"

"Oh, no! This is quite unofficial. In fact, it's confidential."

"We're not even at war," Sebastian said.

"It looks as if we shall be soon. Don't forget a state of national emergency has already been proclaimed."

". . . *Limited* national emergency.' "

Sebastian leaned forward.

"Tell me," he said, "how do you yourself stand on this?"

Maynard looked at his hands for a moment. They too were

very young. Practically no lines or veins showed on the soft, resilient skin, and they were hairless as a woman's. The shaft of sunlight had moved, and a small vanishing triangle shone on the corner of the desk to the right of his elbow.

"You know how I feel about mixing politics and science—or any academic activity, for that matter."

"And who would you say is doing the mixing, in this case?"

Maynard gave him a disapproving look. "Why, Patterson of course! Who else?"

Sebastian raised his eyebrows slightly. "I thought," he said with a faint smile, "that you might be referring to the president."

Maynard obviously regarded this as an impertinence.

Sebastian continued, "You've just said yourself that you didn't know of Bruce's politics until the president informed you."

"Look here, Sebastian!" Maynard exploded, getting to his feet and burying his hands in his trouser pockets. "This is a devilishly ticklish business, and you should be helping me out instead of trying to trip me up."

His tone was both pleading and querulous. Being put on the defensive seemed to bring out everything that was Boston, Puritan and feminine in his nature. His shiny pink cheeks had a deeper hue, and there were tiny specks of perspiration on the bridge of his nose above and below the gold mounting of his glasses.

"You can't," he said after a silence, "overlook the fact that Patterson is a communist. Leaving aside the matter of the president's list, do you think it fair to send such a recommendation as this without even mentioning to Dr. Deakin—who is re--sponsible for making the appointment, and who is accountable, after all, to his president and to his faculty—the fact that Bruce Patterson is a communist?"

Sebastian felt suddenly hot, as if a pad of steam were pressing on his chest. The shaft of sunlight had moved a considerable distance from the desk, its angle approaching the perpendicular.

He would not be dishonest. Nor would he betray a friend. "No," he said, "it wouldn't be fair."

Maynard looked up brightly. "You agree? You agree to withdraw your recommendation?"

"No! I can't do that. Dr. Deakin wrote me personally to ask me to recommend the best-qualified man among my students for this job; and that is what I have done."

He saw the stirring of conflicting impulses in Maynard's face. And he knew that for him, as for himself, moral scruples were not easily dismissed. He sensed after a moment that Maynard's New England conscience was losing the battle.

"I think I should tell you—this is purely parenthetical, in case I should forget later—that this list . . ." Sebastian was irritated, more than he liked to admit, by this recourse to transparent tricks. ". . . It isn't a part of the list, but attached to it . . . There is a mention of your wife as having had a certain affiliation—a . . ."

"She was, until fairly recently," Sebastian said, "a member of the Communist Party."

"A—yes." Maynard looked politely shocked.

Where did honesty end, and deception begin? Did Maynard have a right to know that he too, whom Maynard regarded as the main showpiece in his department, was a communist?

These questions, besieging, insistent, each following upon the heels of the one before, all had a recurring motif: the relativity of truth. It was a problem that did not arise in the realm of science. In the realm of action all was contingency. The absolute of truth, if it existed—and in a human situation it could exist only as a projection of the mind—was submerged by the sweeping, irresistible flood of subjectivity.

He was a communist, yes. But being a communist, in his own eyes, was something so different from what Maynard would conceive it to be that there was no common measure between the two. To tell Maynard what he believed and why he believed it, to explain to him the direction of his efforts and their goal, to make him really understand and feel what impelled him (which presupposed a state of receptivity on May-

nard's part that certainly did not exist and that would have to
be induced if it was at all possible by a long, persevering and
inspired effort)—to do that would be to come somewhere near
what he held to be the truth. But to tell Maynard point-blank
that he was a communist would create a totally false picture in
his mind. What I am, as I see myself, he realized, corresponds
in so many fundamental respects to what Maynard identifies
with moral and civic rectitude that it could be truer to tell
him that I am a dyed-in-the-wool Republican.

No amount of casuistry, however, could eradicate the fact
that in joining the Communist Party, as in taking holy orders
or in committing murder, one entered a world that separated
one from all those who did not belong to the brotherhood. It
was hard for him to think of himself as a conspirator. Yet the
world that now claimed him, in which he had a place, a function, a reason for being, was the world of conspiracy. Like the
world of the early Christians in the Roman Empire, of the ra-
tionalists under the French Monarchy of the eighteenth century, it was a world of passion, of dedication and sacrifice, and
it bore the future darkly in its womb.

He belonged, inexorably if imperfectly, to the Order of the
Revolution. In the political struggle that divided the world of
today into two warring camps and of which he had only recently become aware, he had chosen the side of the poor, the
disinherited, the oppressed, the hunted, the exiles, the outlaws
—the men and women who filled the prisons, who were being
tortured, who faced the firing squad, the gallows and the electric chair. These were his brothers. To them, all his love and
compassion went out unreservedly. Their triumphs were his
triumphs. Their defeats were his defeats. And their truth was
his truth—not necessarily always the slogans and directives that
they were asked to follow, which could be as often wrong as
right, but the truth of their needs and aspirations, the truth
of the creative ferment that stirred in the hearts of that vast
legion of humanity whose day had not yet come.

Nevertheless, he would not be dishonest.

"I want to be fair with you, as with Dr. Deakin," he said.
"You just mentioned my wife. Any questions you care to ask

about me, if that was your intention, I shall be glad to answer as fully as you wish."

"Heavens, no!"

He was quite sure, from his tone, that his little trick a moment ago had been a straightforward man's inept blundering into deviousness, a thing devoid of malice.

"I intended no such thing!" Maynard gasped.

"Then perhaps we could come back to Bruce Patterson."

He looked at Maynard. The man of breeding, of conscience, was strong in him, but not invulnerable; the scientist was surer.

"You say that before you saw the president's list you had no knowledge of Bruce's politics?"

"None whatsoever."

"All right then, let's just suppose for a moment that you've never seen that list. How would you feel about my recommendation?"

"Well in that case of course I should have no grounds for objecting to it. . . ."

His tone was unsure. He was obviously reluctant to venture far on the thin ice of the proffered hypothesis.

"Let's go just a little further," Sebastian pursued, "and assume that I had not written a recommendation. Whom among our graduate students would you consider the candidate best qualified for this post?"

Again Sebastian read, in the hesitancy registered on Maynard's face, the signs of an inner struggle. It would be easy to suggest several good candidates, as good or better in one or more special respects, almost as good over-all: Roos, Hendrickson, Levitt, Breuer—and Leutner, of course, though he wasn't quite ready for it yet. But this time the New England conscience won.

Maynard made a series of grimaces and ungainly lip movements.

"I'm not saying . . . I don't want to say that we could propose anyone better. In fact—all right, I'll admit that as far as science is concerned—theory—Patterson is the best man we could propose."

"Right," Sebastian said. "Let's just examine this for a moment. We agree that Bruce, as far as his qualifications are concerned, is the best man for this job—or for a similar job. And by the way, that is another reason why I attach such importance to this particular recommendation. If Bruce is turned down for this job on political grounds, chances are he will be turned down for any other job. As scientists, then, when we recommend a scientist we know what we are talking about. Do we know what we are talking about when we say that because a man is a communist he is not fit to do a good job as a scientist?"

Maynard was fidgeting with papers and pencils on his desk. After a moment he said, "I don't know that we're going to get anywhere by talking. We look at these things differently. Suppose your brilliant scientist was a criminal, or a lunatic—that is of course possible. Wouldn't you take that into consideration?"

These, thought Sebastian, are the natural associations of ideas among the vast majority of our fellow citizens. A man who challenges property rights, an order of things regarded as immutable, is regarded as being in the same class as the criminal and the insane.

"I don't think the cases are exactly comparable," he said.

He felt a sense of outrage. Yet he knew that Maynard had made these associations in utter innocence, the kind of innocence he himself had once had.

For a moment, neither said anything. Then Sebastian continued: "I've suggested that I think we lay ourselves open to attack whenever we undertake to judge a fellow scientist on other than scientific grounds. By this I don't mean that we should not have feelings and ideas, and even convictions, on matters outside our special province. We should certainly have these for ourselves, and even communicate them to anyone who is interested. But by the same token we cannot allow ourselves to *impose* them on our colleagues or apply adherence to them as a criterion in anything connected with our work. I am convinced that upon this depends the very freedom of science: that a man, of whatever persuasion—political, religious or anything else—should be permitted to make the contribution to science that his gifts and his training have prepared him to make. No matter how we may personally feel about a given philosophy, we have no right, in the absence of other proof, to assume that holding it will affect a man's work adversely."

Maynard said nothing for a few moments. With his elbows on the shiny desk, his long fingers drooping from his chin, his narrow shoulders, his glasses that reflected a reflection of the vanishing shaft of sunlight behind him so that his eyes were invisible, there was something about him that suggested a grasshopper.

Finally Maynard said: "If you go ahead and send this recommendation, what do you expect me to do?"

Sebastian knew he had won.

"All of us," he said, "who have administrative duties have a strong prejudice in favor of handling business according to established rules. We prefer not to have to make decisions that fall outside the routine pattern."

He looked at Maynard and contemplated his candid, almost infantile face, which seemed to symbolize the sheltered life of the academy and betokened a career dedicated wholly to scholarly pursuits, into which politics had never entered—no politics, that is, except the rock-ribbed, righteous and unalterable republicanism to which he was born; and he felt a surge of kindliness and sympathy for the older man.

"That was all right until fairly recently," he went on.

He noticed that Maynard had not heard him, and realized that his voice had dropped. He repeated it, but what he had to say seemed so obvious that he was diffident about expressing it in anything much above a whisper.

"It was possible to operate that way because the accepted rules and patterns took care, by and large, of most of the situations that had to be met, without creating any acute moral conflicts."

He got up for the first time since he had come into Maynard's office, and began to pace.

"That is no longer true," he said.

He stopped, facing Maynard across his desk.

"Take that list of the president's. There is a well-established, in fact a sacrosanct procedure for dealing with such cases as this —recommendations for outside posts, for fellowships, promotions, and so forth. The heart and core of that procedure is the protection—on the one hand, of the individual, and on the other, of the academic community—by providing guarantees against the arbitrary exercise of authority. The president's list, don't you see, is precisely such an arbitrary exercise of authority."

"It's only a suggestion," Maynard said a little weakly.

"Meaning?"

"It isn't an order. The president merely gave us the list and suggested . . ."

"Yes."

Sebastian had uttered the word softly, but Maynard looked startled. He put both his hands flat on his desk top, elbows raised, and his face distorted in a painful grimace. The sun had moved out of range of the tall windows, toward noon, and the light in the room was now more evenly distributed, eating the shadows.

"All right," he said. He looked at Sebastian half grudgingly, half admiringly. "You could probably convince the devil himself. I'll do whatever you say."

He got to his feet heavily.

"I wish I could feel better about it, though," he sighed.

Sebastian felt no sense of elation.

How many such victories could he afford?

Chapter 4

THE summer brought Mark a promise of respite from his dilemma. A cousin of his who had an apple ranch near the coast in the State of Washington invited the family for an indefinite visit. As soon as examinations were over in early June, he, Eve and Jimmy piled into the old Dodge and drove west, and they stayed through August. He took along a pile of books—economics and Marxist writings.

So now he was far away from both the Chief and Sebastian Bloch. Would he at this distance be able to see things in perspective? The trouble was that he was at the same time closer than ever to Eve; too close to work things out in his mind with the serenity he felt he needed. There were no classes that he had to attend here, no office hours, meetings, studies to take him away from her during most of his waking hours. And he discovered, to his stupefaction, how far they had grown apart. There had always been an intimate communion between them, an understanding that needed no words and that made them a perfect team. But since Mark had taken on his new assignment there had been a progressive drying up, not only of the current of meanings and associations that nourished their common life, but also of the flow of feeling between them.

The pattern of their life during these months was a physically healthy one. The country was wild and mountainous, and the ranch had been hacked out of virgin forest. A series of clearings on an area of steep rounded slopes had miraculously yielded a thriving orchard. The Ampters had a cabin to themselves, not far from the main house where his cousin Jack Gifford lived. They would spend all day outdoors, helping out on the ranch, taking hikes in the mountain or driving down to the coast, a twenty-minute ride away, where they would picnic on one of the many beaches in the rocky coves. And at night he and Eve would abandon themselves to physical intimacies that were lustier than any they had enjoyed during the past year and that were, in a measure, a compensation for a growing estrangement that had manifested itself between them on other levels and that they both seemed, with a kind of desperation, to hope to overcome through a communion of the flesh.

For the first time Mark faced a serious problem that he felt unable to discuss with Eve. And when he tried to analyze the reason that he felt this way he had to recognize that it wasn't because, as a man might be tempted to say in such a case, "she wouldn't understand," but rather because she would understand only too well.

She had never formulated it, yet he knew with absolute certainty that if he were to ask her point-blank what she thought he ought to do she would say, "Quit!" But she knew that he wouldn't, and that the reason he wouldn't was the Chief. And often, in the calm of these summer months, when he was alone, lying sunning himself on a beach, sitting in the shade of an apple tree and letting his mind drift after a spell of reading, or perched on a crag to which he had hiked, looking out over a wild stretch of country falling away in a broken line to the sea, he found himself thinking about the Chief, and about the compelling power that he exerted.

The return of the fall session brought him back to his dilemma in all its acuteness. He had been out of touch with Sebastian during the whole summer period, except for checking his movements through the various offices, and now it was urgent for him to send the Chief a report. The first opportunity he had of seeing Sebastian at some leisure was a dinner at his house to which Eve and he were invited. The Blochs were both so warm and friendly, and Tanya had so obviously put herself out to prepare a festive evening, that as he plied Sebastian with question after question on touchy political subjects so as to be able to pad out his report he felt like an utter heel. And Eve was no help.

In every other way, it was a pleasure to get back to university life. There was no denying the fact that he found the atmosphere, the flavor, of academic surroundings peculiarly congenial. He enjoyed teaching, and he enjoyed research. One day an odd thought occurred to him which, however, he dismissed a moment later. Suppose, he said to himself, that instead of just going through the motions, I actually went ahead and wrote a thesis and got a Doctor's degree? . . . He had, as a matter of fact, been doing all the required work, and doing it conscientiously, and had been getting good grades. He didn't know quite why. Perhaps it was just because it interested him and because besides it was something honest that he could hang onto.

An unbelievably lucky break came to him a few weeks after the dinner at the Blochs', when Bruce Patterson invited him to have a cup of coffee at the Students' Cooperative and began sounding him out about joining the Communist Party. Mark showed interest without displaying excessive enthusiasm. He asked for a week or two to think it over.

Curiously enough, he had even here a divided reaction. He had not asked who was in the unit, but it was likely that once in the party he would be able to ascertain whether Sebastian was actually a party member or not. But once he found this out he was bound to report it, and this was a far more serious matter than anything he had been able to report on him thus far. At the same time he found himself half hoping that what he would find out would be that Sebastian was *not* a member. And this might very well bring his investigation to an abrupt end, and all his inner conflicts would be resolved.

An incongruous thought grazed his mind as he contemplated taking this decisive step. Joining the party was of course indicated as part of his investigation, and he would be covered by the service. But if he had entertained any idea of seriously studying for the Doctor's degree and going into university work, a record of party membership would be a serious handicap to an academic career.

When he announced his decision to join the party to Bruce he was amazed first of all to have Bruce immediately give him the total composition of the closed unit to which he would be assigned, and still more amazed to learn that Sebastian was one of its members.

A part of Mark's quandary was now resolved. Sebastian *was* a member, and was therefore dangerous. The Chief had been right. Not only that, but the Chief had even named two of the other people in the unit: Professor Cummings and Fritz Leutner. He had also mentioned Patterson who, while not actually a part of the unit, often met with it. The other members, all of whom Mark knew, were Hsueh Ling, a young Chinese political science student, Philip Jones, an instructor in the Spanish department, and Hans Weber and Lou Goldstein, both physics researchers.

Now at last he had something to go on. He was on the inside. He would be able to see how these people operated, observe at its inception the mechanism of subversion, disruption and sabotage.

The first of the weekly meetings of the unit that he attended amounted to little more than a friendly gathering of colleagues, and was very disappointing. After a dozen or more meetings he began to wonder if his immersion in the subject of subversive activities had by this time destroyed his objectivity and robbed him of his powers of observation. For the meetings reminded him of nothing so much as of informal seminars of the kind that were constantly being held on all sorts of subjects among professors and students on the campus. They were concerned on the one hand with ideas and theory, with the analysis of current political problems, and on the other with practical problems, the activity of this or that member in the Teachers' Union, in a professional organization, the planning of public meetings, action to be promoted in regard to an immediate political issue, the support to be given to a labor union campaign, a strike, an individual or group under attack on a civil liberties issue. . . . Try as he might, he was unable to unearth any schemes to sabotage or disrupt the normal and orderly processes of laws and institutions, he could find no trace of collusion with sinister powers, of contacts with foreign agents.

One item did come up in early December that looked as though it might lead to something. The U.S.S.R. invaded Finland on November 30th, and a great furore went up in the Western camp and the Soviet Union was branded as a ruthless imperialist aggressor. At the subsequent unit meeting Sebastian took up the matter.

"Our faculty colleagues," he said, "are confused and badly

misinformed. Worst of all, they never have any opportunity to hear our position on crucial national and international problems."

He proposed that the unit should issue from time to time a brief analysis of immediate situations and problems, in which the position of the party would be set forth in language palatable to cultivated, critical minds. These leaflets were to be printed attractively and distributed not only to the faculty of the University but to those of the universities and colleges of the whole region. Sebastian would pay the cost of printing and distribution, and as it turned out, he did most of the writing as well. It was his baby. A number of these "Reports to the Faculty" appeared over the next few months. They contained no incendiary slogans, no calls to revolt, no vituperative denunciation of the lawfully constituted authorities—merely statements of facts, and cool, rather persuasive analyses of these facts.

Your group sounds like a Sunday school, the Chief wrote Mark in code in a brief message after he had been in the unit for several months. *Try to get the low-down.*

Mark had been sitting for a long time staring blankly at the sheets of paper that he had finished typing. Now he got up, walked heavily across the room and opened the window wide. The lawns in front of the houses on both sides of the street were bright with new grass, the privet hedges showed a tender green, and borders or beds of primroses, daffodils, tulips and other spring flowers shone here and there in the fading light.

He crushed out his cigarette and glanced at his wrist watch. Soon it would be time for dinner. Tonight was the unit meeting, and that meant Eve was going to be harder to manage than usual. He dreaded the thought of going downstairs, of facing her across the table.

. . . Just now, when I need her most. . . .

He went back to his desk and began doggedly to reread what he had written.

CONFIDENTIAL
  Attention: J. W. Gregg.
  SUBJECT: [Here a series of code-numbers identifying Sebastian Bloch and the nature and number of the report] . . .

He had picked up some background material in the last few months that seemed to have a certain interest.

  . . . Dr. Otto Frisch in Copenhagen last year wrote article predicting future application of principle of fission to making uranium bombs. These would be enormously destructive, proposes testing in Pacific Islands . . . Prof. Kapitza in Russia, Werner Heisenberg and W. Bothe, both associates of Prof. Hahn, working on uranium . . .

The report dealt mainly with the fact that "the Subject" was attracting an increasing number of advanced students, and with the influence he seemed to exert over them.

  The first impact is of course the brilliance of his mind, his authority in the field that interests them. But this is immediately overshadowed by the special quality of his personality . . .

Mark picked up all the sheets and tore them to shreds.
"No," he said aloud. "I can't do this any more."
His reports had become increasingly difficult to write, and less and less regular. He gathered the shreds of paper into a ball, was about to toss it into the wastebasket, then changed his mind. He went back to the window, put the ball of paper on the brick ledge, and lit a match to it. It had grown dark enough for the flame to flash its flickering light over the whole window frame. As the last inner folds of the paper and its message were being consumed, he had almost the physical sensation that the Chief was watching him. And he knew at the same moment that he had just performed a decisive act.
A group of young people was approaching on the near sidewalk, students unmistakably, their voices raised in heated discussion. As he tried to catch the drift of what they were saying, the voice of one of the girls plunged him into a state of momentary bliss.

And then he remembered. Eve's voice had been like that once. . . . In the past months a hardness had crept into it, but it had been so gradual that now, as he suddenly heard the echo of what it had been, the contrast startled him. He felt a wave of tenderness. We love each other, he told himself, we've got to work things out. And there was Jimmy, too.

Abruptly he decided that he would not go to the unit meeting tonight. It was more immediately important to try to straighten out the situation at home.

He stopped off in the bathroom on the floor below to splash his face with cold water and wash up, and then ran downstairs, feeling almost cheerful. But before he reached the bottom step he heard a commotion in the kitchen. Something crashed, and then there was a loud wail.

"Well, what's going on?" he called out as he opened the swinging door from the dining room.

Jimmy, sitting at the kitchen table with its white oilcloth top, his face convulsed, eyes closed and mouth gaping wide, was catching his breath for a fresh shriek. An amber pool dripped over the edge of the table, and broken glass and spilt liquid were scattered over the blue linoleum floor. Eve was bringing the floor mop. She was wearing her long wine-colored smock that left only the edge of a navy-blue skirt showing, and against it her face was white and drawn. Her eyes were swollen and her mouth was set in hard lines.

"He knocked over my drink," she said with controlled fury. "He did it on purpose."

Jimmy's shriek broke, rending the air, but he interrupted it after a hysterical gulp to blubber, "She hit me!"

Mark registered the fact that it was the first time he had known Eve to take a drink by herself like this before he joined her. But he was determined to create a propitious climate for a heart-to-heart talk.

"All right, all right," he said soothingly. "No use crying over spilt milk."

"It wasn't milk!" Jimmy bawled.

Mark picked Jimmy up from his chair and, winking half-reprovingly to his son, swung him high in the air. This exercise belonged to the realm of play and usually brought forth squeals of delight; but this time Jimmy was unresponsive, though he stopped crying. Eve was mopping up the floor, gathering the broken glass into a pile.

"A big boy like that, spilling a lady's drink!" said Mark with mock severity, shaking his head. "Tell Mommy you're sorry!"

Jimmy's lower lip was out, and he maintained a stubborn silence. Mark let him down, bringing the boy's face to the level of his own. He playfully pressed down the pouting lower lip with his forefinger and let it snap back, but Jimmy remained solemn. Finally Jimmy said, slowly and distinctly, "I'm not going to be a cop. I'm going to be a robber. And I'll rob all Mama's things!"

When Eve took him off to bed a few minutes later, he refused to hold her hand.

By the time Eve came down again Mark had two glasses and ice and seltzer water and the whisky ready on a tray in the living room. On taking the whisky bottle out of the cupboard he had had the impression that the level had dropped quite appreciably since he had last seen it, but he could have been mistaken. He called to Eve as she turned to go into the kitchen. She stopped reluctantly in the doorway, her face expressionless.

"I have to get dinner."

"Let's have a drink first. There's no hurry. I'm not going out tonight."

"But you told me you were going . . ."

"I've changed my mind."

He got up and went over to her. He wanted to put his arms around her, but he did not touch her. She would probably have fought him off.

"I've been thinking," he said. "We've got to talk things over. I'll stay home and forget about my work for once, and we'll have a quiet, relaxed evening just to ourselves with plenty of time, and maybe we can get a better perspective on things."

"Talking isn't going to do any good," she said.

There was a deadness in her voice, and in her whole attitude. She looked utterly exhausted. But she took a step into the room, and he turned to the tray on the low table in front of the fireplace and poured out two drinks.

With mechanical eagerness she took the glass he handed her and raised it to her lips immediately. She's been living on her nerves for weeks, he guessed. He made her sit down in the armchair by the fireplace and sat down himself on the sofa opposite.

"You remember the day we decided to get married?" he said, putting his glass down. "We both did plenty of talking—I especially. And it took a lot, too, because you had made up your mind you just weren't going to marry me."

"Maybe I was right," she said, unhelpfully.

"Maybe so, but in that case . . ." Mark threw up his hands. "Look here, hon, are you trying to wreck our marriage?"

"It's pretty well wrecked already, as far as I'm concerned."

Mark glanced at her searchingly. She had spoken in a matter-of-fact tone and she looked dead serious.

"Eve, darling," he said, "let's stop beating around the bush. What's wrong?"

She stood up. She had already half finished her drink, and she took another swallow. "You know just as well as I do what's wrong," she said, and went out into the kitchen.

Mark resisted the impulse to follow her out immediately. He was too stunned for the moment to think out his next move. He had had no idea that Eve was in such a bad way.

What an idiot I've been! he thought to himself. As if he had not always known that Eve was not a girl who could be expected to just stand by and not be affected by what was going on in her immediate sphere.

When they sat down to dinner a little later he knew that he had to bring out into the open what was certainly the heart of the problem, which he had dodged discussing with her all these months.

Eve had prepared a salad of sliced avocados and canned grapefruit as a first course. She had poured herself a second drink and it stood half emptied beside her water glass.

"All right, I know what's wrong," he said. They had not

spoken since she had left the living room. "You don't like the job I'm doing. Well, neither do I. Let's start from there."

Eve looked at him without surprise, but her deep blue eyes showed no hostility.

"Go on," she said.

Mark hesitated.

"I—I started a report to the Chief this afternoon."

He felt his cheeks flushing.

"I tore it up."

"Why?"

He did not answer immediately.

No, he couldn't tell Eve that the reason he had torn it up was that as he had tried to describe how the young physics students looked up to Sebastian Bloch he had been stunned to realize that he was himself beginning to look up to him in much the same way.

"Probably for the same reason you would have," he said lamely.

But he realized that evasiveness would get them nowhere.

"I don't like this job I'm doing. I told the Chief that, a year ago. But I've taken it on and I can't just walk out on it. What I *can* do is—well, I've decided to use a less personal approach, leave the private life alone—that's a man's own business. But there are certain things we *do* have a right to know about. I'm not explaining myself very well . . ."

"It's quite clear," Eve said, very calm now. "It's what I meant when I said it was no use talking. You refuse to quit."

"I can't."

"Why not?"

"Not right now, anyway. Listen . . ."

"I know. You've fallen for the boy wonder, just like everybody else, and now you can't bear to be separated from him."

Mark gave a forced laugh. "I'm glad to see you've got your sense of humor back."

"Sense of humor my eye!"

Unexpectedly she reached for a cigarette from the pack that was lying on the table and put it between her lips. While one part of him noted and wondered about the unusualness of this act (she had not finished her salad), another part of him—his right hand—reached into his coat pocket for his cigarette lighter, whipped it out, deftly lit it and held it to the tip of her cigarette.

"You see," she said, after taking a puff, "you even imitate him."

He looked at his lighter with a new kind of recognition.

"Yes!" she went on, raising her voice. "His mannerisms, and his way of talking. I've been noticing it."

He studied the lighter, at the same time marveling at Eve's disconcerting trick of seeing through him. It was a neat, expensive lighter of a special make. On one side were engraved the initials *M.A.*—which were his own, but which also meant Master of Arts. On the other side were the letters *Ph.D.*—Doctor of Philosophy. It was a gift from Sebastian for his last birthday, and the inscription was Sebastian's way of reminding him to concentrate his time and energies on getting his Doctor's degree.

But Eve's insinuation had kindled a spark of anger in him too.

"What have you got against Sebastian anyway?"

"I told you long ago I refused to discuss him."

"Well, a lot of things have happened since then. Now this thing has come between us and is messing up our lives, and I feel it's your duty to tell me what's in your mind."

Eve took a drag from her cigarette and blew out the smoke gently, looking down at her unfinished salad.

"I can't tell you," she said, almost as if to herself, though there was a sharp edge to her voice. "I can't tell you because I don't know—it's just something I feel. But I know it that way. I know it for myself." She looked up. "I can tell you one thing, though; he despises women."

"You mean . . . ?"

"No, nothing like that. He only goes to bed with women. He goes to bed with them, but he doesn't love them."

"You're crazy. He certainly loves Tanya. I've never seen a man so—"

"Did it ever occur to you that he only married Tanya because he had got her pregnant? He was interested in plenty of other girls at the same time."

"How do you know?"

"About Tanya's being pregnant?"

"No, not that; I can count too. But how do you know he wouldn't have married her anyway? And how do you know about the other girls?"

"All right, he might have married her anyway. But the fact is that up to a couple of years or so before that he had had absolutely no experience with women. Then he discovered sex and went overboard and had one affair after another. Tanya just happened to be the first girl he got pregnant. You can draw your own inferences."

She crushed out her cigarette, got up and took the two salad dishes.

"How do I know it?" She started toward the kitchen. "I've spoken to some of the girls."

While Eve was in the kitchen Mark tried to get his bearings. It was hard to swallow the fact that Eve, who had reacted to Sebastian Bloch in a wholly negative way from the beginning, who had shown a complete indifference to him and seen very little of him, seemed to have a deeper understanding of him and to know more about certain intimate aspects of his life than he did.

But she could be wrong, couldn't she?

She reappeared, bringing two serving dishes.

"You forget one thing," said Mark. "He never gave any other girl a grand piano."

Eve put the steaming dishes down.

"Maybe not," she said. "But he gave one of them a Nash coupé. And another he's putting through five years of medical school . . . to say nothing of the jewelry and clothes he's lavished on every one of them."

Mark felt an inexplicable irritation mounting.

"Generosity is hardly a fault. And besides, he helps out a number of male students, too."

"That's true. And he *is* generous. But this is something else. It's almost as if he had a sense of guilt toward women."

"Guilt? Why should he have a sense of guilt? And anyway, that's quite a different thing from despising them."

"Different, yes. But the two can be connected. To overcome his sense of guilt on one level he despises them on another."

Eve had an uncommon way of sizing up people, but he was unwilling, in the present case, to admit that the picture she was drawing had any validity.

"I don't know how you can say he despises women," he ventured. "I would say rather that he was too soft, too much of a gentleman."

Eve, still standing with her fingers resting on the edge of the table, looking even taller than usual, gave him one of those enigmatic smiles he had sometimes, but not often, seen on women's faces. It served now as a mocking reminder of the fact that for over five weeks she had in one way and another been managing to circumvent all his attempts at love-making.

"I can't explain it. And perhaps it's hard for a man to understand . . ." She glanced down. "Our food's getting cold." Then she looked at him again. "Your Sebastian is—well, he's special, all right; quite out of the ordinary . . . He frightens me. You can't see him as a woman does. But do you imagine it's easy—or perhaps even possible—for a woman who has been with him intimately ever to be happy with anyone else? The thing is that he knows it. Women attract him, but he resents it. So he has to punish them. Oh, I don't mean that he wants to. He despises them but he doesn't want to hurt them. Yet he does. All of them. It goes back to his sense of guilt."

"But why in the world should he have a sense of guilt?"

Eve was leaning heavily on the table with both hands. It struck Mark that her posture, the look in her face, was quite unfamiliar to him. Was it possible that the Eve he had known practically all his life, to whom he had been married for five years, could have kept that particular look concealed from him all this time? She looked now, he thought, like some ageless sibyl through whom an oracle spoke.

"He must have done something—oh, not deliberately, not even consciously perhaps—something that he senses to be a crime, perhaps an inexpiable crime, against all womankind."

Mark shook his head, as if to shake off a sense of unreality that he felt creeping over him. "Such as what?" he said in his hard police voice.

Eve picked up the kitchen towel she had hung over the back of her chair.

"I don't know . . . I guess the extreme case would be if a man, a sensitive man, had murdered his mother; or if his mother had died in giving him birth. I'll bring the veal chops."

They ate for several minutes in silence. Mark was in a state of almost unbearable agitation. For no reason that he could explain, he violently resented everything Eve had said about Sebastian. If she was wrong, as she surely was, what did it matter? If she was right, what she had said simply filled out the picture, and he should have welcomed it. But its actual effect was to throw all his emotions into a turmoil. And what he needed right now was not new complexities but simplification, clarity.

The smothered veal chop was tough and the mashed potatoes were soggy. It wasn't often that Eve spoiled a meal, and he decided, in a mood of vicious self-indulgence, that she had done it this time on purpose. But in any case he wasn't hungry.

He took hold of himself. The evening had got off to a bad start, but perhaps it could still be salvaged. Oddly enough, the things she had said about Sebastian, while they incensed him, had stimulated his desire for her.

He broke the silence.

"I don't suppose Sebastian's feelings about women have anything directly to do with your being so upset about my connection with him . . ."

"No." She had become withdrawn again.

"Yet it seems to me that the fact that you dislike him so much might make you object less to . . ." He couldn't find the words to finish what he had started to say, but Eve interrupted him.

"I don't dislike him. Sometimes I think you're terribly obtuse. I can understand girls falling in love with him, and men too: all his students, and even you—"

"Aw, cut it out!" he protested feebly.

"It isn't anything to be ashamed of. It's true of men twice his age and twice as eminent. He exerts a real fascination. Don't think I don't feel it too!"

"Well?"

"Well, I won't let myself go." She drained her glass, which by now was mostly melted ice. "I don't know how to explain it." She frowned with an effort of concentrated thought. "I've never met Einstein," she said in a hesitant tone, "so perhaps it's unfair to make a comparison. But it's occurred to me often. I dare say Einstein is as much of a genius as Sebastian Bloch is. But what I know is that I would never be afraid of him in any situation. I would trust him with my life. He's—what is the word I want? Yes: he's innocent—innocent in the sense in which the first man was, before evil was introduced into the world. Sebastian Bloch is *not* innocent. He has tasted of the forbidden fruit. And," she added, looking at Mark with what he took to be a spark of malice, "he rather likes the flavor."

Mark felt himself bristling again.

"You keep harping on the same theme. Well, if he has such a sense of guilt, if he is so lacking in innocence as you say, you shouldn't be objecting so strongly to my—professional interest in him."

Eve weighed this for a long moment.

"I think we're talking about quite different things," she said finally.

Suddenly she lost control. Her face contracted in a grimace of pain and frustration, and tears shot from her eyes.

"Can't you see?" she screamed. "I don't give a damn about him! It's us I care about!"

Almost immediately she recovered her composure.

"I'm sorry." She wiped her eyes with her napkin. "But I can't go on like this any longer," she said softly.

It wasn't like Eve to go to pieces in this way. Again he had an impulse to take her in his arms. But there were too many things churning inside him.

"Tell me," he said, and he kept his voice gentle. "What do you want me to do?"

"Anything—I don't care what—so long as we stop leading this double life!"

Mark remembered their first quarrel over the new job that Thanksgiving night, just before the Spanish party at which they had met Sebastian. Never before that had they had the slightest misunderstanding. But in the eighteen months since then things had become progressively worse. The bonds that held them together were straining to the breaking point. "I'll be a good sport and I'll tag along," she had said that night at the Spanish party. She had kept her promise, but it was telling on her, driving her to distraction. She had reached her limit. It would take a powerful stimulus to make her hang on a little longer.

"Well, as a matter of fact," he said slowly, watching for her reaction, "I feel pretty much the same way."

Eve betrayed both interest and surprise, and he paused a moment to allow his words to take effect.

"I've been thinking about it a lot."

Eve was looking at him, and he knew from the fact that she did not say anything that she was receptive. Once more he hesitated, knowing the moment was crucial.

They had both stopped eating. He offered her a cigarette and took one himself. He looked at the lighter a little self-consciously, and his eye caught the *Ph.D.*

"I've made a decision," he said finally.

It hurt him to be not quite honest with her, but he saw no other way. "Decision" was a big word. He was far from having made it.

"You know," he went on, "I had forgotten the appeal of the academic life. But after all, I first came to college all of twelve years ago, and more than half my time since then has been spent on the campus. I feel at home here."

He drew on his cigarette, and blew the smoke out slowly, alert to Eve's reaction. She was listening eagerly.

"I like research. I like teaching."

He looked at her affectionately, yet feeling like a man handing a piece of poisoned candy to a baby.

"How would you like to be a professor's wife?"

"I'd love it!" she said, grabbing the candy and putting it in her mouth.

"I figure I'll be able to get my degree in just about a year and a half. Of course it's impossible to make hard-and-fast plans these days, with the war clouds gathering. But if all goes well I have a good chance of being offered an instructorship a year from next fall. And then," he said triumphantly, even as he dreaded her reaction, "I'll quit the agency!"

Eve looked at him for a moment incredulously, shaking her head ever so slightly.

"You don't mean," she said slowly, her head shaking more vigorously, "you don't mean you're going to go on with this for another year and a half!"

All the light had gone out of her face.

"Listen, darling. We have to be reasonable and practical. The fact that I'm quitting is the important thing, and it should make you feel better about it. I can't quit my assignment right now. I have a commitment and a responsibility. And besides" —it was a piddling argument, but one that might appeal to her sense of realism—"it's the money that I'm getting on this assignment that's paying for this house and the maid and the car. We couldn't possibly get along on my teaching assistant's salary. The fact is that we can't afford to quit right now."

Eve's look of contempt came as such a shock that he could not meet it and had to drop his eyes.

"So you'd sell your birthright for a mess of pottage!"

She rose slowly from her chair, and he rose too, full of self-loathing.

"I'm sorry," he said. "That isn't really a reason. I—"

No, it was no use trying to justify that particular argument.

"But seriously, this is a matter of duty. I don't mean just a job or having given my word, or anything like that, but a civic —a *patriotic*—duty. I have no right to back out now. I know it's unpleasant as hell, and believe me I don't like it any

more than you do, but it—" He remembered the sense of dedication that had filled him the morning the Chief had first briefed him on the assignment and he had decided to take it on. "It involves matters of such vital importance to the country's security that if I were to pull out now I'd be—I'd be practically a deserter!"

"Hocus-pocus!"

She practically spat the words at him, with a venom he would never have thought her capable of.

"What . . . what in the world?" he stammered.

"Yes, hocus-pocus!"

She began to move, not back and forth, but in a senseless, erratic way, in all directions, taking long steps, waving her arms and seeming unable to control her movements.

"Patriotic duty—hocus-pocus! The country's security— hocus-pocus! This whole thing that you and your Chief have cooked up is just an elaborate game of hocus-pocus!"

She kept pacing in that peculiar, insane way.

"I don't know what you're up to and I don't want to know. But I've seen you at work, and I say it's a lot of hocus-pocus!"

"I suppose communism is hocus-pocus too?"

"You ought to know. You must have become quite an authority on it by now."

Mark could ignore the sarcasm in her tone, but her words held a challenge that he could not let go by.

"So far as I'm concerned," he said, "there are two things. There's a political philosophy, a way of interpreting history and society—in other words, a theory. That's one thing. And then there is a program of action, an organization, a movement. That's the other. And this other, because it's subject to the dictates of a foreign power, or at least sensitive to its interests and responsive to its persuasion, is a threat to this country's security. This is in our bailiwick, and this is what I'm interested in. I'm not at all interested in the political aspects of the matter. In fact I'm not interested in politics, period!"

"Oh, you're not?"

Eve had been walking, in the same unnerving, stiff-legged

way, toward the other end of the room as he had been talking, and she now abruptly turned around and, still clutching her upper arms with the fingers of either hand, began stalking toward him.

"So you're not interested in politics!"

She gave a forced laugh, stopping in front of him, and eyed him from head to foot with an insane stare, while Mark felt a tide of anger rising in him that was becoming harder and harder to control.

"And I suppose," she said, "when you go snooping into the business of private citizens for the sole reason that they happen to hold political opinions you don't approve of, that isn't politics! I suppose when you spend your time compiling lists of hundreds of people who happen to attend certain meetings or who happen to be seen in the company of certain individuals and you turn in their names so that at some future time it can be used against them and perhaps ruin their careers and their lives, that isn't politics!"

Her voice had risen, and she was practically screaming.

"Well, let me tell you something, Mark Ampter, Secret Agent. In your language you may be a soldier of freedom and a defender of your country's security and a hero, but in *my* language you're an informer and a rat!"

Walking in the night minutes later, Mark tried to reconstruct what had happened. A tingling, burning sensation around the knuckles of his right hand kept throbbing the message that it was this same hand that had struck Eve across the face and brought blood oozing from her mouth. This, visually, came back more and more clearly through the fog in his brain. But the rest was blurred. He had hit her, and now he was here walking down a quiet and probably familiar dark street, and he was filled with a consciousness of failure and a sense of shame. Everything had gone wrong.

Walking aimlessly, but with the purposeful pace of one who has a fixed destination, he doggedly concentrated on driving away the image of Eve with her mouth all bloody.

Grass, flower beds and shrubs lined the street on either side, except for an occasional vacant lot overrun by weeds. Lights shone here and there in most of the set-back houses, and a kind of well-bred, suburban peace hung over the scene. He tried to visualize the professor, the doctor, the engineer, the retired colonel, the manufacturer, the banker, the state senator, who lived in this or that house—sitting relaxed in an overstuffed armchair surrounded by family, friends, all his household fetishes. He imagined the consternation he and his neighbors would feel if they were suddenly told that in the street just outside a man was walking, heading for nowhere, in the throes of an agonizing torment over a decision that could conceivably have far-reaching consequences for them as well as for himself, and that a telling factor in this decision was a woman. Within the framework of the security system on whose alertness and efficiency they relied, this man had become prey to grave misgivings as to the validity of a highly confidential mission with which he had been entrusted and was at the same time, and irrespective of this, faced with the choice of abandoning this mission or seeing his home broken up.

That was what it came down to, Mark realized once again as his mind flashed back to the memory of Eve as he had left her standing in the living room, her face white and accusing, with blood trickling down her chin.

It was only now, as he recognized a certain dogwood tree whose generous bloom had a delicate pink glow even in the weak light cast by the corner street lamp, that he became aware that he was walking in the direction of the campus. He stopped. He found he had come out without hat or coat— or, as he discovered when he felt the breast pocket of his jacket, his wallet.

It was a mild spring night, with stars in the sky between the branches of the trees that were just showing their first timid leaves. He had walked a considerable distance yet he had met no one; not even a car had passed in either direction. It could not be much after eight, yet the town, if not asleep, was composed for the night. Sounds dwarfed by distance, reminders that somewhere boilers and pistons and dynamos were turning wheels to service an endless chain of human needs, gnawed at the outer edge of the silence.

He stood hesitant at the corner, his eyes caught by the great panoply of lovely dogwood blossoms. He had already walked many blocks. He must have turned this way through sheer force of habit. It occurred to him now that this was also the way to the Leutners', where the unit meeting was at this very moment being held.

He looked at the dogwood tree, and a feeling of relief, of serenity, almost of happiness, came over him as he gazed, noticing how the blossoms arranged themselves on the tree's outer twigs. The blossoms—four large petals, light as swan's down, of an ethereal pink in the ghostly semidarkness—spread their loveliness in upflung billows and sprays of an airy insubstantiality that seemed to defy and contradict the rigorous black skeleton, now invisible, that bore them. For some reason the pleasure of contemplating the beauty of the arrangement of the blossoms on the periphery of the tree made him think of Sebastian. If only his problem had been one that he could have discussed with Sebastian, how he would have loved to observe his mind grapple with it, and how much clarity and wisdom Sebastian would have brought to it! As he was thinking this he began to walk on again slowly, in the same direction as before.

But of course Sebastian was the last person in the world he could confide his present troubles to. And now it came home to him that he could turn to none of the three people to whom—to one or another of whom, depending on the case—he would instinctively have turned for advice on a difficult problem. The Chief, Eve and Sebastian—all were involved in his predicament. And all of them he had double-crossed. And, he realized with a kind of helplessness, he was probably going to go right on double-crossing them for quite some time.

As he walked on he was conscious of the fact that his steps were taking him in the direction of the Leutners' house. He looked at his watch by the light of the next street lamp. Eight thirty. It was not too late to attend the unit meeting. He stopped again and hesitated. He wanted to go back to Eve, to put his arms around her, to beg her forgiveness. But somehow this was not possible. The gulf that separated them now could not be bridged by a gesture of love.

He walked on mechanically. Presently he made out, down the street ahead of him, the faint outline of the two-story stucco building of which the Leutners occupied the upper floor. The meeting would be well under way. He visualized the familiar, friendly faces. And suddenly he had an odd feeling. He belonged in that meeting; the people there were his comrades; the business they were discussing concerned him.

He headed up the cement walk leading to the front door. He would be able to forget his personal problem for a little while—and see Sebastian.

The moment he stepped into the smoke-filled room he sensed that this was no ordinary meeting. The eight members of the unit, now that he had arrived, were present in full force. But there were several other figures in the group that crowded the Leutner living room.

When he saw who they were, he immediately realized that the occasion must be one of exceptional importance. For in addition to Bruce Patterson, the group's regular contact with the party, there was also Bill Parrish (and this was the first time both had attended the same meeting), and besides these Mark was amazed to see not only Max Baum, the regional secretary of the party, but Leo Vorontov, the district treasurer. Led in by Fritz Leutner, Mark was first introduced to these two functionaries who he noticed gave him a wary once-over; shook hands with Bill Parrish (with whom he had not spoken since the night he had first met Sebastian, after the Spanish party); and exchanged nods of greeting with Professor Cummings, Hsueh Ling, Phil Jones, Hans Weber, Lou Goldstein and Bruce in turn. Sebastian greeted him with a warm smile that was more expressive than any words.

The introduction over, Mark took a seat on the floor rug,

along with Fritz and a couple of others, since there were not enough chairs to go around, and the discussion that he had interrupted immediately continued. He gathered that it had been going on for some time and had reached a decisive phase.

"That is what we should all like to believe," Sebastian said in a voice that was little more than a whisper, in reply to a long speech by Baum analyzing the war situation, during which he had shaken his head imperceptibly, with an expression of deep melancholy. "But you see, it isn't so, and we must know that it isn't so." He leaned forward, his left hand tightly clutching the bowl of his pipe. "Of course we want peace. And we must say so. We must never fail to make our objective known. But we must also be very clear as to what is possible and what is not possible. I think that anyone who looks at the world today with such knowledge as we possess must recognize that war and not peace lies ahead, not only for Europe but for us as well. And that it will be a long and desperate war, and that the outcome is far from certain."

As the discussion continued it became clear that it was essentially a debate between Sebastian and the party officials. The members of the unit who spoke up—Cummings, Ling and Weber—tended to side with Sebastian. The party, Mark thought, certainly seemed to take Sebastian's views pretty seriously.

Vorontov spoke very little. Mark remembered that he was regarded as one of the party's leading theoreticians and he was said to have known Lenin. He threw in an occasional observation or two, speaking with a heavy accent. He was short, almost dwarfed, with a very Asiatic face. The light from the ceiling accentuated his cheekbones and the narrow slits of his eyes and shone on his completely bald head as on a sphere of polished ivory. His thin drooping mustache beneath his small flat nose gave him a villainous look. Hsueh Ling, by contrast —who at twenty-two looked much younger—was imperturbably cheerful and would punctuate his comments on grave international events with bursts of boyish laughter.

The argument seemed to be whether or not the communists

should recognize that the war in Europe was an antifascist war, that it could be ended only by the defeat of Hitler and Mussolini, and whether, recognizing this, they should make their position known.

"You must understand," Baum said, "that it would be unprincipled for the communist parties of the world to advocate or support the active pursuit of war against Germany when the Soviet Union is bound to it by a nonaggression pact."

"But a nonaggression pact," Phil Jones pointed out, "isn't an alliance, after all. Fighting Hitler isn't going to hurt the Soviet Union, quite the contrary."

Hsueh Ling joined in the discussion. "When you talk about an antifascist war," he said, "you have a very big subject." He laughed, not because it was a joke but because he had a lot of vitality and a happy disposition. "Look at the communists in China. They are fighting the Japanese invaders alongside the armies of Chiang Kai-shek." His face bubbled over with mirth. "The government of Chiang Kai-shek is just as fascist as the Japanese government. But it's still an antifascist war. It is a nationalist war with an antifascist core."

"The situation isn't the same, comrades," Baum put in. He was massive and square, with a thick shock of close-cropped white hair. "In Europe you have, so far, only a phony war. There are no clear issues. England and France, who refused to go to war to keep their pledge to democratic Czechoslovakia, have gone to war to try to save feudal Poland. Actually, England and France can't save anyone, perhaps not even themselves."

Bill Parrish now spoke up for the first time. "Let me try to put it in another way. We know Hitler is going to attack the Soviet Union sooner or later. *Unless* the war can be brought to an end before that happens. And that's what we have to concentrate our propaganda on at this time."

Sebastian's face and his whole manner took on an extraordinary sharpness. "This, you see," he said, "is what I think is so wrong. I agree that every effort should be made to end the war, and that even in a cause as hopeless as this such effort should be exerted in good faith. But the great danger that I see is that while we are talking peace and weakening the democratic resistance to fascism and the will to fight it, Hitler will continue his aggressive campaign, vastly extend his power, and make our position a truly desperate one."

As the battle went on it seemed to Mark that all the arguments were in Sebastian's favor. But neither side would yield. Mark looked in turn at Baum, at Parrish and at Vorontov, and noticed that all three had broad, solid necks, especially Baum, who had done most of the talking, and whose neck looked strong as a bull's. Sebastian's, by contrast, was emaciated and fragile-looking.

Mark became conscious of Vorontov. The old man pushed himself forward to the edge of his chair to make his feet reach the floor and rested his right hand, palm down, on his right knee.

"Let me tell you something," he said, addressing Sebastian. "I am an old man. I have lived a long time, and I have had a close view of a good deal of the history of this century. You excuse me, no? for talking to you a little like a grandfather, and don't think I don't respect your great intelligence and your very special gifts. I am prepared to say that your analysis that you have given us is essentially correct and your predictions as to the war development are almost certainly right. But in politics, in everything connected with the dynamics of masses of people, there is a most important factor, which is not logical but psychological. And that is ripeness. For a certain evolution to take place a situation has to ripen. You can sometimes help the process a little, hurry it up, but it is an indispensable condition for success. Patience is needed. Sometimes opportunities are lost. The situation now is simply not ripe to commit our party to a war against Hitler, which could easily, as in Finland, be turned into a war against the Soviet Union in which Hitler, after a patched-up peace with the Western allies, would be sure to join. This is not just fantasy. It is a real danger. That is one thing."

Mark was watching Sebastian, but nothing in his expression

betrayed his reaction. His black eyes were directed at Vorontov, but they seemed also to envelop him, to look beyond him as though they took in all the years of this man's life and all the experiences that had filled it.

"There is another thing," Vorontov continued. He had a deep voice, and though he spoke with little emphasis, he commanded attention. "The people. You said a while ago that we put our trust in the people. This question is something the people instinctively understand. We must try to understand it too. Very important." He peered at Sebastian between narrowed eyelids, and he curved his mouth downward in a grimace that looked positively sinister. "Do you know what is the greatest power on earth?" He held the question in mid-air, suspended, and his eyes were mere yellow glints. "Not knowledge. Not intelligence. Not piety. Not faith in yourself or in others. But humility. The people—who are nothing, who have nothing—they have a kind of wisdom, and in their wisdom a strength that is irresistible. That wisdom is the sense of their human condition: not resignation, but recognition. The recognition of necessity. On this and only on this is it possible to build. To build a society. Theories, constructions of the mind—" He flung up his hands. "Nothing!" He shook his head. "There is nothing more dangerous than pride." He looked meaningfully at Sebastian, his face by now screwed up into a mask which, though a hideous distortion of his features, somehow expressed compassion. "It is a danger to which intellectuals are particularly exposed."

Now a change did come over Sebastian's face. A shadow fell across it, and then it was gone and a kind of innocence shone from it. He nodded his head.

"I know," he said. "But I have known it only recently. I used to think that the individual was self-contained. That the individual was free to the extent that he could feel, think and do for himself alone, and that like a runner he could go farthest and fastest if he had the strength and the vision and the courage, when he was alone, and that a man's most worth-while aim was to outdistance all others." He looked at Vorontov, then at

Baum and the rest of the group, with a wide-eyed candor that to Mark was like a window open to the blue of heaven. "It has become clear to me how illusory this freedom of the individual is and to what extent it rests on the 'unfreedom' of the many. And it has become clear to me that in a world beset with economic crises, vast inequalities, flood and famine, fascist conspiracies and the ravages of war, the scientist who cares about his science has to fight to defend it, to safeguard it from misuse—and the only allies to whom he can turn are the people."

A silence followed, which no one seemed willing to break. Finally Vorontov spoke.

"You understand, then, that the time has not yet come to give open support to the war?"

Mark was taken by surprise. He had not gathered from anything Sebastian had said that he had changed his views.

Sebastian nodded his head gravely. "I see it now." Mark was struck by the tone of finality. "I should have seen it before." He looked at Vorontov with a boyish air of contrition. "You realize that I am rather new to all this."

Vorontov slipped his feet to the floor and stood up. Baum got up too. The older man was two heads shorter than he.

"We must go now," said Vorontov. "We should not have stayed so long." He held out his hand to Sebastian and smiled knowingly. "It is unfortunately true that a worker understands certain things more easily than—than we do." He took the threadbare gray coat and tired black hat that Fritz handed him. "This can be a lesson in humility," he said as he turned to leave.

Bill Parrish got up shortly after Fritz Leutner had escorted the other two downstairs.

"I may not see you again before you go east," he said to Sebastian.

Mark found himself wondering how much Sebastian knew about Parrish's past relations with Tanya. Everything, he decided; but in the light of this he could not account for Sebastian's cordiality.

Parrish looked at Sebastian probingly, while his lips broadened in a good-natured smile. "The old man is right, of course. But he has often been wrong, too, as all of us have." He laughed as Fritz helped him on with his coat, an officer's trench coat. "People fool themselves when they say communists claim infallibility. We claim to be *better* than infallible. Because even the infallible make mistakes, as any Pope will tell you, off the record. We communists make plenty of mistakes, unfortunately—as many as our enemies, perhaps more. After all, we have nothing like their resources. But we have one supreme advantage: we know how to recognize our mistakes, and correct them, and learn from them." His strong face was still sparkling with good humor as he shook hands all around. "Sometimes we even admit them!" he added, and was gone.

The formal part of the meeting was over. Fritz was bringing coffee and sandwiches, and Bruce Patterson had begun to go around collecting dues and distributing literature. As usual, he passed Sebastian by. He came to Mark, and Mark reached into his inside coat pocket for his wallet.

"I—I haven't got my wallet," he stammered. "I must have left it at home . . ."

Suddenly he remembered Eve's face, with the blood trickling from a corner of her mouth, the churning violence that had gripped him. And he knew that when he left this meeting all his worries would still be waiting for him outside.

Chapter 5

EVE could not imagine how she had been able to stick it out till exams were over in early May. Those weeks had been a nightmare. She and Mark had lived in the same house, had shared meals, had carried on a semblance of conjugal life, they had tried to pretend in front of Jimmy that everything was "as usual." But even a child of barely four can sense tension between his parents, and when they no longer even sleep in the same bed he knows that something is radically wrong.

She had done everything she could during those weeks to keep from going crazy. She had indulged in fantasies, drugged herself to sleep, drunk herself into a half stupor during her waking hours to try to keep her mind from facing facts.

She had wanted to leave the very night it had happened, and had even started to pack her suitcase. But there was Jimmy. She knew it was all over now, because she couldn't go along with Mark any more as long as he stayed with his dirty job. But in the back of her mind the hope persisted that the scales would fall from his eyes, that he would wake up to what he was doing. Besides which she loved him, she had always loved him, and always would, and she shrank before any irrevocable gesture.

It was funny: even though she had been a member of the University community for only a short time, she felt herself bound even by some of its more superficial conventions. While marriage difficulties and irregularities were disapproved of at all times, a separation or divorce during academic sessions was particularly frowned upon. And yet this was not enough to explain how she had stood it all those weeks. She had been so wrought up—she still was, even now that Mark was away—that none of her reactions, nothing that she had done, had been normal.

The last words that Mark had spoken to her that mattered had been "You bitch!" And then he had hit her. Everything that he had said after that she had just sloughed off. She had been immune to all the words that he had uttered since, they had had no effect, she had hardly heard them. And now he was away, she didn't know where.

Of course she knew that he was unhappy too. And deep down she knew that he wasn't wicked or rotten or any of the nasty things that would come to her mind while she was eating her heart out and trying to keep herself from going to pieces. Where had he gone? He hadn't said. He had said he would be back, she remembered, before he had driven off in their old Dodge. She had a vague impression that he had also said something about having to do some research somewhere. Perhaps he didn't know himself where he was going. She hadn't told him that when he came back she probably wouldn't be around.

She had been in a kind of torpor for several weeks after he had left. It had been a relief, of course. An enormous relief. She could breathe freely, she didn't constantly have to be watching herself, be on the alert for his comings and goings, wear a mask, tremble on the edge of uncertainty as to what he would say or do next. There was just Jimmy and herself. The two of them in the big house.

But she had been under too great a strain for too long a time, and now she was exhausted. The least motion was an effort. She didn't need sleeping pills or whisky any more. But she had just enough energy left to take care of Jimmy and to get through the day.

One day at last she had a word from Mark—a postcard from somewhere near Los Angeles. For some reason it snapped her out of her lethargy. She decided that she would go back to her mother. She would give up the house. This phase of her life was over. She wasn't closing any doors. Mark could do what he liked. But she would never go back to him as long as he was a secret agent.

Mark had landed in Los Angeles to find it in the midst of a war production boom. But when he had set out on his journey he had had no destination in mind. He had simply run away—it had literally been a flight, unpremeditated, sudden. He had run away from Eve, from his marriage, from his problem. But at the same time his flight was not entirely an escape. He was looking for something, and he needed to get away to be able to think about it clearly. The Chief and Sebastian. Two poles. Did it have to be one or the other? That worried him too. He had looked up to the Chief. Now Sebastian seemed to be pushing the Chief into the background, to be taking his place.

So he had landed in Los Angeles, just at the time when most of the remaining free countries of Europe were being crushed under the Nazi war machine: Norway and Denmark had already been overrun, then Luxemburg, Belgium and Holland, and now France.

Defense industries were mushrooming in southern California, a series of new aviation plants—Douglas, North American, Vultee, Lockheed—were being built. He had taken a job on the production line and in order to do this had had to join the CIO union, which was organizing all the plants in the area. It was on the job and at meetings of the local that he heard about the strike at Santuro.

Santuro, a small company town lost in the arid wastes of the Mojave Desert, was the world's largest producer of potash, borax, boric acid, soda ash, salt cake, lithium and bromine. The twelve hundred workers of the U.S. Potash, Borax & Chemical Corporation had been out on strike for over three months. Their situation was said to be growing increasingly desperate.

On an impulse Mark decided to drive out there and see the thing for himself. He knew the impulse was irrational. What did he really hope to find? He had seen strikes before.

The impulse certainly had something to do with Sebastian. Mark wanted, in his own way, to confirm something, perhaps to test himself. Why had the country experienced the remarkable insurgency of labor in the last few years, millions of unorganized men and women joining unions, becoming politically articulate? Did all this have something to do with the values that Sebastian said resided in the masses, that fertilized not only social action—the everyday life of people in their work, in their relations to one another, in their institutions—but the arts and the sciences as well? Sebastian had come to this knowledge in his own way, directly, by a leap. Mark did not function in that way. He had to see things for himself, work them out step by step.

So he came to Santuro, not because he had been sent here

to do a job, not to prove anything, but to learn what he could.

He had not thought too much about how it was going to work out. He would arrive, he would look the situation over, he would talk to people, he would try, by conscientiously exploring all the factors, to understand the issues of the conflict. He went to the strike committee and offered his services. "I want to help you win your strike," he told them. He would give his full time. He would pay his own way. He would contribute to the strike fund.

The strikers, however, were suspicious. "We got plentya people," they said. "More than we know what to do with. And anyway, we don't know you."

As it happened, Norberg was scheduled to arrive the following day to address a meeting of the strikers, and once he had vouched for Mark there was no longer any problem. Mark was put to work immediately, and for the next six weeks he hardly had time to catch his breath.

The job that had to be done, in which Mark quickly came to take an important part, was to inform the world of what was happening in Santuro—to publicize, to solicit funds and contributions in kind, to keep up the morale of the strikers.

From the first day, Mark went to work with the fervent hope that the strike would be won and that his efforts would contribute to the victory. His involvement was a necessity, immediate, all-embracing, and there was no question, no detachment, no temptation or even time to take notes, to analyze. He was immersed, swept up into a situation of great urgency, and the only reality that had meaning for him was composed of the men and women whose cause he had made his own.

The experience left a deep mark upon him. At the end of the six weeks he felt he had been seeing and hearing and walking like a man for the first time.

The miles, as he drove home, lulled and yet sustained his growing eagerness to share his experience with Eve, with Sebastian and with Anderson, and hummed a refrain of joy and new-found strength.

And this, he repeated to himself as the towns and the fields and the rivers and the hills whirled past, this I owe entirely to Sebastian.

When he got home he discovered that he had no home. Another family occupied the house. Eve and Jimmy had left in July, and the forwarding address that Eve had left was her mother's.

He put up in a hotel that night. The next day he drove into town. Eve had gone back to work as a secretary for a law firm —the same job she had had before she married him. Jimmy was in nursery school.

"You might at least have told me this was what you wanted to do," he reproved her. "We could have talked it over."

"You didn't consult me when you took on an assignment that's ruined our marriage."

"You didn't even write and let me know how things stood."

"I didn't want to spoil your fun."

"Fun, hell!"

They parted in anger, but their quarrel had cleared the atmosphere. Mark got himself a room and went back to a routine of teaching and study. Anderson was away in Wisconsin for the fall semester on a visiting professorship, but Mark had plenty of work mapped out to keep himself busy while he was gone.

His experience in Santuro had crystallized many things. He knew now that he belonged to Sebastian's world and not to the Chief's. His long agony of indecision on that score at least was ended. It was supplanted however by another worry, of equal if not deeper gravity.

When he had first taken on this assignment to investigate Bloch he had completely approved of its objectives and had felt that it was not only a proper but a worthy activity. But now his entire outlook had changed, and he could no longer accept the assumptions on which his assignment was predicated. In the light of his new outlook the role of informer that he had played in relation to Sebastian and all his new left-wing friends no longer appeared as a laudable service in his country's interest, but on the contrary as a violation of trust, as a betrayal, of a peculiarly despicable kind. His first impulse, on returning from Santuro, was to quit immediately, to tell the Chief he was through. That would have, to begin with, the immediate advantage of straightening things out so far as his marriage was concerned, for he was sure Eve would come back to him at once. They would have a hard time making a go of it financially, of course, and Eve would probably have to go on working until he got his Ph.D., but she would be game. And he would be able to face Sebastian and the others with a clear conscience.

But after thinking about it a little he discovered that things were not that easy. All those reports that he had turned in to the Chief were on file in the office and were a matter of record. They were dynamite. They could ruin Sebastian's career. How could he undo the harm that he had done?

An idea came to him, one day, that gradually took root. During all this time he had built up a picture of a man more and more deeply involved in activities regarded as "subversive." Perhaps—yes, perhaps he could modify that picture, subtly at first, showing the subject hesitant and uncertain on a number of questions on which the party had taken a position, holding unorthodox views, taking issue with the officials, becoming less active, manifesting less interest in politics in general and in the party in particular. This could conceivably make a substantial difference in the over-all effect that those reports would have.

As the semester got under way he began sending the Chief more frequent and regular reports. The curious thing was that he found plenty of material that by a slight alteration of emphasis, by mere statement of fact without interpretation, suited his purpose perfectly. He had decided now definitely to become a candidate for the Doctor's degree and proceeded to pursue that goal in earnest.

He saw Sebastian more or less regularly at the weekly unit meetings, at Teachers' Union meetings and at meetings of other organizations. But Sebastian was often away now on mysterious errands which, from his sources of information, Mark knew had to do with strategic weapons research. A voluntary censorship of atomic information had been instituted in the spring, and in the course of the summer a National Research Council had been set up. Mark realized that from the service's point of view this was a time when he should be watching Sebastian more closely than ever. The war outlook, both in Europe and in Asia, was darkening.

Despite the fact that Mark was no longer communicating derogatory information in his reports, he found the strain of seeing Sebastian becoming increasingly great. In a curious way it was aggravated by the rift between himself and Eve. He had had to tell Sebastian and Tanya, of course, about the separation when he saw them in the fall. Tanya told him then that Eve had come with Jimmy to say good-by before she had left. Both Tanya and Sebastian showed such concern and solicitude that it positively embarrassed him. Worst of all, for some reason they both seemed to act as though they were in great part to blame for what had happened. Because it was in a way so close to the truth, Mark found it peculiarly distressing.

The war went on, with the Japanese moving into Indo-China and the bombing raids on Britain becoming ever more intensified. Franklin Roosevelt was elected for a third term, and the semester came to an end. By New Year's Eve, which he spent, rather miserably, with Eve and Jimmy and the combined families, he had reached a point where he felt he could no longer continue this divided life that was tearing him apart. At the stroke of midnight, when his father raised his glass of champagne and invited everyone to make a good New Year's resolution, Mark solemnly resolved that at the first opportunity he would tell Sebastian the whole story.

Chapter 6

THE spring semester began in the usual rush and confusion
—new students, new classes, long office hours taken up with
helping students with their study programs, appointments with
professors. Only after many attempts did Mark finally manage
to get in touch with Sebastian, and make a luncheon date with
him. But on the very morning of the appointed day, which
happened to be Inauguration Day, Sebastian phoned him to
say he would be unable to make it because an official from
Washington had turned up unexpectedly and could only see
him during the luncheon hour.

Later in the morning Mark ran into Tom Anderson, just
back from Wisconsin. It was the first he had seen of him since
his return, and as Anderson happened to be free that noon they
arranged to lunch at the Faculty Club.

The place was more crowded than usual, there were no private tables available, and they just managed to find two places
at one of the long tables. It was impossible, amid the roar of
topical discussions all around them, to carry on a private conversation. "After lunch," said Anderson reassuringly, "we'll
find a quiet spot where we can talk. I'll have a few minutes."

Mark caught sight of Sebastian passing through the huge
dining room, probably on his way to meet the Washington
notable, and at the same moment Sebastian's eyes, as if mag-
netized, alighted on him.

Sebastian came over to say he would be free at two, and
would have a little time before going to a seminar. "Perhaps
I could meet you in the library upstairs? We could walk over
together."

Although he had an office hour then, Mark was determined
not to put off his confession any longer.

"O.K.," he said.

The students could wait.

Immediately after Sebastian left, the conversation at their end of the table, which up to that point had been concerned with the Far East and Japan's plans for a Greater East Asia, turned to Bloch. Mark had of course often listened in on conversations about Sebastian. It always surprised him that he should react to them in such a personal way. But as he listened now his feeling was one of resentment, even of indignation, while he tried to gauge the ingredients of fatuity, jealousy or downright rancor that went into the remarks.

"He's not looking well," commented Joe Brand, the law professor, the moment Sebastian's back was turned. "He has fantastic nervous energy, but he's driving himself too hard." And he went on to enumerate some of Sebastian's many activities.

Everyone had a pet idea that he was bent on expressing.

"There's no denying his brilliance," said Sutherland the historian, during a momentary lull. "Perhaps he's more brilliant than Einstein. What disturbs me is that he has made no comparable contribution. Remember that Einstein had already published his restricted theory of relativity at twenty-six, and that by the time he was Bloch's age he was almost ready to bring out the generalized theory."

"What disturbs *me* most," said Cory, Mark's chairman, "is his leftism." He had a petulant old-womanish voice. He turned to Joe Brand irritably. "*You* may attribute his communistic ideas to his 'social imagination,' as you call it. Personally I put them down to sheer irresponsibility. A man in his position has no right to play around with the Left the way he does."

"Oh, but I'm certain that he is perfectly sincere," put in Alvarez, speaking carefully and with a strong Castilian accent. He was an instructor in Spanish, a Loyalist refugee.

"Fiddlesticks!" Cory snorted. "The trouble with Bloch is that he's too damn rich. He's a playboy. I'll tell you what: he's a twentieth-century Alcibiades. He's a good physicist, all right —how could he help it, with the brains he's got?—but he doesn't even take science too seriously. He'll always remain an inspired amateur."

Mark could feel himself growing tense.

Then Anderson spoke up for the first time. "The real trouble with Bloch," he said, "is that he's too damned brilliant for his own good. Everything is too easy for him. He's never had to struggle and plug and sweat to grasp an idea or master a subject, any more than he's had to work for a living."

Anderson's words came out like hard jabs, and he had the same angry look on his square granite face that he had when he lectured. He went on:

"He may come up with the right answers all right—he usually does—but what he misses is everything that leads up to them, the whole process that gives them their human content, the searching, the patient work, the tension, the frequent failure. That's why he'll never really understand the economic and political facts of life."

There was time for a bit of talk after lunch, and Mark and Anderson looked into one after another of the various rooms for a quiet corner where they could sit undisturbed. The library upstairs proved to be deserted, at least for the moment, and there were a couple of comfortable armchairs in a small alcove that was out of sight of the rest of the room. A ceiling-to-floor window gave a view, across rolling lawns dotted with tall pines and edged with beds of shrubbery, that took in several of the white stone buildings of the campus. The grass, though it still kept a trace of green, had a shriveled winter look and the sky was leaden. Here and there a figure could be seen moving briskly along one of the cement paths.

"Let's save your thesis for another time," Anderson said as they sat down. He reached in his pocket for his cigarettes and offered Mark one.

Mark whipped out his lighter, holding the engraved *Ph.D.* toward his teacher as he lit his cigarette. Anderson acknowledged it with a smile.

"I haven't had time yet to read the material you've turned in, and I haven't had much of a chance to think about it. We'll arrange for you to come over for dinner some time next week and we can go into it thoroughly then."

There were the past six or eight months to catch up with—Anderson's impression of his native state (he was from Oshkosh) during this critical period, Mark's experience with the Santuro strike and his separation from Eve, which he played down—but he was anxious to bring the talk around to the subject that was uppermost in his mind: Sebastian. He hadn't liked what Anderson had said about him at the luncheon table. But it was consistent with remarks that Anderson had let drop on a number of other occasions. He had a chip on his shoulder so far as Sebastian was concerned, and Mark was hoping to get some kind of clue as to why.

"I notice you keep taking pot shots at Sebastian Bloch," he said. "What have you got against him?"

Anderson gave him a rather mysterious smile.

"Funny," he said. "I was just going to mention Bloch." He swung one leg over the arm of his leather chair, assuming a most unprofessorial posture. "I haven't got anything against him. I just don't think he's God."

"Is it your impression that he does?" Mark felt strangely ill at ease.

"No, I'm sure not. But there are plenty of people who do. This is something I've been wanting to talk to you about for a long time, by the way," he went on, completely serious now. "It's none of my business, of course, and you're not going to like it. But I think I ought to tell you anyway, for your own good."

He was silent for a moment.

"I don't know exactly how to put it. You ask me what I have against him, and I haven't any good answer. I guess it's in large part intuitive. Certainly if I tried to explain it, it might not make too much sense. To sum it up in a phrase, I'd say that he flies too high. You know about birds of a feather. He just isn't my kind of bird. And I don't think he's yours."

"If you mean that I'm not in his class, of course I'll agree—"

"It isn't just that . . ." He brought his leg down and sat

forward a little, looking at Mark hard. "You've become pretty friendly with him, haven't you?"

Mark became wary. He had always remembered something the Chief had once said about Anderson: "He'll be very useful." He had dismissed it, yet he couldn't forget it. And he was professionally conditioned not to trust anybody.

"I like him a lot," he said.

"And he likes you."

"I can't vouch for that."

"I just don't like to see you get hurt." Anderson's tone, as well as his words, startled Mark.

"Get hurt? Why should I get hurt?"

"Because he's lightning."

Mark stared at him.

There was a long silence, then Mark became aware of someone—though footsteps were all but inaudible on the thick carpet—coming into the library. An odd little wizened face, which he recognized as that of a mathematics professor whose name he didn't know, came into view around the angle of the nook and peered at them for a second, then vanished.

"All right," Anderson said finally. "I'll tell you a story." He glanced at his wrist watch and Mark, by a reflex, looked at his own. There was still quite a bit of time before Sebastian would turn up.

"I've never told this to anyone except Helen," Anderson began. He looked hard at Mark. "This is just for you. I'm not making any comments, I'm drawing no inferences. I'm just telling the story straight."

He passed his hand over his chin, stroking it.

"Ever heard of Leo Hirschberg?"

Mark shook his head. "I've heard the name, that's all. A young physicist, a student of Bloch's."

"Yes. This was before you came here—or came back, I should say. Three or four years ago. I hadn't known Leo before, but he came from my home town in Wisconsin, from Oshkosh. His father was a doctor, and he happened to take care of my father in his last illness. So when Leo came here he looked me up, though he wasn't taking any economics courses. We got to be good friends. He was just twenty-five.

"Leo was nothing to look at. He was short and didn't carry himself well, he had bad eyes and wore thick glasses, and he had a funny rabbit look around the mouth. But you only had to be with him a few minutes to discover that he was a rare human being—sensitive, generous, kind. You just couldn't help liking him. He had a hell of a good mind and was a first-rate physicist. Bloch was crazy about him and considered him one of his most promising students. They did some experiments together on hard gamma rays and published a couple of papers in *The Physical Review* that Bloch cosigned with Leo Hirschberg. A great honor.

"There was only one thing wrong with Leo; he was terribly shy. He thought of himself as unattractive and devoid of any kind of appeal, especially for women. It was a well-defined case of an inferiority complex and he was rather unhappy a good deal of the time, though he kept it pretty much to himself, and he was generally regarded as a fairly well-adjusted guy.

"The big thing in his life was Sebastian Bloch. Like so many of the physics students, he worshiped him, and the fact that Bloch seemed to single him out for special attention did a lot for his ego. And then, as if that weren't enough, something else came his way that was quite unexpected, and that seemed to promise him lasting happiness."

Anderson took a last long drag on his cigarette, crushed the butt in the ash tray by his side and slowly blew the smoke out. Mark became aware that his body was all tense, and he consciously relaxed his muscles.

"Estrellita. I don't know if that was her real name, but that's the name she went by. I don't even remember her last name. She was a Mexican girl, from Cuernevaca—good family, I believe, though why they allowed her around loose will always remain a mystery to me. She was only nineteen, twenty at the most, and she was one of those women that men leave home for. She was a magnificent creature—jet-black hair, enormous dark burning eyes, small even teeth that flashed white in her red mouth. Her skin was tawny with a flush of pink, and smooth as a shell. The curves and movements of her body were soft and graceful as a cat's. And they had the same suggestion of steel-spring tautness and strength. There was witchery in her laughter, and you couldn't look at her without your pulse starting to race. She had sex written all over her.

"Well, for some mysterious reason she took to Leo. I have no idea how they met. As I said, Leo was not unattractive and he was lovable, and Estrellita had a pretty good head on her lovely shoulders. But there was something wild and reckless about that glamorous beauty of hers. It was hard to think of her tying herself down to any one man, and Leo was the last man you would think of to pair with her. But they seemed to hit it off. They went together for several months, and then at the end of that spring semester they became engaged.

"This, you understand, was a proper, conventional courtship, with no jumping of the gun on the wedding ceremony. Leo was old-fashioned about some things. I don't know whether he had ever gone to bed with a woman—I suspect not —but in any case he would have thought it dishonorable to have such intimacy with the girl he was going to marry. He was a little dazed by his unbelievable good luck. He was like a kid with a new toy. He was the happiest man you ever saw. He went around beaming, he was working well: no more inferiority complex, everything was clicking. They were going to be married at the end of summer.

"For some reason which also is not clear to me, Bloch does not seem to have been told about the engagement. In fact I'm quite sure he knew nothing about it. Everyone else of course knew. Perhaps Bloch had been away just when they were engaged—he *had* met Estrellita, and had seen her and Leo together a number of times, just enough to know there was some kind of connection—and later, things were sort of hurried. Or perhaps—I'm just guessing—perhaps Leo had a feeling, some premonition . . . no, forget it.

"Just at the end of the semester Bloch got an urgent call from one of the big industrial laboratories—General Electric,

I think it was—for a man to head up a special research project. They were offering a three-month contract. Good pay, a lot of prestige, a wonderful opportunity. Bloch gave the chance to Leo, who jumped at it. So everything was working out beautifully for him. He had one of the world's great physicists as his best friend and teacher, he had just been given his first chance at an important professional job, and best of all he was going to marry the most beautiful girl in the world.

"He didn't like the idea of the three-month separation, of course. But on the other hand the last months of an engagement are apt to be pretty trying, when the two see each other all the time and are being proper about it. Besides, Leo would be able to concentrate fully on his difficult job, and Estrellita would have plenty of time to go back to Mexico for a visit with her parents, get her trousseau together, or whatever. I saw Leo just the day before he left for the east. He was a happy man."

Anderson lit another cigarette, taking it slowly, and blew out a big puff of smoke. Mark had to stretch out his left leg which had begun to ache.

"Estrellita didn't go down to Mexico. A few days after she had said good-by to Leo she telephoned Bloch one evening at his apartment and said she wanted to see him. Leo had talked about him so much that he had undoubtedly aroused a violent curiosity in her, and perhaps more than curiosity. Bloch went to fetch her in his car at her boardinghouse and brought her to his apartment. She stayed the night."

For a moment Mark felt as if his bones were turning into water. He had to take a firm hold on the arms of his chair.

"The affair lasted the major part of those three months," Anderson continued. "By all accounts it was a passionate and colorful romance. Bloch never does anything by halves, and apparently he put everything into this. They did a lot of traveling in his big roadster, all over the countryside and out to the coast, putting up at ritzy hotels and resorts, taking in concerts and shows, dancing, riding. He bought her scads of exotic-looking clothes and flashy, barbaric jewelry. And then one day he decided it was enough. He bought her a lot of expensive presents and told her in the nicest way he could that he was through.

"The trouble—" Mark could feel that Anderson was watching him closely. "The trouble was that in the meantime Estrellita had fallen in love with Bloch. For her the romance was just beginning, and it wasn't ever supposed to end. There were violent scenes in which she tried, by cajolery and threats, to make him take her back.

"Then one day, in desperation, she told Bloch the truth about Leo and herself. That was the last time Bloch saw her: he threw her out. According to her, he refused to believe it and thought she was concocting the story for some malevolent purpose of her own. 'I'll believe that if Leo himself tells me,' she quoted him as saying.

"Well, Leo never did confirm her story, because he and Bloch never saw each other again.

"When Leo came back he was already in a badly agitated state of mind. While he had been gone he had hardly heard from Estrellita in answer to the dozens of passionate and increasingly worried letters he had written her. Just two or three noncommittal notes. He knew she hadn't gone back to Mexico to get ready for the wedding. The very first time he saw Estrellita after he got back she told him exactly how things stood. I guess she did it pretty brutally—how she had been living with Bloch, and fallen in love with him, and he had rejected her; that she no longer loved Leo, and couldn't go through with the marriage, and of course she was sorry . . .

"I didn't see Leo myself after he got back, and I don't know anyone else who did. He was found dead in a room in a cheap hotel in town two days later. An overdose of Nembutal.

"He left a note for his father, the doctor, back in Oshkosh, which I had the sad duty of sending to him. I don't know what he said in that note. But he also left one for Estrellita which she showed me."

Anderson paused, and Mark had the impression that he was making an effort to control his emotions.

"You probably think of me as a hard-boiled old cuss, and I suppose maybe I am." He paused again. "But that last note of Leo's shook me."

He looked at Mark, and there was an expression almost of compassion in his eyes.

"Bloch wasn't to blame. He can't help being what he is. But because of it, people close to him are apt to get burned. What Leo said, in effect, was this. Losing Estrellita was a terrible blow. But that he could have stood. He knew he didn't deserve her, and deep down he had always known that he was not the man for her. At least she had given him a few months of happiness. And if he had to lose her, there was no one he could have chosen whom he would rather have seen her marry than Sebastian. But what he could not live with was the thought that Sebastian should have sent him away purposely in order to have her to himself and enjoy her. Yet he might even have taken that, he said, if Bloch had done it out of love and had intended to marry her. The fact that he had taken from him the being whom he cherished more than all the world and been intimate with her, and had then discarded her—that he couldn't bear."

Anderson got to his feet.

"That's the story," he said, "as I got it from two of the three interested parties." He began to walk slowly toward the carpet. "I don't know what happened to the girl. She disappeared—"

At that moment Mark became aware of another presence. He looked around.

Sebastian was standing at the entrance to the alcove. He did not move, and he looked as though he might have been there for a long time, though Mark was sure he had not been present the moment before.

Mark felt like a small boy caught in a shameful act, and Anderson too was visibly ill at ease. How much had Sebastian heard? He could have been behind the bookcase for a long time. But it was impossible to think of Sebastian as eavesdropping. (And yet, why not? Mark found himself thinking. Wasn't that what he himself had been doing professionally for years?)

"I hope I'm not interrupting an important conference." Sebastian looked benignly, and with a half-smile utterly devoid of guile, first at Anderson and then at Mark. He had the face of an old man who has plumbed the depths of human tribulations and sorrows and who in his declining years can still contemplate life with serenity.

"Not at all," Anderson said, quickly recovering his composure. "We had finished our business, and I was just telling a story to make a point." He turned to Mark. "I don't know if I made it."

"As far as you went," Mark said. He was sure now that Sebastian must have heard enough to know what the story was. "But there was a third interested party, remember. That shouldn't be overlooked."

Anderson shot him a quick luminous look, like a chess player acknowledging a good move by his opponent.

"Quite right," he said. "And I'm sure you won't overlook it."

As he and Sebastian walked away from the Faculty Club after taking leave of Anderson, Mark remembered that this was the moment he had been looking forward to for so long, both eagerly and with dread, when he would make his confession to Sebastian. But the story of Leo Hirschberg had shaken him. David and Absalom.

Sebastian made the little sound of clearing his throat that Mark knew so well.

"This perhaps isn't the best time," he said, glancing at his wrist watch. "I have my seminar. But you will certainly want at least a brief statement immediately from the 'third interested party.' "

Mark made a vague gesture of remonstrance. He felt embarrassed.

He had felt embarrassed when Anderson had told him the story although it was a story that he would have reveled in two years before and have written up in full detail in one of his regular reports to Gregg. But just now he had listened to it

reluctantly, feeling he had no right to hear it, at the same time
that it filled him with an unaccountable distress. He felt an
obscure sense of having been guilty of disloyalty toward Sebastian, not so much in listening to the story as in having, even
with reservations, accepted it and having allowed it, however
slightly, to shake his faith in Sebastian's integrity, humanity
and wisdom.

Sebastian slowed his pace. Mark, wearing a hat and a heavy
coat, still felt the penetrating January cold, but Sebastian, coat-
less and hatless, seemed impervious to the weather.

"Anderson's voice, as you know, carries like a foghorn," he
went on. "I couldn't help hearing a few words as I stepped
into the library. I would have joined you right away without
listening if I hadn't caught Leo's name. Then I hesitated. I
gathered immediately that he was telling you the story by way
of warning you against me. And I decided it wouldn't be fair
to interrupt, that I should let you hear his version through to
the end."

Mark glanced at Sebastian out of the corner of his eye. He
was having difficulty holding himself back to Sebastian's slow
pace. The sharp, ascetic face was bloodless and blue-tinged
with cold, but beneath the tired skin there was the suggestion
of an inner fire.

"But why," Mark said, "didn't you say anything to Anderson about it? He must have guessed, as easily as I did, that you
heard something of what he was telling."

A suggestion of hardness came into Sebastian's face. "I preferred not to discuss it with him." He was silent for a moment.
"There's too much to say."

They walked on a little distance without speaking.

"Anderson said I wasn't to blame," Sebastian said finally.
"That's where I came in," he added parenthetically. "Actually
I *was*—very much to blame. But in another way."

He looked at Mark earnestly, and shook his head.

"I'm sure this is not easy for you. I would certainly rather
you had never heard of it. I—I'm afraid I didn't behave very
well. But you must form your own judgment."

Mark sensed that Sebastian was trying hard to conceal how

painful the subject was to him and how doubly painful to say what he felt he had to say about it.

"I don't know exactly what Anderson may have told you, but I can guess." He cocked his head a little to one side and shook it slowly. "It wasn't exactly like that. The girl never loved poor Leo. She was a terribly mixed-up creature. Not vicious, but spoiled—spoiled by her outrageous beauty, by her parents, and completely wild. She had got into trouble back home in Cuernevaca, and disgraced her family, and they had sent her up here chaperoned by an old aunt who had instructions to marry her off as soon as possible. Leo was probably the most unlikely victim she could have hit on. The aunt, finding him eminently respectable, gave her approval. And Leo, in his innocence and complete lack of experience, believed that she was a virgin and that she cared for him and he was going to marry her.

"The way I became involved was this. The girl, though she was a nymphomaniac, had decent impulses and was good-hearted when she wasn't thwarted. By the time she and Leo became officially engaged she had come to like Leo too much to want to play the dirty trick on him that she had planned. And by the time he left for Schenectady she had decided to break off the engagement. But she wanted to do it without hurting him."

Sebastian was talking in such a low voice that Mark had to strain to hear him.

"I am reasonably sure that she was telling the truth when she said to me, weeks later, that her sole purpose in phoning me that first time was to get my advice as a friend of Leo's. She had assumed, as a matter of course, that I knew all about their engagement and would therefore regard her as completely taboo. It took her no time at all to discover that I knew absolutely nothing about her relation to Leo. She decided then and there to make a play for me. As it happened, at just that point I was a pushover for such an adventure. The girl was terribly attractive, and she was the kind who played around, so I knew there wouldn't be any broken hearts. We had an affair.

It was perfect in its way while it lasted. What happened later, of course, completely spoiled it.

"When I decided that the affair had come to its natural end she proved to be a bad sport and pretended that she had fallen in love with me. She had enjoyed our rather extravagant fling, and I guess wasn't ready to have it end, as she knew it had to. Also, I think it hurt her pride that I should have made the first move, though I tried to do it as gently as possible. She became difficult and I was forced to handle her a little roughly. It was then, and only then, that she told me about being engaged to Leo.

"Like all such women, she was a terrible liar. She told me half a dozen contradictory stories, and finally decided to stick to the one to the effect that she had fallen in love with me and because of this wouldn't marry Leo. I threw her out for good when I realized she had become hopelessly unreasonable. My one concern from that point on was to get hold of Leo before she did and set him straight. I tried to phone him while he was still back east, but was told that he had already left Schenectady. And he was not returning by train or by plane, but had bought a car and was driving, so that there was no possibility of reaching him while he was on his way or of knowing exactly when he would arrive. I realized later that I should have had him traced, but I had no way of knowing how desperate he already was. I didn't know that he had hardly heard from her all summer and that he had been writing her increasingly frantic letters. Actually he was in such bad shape that he had a couple of accidents, abandoned his car in Cincinnati, and flew the rest of the way.

"I had left word for him in his apartment and had people on the lookout for him. But he didn't even open his mail when he came in. He must just have stayed in the apartment long enough to phone and make a date with her. You know approximately what she told him."

They walked on in silence. Was that the end of Sebastian's story? They had passed the Astronomy building and skirted Bosley Hall and were approaching the Physics building.

"You may have wondered," Sebastian said, "whether I knew about the contents of the note Leo left for her." He shook his head, and his lips parted in a mirthless smile. "She sent it to me, with a notation to the effect that it apparently concerned me more than it did her, so she was passing it on to me. That is the last I heard from her."

They had reached the pyramid of granite steps leading up to the entrance to the Physics building, and Sebastian stopped.

"Seen from a certain angle," he said, "the whole thing has the earmarks of an obscene joke played by fate on three people, each afflicted with his own blindness. What is so particularly rotten is that the only innocent one of them should have been made to pay the greatest penalty. Leo's death was a terrible blow to me. There is nothing that I wouldn't have done to save him. The realization that if it had not been for me he would probably be alive today is a weight that I don't carry easily. I say 'probably,' for without wishing to minimize my own guilt, there was in Leo a certain element of self-destructiveness. For some reasons that are easy to guess, and others that are more obscure, he took elaborate precautions to keep the knowledge of his engagement from me. And I was the one person who should have known. What I blame myself for most is this ignorance. He needed more help and protection than I gave him. I failed him. And the bitterest of all is the knowledge that he died because he thought I had betrayed him."

He put one foot on the first step to the building. "Here I've been unburdening myself and doing all the talking, and I haven't given you a chance to tell me what you had on your mind. Will it keep?"

The chimes of the college chapel rang out their eight preliminary notes, then pealed the hour of two.

"Yes," said Mark. "It will probably keep a long time."

He suddenly knew that he couldn't, either now or in the predictable future, tell Sebastian what he had planned to.

"I'm glad you told me," he said. "I—" There were many things that he would have liked to express: his inner turmoil, a vague unhappiness bred in large part of his own unworthiness, but also the revelation of shadows where he had not expected them, and with this a communion born of the flesh and its snares. But he could find no words. "I just don't—"

"That's all right," Sebastian said, putting his hand to Mark's arm and pressing it gently. "I know it isn't easy. Just take your time. Whatever you decide will be right."

"Don't worry about me . . . I—"

"Oh, one more thing," Sebastian put in. "Perhaps it's important." He looked down, chewing his lower lip. "All this happened some three or four years ago." He looked up again and his fathomless eyes met Mark's. "It couldn't happen today—" He broke off abruptly. "I must run, now. Call me."

They shook hands, and Sebastian, stooping slightly, one shoulder higher than the other, a loose-jointed, somewhat ungainly figure, hurried stumbling up the steps and was quickly lost in the crowd of students.

Chapter 7

LIGHT so dazzling that it made a night black as the thrust of white-hot daggers through the retinas of both eyes; blackness so deep that its intensity shone with the blinding violence of a thousand suns . . .

It had been a frightening dream. Or was it a dream?

Sebastian opened his eyes, but they encountered a darkness as great as he had just leapt from, and he immediately shut them again. His head was a little knot of hardness, much too explosive for sleep, a knot that was prolonged by an awkward spine to which an odd assortment of organs and parts was attached, each of them a point of attack for discomforts, strains and aches, distracting the head from its pure obsession.

After a time—how long?—the elements began slowly to untangle. A military operation, a vast wheeling movement hinged on a key Russian city—Lenincow or Mosgrad—became an acute twinge in his right hip that required a slow and careful rearranging of his whole body. This took some time, and when his eyes opened again the dark was less opaque. Now he seemed to remember that while the momentous happenings were unfolding he had been aware of a man (whom he knew well but did not recognize) who was trying with some urgency to reach him, but who was perpetually foiled. A turn in the road, a closing door, a crowd pressing ahead of him. Who was he? What did he want? There were too many generals. Now, with returning wakefulness, it was clear that it was Mark. But what did he want? Oh yes, of course it was just a dream.

At the same time he had the impression that he had been awake for hours. In which case he could not have been dreaming. He felt utterly exhausted, though his nerves were quivering, his muscles taut. For a week now he had felt this tension, and sleep when it had come had been this same fever filled with visions of violence. Yet the news of Hitler's attack on Russia had been long expected and had none of the effects of surprise. But it brought the need for decision one fateful step closer.

There was an ache, a curious hollow ache inside his right shoulder, and he turned his body again. He felt Tanya's nakedness stir in response to his movement and her warm buttocks snuggled into the hollow of the angle formed by his belly and his thighs. He remembered last night's party. Why had he had, for the first time, the feeling that Tanya was *too* beautiful, that she seemed out of place? He had insisted on candles—there had been over a hundred in the living room—and he had known later when he had looked at her across the room, standing in the center of a group of physicists, most of them foreign, in tuxedos, that he had meant the many-tongued light to lick her bare throat and shoulders and arms in just that way to give her skin that soft glow against the glistening white silk of her low-cut dress. So that perhaps it was not she, but all the others who were out of place? Who belonged where?

Now they were moving into a time of boxes within boxes, of compartments, overlapping perhaps, but impermeable to one another. The twelve physicists, from Britain, Sweden, Germany, Hungary, Italy, from Columbia, Wisconsin, California and the University, had had a three-day conference on the uranium headache. Porter had of course been a part of it, and Maynard Reed had sat in on it. Bruce Patterson and Fritz Leutner, who had been working not only on thorium and protoactinium but on isotope separation and knew most of what was known in the field, were not in on it but would be told about it. Goldstein and MacAvoy and Weber, who were working on moderators and gadgets, would be told something but not all. The others among the thirty-odd physicists who had attended the party (not counting a dozen wives) would know no more than they could guess, which in some cases would be a good deal.

Had they drunk too much champagne? He had an impression that he had had to open a third case, but he wasn't sure. A special edition of Moët & Chandon's 1923 vintage, from his father's cellar. When one of the Britishers had raised his glass and proposed a toast "to 93," Sebastian had quickly interposed, "A good novel. But of all Victor Hugo's work I prefer the early lyrics. However, if you insist on a novel, why don't we drink to *L'Homme qui rit*? And in this case we mean the *first* man who laughs, because he is quite likely also to be the last and *only* one."

It was a poor joke, he recognized now, but even Fenway's cryptic reference to the first transuranic element (if it were found to exist) had seemed to him fraught with danger. Yet in a sober light the danger appeared all but chimerical. That U-238 by absorbing one neutron would pass through the stage of neptunium to become fissionable plutonium had by no means been proved. And the Geissler tube method of separating U-235 being used at the University of Minnesota and General Electric—the only method found so far—that yielded 1036 millionths of a gram every ten days, would take 26,445 years to produce one gram, and 11,995,074 years to produce one pound.

Sebastian sighed. Perhaps it couldn't be done. He shook his head. It *could* be done. The question was: *should* it be done?

His hand sliding down the smooth flank seemed to release a soft spring that caused Tanya's body to turn gently upon itself. She was surely not awake, yet the touch of his hand as it grazed the feathery tangle of hairs and slipped between her thighs set off pulsations of desire. She drew him onto her and enfolded him, as if to capture him and carry him off into a golden dream from which dark broodings and sinister devisings were rigorously banished.

For a moment he held back. Why? Not because the pleasure of a woman's embrace, so long shunned, was still accompanied by a morbid sense of sin. But it seemed to him now that the solemnity of responsibilities to be assumed, of decisions to be made at this juncture, called for a state of grace with which sexual indulgence was incompatible.

It was too late. Her legs were locked around him and his prodding flesh, unguided, had found its way into her and he was swept by the headlong cavalcade of the senses. I could lose myself, he thought, responding now to the lurches and twists, the contractions and thrusts of the palpitating body beneath him. This alone could be real, and the rest shadows. . . .

Yet no magic door opened to admit him to that golden dream which held her apart from him. Could she really still be asleep? No word of tenderness issued from her lips, but her breath came in little sighs and gasps that were like a secret language of ecstasy. In the half-light her face, with her eyes tightly shut, had a look of concentrated expectancy.

Desire in him gave way to a kind of fury. The mechanism of her dream, he supposed, was so contrived that she was geared to reach the climax of her pleasure without awakening. He suddenly decided to wrench her out of her dream by the very violence of his embrace.

The first gulp of steaming black coffee burned his throat as it went down, but it effectively dispelled the last shadows left by the phantoms of the night. The papers spread out before him, independently of their political color or their contents, had a reassuring today-is-another-day look.

He and Tanya were breakfasting out on the terrace, their slippered feet bathed in morning sunlight. The shadows of the camellia bush fell across the pale blue folds of Tanya's crepe-de-Chine dressing gown over the even paler blue of the sheer, lace-edged nightgown that she had slipped on after getting out of bed.

She had got up this morning a little sleepier perhaps than usual, looking a bit tired even, but without the slightest self-consciousness, making no allusion to what had happened in bed.

It was a radiant morning. There was dew on the grass, a glittering web of diamonds, there was a hum of bees among the yellow roses overhead, and the smell of the earth and the fragrance of growing things had an indescribable freshness. The Germans reported that they had taken Vilna, Kauna, Brest-Litovsk, had passed Minsk and were approaching Lwow. The Finns were attacking on the north.

"You should see the living room," said Tanya. "The house is a shambles."

He could imagine it—the burned-down candles, the glasses, the bottles, the dishes and remains from the buffet supper, the ash trays, the floor littered with crushed butts . . .

Roosevelt had ordered 900,000 more men inducted into the army.

"I hope you're not completely worn out."

"Well—" She wagged her head and rolled her eyes upward while a perverse smile played over her lips. "If only we didn't have to do any more entertaining for a while or have to see people or be polite. I've had hardly a moment to spend with Gino for a week."

"I know. We've been working you too hard. But today's lunch will be your last chore, and after that—"

"*What* lunch?"

"Don't you remember? We have to feed Gröndahl."

"Oh, heavens, I'd completely forgotten! What are we going

to do? There'll barely be time to get the house cleaned up."

"It doesn't matter. He takes things as they come. You won't have to put yourself out."

"Couldn't you both eat out? It's going to be one hell of a rush, and I have no idea when I'll even be able to get into the kitchen."

"I'm afraid not . . ."

He hadn't yet resolved the problem of what to tell Tanya. Gröndahl was conducting a survey of the country's scientific resources with a view to making recommendations as to the most judicious allocations of such modest funds as were being made available by the National Emergency Research Council for uranium research. The University was trying to get a sizable contract for a project on one important piece of the nuclear puzzle, and the Physics department had delegated Sebastian to negotiate it. He was going to see the president this morning to prepare the ground for Gröndahl's interview with him this afternoon. But Gröndahl didn't want any publicity. He didn't want to be seen, especially not with Sebastian, in a restaurant.

". . . Just this last little lunch—all we need is some French bread and cheese and a bottle of wine; that's what we often had when we saw each other for lunch in Paris—and then no more entertaining, no more lunches, no more dinners, no more cocktail or evening parties . . ."

"Until when?"

"Until— I'll tell you what: tonight, unless something quite unexpected—"

"No, thank you! I'm not going to be dragged into any more plans that turn out at the last minute to be no plans at all."

She certainly had a point. "All right," he said, "we'll make it definite." After all, he was entitled to a private life. "Tonight we'll have dinner out—anywhere you like. We won't invite anyone to the house for at least a week."

Tanya gave a great sigh. "How heavenly!"

She poured out more coffee into both their cups.

"By the way," she said, putting down the cup that she had started to raise to her lips, "what in the world has happened to

Mark? I haven't seen him since I don't know when. You were going to have him over."

Sebastian put down his cup and looked up from the papers. "I'm worried about Mark."

"What's wrong with him?"

"I don't know. He's unhappy. He isn't himself. He's gone limp. Something is preying on his mind. A part of his trouble certainly has to do with Eve. But I'm not sure that there isn't something else."

"Have you tried to talk to him?"

"He won't talk about it."

"What does he say?"

"I don't want to ask him. He'd tell me if he was willing to talk about it."

"Yes, I guess he would. I can hardly imagine him keeping anything secret from you."

"One explanation would be that he doesn't want to embarrass me. It must have something to do with me. And the only thing connected with me that could possibly cause him to have qualms is the matter of party membership. I can see that that might have a lot to do with the difficulty between him and Eve. But I think there must be something else."

"I wonder . . ." Tanya took a cigarette, and Sebastian's hand automatically reached into the pocket of his robe for his lighter. "You'll probably say I'm crazy, but it's something that occurs to me . . ." She leaned forward toward the flame of his lighter. "Suppose Mark joined the party only because of you. He's crazy about you, you know, and it's a sure way for him to see you often and regularly. Maybe he's unhappy about being in the party but can't bring himself to pull out, because of you."

Sebastian shook his head. "I think we can rule that out. He's too levelheaded. Joining the party is a serious step, and he has a strong sense of responsibility about his family."

But on second thought he was less sure. He lit a cigarette for himself and frowned.

"I can't help feeling, though," he said, "that it's all my fault and that I ought to do something about it."

"What can you possibly do, if you can't talk to Mark?"

Sebastian watched the smoke curl upward from his cigarette for a moment. "There's Eve," he said.

"Oh, but—"

"I know."

After a silence Tanya asked, "How is it between them now?"

"They see each other once in a while. Mark drives to town and pays a call every two or three weeks, takes Jimmy out occasionally on Sundays. It's . . . pretty sad."

"But she still isn't asking for a divorce?"

"No. As a matter of fact, Mark seems to think that once he gets his Ph.D. everything is going to be all right, and that she'll come back."

"And when is that supposed to be?"

"His oral is down for November. He's passed his French and German examinations, and he's planning to finish his thesis this summer. So if all goes well he should have his doctorate by the end of November."

"And then she's supposed to come back?"

"So he claims."

"That's only about five months off. But surely her leaving him had nothing to do with his having or not having a Ph.D. That's too absurd!"

"Exactly. So if she does come back as he says she will when he gets his degree, it can't possibly be because of the degree itself nor, I think, because of the instructorship that he'll certainly be offered. It must be because of something else that is supposed to happen at the same time."

"Something having to do with you?"

"It doesn't make much sense, does it?"

There was another silence. Sebastian cocked his head. He was remembering Leo Hirschberg. He was remembering a long succession of individuals going back to his earliest childhood, men, women, girls, boys, who in one way or another had been associated with him and who had come to greater or lesser grief through no fault of his, yet somehow because of him. That remark of Anderson's which he had overheard that day in the library of the Faculty Club . . . It was nonsense of course, but he didn't want anything to happen to Mark.

"Perhaps," he said, "everything is going to be all right, as Mark seems to believe. But I think it would be wrong to sit back and do nothing when there's even a bare possibility that I could do something to help."

Five minutes later he was talking on the telephone to Eve— Tanya, remembering that Eve's maiden name was Loasby, had found the number in the telephone directory. Eve was startled by his ringing and was obviously extremely reluctant to see him.

"She didn't want to see me, but I twisted her arm," he said, grinning, when he came back to the terrace. "I'm to go to her house at five this afternoon."

The pale blue crepe-de-Chine gave a wispy, ethereal quality to Tanya's body that contrasted startlingly with the tactile memory of the night.

"God knows," he said, "I have no great yen to see her either. But in any case I'm not going to have much time to think about it between now and then."

He did catch himself thinking about it again, however, several times during the morning. The thought that because of him some deep misunderstanding had arisen between Mark and Eve seemed just to have come out into the open at the prompting of Tanya's questions, but he recognized that he had carried it deep within him for a long time.

Dr. Gröndahl appeared promptly at 12:30, and Sebastian introduced him rather hurriedly to Tanya and Gino. "We're going to go into a huddle for a while," he told Tanya as the two men headed for the study. He was anxious to get the serious business over with before lunch so that they could enjoy a relaxed sociable visit afterwards.

"Well, I see you've changed your style of living," Gröndahl said, taking in the room, the book-lined walls, the large Kazak rug, the comfortable furniture, the pictures, the knickknacks. He was referring to the time when they had seen a good deal of each other in Paris, where Sebastian had lived in a small rented room near the Porte d'Orléans—bare walls, curtainless windows, an *armoire*, a table, two chairs, a blackboard, a cot, a sink with a cold water tap in one corner; never more than one or two books which he would get rid of as soon as he had absorbed them. He had wanted no possessions, no attachments. He had reduced food, sleep, indulgence of every kind to the minimum, his whole being dedicated to exploring the vast realms of speculation opened up by the new findings in atomic science. Perhaps Gröndahl was remembering what Sebastian had said late one night when they had walked along the quays after a lecture at the Collège de France: "I want my life to be stripped of everything but the essential, like a bleached bone." That was a long time ago. It belonged to another world.

"The books are from my father's library," Sebastian said now as they sat down.

Gröndahl listened dutifully to his careful report on the uranium symposium. But he had not lost his habit of looking a little bored and restless when he himself was not talking, and he apparently had something on his mind to which this was only a prelude and which he was anxious to get to. Yet the developments on which Sebastian had to report were of considerable interest. The lattice pile at Columbia was practically completed and work could soon go ahead on determination of the multiplication factor. At California they were working on U-238 and the capture of fast neutrons. Elsewhere projects were moving forward on isotope separation with the mass spectroscope, by centrifuge and by gaseous diffusion, and other methods were being tested.

"We never kidded ourselves that it was going to be easy," Gröndahl grumbled, "but it looks as if it's going to be even tougher than we thought. How are the calculations?"

"Not very good." Sebastian gave some typical estimates of plant requirements.

"It means money," Gröndahl said, getting up to study a Cézanne landscape that hung above the fireplace. "A hell of a lot of money."

He turned, with both hands in his trouser pockets, and faced Sebastian.

"Tell me, how do you really feel about this?"

Sebastian met his gaze. What he liked about Gröndahl was

his utter indifference to persons or personalities. Whether he spoke to Roosevelt or Churchill or Einstein or his wife or a student or a taxi driver, he would have the same rasping, slightly disparaging approach.

"If you want a straight, simple answer," Sebastian said, "I'm afraid of it."

"That's no answer. What I want to know is: what are you going to do about it?"

Yes, it came to that. The question was becoming more and more insistent. Hitler's invasion of Russia had brought it still closer.

"I've been helping," he said softly. "Of course I'll continue to help in any way I can."

"Help!" Gröndahl exploded. "Hell, man, what we need is your leadership!"

"Let's not lose our heads." Sebastian gave a slight edge to his voice. "We're still a long way from anywhere. Let's wait and see where we're going." As a scientist he was challenged and excited by the breath-taking possibilities inherent in harnessing the energy of the atom, though this was incidental to problems of far deeper import. But behind the war clouds that were rapidly approaching stalked terrifying phantoms.

Gröndahl stuck out his jaw aggressively. "You think we have a lot of time to throw away?" He came a step closer, glowering. "We've just had word through intelligence"—he had dropped his voice, but his tone was ominous—"the Germans are working on uranium. Hitler has given orders to go all-out. A whole big section of the Kaiser Wilhelm Institute is being given over to research."

Sebastian got up and walked over to the window. If what Gröndahl said was true, there was no longer a choice.

He turned into the room. "Are you pretty sure of this?"

"Am I *sure?*" Gröndahl's voice rose again, but he checked himself and sat down. "The source is unimpeachable."

Sebastian frowned. He visualized Hahn, Heisenberg, their many co-workers, as he had last seen them.

"This is terribly serious," he said.

"That's what I'm telling you."

The first thing to do, Sebastian decided, was to try to check the information. The possibilities of doing this, however, were slight. He considered the full implications of the news. Such a report could of course easily be wrong, yet the risks were so great that if the slightest doubt existed one could not afford not to assume it was true.

He wondered if Gröndahl's commitment was as complete and unconditional as he made it seem. While a veil of secrecy hung over uranium research, an impenetrable blanket of discretion seemed to envelop the private thoughts of almost all the scientists involved in it. They were enthusiastic about the possibilities, yes. They would discuss feasibility. But how did they actually feel about the creation of an instrument of wholesale devastation that would unleash a holocaust of incalculable horror? How did they feel about the possible use of this instrument as a weapon in warfare? And, more prosaically, how many of them would be willing to drop their own research projects and devote their full energies to bringing this monster to birth? Everyone so far seemed to be feeling his way, looking only at the immediate and concentrating on the next step. Was a chain reaction possible? That was now the big question. So far as the project was concerned, the Government was thinking mainly of cost, the military was cautiously interested, the Europeans who had come over were almost desperately eager, the Americans remained noncommittal.

"Suppose—just for the sake of argument—let's suppose it isn't true. . . ."

Gröndahl looked at him with something like exasperation. "Look, Sebastian, let's not play games. This is very serious business. All we have any right to ask ourselves is, Is it possible? Can it be done? And if the answer is that it *can* be done, then we have to go ahead and do it. We have no choice. As scientists we can't turn our backs on a line of investigation that holds out staggering possibilities. And as members of a community of men, we know that what is possible for us is also possible for scientists in other communities, and we can't afford to let them get ahead of us."

There was no angle of this problem that Sebastian had not considered a dozen times, and he knew that no amount of pondering, no arguments, would dispel his misgivings. It did not seem possible that Gröndahl could be wholly untroubled.

"The release of new energy is one thing," he said in a low voice. "The making of the Weapon is another. What I was trying to ask was whether you would be in favor of going ahead with the Monster even if you knew no one else was working on it."

Gröndahl started to answer, but Sebastian went on.

"Of course," he explained, "there's nothing that is really secret about any of this. The thing has been talked about pretty freely up to a little over a year ago, and a lot of people have been thinking about it. Sooner or later, certainly, someone is bound to have a try at it. I'm talking about right now. Could you in good conscience go ahead and let this thing loose upon the world, knowing its terrible power?"

Gröndahl looked at him for a long moment in silence and slowly shook his head. "I'm afraid I'm going to have to talk to you like a Dutch uncle." He smiled awkwardly. "This is no time to indulge in the private luxury of qualms of conscience. You know perfectly well that the way you or I happen to feel is quite beside the point. We've stumbled on this thing—and when I say 'we' I mean scientists all over the world—we've stumbled on it, and there it is challenging us. An instrument of wholesale destruction. An incalculable potential for good or evil—or just for evil, if you like. All right. I hate it as much as you do. But do you think you could possibly stop it? You know damn well you can't."

Sebastian felt himself nodding, but his mood was of denial. He fumbled in his pocket for his pipe, which he hardly ever smoked any more. It wasn't there. He walked slowly over to the fireplace and in his turn looked at the Cézanne. He was looking through it rather than at it, and a corner of his mind worked on the thought that Cézanne had destroyed painting, had begun the process leading to the disintegration that made the exhibits of modern painters look like the cemeteries and ossuaries of art. But what a marvelous painter he could have made!

"Maybe you can't stop it," he said, turning again to Gröndahl, whose huge form filled the armchair to overflowing. "But as you yourself observed, you can't go ahead either—without money. A lot of money. As you know, science has to plod along on a shoestring most of the time; and partly because of that, fundamental research in this field is some fifty years behind where it should be. I dare say money will be forthcoming now. But we can't shut our eyes to the fact that it's primarily an investment in death. If the money is raised it will only be because shrewd businessmen are convinced that we've hit on a gadget that will destroy people and property more economically and more efficiently than conventional weapons."

"You're damned right! And that's the beauty of it! We have this opportunity that otherwise we might not get for years. Once we have the plant, all possibilities are open. As for the Weapon—the Monster, as you call it—chances are we'll never have to use it. If we get it too late, of course we're sunk. If we get it by the time the Germans do they won't dare use it. If we get it *before* they do—well, they'll know what they're up against, and we can dictate the peace. That's why we have to go ahead without losing a moment."

The compelling argument was the information that the Germans were actually going ahead. All others could be dismissed, except the one to the effect that the Thing might be the only means of averting a fascist victory. In which case, too, there was no choice. But were the Germans in a position, with their resources strained to the breaking point, to make the staggering investment in capital and manpower that would be required? It did not seem likely. Moreover, he knew no German scientist who, even if he were given the means, the authority and the freedom, would be capable of co-ordinating and directing the multiple phases of the work with the speed and efficiency that would be required.

"With luck," Gröndahl said, as though reading his thoughts, "and if we don't waste any time, we should beat the Germans to the draw. I'm not denying that it's a desperate gamble. But the stakes are high, and if we win . . ."

"If we win." Sebastian shook his head slowly. "That is something I worry about too. I can conceive of circumstances under which victory might be almost as disastrous as defeat."

"Frankly, Sebastian, I don't like to hear you talk this way. We're going to be in this war any day now—I give us six months at the outside—and this kind of talk from you . . ."

Sebastian remembered their earnest, impassioned discussions of six years ago in Paris. They had not talked of politics and war then, but of life and death, of knowledge and progress, of books and art and music. There had been an adventurous excitement about those talks that sprang from the fact that while their temperaments and their views on most things were poles apart, they were able to exchange ideas with vigor and frankness, each could listen eagerly to what the other had to say, could respect the otherness of the other. There was a different note in Gröndahl's speech now, yet Sebastian could not imagine speaking to him with any leashing of candor.

"You are perhaps the only person I could speak so freely to," he said. "I have kept these things to myself. But they trouble me, and I need to share my misgivings."

Gröndahl's face was dark. "We're living in a critical time, Sebastian, and it behooves us to be tough. This goes for all of us, but especially for those who may be called upon to play a crucial part in what is shaping up to be one great irrepressible conflict of this century."

Sebastian knew now what Gröndahl was coming to, and he wondered what his angle of approach would be.

"You mean the war against fascism?" he said.

"Let's say the war against totalitarianism."

Gröndahl got up, lifted to his feet it seemed by an inner excitement. He was no taller than Sebastian, but with his heavy features, his massiveness, his long arms and huge hands, he looked by comparison like a giant.

"Look, Sebastian . . ."

His voice partook of his bigness, and even when he tried to speak softly there was a powerful reverberation beneath the husky whisper. Sebastian was reminded again of the military man.

"I'm glad to have this opportunity to talk to you. I've been very much disturbed by certain rumors . . ." He held up his enormous hand, the palm of which, with its network of lines, looked like the map of France. "I don't want to go into that. I don't want to know about it. Let's not talk about yesterday. Let's talk about today—and tomorrow."

He looked at Sebastian, and Sebastian had the impression that he must have made many speeches somewhat along this line recently, but that he was hesitating now to find the most appropriate approach.

"This war that's going on," he said, "and that we're soon going to be drawn into, is just a beginning. The battle today is against fascism as it has grown up in Germany, Italy and Japan. We've got to win that battle, and to win it we need Russia's help, and we probably will not win it even so without the Weapon. But once that is over we'll still have to settle scores with Russia. And that's going to be the decisive conflict. There will be no escaping it. It will be them or us. And we have to see to it that we have as many winning tricks as possible in our hands."

Sebastian nodded slowly, not in assent but in recognition. This was pure State Department doctrine, and it made him wonder how spontaneous the little briefing was.

"We must first be sure we know who 'we' are," he said, by way of a surface response to Gröndahl's last words. But he was deeply upset. Gröndahl was after all a physicist and not a State Department career man. Sebastian remembered the excitement with which he had read his papers on the polarization and spectra of X-rays and on the specific heat of solids some twelve to fourteen years ago. There was no one else at a high official level with whom he could discuss his predicament with any hope of being understood.

He paced over to the window, then came back.

"Sit down, Hjalmar," he said, using Gröndahl's given name for the first time. "I have something important to tell you."

Gröndahl looked at him sharply for a moment, then the lines of his face smoothed out. He smiled. "We've known each other a long time, Sebastian," he said. "I think we understand each other better than most people. Yet actually we know very little about each other." He came a step closer. "Let's leave it that way. I'm sure what you want to tell me is important. But I'm just as sure that it isn't important for me to hear."

Sebastian was startled. "But it's something I think you have to know!"

"I don't have to know anything. Listen—"

"But suppose I were to tell you—"

"Well, just don't!" He grasped both Sebastian's shoulders, holding him at arm's length with his powerful hands, and Sebastian felt a little quiver pass through them, like an electric current.

I must tell him, Sebastian thought. I must tell him now. I must tell him that I am a communist, and that anything I may do about the Monster will be conditioned by that fact. And if they want me to work with them in the light of that, it will be all right, and if they don't it will be all right too. I must tell him *why* I am a communist. I must tell him how Marxism has illuminated for me the political history of our time, and how, in the light of it, I view the present conflict. I must tell him especially why, as a scientist, I have become convinced that only in a classless society will it be possible to solve the crisis that science finds itself in today, which is in fact merely a reflection of the crisis that besets our whole society. Hjalmar, who sees as clearly as anyone how increasingly unstable the integrations in physics are becoming, in mechanics, field physics and atomic physics, as he has shown in his analyses of the implications of the Fitzgerald contraction and the Clerk-Maxwell electromagnetic equations and other brilliant early studies, who is aware of the need for synthesis and of the shakiness of our metaphysics, will understand this best of all. But he will be deeply disturbed by all this. He has no idea how far I am committed or how important this is to me. He probably thinks it is a purely emotional excursion, that I have let myself be carried away— by generosity, humanitarianism, or a misguided sense of fair play. At worst he regards me as a parlor pink or a fellow-traveler. But this above all I can't allow. I can't judge how useful the things I have been able to do for the party in the past three years have been in a small way. I should not want them to be made to seem still smaller by being attributed to any kind of misapprehension or irresponsibility. So I must tell him. I must tell him now. For I want no misunderstanding. If he expects to use me he has a right to know what he's in for.

Gröndahl's powerful hands were holding him at arm's length, the pressure of his fingers on Sebastian's shoulders was almost tender. A smile—an inner smile that was half reminiscent, half expectant, friendly, confiding, full of gravity—communicated itself ever so faintly to his heavy lips and lighted up his deeply shadowed gray eyes.

"There!" he said with finality. "We have enough worries ahead of us to keep us busy for a long time to come. No need to go rummaging for them in the past." He gave Sebastian's shoulders a final squeeze and folded his arms. A quite different look came into his face, which became a slow grin that broadened it and accentuated all the deep wrinkles. The moment of intimacy had passed. "You're a hell of a host," he said in a deadpan voice. "You've kept me busy talking here for an hour and you haven't even offered me a drink."

Now, thought Sebastian, *now* is the moment, for here we are on the threshold, and what is said or not said now will set the pattern of my future involvement. Now I can tell it cleanly, as it should be told, with no reservations and no apologies.

But he knew that it was too late; and that even if it had not been too late, it would have been wrong. Gröndahl was making it clear to him in his own way that anything he told him would tie his hands, and that he didn't want his hands tied. "This is no time to indulge in the private luxury of qualms of conscience." Gröndahl had said that straight, without irony. Sebastian had never regarded such qualms as a private luxury. But now? If he were to tell Gröndahl the one fact of his life that was the most meaningful, to him the most triumphant, he might easily jeopardize his future usefulness in a venture that could affect the fate of the world for all the generations to come.

Tanya brought in the silver tray with the martini makings. Wearing a white embroidered blouse and a full green-black-and-gold striped skirt with a belt of tooled silver spangles clasping her incredibly slim waist, her feet encased in glovelike red kid pumps that made her steps noiseless on the tiled floor, she struck Sebastian as having a little the look of a child out of a fairy tale who had strayed inexplicably into an all-too-real world. But why, all of a sudden, did she seem so persistently to elude him, to escape into *another* realm? He found himself longing to hear her play.

Tanya was about to leave them again when Sebastian said, "Don't go." He turned to Gröndahl. "I think we've taken care of all our tedious business?"

"I'll just get some potato chips," Tanya said, disappearing through the doorway. Gröndahl's eyes followed her, his whole face rejuvenated.

"She's a rare girl, Sebastian," he said approvingly.

He came over to where Sebastian was mixing the cocktails at a small table by the window.

"By the way," he said, "when I discuss that contract with your president this afternoon, I'm going to tie one condition to my recommendation, and that is that you have full charge of the research."

Sebastian looked at him, surprised. "I was thinking of Porter for that."

"There's nothing wrong with Porter. But I want you. I think you understand why for strategic reasons it's important to have you in a key position as soon as possible."

Tanya came into the room again, carrying a Chinese oxblood bowl piled with crisp chips.

"We'll have to see—" Sebastian had started to say. But perhaps the decision was already out of his hands. He was stirring the drink with the long stainless-steel spoon, and the ice cubes tinkled faintly as the campus chimes began to ring forth. "This is the one important skill I have acquired since I last saw you," he said, pouring the pale crystalline liquid into the glasses.

"I suppose you're wondering why I wanted to see you," Sebastian said when he and Eve were settled at last on the wide front porch overlooking the little dead-end street. She was sitting in the hammock, and he was trying to manage an unruly rocking chair that he found excruciatingly uncomfortable.

It was a stiflingly hot day. Partly no doubt because he was unsure of himself, he had come bringing a huge sheaf of red roses, which the moment he arrived he felt to be peculiarly inappropriate. He had met Eve's mother, a pleasant-faced, bustling woman who had affected him, as all mothers did, in a vulnerable secret area of his being. He had tried to make small talk and draw Eve out a little, but it hadn't worked.

"I have to tell you first of all," he went on, having thus far received no help from her at all, "that this is entirely my own idea, and that Mark knows nothing about it. I've felt great hesitancy about coming. The last thing I want to do is to interfere with your private life—yours and Mark's—in any way. In fact the one reason why I finally decided that I had to see you was that I have a very strong suspicion that I am perhaps to a certain extent responsible for the situation that has—"

"Oh, no! You mustn't think that!"

"Let me just explain—"

"No, it really has nothing to do with you, I mean—"

"But just let me explain—"

"I really can't discuss it, but—"

"I'm not trying," he broke in firmly, "to make you listen to something you don't want to listen to, or say something you don't want to say. What I have in mind actually does concern myself rather than you or Mark, and there is one thing in particular—"

"But you don't understand." Eve sat straight up in the hammock. A flush had come into her face, and a deep intake of breath betrayed her agitation. "So far as I am concerned, this is something entirely between Mark and me. If you come into it at all, it's on Mark's side, and you'll have to discuss it with him."

"That's just it," he said soothingly. "It wouldn't do any good to discuss it with Mark. He's too generous, and he wouldn't admit I was at fault." He looked at her pleadingly. "Don't you want to help Mark?"

"I can't explain," she said breathlessly. "There's just nothing I can say."

She looked quite upset. She's hiding something, he thought. Something she's ashamed of. Something about Mark. But she's wrong.

"Then," he said, "will you let me say just one thing—"

"No, please! I—"

At this moment Sebastian heard a tinkling of glass, immediately followed by the chirp of the spring on the screen door. He wrenched himself to his feet with an agonizing effort, and went forward to meet Eve's mother, who was carrying a tray with a glass pitcher full of lemonade and floating ice cubes, glasses, and dishes of cookies and candy.

"Excuse me for disturbing you folks," she said cheerily, and he noticed that her voice was low and warm, and she was a little out of breath. "I just thought you might be thirsty and this might cool you off."

Sebastian took advantage of the opportunity to go to the other side of the porch and fetch the card table, and while Eve and her mother were deciding to call Jimmy in for his bath he went back and got one of the straight-back chairs.

"How's my daddy?" was the first thing Jimmy said when he finally appeared, all out of breath, in T shirt, and shorts and sneakers, dirty and disheveled but radiant. Sebastian was surprised that he had recognized him so quickly. "Boy, that's some car you got!" the boy bubbled over in pure admiration. He was all Mark's, Sebastian decided, except for the eyes which were like his grandmother's, candid and disarming.

While Eve's mother bustled Jimmy and herself in, after insisting upon his tasting the lemonade to see that it was right, he became prey to a growing sense of frustration. Ever since childhood he had been pursued by the feeling, sometimes amounting to conviction, that a kind of corruption lay at the heart of every human relation, dooming it to failure and unhappiness. For a time he thought he had escaped the circle of futility. But recently he had had moments of uneasiness. Today had been a series of miseries.

The cool acid of the lemonade slid deliciously down his dry throat, and the straight chair, though it was rickety, felt good to his back.

In a few minutes he would be saying good-by and he would leave. He would have exchanged words with this person, a virtual stranger, but nothing would have been communicated. She was unhappy, and her husband, who was his friend, was unhappy, because of an undoubted misunderstanding. He had wanted to ask questions and to answer questions and he was confident that from the answers to these questions a clarity would have emerged and torments would have been ended. But Eve was afraid. Afraid of knowledge that might perhaps save her marriage.

As for himself, if he was anxious to know, as Eve could quite possibly have told him, whether Mark had joined the party solely out of intellectual conviction or had been to a significant extent swayed by his influence, it was in a more immediate sense for the sake of friendship and in the hope of finding a solution. But it was also because of a more general problem that had begun to worry him lately. Although it was a constant temptation to dismiss it from his mind, because it implied attaching a greater importance to himself than he thought warranted, it was impossible for him not to recognize that four out of five of his brightest students had become left-wingers, many of them party members, because of him. It had pleased and flattered him at first, but now with the approach of war it was causing him some uneasiness. It was reassuring that the Soviet Union had become one of the Allies fighting Hitler, yet he knew—and his conversation with Gröndahl today had confirmed it—that the moment the U.S. got into the war there would be a close surveillance of all communists. They would be subjected to various kinds of harassment, they would have an increasingly rough time of it—unless of course the determination of the capitalist governments to turn the antifascist war into an anticommunist war at the first opportunity could be thwarted. This was the great uncertainty, but also the hope. In any case the war was going to call for some drastic decisions, both on the organizational and on the personal level. And come what might, he didn't want Mark, or any of his students, to get hurt.

Eve had recovered her serene composure. Sebastian was often able to read people's thoughts—it was a gift that was at times even embarrassing. But behind Eve's smooth forehead above the beautifully arched black brows that contrasted with her wavy blond hair the enigma was complete.

"I hope you don't feel too badly about my coming," he said.

"I didn't want to tell you not to come," she answered. "But I couldn't encourage you to come either. I'm sorry."

"I had hoped to be of some use," he said. "But of course I realized that it might not work."

"I guess it can't be helped."

Chapter 8

THE Bloch file—a stack of folders ten or more inches high—was piled on the blotter in front of the Chief. He had spent the morning going through it. On top of it lay the most recent picture of Sebastian Bloch, blown up from a snapshot, and the Chief studied it as he listened to the radio on his desk.

He had had the radio put in only very recently, and for occasions just like this. Hitler's attack on Russia on June 22nd had caught him off his guard. Now on Sunday afternoons he could keep in touch with what was going on without leaving his office. Besides, occasionally important policy statements were broadcast on weekdays that could provide valuable background to directives from Washington.

For a week now, since about Labor Day and the second anniversary of the war, attention had been more sharply focused on the Russian front where the Germans were advancing toward Moscow, and it looked as if the capture of Leningrad was imminent. But according to the newscast the city's defenders were still holding off the Nazi troops; there were no sensational developments elsewhere. The Chief turned the radio off.

He was thinking, looking at the snapshot, that during all the time that Ampter had been working on the case—it was nearly three years now—he himself had never once laid eyes on Sebastian Bloch. Whereas Ampter had seen him hundreds of times, had become intimate with him . . . too intimate.

The Chief looked at the blown-up snapshot. For a moment or two by dint of intense concentration he would have the illusion that it was alive, an illusion helped rather than hindered by the imperfections of the print with its blurred lines and blotched texture. What made it alive, more than anything else, was the baffling mystery that those eyes concealed, which would perhaps be even more baffling if one were looking at the man face to face.

It was odd that Ampter had not been able to get hold of any proper pictures of the man—photographer's portraits, pictures to go into yearbooks, official records. Bloch must be camera-shy.

There were of course two men in Sebastian Bloch—at least two, as with all men. One was the scientist, to whom the Chief took his hat off without any reservations. Ampter in his reports of recent months had put in many things that seemed almost intentionally to belittle him—critical remarks by colleagues, the relative slightness of his original work, the total absence of new fundamental discoveries or concepts comparable, without mentioning Einstein, to those made or put forward by a number of his immediate contemporaries, such as Dirac, Heisenberg, Fermi, Oppenheimer, Schrödinger, the Joliot-Curies. That didn't bother the Chief. The contributions being made every day by his students told the story. It was obvious from everything in the record that Sebastian Bloch, by virtue of the immense range of his mind, his power of analysis and his phenomenal insight, was right up there among the giants.

But there was another man in Sebastian Bloch, and that was the human being. It was he who fascinated the Chief to the point of obsession and whom he had singled out for his quarry. For of one thing he was sure, and that was that the mystery behind those eyes in the photograph was not the mystery of innocence. Pathological delusion? Ruthless ambition? Inordinate pride? He didn't yet know.

And Ampter had ceased to be of much help. For the purpose of the service he had become practically useless on the Bloch case. The Chief had seen it coming for a long time. He had been aware of the danger. Now he was going to have to write him off.

But not right away.

That was why he was calling him in today. Zelinski's report worried him. For the first time he felt not quite sure of himself in relation to Ampter. It had never occurred to him that he might want to quit on his own.

He had immediately decided that he must see him. The idea of meeting him here in the office—on a Sunday, when there was little risk of his being seen by anyone who might recognize him—had occurred to him as a way of reviving whatever loyalty to the organization he might have left in him. It was funny to think of a thing like that in connection with Ampter. What he would tell him was another question. Ampter was holding all the cards.

He needed him badly. With the war coming on, Sebastian Bloch was going to be plenty hot; and Ampter, who controlled the one direct line right into the heart of the enemy territory, was letting him down just when he needed him most. The fear that haunted him was that one of the other intelligence services—they were already putting out feelers—would decide to take over the case. It was a possibility that he refused to contemplate.

Ampter would be coming any moment now, and Gregg hadn't yet fully made up his mind what line to take. As chief of the bureau agency his duty was clear. Ampter had fallen down on the job. He could no longer be trusted. He was withholding information that he was being paid to deliver. And now he was trying to do a whitewash job on Bloch. What Zelinski had reported about the role Ampter had played in the Santuro strike had come as a deep shock. Ampter had merely written that he had gone off into the desert "to get a fresh slant on things." Well, he had come up with a fresh slant, all right.

Gregg had every ground for firing him. He had been tempted to do just this many times in recent months as Ampter's increasingly fuzzy reports had been coming in. What had held him back each time was Sebastian Bloch. Ampter, however unsatisfactory, was his one direct link with him.

He knew that Zelinski could never take his place. The White Russian was smart, he had good connections, and for Gregg's purposes he was reliable. The fact that he held down a responsible job as an electronics engineer with Standard Development made him very useful. But so far as Bloch was concerned, he was a total loss. In nine months he had barely reached a bowing acquaintance with him. His approach had been through Mrs. Bloch's father, Krylenko, who liked to talk Russian with him, and in his bookshop Zelinski had run into Sebastian a few times and had exchanged a casual word or two at some of the big social parties given for political causes. But it hadn't led to anything, and never would. He didn't have the personality. Invaluable though he would be in another way, he was no substitute for Mark.

The Chief put Bloch's snapshot away in the middle drawer of his desk. He needed Ampter just where he was. However meager the information he was feeding him now, however insubordinate he had become, every little item contributed to building up the picture for him, and as long as Ampter kept up his intimacy with Bloch he must hang onto him. At least until the United States got into the war.

The buzzer inside his desk gave its muffled signal. He pressed the button above his right knee to signal back that all was clear. As he waited for Ampter to appear he mentally reviewed Zelinski's recent reports. Ampter had never mentioned that his wife had walked out on him or that he was planning to get his Ph.D. this fall.

Well, he wasn't going to try to pump him.

Mark had been dreading the interview, and during the whole drive from the University he had wondered nervously why in the hell the Chief had chosen his office as the meeting place. He's going to fire me, he had decided, and he wants to stage it in the most effective setting. The fact that it was a Sunday, when nobody would be around, was in itself far from reassuring. He was obviously planning a showdown.

But as he stepped into the office the familiar excitement which he had always felt in the presence of the Chief, and which today he had not even guarded himself against because he thought he had long since outgrown it, surged over him again, and before it all other emotions faded.

When he came in he went through the motions of carefully closing the door behind him, though he knew it had one of those fancy hydraulic spring devices that shut doors efficiently and noiselessly; he was watching the Chief for a clue as to how he should act.

"Hello, Ampter." The voice was cordial.

"How do you do, sir."

The Chief put his hands on the arms of his chair as though he were about to get up, seemed to hesitate, then dropped his arms. "Have a seat," he said.

So it was not to be one of those lightning interviews, though Mark wondered about that moment's hesitation. He pulled out a pack of cigarettes.

"Do you mind?"

"Go right ahead."

Mark noticed the radio on the desk. He felt a little bolder than he had felt the last time he sat here. It was the only new item in the room. Except for the stack of folders, which would be some current business. He remembered that he was no longer committed to the secret service. How different everything was, now. Then, to the Chief particularly, his life had been an open book. Now great areas of it were closed to him. At the same time, Mark felt exposed and vulnerable.

The Chief pulled the same square heavy glass ash tray from the same drawer.

"I'm glad to see you," he said. "I hope I haven't inconvenienced you by asking you to come here—"

"Not at all," Mark put in in a muffled voice.

"Fact is, I'm up to my neck in work. With this war coming on we're feeling the pressure, and we're having to increase our staff. Actually it's one reason I wanted to see you. And anyway, it was about time we got together and had a talk, don't you think?"

"Yes," Mark said. "Yes, I've kind of been thinking that myself." (Now it's coming, he thought. And he remembered Eve.)

"Not that there's anything special I had to tell you," the Chief went on hurriedly and as if reassuringly. "Just that I thought it would be in order to exchange ideas and see where we stood."

"Yes," Mark said, blowing out a big cloud of smoke, "I think it's a good idea."

He felt very nervous, and it infuriated him to feel that way because underneath he felt more sure of himself than he had ever felt when he had worked out of the service. He wondered how much the Chief knew about his plan to make a break.

The Chief put his hand admiringly, almost reverently, on the high stack of folders in front of him.

"Here's the Bloch file," he said, with a warmth that he rarely showed. "I've spent some time going over it today. This is your work, Ampter, nearly all this pile of material. Three years of work."

Mark waited anxiously.

"I think on the whole you've done very well," the Chief went on after a pause. "As well as we had any right to expect. And you're to be congratulated."

He tapped the folders meaningfully.

"This is an important file," he said, seeming to weigh his words. "Perhaps the most important file this office has produced."

Mark had always had enormous respect for the Chief's astuteness. He was startled now to hear him express even qualified satisfaction with what he certainly knew to be an elaborate piece of double-dealing. The Chief's acid comments on individual reports as they had been sent in had shown quite clearly that he wasn't being taken in. He obviously had some trick up his sleeve. Mark muttered a lame acknowledgment of his remarks.

"You understand, of course," the Chief said, "that as the situation comes to a head in Europe and we are dragged further into it, this particular case will become increasingly important. We have to be prepared for eventualities, and we mustn't have a too mechanical approach. That's why I've been particularly interested in your reports of the last ten or twelve months, which I wasn't prepared to accept at their face value at first. I'll admit that I thought for a while that you were succumbing to influence. But I see now that I was wrong. According to what you report, there has been a fundamental change of direction."

Mark was sure now that the Chief was laying a trap.

"That's a healthy sign," the Chief continued, "though it's too early yet for us to be sure it's genuine."

He looked at Mark sharply.

"You still don't think he has any suspicion of you?"

"Oh, no!" The question took him by surprise. "I certainly have no reason to think so."

Yet how could he be sure? How could he be sure of anything, or of anyone? Even Eve had let him down when he needed her most. But his deepest misgivings arose from the knowledge of his own duplicity. If he could not be sure of himself—he had come to mistrust his own most generous impulses—how could he be sure of anyone else?

Sebastian alone seemed to be beyond the reach of such doubts and questions. Of him he could be sure.

He suddenly felt wretched.

The Chief was charting the likely evolution of Sebastian's political views.

"The party turnover is enormous," he explained. "Fifty or more per cent of the people who sign cards and are listed as members in the official records drop out before they have been in a year. So even if the membership is growing, as it's still doing because of Roosevelt, it's a raw army of misfits and malcontents with just a small hard core of Moscow-trained thugs and bureaucrats. The trouble is that when a member drops out he doesn't thereby automatically become clean. He doesn't necessarily turn anticommunist. He's still on the fringe, still susceptible to the propaganda, an unreliable element. There's only one way that a onetime commie can prove that he's become a good American, and that is by showing his willingness to help fight communism. That goes for Bloch as well as for anybody else."

Does he really believe those reports? Mark wondered. He had wanted him to believe them, and now the mere possibility that he might struck him as a monstrous absurdity. No, it's impossible, he immediately decided.

"Bloch is an intelligent man," the Chief continued. "There are all sorts of reasons that could make such a man fall for communist ideas for a while. But being an intelligent man, he was bound to see through all the fallacies sooner or later. That was to be foreseen. And it wasn't because Bloch in himself represented a danger on that score that we originally decided to put him under observation. It was because of his influence, the amount of damage he could do during the longer or shorter time that he went along with those ideas."

The Chief slid forward to the very edge of his chair, leaning toward Mark.

"Now this is the point," he said in a low voice, tapping his clenched left fist into his right palm. "Bloch is at last coming back to his senses. We don't really have to worry about him any more. Keep an eye on him, yes, as much for his own protection as anything else. But—and here's the point—Bloch has done incalculable harm to his country and its ideals during the past three years. As you have shown in your reports, he has propagandized hundreds of individuals directly, and an inestimable number indirectly, and these are people whom the party ordinarily isn't able to reach, at least so effectively. He's probably done more to promote the cause of communism than a hundred paid organizers, because—remember—his influence has been among key people, each of whom reaches scores or hundreds of others.

"Now, the harm that Bloch has done isn't going to be undone simply by his abandoning today the ideas he was advocating yesterday. The influence that he has exerted will go right on spreading its poison, even though he has changed his views. The only way he can undo at least some of the harm he's done is by joining in the fight against communism in every way he can, like any good American. In other words, the burden is on him to prove that he is a good American."

The Chief sat back in his chair and rested his left arm on the desk, his fingers touching the Bloch file.

"This is something he will naturally understand himself. But it will take more or less time. He may need help. And that's where you come in. You can be of material assistance in making the transition relatively rapid and effective. . . ."

Mark let himself out of the offices, rode down in the elevator the twenty-two flights to the ground floor, and stepped dazedly out into the street.

Was the Chief pulling his leg, or did he really believe those recent reports in which he told of Sebastian's wavering allegiance to the Communist Party? If he was pulling his leg, he could not possibly imagine what the motive might be, and it was unnerving to be left so completely in the dark. But if he really believed the reports, it was absolutely baffling.

Mark realized that he had never seriously expected those reports to be believed. He had merely intended that they should be a part of the record, so that if they were ever used they would, to some extent at least, counterbalance the earlier reports and give a less damaging picture to an outsider. The Chief would not be in a position to refute the information that they contained, always based largely on fact, but he would scrutinize with the most probing eye the inferences that Mark drew from it. And the Chief was not easily taken in.

He turned the corner and headed down the side street where he had parked his car. Whichever way it was, he reflected, he had a little more time to wind up his picture of Sebastian "for the record." If the Chief actually believed it, so much the better. His Doctor's oral was scheduled for November 28th. Right after that he would make the break. Eve would be back. Together they would start a new life.

As he got into his car he could still hear the Chief's voice—hard, cynical, yet persuasive. He had something in the back of his mind, all right. Mark didn't like it. Whatever it was, it spelled trouble.

Chapter 9

FOR months, or so it seemed, they had planned this party. Ever since the beginning of the semester in late August. It was to be a Russian War Relief party, and it was going to be bigger and more chichi than any party they had put on in the last three or four years. A committee had been formed including several eminently respectable faculty wives, and they had met more and more frequently, in an atmosphere of growing excitement, over the weeks. When Roosevelt pledged the billion-dollar

Lend-Lease aid to Russia on November 6th, the committee had finally decided that it must set a date, and they agreed to make it Saturday, November 29th.

As it happened, Mark had planned if he passed his Doctor's oral on the 28th to give an impromptu party to celebrate his new status that same Saturday evening. But as all the people he would want to invite would be attending the Russian War Relief party, and as both occasions would call for serious drinking, he hit on the idea of making it a party within a party.

It was Mrs. de Rivas (whose husband had died of a heart-attack some two years before, on the eve of the surrender of Madrid) who had thought of the Outland house as the stage for the party.

"I'll talk to Lily myself," she had announced to the committee.

It was one of the town's show places, a huge, sprawling house on top of one of the hills overlooking the campus, surrounded by lawns and a rambling garden. In addition to the great living room, with a monumental marble fireplace at either end imported from a French château, the library with its famous collection of the English Enlightenment period (sixty-five thousand titles), the music room, dining room and solarium, there was an enormous formal ballroom that Professor Outland used mainly for staging amateur plays, in which staid faculty members and their wives could don period costumes and speak the witty, sometimes ribald, lines of the Restoration comedies. Though in his early sixties, Ronald Outland, the eminent English scholar, had recently married a childhood sweetheart ten years his senior, the lively Lily Bainbridge who had inherited a chocolate fortune. They both adored people and sociable gatherings, and when Mrs. de Rivas proposed the Russian War Relief party to them they both, though they didn't have an ounce of politics in their bones, enthusiastically embraced the idea. Ronald, conscientious scholar that he was, immediately went to the University bookstore and bought all the books on current Russia that he could get hold of and spent his spare moments reading them in preparation for the event.

Mark had kept his secret from everyone except Sebastian and Tanya, and when he appeared at the party with Eve in tow, it created the sensation he had hoped it would.

They were pulled into the reception hall to make room for the other people who were just arriving. Eve and Hannah Leutner fell into each other's arms as Mark was assailed by half a dozen young beauties in party dresses with trayfuls of orchids and made to buy one. Then he and Eve were swept to the nearest bar and the first toasts were drunk. They ordered vodka.

People were arriving by twos and in groups.

"To the newlyweds!"

The glasses went up.

"To the new Doctor!"

Mark raised his glass, and Eve followed suit.

"To the success of the party!"

More and more orchids were appearing on female bosoms. The bar at the other end of the big room was beginning to do business.

Someone standing beside Mark pulled a fresh cigarette out of a package and brought it to his lips. Mark brought out his lighter and flicked it on. He recognized Erasmo Alvarez.

"*Gracias,*" the Spaniard said, taking hold of Mark's hand. He held it, looking at the lighter. "Ph.D.," he said. "It is a new present? Congratulations."

"No," Mark said, looking at it in turn. Sebastian's gift. "I've had it for a long time. It's been a kind of talisman. It was meant to spur me on. It did."

"And what will it mean now?"

The question hadn't occurred to Mark. But it was a real one.

"Come on," he said to Eve, after they had had three drinks and the excitement had died down. "Let's case the joint."

Neither of them had been inside the house before.

This was the big night. Mark knew he was going to get drunk tonight. Yet not too drunk, because this was the first night he would be spending with Eve in a year and a half, and he didn't want to spoil that. Those three vodkas felt good. But he needed another one.

"You see what a fine house we'll be able to have when I'm a professor?" he said, squeezing Eve's arm.

"If you're careful to choose the right parents and marry the right girl," she said. "Heavens, look at all those books!"

"And look at that bar!"

They had another drink.

"You're really going to become a professor?"

"If you're willing to become a faculty wife."

Eve assumed an expression and an attitude of supercilious primness.

"How can you question it, Doctor?" But she immediately switched back to her natural manner. "You haven't told me about your examination."

"And you haven't told me what you've been up to all these months."

"We have so much to catch up on! When are we ever going to?"

"Certainly not here, in this crowd. Look at the way they're piling in!"

"Just when it would be so nice to be alone!"

They came to a recessed angle of the room which formed a relatively sheltered nook, unoccupied at the moment. Mark dragged her behind the tall book cabinet, out of sight of everyone, and put his arms around her.

"Kiss me!" he said. She gave him her lips, timidly at first, a little stiffly and half holding back. But he was clasping her tight, his hands hard against her back, caressing her, and as his lips pressed hers eagerly, a great tenderness welling up in him, he suddenly felt her melt and her heart spilled into her lips. She murmured "Oh darling," without separating her lips from his, and for a brief second it was again as it had once been.

Shuffling footsteps on the hardwood floor, accompanied by a low whistle, broke the spell. Eve smiled at him—a smile he had forgotten, a girlish smile that at the same time glowed with the warmth of intimacies shared. Her eyes were moist.

"We mustn't be in too much of a hurry," she said. "We have

plenty of time. Now that we know everything is going to be right."

"But it's been so long, darling!"

"I know. I've missed you terribly. But we're together now. That's the main thing."

An elderly couple whom neither of them recognized waddled into the nook and out again.

Eve put her hand up to Mark's face and stroked it. "So you got your Ph.D.," she said musingly. "That's wonderful! I know it wasn't easy, and I'm proud of you. And you had a lot of problems to make it harder, including me." She dropped her hand to his arm, letting it rest there, and smiled at him again. "You're a Doctor now. Dr. Ampter!"

They both laughed.

She became serious again.

"About tonight," she said, and hesitated. "I didn't want to tell you. It seems like such a dirty trick, but it isn't my fault." She glanced down for a second, then looked at him directly. "I've just got the curse. I'm so furious. It's two days early."

"That's all right."

The announcement gave him a jolt, and yet it brought a kind of relief. He still felt terribly keyed up, and he realized he had been worrying a little about tonight. He wanted her more than anything, but he remembered their wedding night and what a flop he had been. This was sort of another wedding, and he had been worrying about it.

"You know," she said, before he had a chance to say anything else, "I think we have to realize that we're not going to get back to the way we were before right away." She gave him a tender smile. "It'll take time." The sound of voices, of people being sociable and convivial and loosening up, had become a steady hum, and the volume was rising. "What was so wonderful in what we had before was that we had a perfect trust and understanding of each other. And then we lost that. We've got to get it back, and it will take a little time."

"Yes," he agreed.

"I think," she went on, "part of our effort at getting it back means recognizing that we haven't got it yet. But I truly believe we will be able to, don't you?"

"Oh yes!" Mark said feelingly.

"You *have* definitely quit the agency, haven't you?"

He recognized Eve's flat-footed yet devastatingly honest way of getting right down to realities. He accepted it.

"Yes," he said. "I'm through. No more reports. No more snooping. That's all in the past."

He knew this was so. But it was the first time he had said it —to anyone. And it made it more real.

"But you haven't told the Chief yet?"

"No . . ."

"Why not?"

"Look, it was only yesterday I took my oral . . ."

"I know—you haven't had time. And I'm not blaming you."

She looked at him in that probing way she had.

"But that isn't the only reason, is it?" she said.

Mark realized again, as he had many times before although he kept forgetting, that he had never really deceived Eve because she had always been able to see through him.

"No," he said.

"When are you going to?"

It was the question he had been asking himself for weeks. And he hadn't found the answer.

"Don't worry," he said, a little belligerently. "I haven't changed my mind, and I'm not going to."

He seized her by the wrist of the hand that was still resting on his arm and, trying not to seem to be rejecting her, released himself and took a few steps away from her.

"The problem is not whether to quit. The problem is *how* to quit. That's rather important, and I haven't had time to figure it out. I'll tell you what," he said, suddenly brightening. "Next week is examination week. I'll be busy reading papers day and night. I've got to turn in all my grades by Friday night. Saturday—that'll be December 6th—we'll go away somewhere, take a little trip for a few days, just you and I. We'll talk the whole thing over and decide then."

The Man Who Would Be God

"A wonderful idea! Oh, darling!" she said, slipping her hand under his arm. "I think I'm going to like being a professor's wife!"

"Good!" he said. "And now I think we owe it to our public to circulate a bit."

And he badly wanted another drink.

Alexander Zelinski loved to have people call him Sasha. But there was probably no one here who would. He was being crowded away from the bar in the ballroom by people pressing to either side of him trying to order drinks, and he clutched his highball protectively as he was being edged back, taking an occasional slow sip from the tall glass. He preferred vodka, but vodka had to be drunk in one gulp, and he needed a drink that he could work on slowly. The balalaikas behind him were playing a haunting air that brought back memories. He found himself wishing that there were someone here who would call him Sasha. In his heart was a great love of humanity. And the sad thing was that he was everywhere misunderstood.

Sasha sometimes said to himself that he should have been a poet. Or perhaps even better, a story writer like Chekhov or Maupassant. He had a passion for observing people, the way they talked and acted, their habits, their relations, their little eccentricities. But his father, God rest his soul, had decided that he should be an engineer, so he had become an engineer. It was a satisfactory occupation. He had a natural bent for it, and it paid well. But it left a whole essential side of his nature unfulfilled.

Now, by an extraordinary stroke of luck, he had found a fertile outlet for his secret talents. He owed it all to that first chance meeting with Gospodin Gregg, as he liked to call him, in a restaurant two summers ago at the time of the fall of France. Gospodin Gregg had even offered him money, but Sasha had indignantly refused. "What do you take me for?" he had said with hauteur. And he had made him understand that anything he might do along the lines Gregg suggested would be on a voluntary basis, as a patriotic service to his adopted country. He had not thought it necessary to inform him that it would also give him a deep intimate satisfaction and invest his life with a purpose that it had always lacked.

As he looked around the huge ballroom he saw hardly anyone whom he even recognized. It was still nearly empty, but there must be at least two hundred people clustered around the two bars. It was not the crowd that usually turned up at these left-wing parties. It had much more class. Everything here surprised him. The elegance of the house. The Outlands must have lots of money. And those girls selling the orchids— where had they ever found such beautiful girls? If he could only get to know such a girl!

He caught sight of old Krylenko over by the orchestra and he drifted casually in his direction. They shook hands, but the old man seemed to have things on his mind.

"A fine crowd," Sasha said to him in Russian.

"*Da, da,*" said Krylenko distractedly. "Russia has many friends."

Sasha had noticed that the old man always acted as though he were anxious to be somewhere else than where he happened to be.

"I haven't seen your daughter," he said.

"She'll be here," Krylenko said gruffly. "She had a lot of things to attend to."

"You haven't had a drink yet," Sasha remarked, having just finished his whisky. "Why don't you come and have one with me? We'll drink a toast to the victory of Russia." Perhaps with several vodkas in him Krylenko would become more friendly and call him Sasha.

"You must excuse me, but I cannot leave my musicians. They may need me."

So even old Krylenko was giving him the cold shoulder.

Over by the other bar things looked fairly lively. But he knew no one here. Some smart-looking women: the men with them obviously had plenty of money. They seemed to have come in groups of four to eight couples that kept pretty much to themselves. This was for them the early part of a Saturday binge that had begun with the football game from which they had come (some of the women were wearing the University's purple chrysanthemum), would continue at some swank roadside inn with a French cuisine, and end up in one or more of the night clubs in town before each couple retired to its respective legitimate or illegitimate bed.

Sasha ordered another highball and tried to catch the drift of the talk. It was mostly anecdotic, although now and again one of the men would bring forth some ponderous remark about the war situation, which would land like a huge stone in the pool of lively chatter. While he was catching stray references to Litvinov being in Singapore, to Rommel's Afrika Korps being pressed south of Tobruk, to Argentina's decision to sell all its tungsten to the United States, his eyes were fascinated by a stunning-looking woman around whom a circle of admiring males had formed. She had golden-blond wavy hair and wore an outrageous décolleté and form-fitting gown that exhibited the most magnificent woman's body Sasha had ever seen. What was particularly sensational, even breath-taking, was the luminous amber color of her skin, a skin satiny and smooth beyond any imagining.

But he was here for a purpose, he remembered. He must pull himself together. He got out a cigarette, put it between his lips and felt in his pockets for a match. They were talking about her tan, and the exchanges, in which the word "sun lamp" came up repeatedly, were punctuated by gales of laughter.

As he was still feeling for a match, a lighter suddenly appeared before his eyes and gave forth a flame. He looked up and recognized Mark Ampter grinning down at him, looking very happy. But as Sasha lowered his eyes to take advantage of the proffered light he had the impression that Ampter had not recognized him until he had looked up and that then Ampter's expression had changed. He lit his cigarette, his eyes caught by the engraved letters *Ph.D.*, and looked up again.

"Hello," he said. "Congratulations. I hear you got through your exam with flying colors."

He noticed the tall, handsome girl whose arm was locked in Ampter's.

"I don't believe you've met my wife," Mark said, and introduced them. "Mr. Zelinski. Alexander Zelinski."

Sasha bowed and took the hand that Mrs. Ampter held out to him in a forthright, friendly gesture.

"My friends call me Sasha," he said.

"Nice party," said Mark. "You Russians ought to feel pretty pleased."

Sasha was wondering how to steer the conversation into friendly, confidential channels.

"Your husband certainly missed you while you were away," he proffered. It was a stab in the dark, but it yielded nothing. He was mystified by Mrs. Ampter's return. The two seemed to be on the best of terms. What had happened? His guess had been that she had left her husband because she disapproved of his political ideas. That at least was what he had told Gospodin Gregg. But if they were back together now he must have been wrong. Or else Ampter had changed his views. No, that didn't seem likely. Perhaps *she* had . . . Sasha was at a loss.

"We'll be seeing you," Mark said as the two of them started to leave.

"Oh, by the way—" Sasha had just thought of another tack. "I'd like to talk to you sometime about something that might interest you. We're trying to form a union. Engineers, technicians, taking in quite a wide field—architects, chemists. We want to go in with the CIO. I thought Bloch might have some good ideas. Maybe he could meet with us sometime."

"You'll have to talk to him. He's a pretty busy man these days, you know."

"What do you think of the idea?"

It had been Gospodin Gregg's idea that Sasha should involve himself in some left-wing activity. "It will make it easier for you to meet all those people," he had said. "They'll have more confidence in you." So Sasha had found out about this union that was being organized through some colleagues and was now actively promoting it.

"I'd have to know more about it," Mark said. "It should be all right. I'm all in favor of unions."

"You think Bloch will be interested, don't you?"

Mark grinned. "I can't speak for him. You'll have to ask him."

The Ampters left.

Alone again, Sasha began to make his way toward the other end of the house. There were more and more people. Lights were being turned on, which made the out-of-doors seem suddenly dark. He had an odd sense that he was living history, that what was happening around him was somehow momentous. Yet while he felt that he was a part of it and was playing a role in it, he was powerless to affect it, and in fact had no notion of what was happening.

In the doorway to the library there was a crush, and as he tried to get past he found himself up against Mrs. Leutner.

"Oh, hello," he said. He knew she was more or less in charge of arrangements. "How is the party going?"

"Well, I guess you can see for yourself," she said and laughed. She was all keyed up, and her eyes shone brightly. "Imagine! We've run out of orchids! We could have sold lots more . . ."

She was gone before Sasha could make any comment, and he found himself pushed into the midst of a group in which a very positive, carefully made-up woman was saying, with a metallic edge to her voice, "All I hear is Sebastian Bloch, Sebastian Bloch! What's so wonderful about this Sebastian Bloch, anyway? If he's so important, why isn't his name ever in the newspapers?"

Sasha caught sight of several young physicists over by the bar, and he suddenly wanted another drink. He said hello to Hans Weber, Ed MacAvoy and Bert Musing, all students of Bloch's.

They had a round of drinks.

Sasha was feeling better. There was something essentially warm and friendly about physicists. He tried to stir Leutner and Patterson to some enthusiasm over the scientists' and technicians' union, but they merely registered polite interest.

He began to circulate. The place was getting more and more crowded. The doorways were jammed. In the huge living room he caught sight of Jane Middleton talking with Professor Outland, who was obviously flirting with her. Did he know she was a communist? Sasha wondered. And his wife, who was gaily chatting with Leo Vorontov . . . It seemed to be in the spirit of the party.

In the milling confusion he became aware of a slight change of key in the prevailing din, of a new note in the polyphony of excitement. The stir in the entrance hall did not seem to have increased appreciably, yet he sensed an imponderable heightening in the emotional register while he watched Professor Cummings, who was talking to a couple of women, suddenly pause in the middle of a sentence and look blank for a moment, then continue. A wave of movement that seemed to have begun over there in the dining room, communicated itself to where Sasha stood, and as he was caught in the eddy he saw that it was caused by one of those gorgeous girls, followed almost immediately by another, and then by a third, each carrying a wide trayful of orchids. At the same time he thought he heard the name of Bloch whispered around him and then, as his gaze plunged into the shadowy dip between the curves of the breasts of the girl advancing toward him, he knew that Sebastian Bloch must have arrived.

As they stepped up to the front door Sebastian said to Tanya, "Now we're going to leave all our worries and troubles here on the doorstep. We needn't be afraid that anyone will steal them. They'll be right here for us to pick up again when we come out, but we don't want them around while we're at the party."

"Right," said Tanya.

Hans Weber and Lou Goldstein had preceded them by a few minutes with the crates containing the hundred extra orchids that Sebastian had wheedled out of Nicodano, though this time he had paid the wholesale price of two and a half dollars each for them. Weber and Goldstein were working out a new method of purifying beryllium for use as a moderator and had been able to knock off the project for the weekend just in time.

As Tanya and he slowly made their way into the living room, surrounded by beaming faces, Sebastian was struck not only by the size of the crowd but by its composition.

"Why, it's a real united front!" Tanya exclaimed enthusiastically as they were being steered toward the nearest bar.

A score or more of glasses went up as Sebastian and Tanya took the drinks that were handed them across the bar. Sebastian could feel the weeks of accumulated fatigue sloughing away. The place was packed. Never had they given a party that had drawn such a crowd.

"This is what we've been fighting for all these years!" said Bruce Patterson.

"It's a beginning," said Hsueh Ling.

Sebastian emptied his glass and smiled. It was a long time since he had felt so relaxed. Perhaps he would get just a little drunk tonight.

The roar of voices was deafening, and there was a constant movement of people weaving their way through the tight crowd. Sebastian looked into Tanya's eyes, and as she returned his look he felt a wonderful inner warmth. It seemed peculiarly appropriate that this party should be held here and now, bringing together all these people who had never been together before and perhaps never would be together again, at least not for a long time, but whose being together symbolized something important and strong in American life and perhaps in the rude shaping that the world was undergoing. In a rather absurd way that was none the less real, the presence of each of these persons was a political gesture. But the warmth that he felt was of a more personal kind. The future was beset with difficulties of every sort, difficulties that would have overwhelmed him three years before, that he would have been utterly incapable of coping with. Today, thanks to the experience of these years, he was equipped to deal with them. He had broken through the wall of that magic but sterilizing cocoon

of solipsism that had enveloped him all his life. He had become
a human being. He had even acquired weaknesses. He glanced
at Tanya and smiled again.

Backed into the corner formed by the bar and the wall, holding his empty glass, with Tanya beside him, he had for some
minutes been obscurely conscious of a half-casual, half-persist-
ent edging and shuffling in the shifting clusters of people close
to where he was standing. Unobtrusively, silently, one after another, Fritz Leutner, Bruce Patterson, Hans Weber, Ed Mac-
Avoy, Bert Musing, Roos, Levitt, Hendrickson and a score of
others of his students had gathered around him. They all had a
look on their faces that he recognized. They were not talking,
they were not even looking at him, though they were alert to
his every movement. They were just waiting.

Sebastian marveled. How could they have sensed it? He
knew that there could not possibly have been a leak, that they
couldn't have the slightest inkling of the news that he had just
brought back: that the California group had established that
U-238 with the capture of one neutron did go through
neptunium to form plutonium, and that plutonium did fission
with slow neutrons like U-235. Yet there they stood, without
any foreknowledge, without prearrangement, all of them looking absent, sly and a little sheepish, waiting for him to tell
them.

He glanced at Tanya out of the corner of his eye, and saw
that she was totally unaware of what was going on. Then he
looked down into the bottom of his empty glass, put it on the
bar and asked for a refill. Unobtrusively they all stepped up to
the bar, two or three of them at a time, and put down their
glasses.

They took their fresh drinks without putting their lips to
them, stepped back and stood, without a word, waiting.

Sebastian looked at his glass.

"I think you would like to know"—he kept his voice low,
but they seemed to hear him, despite the din—"that a brand-
new and very healthy baby has just been born in Berkeley.
He's the ninety-fourth in the family, they've named him

Pu-239, and he seems to do everything that was expected of him." He raised his glass.

No one said anything, but a secret, hardly perceptible smile stole into the faces of all the young physicists. They drank silently.

Several times, during the Blochs' first hour at the party, they had run into the Ampters. Tanya and Eve had embraced, Mark and Sebastian had clasped each other by the shoulders, and then they had been separated by a surging movement of the crowd and had shouted or signaled that they would get together later. They met again now in the dining room, where the voices were a little less deafening since most of the people here had their faces stuffed with food at least part of the time. Hot dogs and buns, sandwiches, cake and coffee were being served and were selling at a lively rate.

"Darling, do you realize," Tanya said to Eve, "that it's a year and a half since we've seen each other!"

"Oh, I know! It's been a long purgatory. And yet, the minute I got back I felt as if I'd never been away."

They were all ravenous. Perhaps because the voices around them were becoming increasingly raucous and people were letting themselves go more and more, the four of them hardly spoke as they munched frankfurters and sandwiches. By a mere "How did it go yesterday?" Sebastian conveyed all the real joy that he felt at Mark's success. And Mark's laconic "All right" was charged with all the labor and anxiety that had gone into a long and arduous ordeal.

"When can we all get together?" Tanya asked Eve. "Here it's obviously impossible even to talk." She immediately added, "Tomorrow is out, because Sebastian is having some physicists over. Sometime next week?"

"Mark has exams all next week and has to read papers every night," Eve replied.

"Next weekend, then?"

"We're leaving Saturday for a short trip. We've promised ourselves . . ."

They found that the best they could hope for was lunch sometime in the course of the week. They would call each other on Monday. The following week Sebastian would probably be going off again.

Sebastian bowed his head a little to one side and shook it slowly and sadly. "You see, I'm very much afraid that this— No." He broke off and looked up with a smile. "I'll tell you what," he proposed. "Let's all go to the bar in the next room and order ourselves a round, and we'll drink a silent toast."

In the living room a string of well-groomed people were slowly making their way through the tightly packed crowd toward the entrance hall, from which a number of late arrivals were working their way in the opposite direction. The hubbub was deafening. Jostled into a tight foursome ("like a four-leaf clover," said Eve) the Ampters and the Blochs got their drinks and held them protectively close to their chests.

Here they were—Sebastian, Eve, Tanya and Mark. They looked at one another and each was filled with his own thoughts. But the thoughts that were uppermost and perhaps deepest in the mind of each of them were those, so different for each of them, that also involved the other three. The strands of their lives had become oddly interwoven. They looked at one another. There was a very pure moment, during which their hearts seemed to unite in a communion of faith and affection. Undeniably they all felt, in that moment, that in whatever lay ahead for each of them their fates would somehow be linked, for better, for worse.

They lifted their glasses and drank.

"Will you give me a light, darling?" Eve said, putting a fresh cigarette between her lips. While Mark's hand was still up she held it for a moment in her own, stroked with her forefinger the letters *Ph.D.* engraved on his lighter, and smiled. "It's still true," she said, and squeezed his arm as they continued to stroll slowly across the library.

Mark tried to rouse himself to the sense of elation he had felt at the beginning of the evening. But there was something leaden in him that would not let itself be lifted. He had drunk a lot and talked a lot and danced, surrounded by kindred spirits. It had been a wonderful party, and he had had a good time. . . . Yet for the last hour or two he had felt himself succumbing to an increasing sense of gloom.

The floor was littered with cigarette butts, crumpled paper, ashes, and here and there a trampled orchid petal. The crowd had thinned out considerably. People still stood about in clusters, but the talk had become more desultory. The bars were doing very little business.

In the long gallery that gave access to the solarium, the music room and the ballroom, Tom Anderson, Jo Brand and Bill Parrish, with Zelinski standing on the fringe, were discussing Wendell Willkie's decision to defend William Schneiderman before the Supreme Court. In the ballroom things were still lively, but the orchestra was showing signs of fatigue and was taking longer rests between numbers. They had just begun playing again when Mark and Eve entered. It was a waltz.

"Let's dance," Eve said.

They danced attuned to each other, responsive to each other, with utter ease, carried by the music, their feet and their bodies obedient to its rhythm, their thoughts hypnotized by it but obedient to laws of their own, spinning away into other realms.

Most of the strangers had left by now, and those who were dancing were almost all people he knew. They flashed on his eye as he whirled around with Eve in his arms, her breasts gently pressing against his chest; flashed on his eye, and for each a trigger mechanism registered a name and assorted data in a special compartment of his mind.

"What's the matter?" Eve was all anxiety. "Aren't you feeling well?"

He had suddenly stopped dancing, overwhelmed at realizing what he was doing.

"It's all right. I'm all right."

He started dancing again, but it didn't go, he was stepping all over Eve's feet, and they dropped out and sat down.

"You've had a little too much," Eve said.

"No, no it's not that . . . It's just—everything."

"Are you sure you're all right?" She looked at him anxiously for a moment. "If you are, maybe you'd like to be alone for a few minutes? I see Tanya's father over there. I haven't had a chance to say hello to him yet."

It was uncanny, the knack she had of sensing his moods, of doing exactly the right thing. As he watched her disappear in the crowd in the direction of the orchestra he wondered if perhaps she had even guessed what he had just discovered. But it wasn't merely the discovery of the unconscious persistence of police reflexes that had upset him just now. He had suddenly seen clearly something that had vaguely oppressed him for weeks, for months, and that he had foolishly imagined would be completely washed away and forgotten once he had reached the present turning point. A new profession, a new relation to other people, a new life. Yes. Except that, looking around, seeing Maggie Garnett, Albert Cummings, Philip Jones, May Barnett, and scores of others, he had suddenly remembered the derogatory information he had collected on all of them, everything that had gone into their files. That wouldn't simply vanish as a result of the fact that he was quitting the security service. It was all in the record, filed away safely in the office for future reference, ready to do its damage. He had done these people whom he now considered his friends incalculable harm. There was no way of undoing it.

He was feeling thoroughly wretched by the time Eve came back.

"Come, darling," she said, taking him by the hand, "sulking period's over. Let's try this Russian rumba . . ."

Her exuberance lifted him out of himself for a moment, but the heaviness was still there. Would he carry it with him forever? Let's think about something else, he told himself, and tried to concentrate on the finicky little steps of the dance. Let's think about Eve. But Eve had the curse, so that wasn't any good either. Why did she have to have the curse just tonight? He looked around. Only sixty or seventy couples still dancing. Scattered groups sitting or standing. The light dripping in thousands of flashes from the cascading crystals in the ceiling, reflected by the mirrored doors. Orchids— And then the thought came to him that probably someone here, one of these people whom he had talked to in the course of the evening, was the Chief's man and was keeping an eye on him. He tried to brush the thought away, but it kept pestering him, like a fly buzzing about his ears. I don't care, he assured himself, it doesn't matter any more. But he knew he was kidding himself. He was not rid of his past.

He caught sight of Tanya Bloch among the dancing couples, swinging in the arms of Bill Parrish. Glancing around the vast room, he finally made out Sebastian's silhouette in an open doorway, half hidden by a cluster of people to whom his back was turned. He was alone, looking out into the night.

The sound of the rumba music grated on Sebastian's nerves. The rhythm was a little off and the instruments weren't right, but that wasn't what bothered him. The fact that Tanya was dancing with Bill irritated him too, for no good reason. Yet it was a relief to be alone for a few moments. He and Tanya had agreed to leave their troubles on the front doorstep when they came, but the strain of keeping the disturbing thoughts from his mind was more exhausting than the burden of carrying them. He was oppressed by sinister forebodings. The shadow of the Monster haunted him.

He lit a cigarette. By contrast with the brilliantly lit ballroom the night was completely black. There were no neighboring houses in sight, and the garden was an opaque mass beyond the glow that fell on the flower beds, the bricks and the grass through the glass doors. A few stars shone faintly in the sky.

What had happened to the elation that had buoyed him up just a few hours ago? He had drunk quite a lot, but after the first few drinks the alcohol had had no euphoric effect. The party was obviously a success beyond all their expectations.

And it had meant a lot to all of them. It was a symbol of a new political climate, a vindication of years of stubborn faith.

The sense of triumph had given way to a growing melancholy. This that should have been—that *was*—the beginning of something that was central to his life now struck him increasingly each moment, as the end. These people would never meet again like this, and he especially would never meet with them again. This was a farewell.

The music stopped, and he turned back into the ballroom. The number of the guests was dwindling. It was way past midnight.

"It's time for us to go home," he said to Tanya as she and Bill Parrish joined him.

He was suddenly very tired. He had been away from his worries long enough.

The Outland chauffeur had been looking for the owner of a car that was parked out on the steep street and that had to be moved in order to extricate two other cars that had locked bumpers. It turned out to be Mark Ampter's car.

Mark left Eve with Hannah Leutner and Genia Patterson, put a cigarette in his mouth and followed the chauffeur out. In the front entrance the Blochs were taking leave of various people. Mark shook hands and bid them a hurried good-by and caught up with the chauffeur as he went out the front door.

Mark got into his Chevrolet, lit his cigarette, and backed the car clear of the two locked vehicles, moved to a space on the other side of the street and went back into the house, throwing his cigarette away after just a few puffs. The Blochs had already left, and the house by now looked practically empty.

"I guess we'd better be thinking about getting home ourselves," he said to Eve when he found her. She was chatting with the Pattersons. Her orchid was crushed and drooping.

"Just one more cigarette, and then we'll go."

He held out his package of cigarettes while he reached for

his lighter. His hand failed to encounter the familiar metal parallelepiped. He pulled his hand out and tapped the outside of his pocket and the whole lower flap of his jacket, plunged his hand into his pocket again. The pocket was empty. Feverishly he tried his right-hand coat pocket, and all his other pockets, while his eyes scanned the floor.

"I've lost it!" he said in a panicky voice.

"Lost what?" said Eve. She had been talking, and had not noticed his frantic gestures.

"My lighter!"

Meanwhile Bruce Patterson had produced his own lighter—also a gift from Bloch—and had lit Eve's cigarette.

"Darling, you can't have lost it! Did you look in all your pockets?"

Practically all the guests had left by now. The bartenders and most of the committee and a few stalwarts, a mere thirty or forty people, wandered about the empty spaces like lost souls.

Everybody began a search for the lighter, in all the corners, among the litter of cigarette stubs, empty cigarette packages, broken orchids and smears of ash and spilled drinks. It was nowhere to be found.

The Ampters were among the last to leave. Mark helped Eve into her side of the car, went around the back and got into the driver's seat. As he pulled the door shut he heard a metallic crunch and felt a resistance that prevented the lock from catching.

He opened the door to see what it was. A mangled lump of metal fell to the ground.

He picked it up. His lighter. It was smashed and twisted, ruined beyond repair. He turned on the dashboard light and looked at it.

"Hell!" he said. "Oh, hell!"

Eve put her hand on his.

"Never mind, darling," she said. "I'll buy you a new one. With a new motto."

Chapter 10

LOOKING back, Mark found it difficult—in fact, impossible—
to recapture the mood of those few days immediately following the Russian War Relief party and preceding the attack
on Pearl Harbor. Nothing had actually happened during that
week to make it memorable, but it had been a crowded and
hectic one, filled with the frustration of suspended hopes and
agonizing strains, dominated by the mounting pressure of an
impending decision that withheld all clue to its issue.

There had been the night of Eve's home-coming, the same
night as the Russian War Relief party. . . . Like the end of
the party itself, like the days and the nights that followed, it
had been terribly mixed up, fate seeming to take away with
one hand what it gave with the other. The blessed state of in-
ebriation that he had so conscientiously built up in the course
of the party had been suddenly dissipated by the discovery of
his crushed lighter, and he had gone to bed cold sober. Eve
was in his arms, pressed close to him, and yet as far away as
the moon, and as untouchable. All night he had tossed deliri-
ously, alternately overwhelmed by joy and despair, triumph
and failure, a clear conscience and a sense of guilt.

"You mustn't brood," Eve had told him the next morning.
"Let's tackle just one problem at a time. They'll all work themselves out."

Everything had been provisional about that week. The
meals were improvised affairs, he caught such snatches of sleep
as he could at irregular hours, every waking minute being
taken up with examinations to give, papers to read, committee
meetings to attend, bibliographies and lectures to prepare for
the new courses he would be giving next semester. And as both

he and Eve were determined to get away for a week as soon as examinations were over, there were the plans and arrangements to make.

Snow had come early this year, and the Colorado ski runs were reported to be in good condition. They had decided to have themselves a fling and had made reservations to spend a week at a first-class winter resort in Rocky Mountain National Park picked out on the strength of the photographs in a publicity folder that they saw in a travel agency.

Mark felt he absolutely must see Sebastian. They made a luncheon date for Tuesday, which was postponed to Wednesday. Wednesday morning Tanya phoned to say that Sebastian couldn't make it; she was in a hurry, she couldn't talk, but she would call back the following day. It was Friday before she called, to say that Sebastian had had to fly east. She sounded upset.

Thursday was the night of the unit meeting. Mark actually could not spare the time to attend it, though normally he would have managed to do so anyway. But this time he had no inclination to go. He would not have had the courage to face his "comrades." What had happened? He remembered the feeling that had come over him on the dance floor at the party when he had suddenly seen his "victims" all around him in a new light.

Getting his doctorate and the instructorship appointment was to have set a seal on that whole phase of the past. But now it struck him that the past was not something that you left behind you. You carried it around with you. It was as much a part of you as your present or your future—more, even, because there was nothing you could do to change it. He could see the forms he would be called on to fill out, an endless succession of them—name, sex, nationality, married or unmarried, date and place of birth . . . and then, inevitably, some such item as *Previous Occupation, if any,* or *Posts Held.* . . . How would *Special Agent* look on such a form? Why was it that this profession, in which he had once taken such pride, now filled him with shame and revulsion?

Certainly this had something to do with the sense almost

of panic with which he looked forward to the inevitable interview with the Chief. His previous occupation was a matter
of record, but the kind of record it would be would depend a
lot on that last interview. And this involved the whole matter
of his reports. What was going to happen to them? How were
they going to be used?

He tried to find comfort by projecting himself into the
future. Once his interview with the Chief was over, he would
be a free citizen once more, with a respectable profession. He
and Eve were together, closer than they had ever been, and
nothing would ever come between them again. They would
devote themselves to Jimmy, perhaps get him a little brother
or sister; he would teach and do research and play an active
part in the University community in which he felt so much at
home; they would get a servant, and Eve would have time to
play the piano, and on weekends he would go back to dabbling
in water colors. . . . But, as he plowed through mountains of
examination books and term papers, he knew deep down that
this was all a pipe dream. Nothing so soft and easy lay ahead.
He didn't know what it would be, but there was a heaviness inside him that nothing would dispel.

The week somehow came to an end—the last examination
given, the last papers read, and the grades turned in to the recorder's office. Little Jimmy, who had found this whole home-
coming week rather trying, had been shipped off to his grandmother's.

On Saturday night, after the train had deposited them at
the small mountain station and they had settled in their luxurious room and had showered, dressed for dinner, and poured
themselves a highball from the quart flask they had brought,
they felt as if they were together for the first time.

That night they made love, and it was good.

They awoke the next morning in a real fairyland. Through
the frost-flowers that adorned the small windowpanes, beyond
the hoar-sprinkled icicles that hung from the widely projecting
varnished-pine roof, stretched a magic white landscape, the
snow-laden boughs of nearby evergreens framing a view of blue-
shadowed slopes rearing to jagged peaks scintillating in the

rising sun. Here, Mark decided, looking out on the scene composed of granite and virgin forest and drifts of snow, of sheer heights and towering grandeur and immaculate whiteness, here, far from human passions and pressures, he would be able to weigh his problem coolly and objectively. They rented skis, and worked out on the more moderate slopes till noon.

"My thighs are a little sore," Eve half-whispered with a smile of secret, happy contentment as they went in to lunch. "But I don't think it's just the skiing."

In the swank dining room the radio was playing soft background music, the waiter had just brought them ice-cold martinis, and Mark was saying, for the *n*th time, and with the same lack of conviction, "I'll just go and tell Gregg I'm quitting. If he wants a reason he can think one up himself"—when the musical program was interrupted by a voice whose ominous solemnity instantly arrested every attention. Suddenly the world seemed to crash. It was not just the shattering details of the death and destruction wrought by the Japanese attack on Pearl Harbor that came over the air in the breathless words of the announcer. Everything that had happened up to that moment went out of focus, became unreal, and the meaning of everything changed.

Mark looked at Eve, as she at the same moment looked at him. Their hands found each other under the table. And as the news of the disaster boomed across the dining room filled with vacationers stunned into silence, Mark knew that what he would tell Gregg was no longer a problem.

Chapter 11

"I've enlisted in the army," Mark announced to the Chief less than a week later, in the latter's office. He had phoned for the appointment, and Gregg had known what was coming—or had thought he knew. Zelinski had informed him of Ampter's appointment as instructor in economics.

"Infantry," Ampter added. "As a private."

The announcement came as a complete surprise. A not wholly disagreeable one, however. Ampter's behavior had confirmed his worst fears. He regarded his subordinate's defection as a betrayal. Ampter had failed him in every way and lost all claim to his consideration. But he could not altogether forget how much he had liked him, what high hopes he had placed in him. And the army seemed a good move. Ampter was definitely too soft. The army might knock some sense into him and make a man of him. He remembered his own war experience, how it had changed his life.

"Congratulations," he said with a show of cordiality. "You might have let us know *before* though, I think. We still have some sort of arrangement, I believe."

"I'm sorry, sir. I wanted to, but—but I was afraid you might try to make me change my mind."

You were certainly in a hurry, in any case, the Chief thought to himself. Pearl Harbor had furnished the occasion, but he was certain Ampter had not enlisted out of sheer patriotic fervor. What had made him do it? A pretty powerful motive, whatever it was. Something to hide. There was always something to hide, something to get away from, something to forget.

"We'll be sorry to lose you," he said—this was at least half the truth. "But in our racket we expect fairly big turnover. We're geared to it: a constant influx of new blood, and those who leave us and go out into the world form a valuable extension of our organization. You know our tradition: once an agent, always an agent."

"Yes, sir." Ampter looked uncomfortable. He was going to be a lot more uncomfortable before the Chief was through with him.

"There'll be certain formalities incidental to the separation," the Chief said. "I want to give you a clean bill of health. First I want you to write a letter of resignation . . ."

"But I already wrote one," said Ampter, "when I took on the assignment."

"That was a phony one, remember? You left under a cloud. We cooked up a rather damaging story. You don't want that to stand, do you?"

"I don't know," Mark said slowly. "You see, I'd like to have my connection with the organization considered severed as of that time. What I've done for you since then—well, you said yourself once that there's no record of my connection with the Bloch case . . . or yours. I want to just blot it out. I've failed . . ."

"Wait a minute—"

"Let me just finish what I wanted to say. All right: I took on this assignment. Admittedly it was very special. I had to resign from the organization. I took a risk. I thought I could do it. I wanted to do it. You warned me about its difficulty, its danger. Well, I tried hard. I put my best into it. I wanted to succeed. I didn't. I was a flop. All right. It was a risk we both took, a personal deal between you and me. Let's leave it there. I'm sorry . . ."

"Sit down," the Chief said gently.

Mark had risen to his feet in his excitement. He was trying to press the issue, taking things a little too fast.

He sat down again.

There was one thing Gregg wanted to find out: had Ampter spilled his guts to Bloch? That would make a difference.

"Let's get things straight," he said calmly. "History doesn't stand still. What was true three years ago is no longer true today. Those reports of yours are no longer a private transaction between you and me. They never were, for that matter, and you know it. The privacy was merely a security measure. Those records are now official. They're out of my hands."

Ampter had always been good at covering up his emotions, but the Chief could tell he was shaken.

"I might as well tell you," he went on, "that those reports are going to be used and that they're considered pretty important."

He stood up in turn and walked around his desk.

"I said just now that they're out of my hands." He looked at Mark sharply. "I may, however, have something to say about how they're used . . ."

He pretended to weigh an idea in his mind for a moment, then went on.

"This is confidential. Bloch is being considered for a highly important war job. Whether he gets it or not may depend on those reports. They'll largely replace the usual security investigation. It has not yet been decided, however, whether when he is interrogated he should be simply questioned as to basic facts brought out in the reports, or whether he should be shown and allowed to read substantial parts of the reports themselves and be asked to comment on them."

He was watching Ampter closely and he knew then, from the slight contraction of the muscles around his eyes at the last words, from a kind of fixed look that came into his face, that he had made no confession to Sebastian Bloch and that there was probably nothing in the world that he dreaded so greatly as that Bloch should find out about the role he had played.

"Then . . ." Mark said in a low voice, hesitating, "that would mean . . . he would know."

"Yes," said the Chief. "He would know."

"In that case," said Mark, "I'd rather tell him myself."

"That's up to you. You're your own boss now." He let the silence settle. "I thought perhaps—for personal reasons—you might prefer to keep it confidential."

Mark said nothing. He lit another cigarette.

"There's another formality," Gregg continued, coming back to his desk and sitting down again. "I want a letter from you formally submitting the body of your reports to this office and stating that this brings your investigation to a close."

"I can't. I can't do that!" Mark burst out.

The Chief let this pass without comment. "I guess I don't need to remind you," he said, "that you have a considerable sum in back pay coming to you. Nearly three and a half years at the increased salary that goes with the promotion."

"I don't want it," said Mark. "And I don't want the promotion."

"Look here, Ampter, let's be sensible. This is a business arrangement. Each of us has certain obligations and certain rights . . ."

"Let me say what I have to say," Mark broke in. "And I have to stand up to say it."

He got up and straightened his shoulders and took a few steps toward the middle of the room, then turned to face the Chief. Gregg found himself feeling sorry for him.

"Let's go back to the beginning. I was assigned to investigate a certain suspect named Sebastian Bloch. The whole idea behind it was that this man, who was an important scientist, might be dangerous because of his political ideas, and it was therefore wise to find out about him. I saw it that way too, and it was on that basis that I agreed to take on the assignment. Now what happened? What happened was simply this: that in the course of my investigation I became convinced that in spite of all the things in the way of associations and activities that looked so damaging in the reports, this man was *not* dangerous, was *not* subversive, but was on the contrary a thoroughly sound citizen—more than that, a man of such integrity, of such deep wisdom in political affairs, that his counsel could be of inestimable value to those responsible for this country's destiny."

He looked at the Chief intently.

"When I went into this I was all for it—I had no mental reservations of any kind. I found out, I think, everything about this man that could be considered most damaging from the point of view of security. Knowing the worst, I have come to the conclusion that he is absolutely trustworthy and loyal." He threw out his arms, the open palms of his hands upturned. "That being the case, you can appreciate the fact that it would be absurd and . . . intolerable for *me* to be the one to point the accusing finger at him, which is what these reports amount to."

Gregg shrugged his shoulders. Ampter's reports proved that

Sebastian Bloch was a communist—and a lot more. Now
Ampter was saying that Bloch was nevertheless loyal. He was
tempted, purely out of curiosity as to what kind of answer
Ampter would give, to ask him point-blank whether *he* had in
turn become a communist. But he immediately dismissed the
idea. He knew what the answer would be. It would be "no,"
but a "no" hedged about with qualifications and reservations.
The real answer was that for practical purposes he *was* a communist; he had gone over to the enemy.

"Let me ask you something," he said. "Those reports: do
they present the true facts as you've learned them and as you
honestly believe them to be—or are they fabrications?"

"Why, they're true, of course, but—"

"That's all that matters. Our job is to investigate—to
gather the facts. It's not up to us to evaluate them. How these
facts are used is not our responsibility. And it isn't our business. Anyway, this is completely out of my hands—and yours.
All we have to do is wind up this case in an orderly way. Now
if you'll let me have those two letters, which I'd better dictate,
I'll have your separation papers made out and write you a letter attesting your satisfactory service, and of course see that you
get your check."

Mark Ampter was shaking his head.

"I can't do it—don't you see?"

The Chief had not anticipated this difficulty. He got up and
crossed to where Mark was standing.

"What I'm asking for is just routine administrative procedure," he said. "And this procedure has to be followed—for
your own good as well as everybody else's."

"I can't see it that way, sir, and I've told you why."

"You'd better think this over very carefully," the Chief said
slowly. "It's only fair to warn you that the consequences for
your own future could be most serious."

"What do you mean?"

"If you go out of this office with a bad record, you know
what that will mean. You'll find yourself behind the eight ball
wherever you go. In the army in particular, to begin with."

Mark said nothing. Gregg's words seemed to have stunned him.

Gregg seized the advantage.

"Be sensible," he went on. "These two letters are just a formality. They don't affect your reports one way or the other. The reports will be used in any case as the Government sees fit. But by signing those two letters you'll be squaring yourself with the service. Your record will be clean, and you won't have anything hanging over you. The other way—well, if you're fool enough to refuse to play ball with us, all I can say is, God help you."

Mark did not reply immediately.

"Think it over," the Chief said. "You don't have to give me your answer now. I know it's a tough decision to make."

"No, it isn't that," Mark replied. "I was trying to think of some way to explain to you, so you would understand. If there was any way of destroying those reports . . . But you say they've become official. So I guess the harm has already been done. But at least I'd like somehow to counteract their effect. I'm trying to think . . ."

Gregg was annoyed. Without those two documents, the reports definitely lost some of their effectiveness and virtually all their legal value. Ampter seemed to be reading his mind.

"As the record stands," Mark said, "I resigned from the service three and a half years ago. There's nothing in those reports connecting my name with them so that they could be used as evidence. The reason I'm not willing to sign those two letters you want is that they would in fact strengthen the effect of the reports."

"Don't kid yourself." The Chief still could not believe that Ampter was seriously intending to refuse. He wasn't going to throw away thirty thousand dollars. He was holding out for something, playing it tough. "Those two letters, as I said, are just a formality for our office. We've got everything we need in those reports. For one thing, we've got your fingerprints on every sheet of paper they're written on. For another, when we confront Bloch with those reports there's not going to be any doubt about their author. And I might as well tell you, in case you were wondering, that I've had investigators out on you too for quite some time. But apart from that, you know better than to think you as an individual can stand up against our whole service. As between your word and ours, you know who's going to be believed. Don't be a fool, Ampter. Let's see if we can't work this thing out. You realize of course that we won't be able to pay you off until the proper formalities are taken care of."

"The money you can forget about," Mark said in a toneless voice.

The Chief was stunned.

"What do you mean?" he said.

"The money," said Mark. "What I was supposed to be paid for writing those reports. I don't want it."

He's crazy, the Chief said to himself. And aloud: "I suppose you think you're going to keep your family on a private's pay."

"My wife will work. That's not the problem."

The Chief went back to his desk and sat down. Though he had himself perfectly under control, he was boiling mad. More even than by Ampter's refusal to write the two letters, he was outraged by his throwing away thirty thousand dollars. Thirty thousand dollars was a lot of money. If that argument didn't convince him . . . His rage was aggravated by having to be contained.

"I'll tell you," Mark said after a pause. "I think I have a solution which ought to take care of both your problem and mine. I'll write a letter of resignation. You say those reports are now a matter of record, so there's no point in trying to pretend that they don't exist. And I'll write some kind of piece to wind up those reports. But I'll write them both myself. With reference to the reports I shall say substantially what I've told you, and in particular that on the basis of my long and thorough investigation I have come to the conclusion that the subject, Sebastian Bloch, is absolutely reliable and loyal, and I shall give my reasons. In my letter of resignation I shall say that I am resigning because I have lost my unqualified faith in the purposes and methods of the service and that therefore I cannot conscientiously continue to belong to it; and that I am not accepting the pay or the promised promotion offered for the successful investigation of Sebastian Bloch, since in the course of working on the case I became opposed to its objective and now regard the entire investigation, and my participation in it in particular, as an error."

"If you write that kind of letter of resignation"—the Chief had to concentrate on holding his fury in leash—"that is of course your own affair. But I warn you that it will mean a record that you will never live down. As for the conclusion to your reports, you can save yourself the trouble. I'll just tear it up."

"Oh, no you won't!" Mark shouted with surprising vehemence. "It's a part of the reports. Either you destroy them all, or you put this with them. If you use them at all you'll use them as I wrote them. I'll have notarized copies sent registered to the proper places, and one kept under seal in my attorney's office. I'm taking no chances."

The Chief felt himself defeated. It was useless to argue further.

So he had lost Ampter. Lost him to Sebastian Bloch.

"All right, Ampter," he said wearily. "You're asking for it. I tried to help you, but you seem to prefer it the hard way. You'll find the going tough, believe me."

"I'll have to chance that, sir," Mark said, his tone again deferential. "I'm only doing what I think is right."

Right. The word sent echoes through Gregg's mind. The moment a man took it upon himself to make his own private decisions as to what was right and wrong, he was headed for trouble.

"I've done what I could for you," he said. "From now on you're on your own."

He felt a faint twinge of regret. But perhaps it was better this way. Because he wasn't through with Ampter. He wasn't through with Ampter, because he was far from through with Sebastian Bloch. Ampter was going to help him just once more. But this time he wouldn't know it. He would probably never know it.

PART II: *Man of the Hour*

Chapter 12

The Monster.

At first there had been only an abstract concept. Without body, without reality: a series of calculations—staggering enough, but purely theoretical—occasional speculations among colleagues, a shadow on the edge of surmise. But as the weeks passed, and the months, as the intimations of Apocalypse became lodged in the mind, and work with pencil and paper, Geissler tube, mass spectrograph and cyclotron brought fresh data to confirm some of the boldest hypotheses, the thing began to assume the fearsome outlines of possibility. In the dark recesses of consciousness the nightmare took shape.

Sebastian had thought of it as "the Monster" ever since his imagination had first glimpsed a breath-taking flash of its awesome features. For monster it was, of a cataclysmic absoluteness that was incommensurable with the letter and the spirit of all the rules by which man lived upon this earth. Its power of destruction staggered the imagination, dwarfed everything man's compulsion to violence had yet devised. It represented a leap beyond the known bounds of nature, a rending asunder of the order and proportions of the charted universe, a pulverizing of the fragile structure of meaning built over the millennia to mirror the enigma of endless worlds whirling in the night, and the even greater enigma of the minute crust of biological proliferation that had manifested itself on at least one of the incidental cooling planets caught up in the infinite galaxy of cosmic dust.

Monster of fire and blast, day-splitting flash, black beast of death rending the air with feet of thunder, body of smoke and dust and ash penetrating and disintegrating corpuscle and tissue, substance and sense.

Its be-all and its end-all was death. But not death as man had ever known it. Not death to crown a life, not death by disease, not death by battle, treachery or poison; not death by faith, by passion or by accident. But a death willed and calculated, and yet so wanton and ignominious that in the obliteration of life it achieved a new dimension. It was death as the ultimate in the denial of humanity—an abstract, mathematical death, a statistical death; a death anonymous, wholesale and indiscriminate, consuming thousands, tens of thousands, in one lick of its searing tongue, men, women, children, devouring all life, spreading poison and pestilence, blinding, maiming, mutilating in a vast sweep of desolation that would extend incalculably beyond the periphery of the holocaust of horror. It would be hailed as a triumph of science and technology, be brandished in the face of the world by politicians and diplomats, annexed with gloating professional complacency by military strategists, who would calculate its effects in terms of megadeaths . . .

The Monster.

He was being asked to assist in the birth of the Monster. And he knew that the Monster, once born, would cause endless havoc. To himself. And to the world. To himself certainly.

He had of course known for a long time, even before the premonitory shadow of its shape first loomed before him, that his commitment to it was inescapable. Yet his whole being rebelled.

It had been so natural, at first, to turn to Tanya. She knew of course that something was brewing, and that there was evil in it. "You understand," he had told her one day, long before that first conversation he had had with Gröndahl last June, when he had learned that the most important decision of his life was one that he had already unwittingly made, "you understand that this work I have been involved in is going to mean some changes in our life."

He had not known how the talk might go, but he had hoped to define as wide an area as possible in which the two of them could still communicate. At that time the thing had been even more remote, the possibility of it as yet almost purely speculative. Hitler had not invaded Russia, and of course America was not yet in the war. The imperatives, though strongly felt by the foreign scientists, had seemed less urgent. The problem then had been for him the relatively simple one of the moral implications involved in creating a weapon so powerful that it could annihilate whole populations and devastate entire nations, and of the role that a man of his convictions could in conscience assume in such a venture.

In talking to Tanya, however, he could not mention that what was involved was a weapon, and this limited the possibility of her grasping the real acuteness of the problem.

It had been a matter of principle with him then, and up to the time of his talk with Gröndahl, that he would consent to work on a government project of whatever kind only after putting all his cards on the table. He would insist that the Government, and the agency concerned, know exactly where he stood politically, what he believed, what he had done. He would agree to cease all political activity, and even to salt away his ideas, "for the duration." But abjure them, no.

Tanya had been full of misgivings.

"You mustn't do it, you must get out of it!" she had blurted out, with unexpected passion, when in veiled terms he had explained the general situation—the danger, the almost-likelihood of an Axis victory, the imminence of American involvement, the certainty that Hitler would soon attack Russia, and against all this the possibility that an "invention" might turn the tide.

"They wouldn't let you!" she had cried impetuously, "and if they did— No, promise me that you won't get involved in it!"

He had not been able to promise, but at that time he himself had been far from certain as to what might develop. He had had the feeling, however, that Tanya was not going to prove too helpful with the problem, and it distressed him.

The feeling had been confirmed shortly after the talk with

Gröndahl. He had been too unhappy about the predicament he suddenly found himself in not to unburden himself to Tanya. He had virtually committed himself to working on the Monster without having clarified his political position.

"But you can't do that!" she had protested, without a moment's hesitation. "Don't you see? You can't do it, as a matter of principle!"

"I know, hon, I've worried about it for hours. I don't see any way out of it."

"There *is* a way," Tanya had retorted. "In fact there are two. You can refuse to have anything to do with it—which is what I think you ought to do. But if you feel you absolutely *have* to get in on it, you simply must do it on your own terms."

What she was saying surely made sense. But there was something in all this that was beyond sense.

"As for refusing to work on it," he had replied, "that's far from simple. In the first place"—he had hesitated here, but had decided that it had to be said—"it's possible, just possible, that if I didn't help on it it might not get done—at least not in time to save us."

"Is that what *you* think, or what *they* think?"

He had tried to explain then that it was something that no one could be certain about, but that the difficulties were so vast, and the time factor so urgent, that every man counted; that if he, who was so close to it and knew so much about it, were to back out it would have a demoralizing effect on the whole scientific community in the country and would result in the refusal on the part of many others, particularly among the younger men, to work on the project. There was real danger that his withdrawal might jeopardize the whole program.

Tanya had been only half convinced. "But then," she had said, after a long pause, "if you are so indispensable, you're in all the better position to make your own terms."

"That's not easy either." There was the fact that this thing was going to involve enormous sums of money and would therefore be subjected to the sharpest kind of political scrutiny. Any suspicion of a taint of communism, especially concerning an important member of the staff, would kill the chances of getting the appropriation. And there was the fact that his colleagues, an overwhelming majority of whom were extreme conservatives, whether they were politically conscious or not, would resent working with him if an issue were made of his left-wing views, and any authority that he might be called upon to exercise would be constantly compromised.

But he realized, as he spoke, that without all the details his arguments were weak and would not convince her. She could have no inkling, for instance, of the terrible urgency imposed upon the project by the fact that the Germans were presumably already working on the same thing. She could not gauge the numerous factors, many of them imponderable, that entered into the problem—the stubbornly held preconceptions and theories of some of the key men, the personal jealousies and hostilities and ambitions, the political pressures . . .

"All I know," Tanya had concluded, after hearing everything that he was able to tell her, "is that it's wrong, and that you're inviting terrible trouble."

As the months went by he found it increasingly difficult to talk to her. More and more of his time was spent away—in Washington, New York, Chicago, and unfamiliar out-of-the-way places where new plants were going up, or old ones were being converted—and when he was home there were many immediate, personal things to discuss. On their rare relaxed evenings together she would play for him. And here, in the enchanted world of music, he could commune with her without any reservations. His tension would relax, the tiredness would flow out of him, the nightmare visions of the Monster would dissolve. A great peace would come over him. The world had ceased to exist: they alone were real, in the heart of this golden sphere of harmony, a man and a woman in a time of innocence.

It was here, in this realm, and here alone, that he found a release from anguish—an anguish no longer purely private but seeming to him more and more to gnaw at the root of life itself. In this mathematical forest of sound all nature's laws seemed magically suspended. Music was a wholly arbitrary re-creation of the world, in which time and space were abolished and emotions were communicated only by means of symbols more abstract than numbers, in a fluid architecture elaborated in terms of a stylization of time that only accentuated its incommensurability with the order of time in which men were born and died. Listening to music, he would reflect that its essence was not sound, but pattern and relationships, and that the ideal music would not be heard at all, even inwardly, but would be felt, as a bat in flight registered the densities of space around him—not with a single organ but with the vital response of the whole being. Purer than mathematics, which depended for its purity on a merely posited negation of both time and space, music existed outside these altogether, outside the very concepts of beginning and end, of being and becoming. The thought sometimes occurred to him that perhaps it was not the sun or the moon, the recurrence of the seasons, or life's brevity; not man's suffering and death; not the acceptance, nor the refusal, of man's fate that had engendered the idea of immortality, and of her stepsister, eternity; but music—music with its rhythms and its harmonies that echoed and re-echoed down the endless corridors of memory and obliterated all the categories that existed only by virtue of what they were not.

With the passing of the months he became ever more deeply involved in the project of bringing the Monster into being. Yet he still had no official connection with it. There was, in fact, no project. There was no organization. There were committees. There were laboratories. There were plants. There was feverish activity in all the research centers, there were hundreds of technicians working overtime on dozens of aspects of the problem, all of them knowing a little, few of them knowing much, about the nature of the goal they were working toward.

Sebastian heard the news of the attack on Pearl Harbor as he was traveling in an army plane from Washington to Chicago. His traveling companion was an ordnance general who served on the Defense Research Committee, and Sebastian was engaged in giving him an elementary lesson in nuclear physics when the radio operator burst into the cabin to make the shattering announcement. The plane carried a full load of army officers, most of them field grade, and the excitement produced by the news was overwhelming. The operator connected up the radio to the loudspeaker, and as the details of the disaster came over the air, broken by static, interrupted periodically by statements from leading officials and finally by the President's message, the tenseness in the cabin—after the first outbursts, the curses, the roars, no one spoke—grew unbearable. Explosive passions churned inside each of the forty-odd officers sitting helpless, impotent, imprisoned in the fuselage of a plane high above the clouds while the American armed forces were being crippled by the worst military disaster in the country's history.

What had happened? Who had blundered? Was there no warning? Where was intelligence? What about those two Jap envoys in Washington? . . . What was left of the Pacific Fleet? The docks and depots and barracks blown up and in flames, the bursting of bombs, the explosions of munitions and fuel dumps, the panic, the screams of the wounded and the dying . . . How many thousands killed? Certainly the Navy had been the worse hit. But the Army already had hundreds of officers and men killed. . . .

Sebastian was caught up by the excitement. It was, he felt, of the same quality and intensity as that of these men. Fury, indignation—the President's words, "a day that will live in infamy"—reverberated within him, but also a grim sense of peril. The Monster. Perhaps the Monster would prove to be the only hope of turning the tide.

He would *have* to decide now.

The weeks that followed were the most agonizing that he had ever experienced. He felt an unutterable sense of loneliness. He desperately needed to talk everything out with someone. But with whom? He could no longer discuss this with Tanya. She did not know enough, and her honesty and concern were too painful to him. He felt much freer with Bruce Patterson and Fritz Leutner. Through him they had a more complete picture of the technical situation than almost any other scientist in the country, though in obedience to the security principle of compartmentalization there were whole areas of the subject that they had no knowledge of. With them, aside from problems of research and development, he could probe deeply the question of their duty—his and theirs—as scientists and as communists. All agreed that they must work on the Weapon. Both Bruce and Fritz felt that they must take their chances on getting clearance.

"What would you say to the idea of telling a straight story, and simply letting them take it or leave it?"

They both made wry faces and shook their heads.

They were sitting in a small bare office of the radiation laboratory. A desk with a telephone, some chairs, an empty wastebasket, a cabinet with a few pieces of unused equipment. The hum from the nearby cyclotron dominated everything, communicated its micro vibrations to one's very marrow.

Bruce eyed the telephone, looked around, picked up his overcoat and piled it on top of the instrument.

"No," he said. "It wouldn't work." He grinned, as he always did when his mind was working hard, and the freckles on his nose shone.

"This is how I look at it. We're all being investigated—or shall be before very long—and they're going to find out enough about us to damn us a hundred times, if they have a mind to. They'll put us down as subversives, but they'll keep the information they collect out of circulation, the really damaging part of it, that is, because otherwise they wouldn't be able to hire us. And they need us—you particularly, Sebastian."

Bruce looked as happy as though he had just discovered a new transuranic element.

"That's the beauty of it, don't you see?" he went on. "That's why you mustn't tell them anything they don't want to know. Because even if you were to go and confess to them merely the things that they already have in their files, and nothing more, they'd have to turn you down. Otherwise you would have a hold on them, and they wouldn't run that risk—not even if it meant scuttling the whole project. What they want is to have a hold on you. They'll let you know that they consider you a dubious security risk, but they'll allow you to work for them anyway. In the meantime there will be that threat always hanging over you. They'll use it. They'll give you no peace."

"It's g-g-going to be hell," Fritz said, somberly, "for you, esp-p-pecially."

"There's this, though," Bruce said, still bubbling. "Your position in another sense is a very strong one. In the first place they need you—need you badly . . ."

He peered at Sebastian through squinting eyes.

"Mind you, I'm not saying you're indispensable. Whether you are or not, no man can allow himself to think that. But apart from your actual usefulness, you have a formidable nuisance value that you can capitalize on if you want to. A lot of people *think* you're indispensable. If you were to be turned down on security grounds, at least half the people we need would refuse to have any part in it—some because they would be disgusted, and the others because they'd be downright scared."

This was an angle Sebastian had thought of, though without too much believing in it. But as Bruce and Fritz said, it gave him a little leeway.

"Just enough," Bruce said, "so that you can keep your honor. Always remember that they know more about you than they want you to tell them. Therefore never tell them anything you don't have to. If they press you, tell the truth. About yourself, that is. About anybody else, you have to be firm from the beginning. That's where you can have the edge on them. There it's going to be tough. But without saying so you can convey to them that you know their game, and if they want to play it they have to let you play yours. Yours has to be that you intend to mind your own business, to stick strictly to your technical job, your job as a scientist. And of course your principles as a scientist. Never let them drag you into any kind of discussion about other people, except on a professional basis. And particularly, don't play into their hands by saying 'I don't know' if they ask you is so-and-so a communist. If you do, you're lost. You're admitting their right to ask the question. The point is that it's none of your business."

Sebastian had always had the greatest respect for Bruce's political intelligence. But now his hard-boiled attitude shook him a little.

"You think that if they ask me if I am, or ever was, a member—"

"They won't ask you," Bruce said. "If they ever do, it means they've decided to junk you, and there'd be no point in not telling the truth. But I'll bet anything they won't, because they need you and they have to pretend not to know it, and they can't afford to have you know that they know. But they'll snarl you up in every possible way."

This however was still only the surface of the problem. And Sebastian found to his distress that with Bruce and Fritz he could not go beyond it. In the depths beneath there lurked some awful meaning that still eluded him.

He was too much away from the University now to handle his courses. He was still able to supervise the research of students working on projects, but he had given over the seminar on photons to Bruce Patterson, and the one on atomic electron velocities to Hans Weber, although he dropped in on both when he could.

I must talk to Mark, he decided one day. The very idea lightened the burden of his problem for a moment. Mark had a purity that would act as a balm to his spirit, and perhaps enable him to achieve a little clarity. He was surprised to learn that Mark had enlisted. It seemed a rather drastic step for him to take, and Sebastian caught himself, oddly, having to suppress a faint feeling of hurt at the fact that he had taken it without consulting him. It was a thing Mark would not ordinarily have done, and Sebastian found himself wondering about it even more than about the decision itself. But this brought him back to his own predicament.

It was the end of January before he and Mark could get together, and this was a not wholly private occasion.

He was a man divided. Inwardly he was distraught and tormented, but outwardly he was self-possessed. He was making all his plans on the assumption that he would shortly be leaving the University for an indefinite period, although he kept telling himself that he had by no means made up his mind, and behind whatever course he might take there gnawed the thought that he would probably be denied clearance. Still he was putting all his affairs in order, even to the making of a new will. He made a number of large donations to foundations that he knew did not need them, made a gift of his father's library to the University.

Whenever he had a free evening sufficiently far ahead he would arrange a get-together with friends and colleagues; he gave several dinners at the Faculty Club; he staged a lively and bibulous party at a downtown night club for all his students. He did not speak of these as farewells but he so regarded them, and he knew as he looked at the familiar faces that belonged to a world he had grown fond of that he would not see many of them again for a long time, if ever, and that when and if he did, so many things would have changed that he would no longer be the same, and they would no longer be the same, and that they would then meet again almost as strangers.

He had arranged a dinner in a private room at the Coq d'Or, the best French restaurant in town, and he had invited, besides Mark and Eve, the Pattersons and the Leutners, Jo Brand and his wife Millicent, Professor William Garnett and his wife, and Albert Cummings. White orchids for the ladies, and a mass of them as a centerpiece for the table. As one of the waiters was expertly carving the charcoal-broiled fillet of beef, Sebastian registered the fact, which had occurred neither to Tanya nor to himself earlier, that they were thirteen at table. He counted again. No: fourteen; for the Monster was always present.

It seemed to be characteristic of these surging times that not even with ultimately important questions was there leisure for the full and easy exchange of views with a trusted friend that he so greatly needed. Mark was required to be at the recruiting center during the whole of the next day, and Sebastian himself was flying east in the morning. He managed to get Mark outside alone toward the end of the evening. They walked side by side down the dark streets, their shoulders brushing.

"I've got a problem," Sebastian said at once. "Maybe you can help."

Mark knew of course that he was engaged in some kind of secret government work, but the only hint Sebastian had given him as to its nature was once when they were discussing the chances of an Allied victory. "In a straight matching of forces we can't win," Sebastian had said, and then added, with a sly wink, "But perhaps we may be able to think up a trick or two."

"I've become involved," he said now, without any further preliminaries, "in a project that is big, difficult, full of risks, but that could perhaps be decisive. My own role in it is uncertain. I may not even get clearance. If it works out, good may come of it, but also evil. I shall be alone. I shall have to forget much. I shall perhaps become quite a different person from what I have been. But I may be able to do some good, although If I do I shall have to pay for it. The question is, how much can I afford to pay?"

They walked for some moments in silence.

"How can I advise you?" Mark said finally. "It all sounds a little frightening." They walked on, again enveloped in silence.

Sebastian suddenly wondered exactly what he was hoping to get from Mark. He had an ordinary, though better-than-average mind, and he was not gifted with any exceptional insight in the realm of the emotions. Mark could shed no light on his problem. Yet he needed something from him—was it reassurance? No, surely something more basic . . .

"I just don't know," Mark said. Then, after a pause: "It's dangerous to be alone." He looked up. "But you'll have Tanya."

"Yes," Sebastian said softly. He would have Tanya. But she was not going to be of much help with anything having to do with the Monster.

"There will be others," Mark went on. "Perhaps colleagues. Perhaps students. The important thing is not to let yourself get isolated."

Sebastian shook his head. "That's not going to be easy."

"And yet it's the main problem, it seems to me," Mark said with conviction.

He was surely right. But if there was no solution? And the decision had to be made at the outset, which would preclude any solution.

They came out upon a brightly lit avenue. Sebastian saw Mark's face clouded over with concern.

"We must get back," he said. He felt an aching emptiness. "Can you imagine a situation in which, for idealistic reasons, for the good of the greatest number, one might have to play the role of a son of a bitch?"

They were walking away from the nearest street light and Mark's face was in the shadow so that Sebastian could not read his expression, but he saw Mark's head turn in his direction with a startled movement.

"No, I can't imagine *you* in a situation like that," he answered at once. More slowly he added, "But I know something about playing the role of a son of a bitch. For idealistic reasons, too, and for what I thought was the good of the greatest number."

He shook his head.

"I'll regret it to my dying day."

He looked up again quickly.

"But anyway, your case is quite different."

Could it be essentially different? Sebastian wondered. He found it equally difficult to imagine Mark in such a role. But it came to him suddenly that no communication was possible in this realm, and that he wasn't going to get anywhere with Mark since there was no way of conveying the nameless anguish that possessed him. Mark could only proffer him the blind gestures of an unreserved friendship and of a touching trust that had almost the impact of a mocking reproach.

"In any case," Mark said, as they rejoined their group in the private dining room, "there's no one whose judgment I have greater faith in."

When Gröndahl called him in to his office in Washington a few weeks later Sebastian knew what was coming.

"We've been playing around long enough," Gröndahl said gruffly as Sebastian sat down. "It's time we set up some sort of structure. Everything we've done so far has been scattered and piecemeal. We no longer know where we're going. We've been struggling along on a shoestring. Now at last it looks as if we're going to be given a chance. The President has given the go-ahead. And now we've got to get ourselves organized. The first thing to do is to get a number of key people together and put them on a payroll. I'm recruiting a skeleton staff for a starter. From now on everything connected with the project is official. Will you join us?"

Sebastian had come fully expecting such an offer and had steeled himself to accept it. But now that he was actually confronted with it he recoiled.

"What we're offering you is nothing fancy," Gröndahl went on. "We'll match your regular salary, but that's all. You'll have to resign from the University for the duration and give us your full time. No fancy title. Just the usual 'research associate,' and a classification number." He stretched out his legs, leaned his huge bulk back in the creaking swivel chair, and looked at Sebastian paternally. "The job has absolutely nothing to commend it. It will be a headache from beginning to end. There's no place to work, nothing to work with, and getting people to join the project is going to be like pulling teeth—and we'll need hundreds before we're through. We'll be snagged at every turn by red tape, inefficiency, suspicion and politicians. The army will constantly be in our hair. There's only one excuse for anybody in his right mind getting involved in this at all, and that is that the thing has got to be done. I've only one excuse for snatching you away from the peaceful glades of academic life, and that is that we desperately need you."

Gröndahl was looking at him, and he became conscious of the fact that he had not yet spoken.

"You've had a lot of time to make up your mind," Gröndahl went on. "I don't know anyone who can think faster, or make quicker decisions. You're not still hesitating?"

"Hesitating? No. But I'm worried. We must make the contraption. There's no shirking that. I'm thinking of afterwards, when the war is won. Who will control the Bolt? Who will control those who control it?"

Gröndahl nodded.

"It's something to think about, all right. It will be a great responsibility. But we'll have to cross that bridge when we get to it."

"Yes. But I think we owe it to ourselves to begin to plan now *how* we contemplate crossing it."

"Perhaps." A spark of humor flashed in Gröndahl's eyes, and he added, "First we'd have to know what kind of bridge it is, and what condition it's in." He became serious again. "There's a more immediately pressing matter, however, that we have to tackle first."

It was curious, after the long span of years, to confront Gröndahl again and to find, not the independent, detached scientist and passionate anarchistic individualist he had once known, but an administrator, an official representative of government.

"I should like, though, to register my concern before we go any further," said Sebastian. "And I should like you to make a note of it, so that it might be a matter of record." He paused and focused his mind on what he was about to say, and at the same time reached into his right-hand coat pocket for a tobacco pouch which he had not carried for perhaps two years. He found a package of cigarettes instead, offered Gröndahl one, took one himself, and lit them.

"This is by no means the first time," he said, "that scientists have been called upon by government to make a special contribution in the interest of national policy. But it is certainly the first time that a considerable portion of the scientific community of a large nation has been mobilized to invent an instrument which if it doesn't destroy us will completely revolutionize the pattern of life, not only in our own country but in the world. Because of this, the most disinterested wisdom is needed in determining the uses it is put to."

He wanted to say here that such a responsibility should never in any case be allowed to rest finally with any government, and most particularly that it should never be related in any way to the pursuit of a purely national policy. But while he knew that he could trust Gröndahl absolutely, he did not want to embarrass him. The old man was going to have a hard enough time with him as it was.

"My concern," he went on, "is that since this power that is to be released, if we are successful, will be the work of scientists, since scientists will in any case have to operate it, and since it may be presumed that, knowing its potential, scientists will have greater wisdom than any layman in defining the area and the limits of its use, scientists should have a major voice in determining the uses it is put to."

Gröndahl was scribbling on a sheet of paper.

"I subscribe to that, of course," he said finally, laying down his pen. "With the proviso, however, that the scientist should never be called upon to make a political decision. His function in this realm must remain purely advisory. Otherwise he loses his independence. All this will have to be worked out. But there's something more immediate that we have to put our minds to right away."

He looked at Sebastian earnestly.

"Before we can begin to talk about anything of this kind, we have to get you approved for the project."

He paused and put the palms of his hands together in an unconscious gesture of prayer.

"Don't imagine it's going to be easy! It's even possible that they may turn you down. If they do—"

Sebastian had of course not only conceived the possibility of his total dissociation from the project, but had for a long time hoped against hope that he could find a way of washing his hands of it. Even now, deep down, he rejected the whole venture; his conscience, his spirit, the effectively human part of him, condemned it. Yet at Gröndahl's words he felt himself breaking into a cold sweat. He could wish the whole idea were just a bad dream. But if it was real, if the project was going ahead, then he must be in on it. The Monster must not be made without him. Such an eventuality was unthinkable.

"—If they do," Gröndahl repeated, after a silence, "I should regard it as a matter of the utmost seriousness. I'll go to bat for you," he said, looking at Sebastian fiercely. "I'll use every pressure, every ounce of pull I've got. It'll be tough, and it may take time. However, I think we'll win out. I'm sure we will. But"— the fierceness in his look gave way to a piercing intentness— "a lot depends on you. You've got to play ball."

He got up slowly and walked over to the cabinet in the corner of the office. His age showed in his way of moving. He took a silver flask and two small glasses and brought them over to the desk. His hand was quite steady as he poured the whisky.

"Here's how," he said, almost perfunctorily, and downed his drink in one gulp. He coughed and sat down.

"As you know," he said, "there are many counts against you. But that's all in the past, and I think we can take care of that. What I'm more concerned about is what happens from now on. I don't think I need to tell you how imperative it is that you keep yourself absolutely above suspicion of any kind, particularly as regards anything pertaining to past political activities and associations. Up to now you've been able to consider yourself more or less a free agent, and anything you did concerned primarily yourself. From here on, what you say and do concerns not so much yourself as the project, your associates, and your country. Another thing: you'll have to resign yourself to the fact that you'll probably be under more or less constant observation. If I were you, I would simply assume that everything you say, and everything said to you, whether directly or over the telephone, no matter where you are, is being monitored and taken down, that your mail is being opened and your movements followed. You're not the only one to get this treatment, of course, though I imagine you'll be watched more closely than most at the beginning. But as the project develops we can expect this sort of thing to become more and more general. I know it's going to be a little hard to take. But remember, the stakes are high. Now, what do you say? Are you game?"

He had planned to make his participation in the project conditional upon the recognition of certain principles that would have strengthened the position of the scientists in relation to the future of the Monster; conditional upon a number of things. But it was clear from what Gröndahl had said that he was in no position to bargain. His position was in fact an extremely weak and vulnerable one. Would he even pass the security check? It was by no means sure. So the first step, and the only possible one, was to take his chances on being cleared.

"I guess game is the word," he said, "since all this involves a considerable element of chance. Yes—I'll go along."

Everything was going to be much harder even than he had feared. He was not going to be able to play the game of take it or leave it. He would not be going in on his own terms. He would be a prisoner. He would be an instrument. That was the price he would have to pay. Those were the limits he would have to work within.

"There'll probably be a good deal of unpleasantness at the beginning," said Gröndahl. "The investigation will take weeks —maybe months. There'll be interrogations." He looked up and grinned. "Meanwhile we're not just going to sit around chewing our nails, are we? Every day, every hour, every minute counts. We've got to get right to work. Might as well get as much done as we can while those jokers try to make up their minds whether they think we're *fit* to work. And first of all, since we're becoming official, we've got to find a code name for the project. Have you any suggestions?"

They named the project "Crossroads." Sebastian had suggested the name. But it remained for a long time, like the project itself, a word on paper, an anticipation.

The vast sprawling enterprise as yet had no head or tail. But there was a great stirring. It extended from coast to coast, and government, army and a rapidly growing corps of scientists, technicians, engineers and administrative personnel and workers of all categories became involved in its elaboration. While the German war machine was rolling the Russian armies back to the Black Sea and toward the Caucasus, while Rommel was smashing at the British across the rim of North Africa and pushing them to within seventy miles of Alexandria, and the Japanese, after overrunning the Philippines, were spreading over all Southeast Asia and reaching toward Australia, the making of the Bolt was going forward with ever greater impetus. The fundamental physics, the engineering planning and the construction of pilot plants were being pressed. University laboratories and research institutions were working with a sense of terrible urgency on dozens of investigations, groups were busy calculating, planning and co-ordinating, material was being obtained, apparatus was being designed and built.

A gigantic operational structure was in the making, with all its implications of policy, finance, priority, control, participation of private industry, politics, personalities, and yet it was still utterly inchoate. To begin with, would the thing work? The best brains were betting on it and there was a good deal of money now behind it, but it was still not proved. Suppose a self-sustaining chain reaction turned out to be impossible? The whole project would then have to be abandoned. But even if the theory should work out, which might involve another year or more of experiment, many months, perhaps years would still be needed to collect material, to process it, and an unpredictable number of other conditions would have to be met before the next stage of the work could begin. It was decided to go ahead on the assumption that the theory would be borne out by at least one of the several slow, costly, large-scale experiments in progress. There were so many quantitative and qualitative unknowns on all levels, the paths that opened up at every step were so bewilderingly varied, that no one could be certain which direction would prove fruitful. And because the time factor was so urgent, it was felt necessary to pursue all lines of investigation that held even a slight promise of yielding results. But this meant infinitely greater resources of money and trained manpower than were available.

Sebastian soon became convinced that very few, if any, of the top men he was constantly conferring with had the kind of grasp, in the large and in detail, of the problem involved in the building of the Bolt which would give assurance that the job would get done in time to be decisive. Perhaps he would have the opportunity to help in this at a later stage. At the moment there was an urgent need for analysis and thinking, there was a tremendous amount of theory to be worked out, some kind of order had to be put into the scattered and haphazard work that was being done in the laboratories, and it was imperative to initiate a number of new projects. In a way he had not so far done, he began to concentrate on the problem of how the Bolt could be made, to make calculations, to bring together a number of key people for intensive study and planning.

Now that he had made his decision there was no longer any wavering. He had made up his mind, once and for all, that he was going to devote every ounce of his energy, dedicate his whole being to the making of the Bolt. Of the possible ways in which he could serve his country, and thereby mankind, this was overwhelmingly the most important. Having so determined, he could admit no conflicting allegiance or responsibility. He had not renounced friend or conviction. He had simply been metamorphosed into another world in which these had no relevance. He had been moved to commit his destiny to the Bolt because he was a communist, because as a communist he had been made aware of the vital necessity to destroy fascism and had learned that his prime duty as a scientist in a time of crisis was to safeguard the discoveries and inventions of science for the service of humanity and to prevent their being exploited by one group of interests for domination over others. But now he was no longer a communist. He had now broken, or was in the process of breaking, all ties with the past, all attachments except those involved in his new task.

And now he was becoming aware of the fact that he was under observation. On stepping out of a taxi at a railroad station, on walking out of his hotel in a strange city, on boarding a plane, he would be conscious of another presence of whose attention he was the object. When he picked up his telephone he would hear a little click, which soon became familiar. When he carefully examined the envelopes of the letters that he received, it became clear to him that most of them had been opened.

He had been forewarned of this and had resigned himself to it, yet the actual experience irked him almost beyond endurance. He had nothing to hide—now, at least—so that being watched was not in itself an occasion for anxiety. He had broken all contacts with the political Left, he no longer saw any of the people he had once been so close to. Mark was the lone exception. His students, whether left-wing or not, continued to be close to him, but no longer did they indulge with him in orgies of political discussion. By tacit consent, all had put politics on the shelf for the duration. He had been tempted, during those weeks when he had been struggling with his decision, to look up Bill Parrish and talk over the problem with him. He was glad now that he hadn't.

It was many months since he had attended a meeting that could in any sense be regarded as left-wing. The Russian War Relief party last November had in fact been a farewell. He had dropped out of all the various political organizations he had been active in, including the Teachers' Union, and requested that his name be withdrawn from the list of sponsors of the various committees and bodies that still carried it. He had allowed to lapse, or canceled, all subscriptions to left-wing or even liberal publications. So now he no longer had any affiliations or involvements that could possibly be considered suspect. Yet the hovering presence of the ubiquitous agents generated a sense of uneasiness that he found all but intolerable.

The fact worried him. Although he knew that there was nothing that those little gray men with slouch hats and soft feet could take exception to in his present life, there was plenty to interest them in his past. Was the past going to trip him up? As he looked back on it now, in the light of his new commitment, he was sometimes a little aghast. He had been foolhardy; had he perhaps even been foolish? But when he faced this question he had to recognize at the same time that it was precisely this "foolishness" that had involved him with the Bolt. How ironic it would be if, because of it, he were to be refused clearance!

Strict security regulations were beginning to be applied to every phase of the project. The code name Crossroads was as yet known only to a few initiates. According to these regulations Sebastian was not allowed access to information in the higher categories of secrecy. Yet most of the important knowledge concerning the project he carried around in his own head, where much of it had originated and from which much more was likely to come out. Gröndahl had to deal with this ridiculous situation by issuing a special order, but Sebastian was constantly running into annoying little snags because of it.

For some weeks he had, with vague misgivings, been expecting a grilling at the hands of the security agents. The first interview was sprung on him at a particularly inopportune moment late one rainy April afternoon in Washington. He had previously been stretched out flat on his back for two days in a solitary hotel room with a recurrence of the spinal ailment that he had suffered from many years before. He had managed to pull himself out of bed to attend a conference on the highest level to discuss urgent matters pertaining to Crossroads. The timetable looked discouraging, and the conference had broken up in a mood of gloom which even the report of Doolittle's raid over Tokyo had done little to dispel. As he came down the granite stairway of the big official building, taking the steps a little painfully, he was accosted by two men in gray and asked to go along with them. He was whisked off in a waiting car to the service headquarters and led into an office on one of the upper floors of the building.

By now he was generally able to spot, in a crowd, those he called "the little gray men" who trailed him wherever he went. They tried to keep out of sight, and they were often not in evidence, but while they did not belong to a single type, they had a characteristic look and manner of behavior that after a time made them easily recognizable to their quarry. The two who now faced him in the office, however—white walls, battle-ship linoleum floor, bare except for the big flat-top desk and three or four chairs—belonged to a different category. The one who sat at the desk and who did all the talking—he had identi-fied himself at the outset as Mr. Dysell—was a tall, robust, handsome man of about forty-five, with wavy black hair, heavy black eyebrows, sharp features, and had an air of considerable authority. The other, Mr. Barber, was a young man still in his twenties, with thinning brown hair, small-featured, effaced-looking, who never spoke except for occasional mumbled exchanges with the other which Sebastian was unable to decipher.

There was some agitation before they got settled. Dysell dis-appeared several times through a second door into an inner office, then Barber went out and came back with a large stack of folders. Dysell had several brief cryptic conversations on the telephone while Barber sat down in an armchair by the door to the inner office.

"Your name is Sebastian Bloch?" Dysell said, addressing Sebastian for the first time since they had come into the office and he had offered him a seat. "Go ahead and smoke, if you like," he said parenthetically, noticing Sebastian's hand reach-ing into his coat pocket.

Sebastian took a cigarette after offering his pack to the others, who both refused but reached for their own packs. Bar-ber got up and lit Sebastian's cigarette.

Dysell went through a list of preliminary questions: date and place of birth, nationality, residence, occupation, titles, posts held . . .

"Now, Dr. Bloch, let's be quite frank," he said, leaning for-ward on his desk and changing his tone to one of great earnest-ness. "The reason we've asked you to come in today is in con-nection with an investigation we're making to determine your loyalty to this country, in other words whether you can be considered a good security risk. As you know, there is a possibility that you may be called upon to do work for the U.S. Government that is classified top secret. But before such a thing can come to pass you've got to be cleared, and it's our job to gather the material on the basis of which such clearance can be considered."

Dysell paused, and looked at Sebastian meaningfully.

"Now, Dr. Bloch, I don't need to tell you," he went on, "that we've found some pretty disturbing things in your record."

He reached out his hand and put it on the stack of bulging folders.

"All this is your file."

He looked at Sebastian piercingly.

"We know an awful lot about you, Dr. Bloch. You'd be surprised how much we know . . . Yes, sir, you'd really be surprised!" he repeated with dramatic emphasis.

He let this sink in a few moments before he proceeded. Sebastian's back ached excruciatingly, and to relieve the double strain he tried to concentrate on a knotty problem connected with the separation of isotopes by diffusion of uranium hexafluoride.

"Everyone can make mistakes," Dysell continued. "A lot of people have done things in the past years that they're sorry for, and that they wouldn't do today. Wouldn't you agree with that, Dr. Bloch?"

Sebastian looked up. He felt humiliated. Did he have to submit to this sort of thing?

"I dare say," he murmured.

"To come a little closer to the point," Dysell pursued, putting his hand again on the pile of folders and looking at them, "would you do today, Dr. Bloch, the things that you did two or three years ago, or even twelve months ago?"

Sebastian felt that the other was trying to push him into a corner.

"No doubt you have specific things in mind," he said in a low voice. "It might be better if we stuck to the specific."

Dysell shifted in his upholstered armchair and assumed a more alert posture. His face took on a look of polite annoyance.

"Dr. Bloch," he said, "I hope you appreciate my position. I'm under orders. I'm not given very much leeway. It's only fair to point out to you that it will be to your interest to realize as quickly as possible that this is an extremely difficult case. Now our investigation falls into two parts. The first has to do with your past activities. The second has to do with your present attitude—and this second part is most important. Most important," he repeated. "So you realize that it makes quite a difference whether your attitude is going to be one of cooperation or one of, shall I say, obstruction. You do realize that, don't you?"

He smiled ingratiatingly, and Sebastian found the smile revolting. He was feeling really very ill. His head and his hands were dry, but under his clothes he felt the perspiration oozing, and there was an aching knot at the back of his neck. Although he was hardly up to it, the moment had probably come when some kind of statement was called for.

He gave what was meant to be an understanding smile. "I know you are only trying to do your duty," he said, "and I want to do everything within reason to help make it easy for you . . ." He looked into space. "What makes this case difficult, as you say—although it is by no means unique in this—is that the facts themselves tell only a small part of the story and perhaps even, if taken by themselves—"

"Excuse me, Dr. Bloch," Dysell broke in, "but I must remind you that *I'm* the one who's doing the investigating here and I'm quite aware of what the problems are. We have our own way of conducting our interrogations. If we want any kind of statement from you we'll see about that later on. Now to come back to where we were. Would you say that, if you had it to do over again, you would do the same things today that you did up to not so long ago?"

He felt humiliated and outraged. Never in his life had he been directly confronted with such intellectual dishonesty, or felt so helpless to meet it. He wanted to answer, This is a question that cannot be dealt with simply . . . and go on to make the necessary explanations. Instead he answered, on the whole truthfully:

"No, probably not. But such a blanket statement is rather meaningless. It would be true of certain things, and not of others."

"We'll come to specific cases in a moment. What I'm trying to do now is get a general picture. Let's put it this way. Would you say it would be a proper thing, or an improper thing, for you to engage in left-wing activities now?"

Sebastian looked up at Dysell resentfully, making an effort to control himself. Never would it have occurred to him to subject even his worst enemy to this kind of infantile catechism.

"Do you think it would be a proper thing?" Dysell pressed him.

"No," Sebastian managed to get out.

"It would be an improper thing?"

"Yes."

"You agree that it would be wrong for you to engage in left-wing activities while working on a secret government project?"

"Yes."

"It would be endangering the nation's security?"

"It *could* endanger it."

"But it wouldn't necessarily?"

"That would depend, wouldn't it?"

"It would depend on what?"

"On the individual, for one thing."

"And do you think the individual, in such a case, should be allowed to be the judge as to whether or not, by indulging in a particular activity, he is endangering the nation's security?"

"No, clearly not."

"So you agree, then, that such activity would endanger it?"

"Yes."

"It would be disloyal?"

"Do we have to use all the adjectives?"

"I'm trying to get a picture. Would it be disloyal?"

"Yes," Sebastian sighed.

Dysell paused a moment, and his face registered a controlled, wholly impersonal satisfaction. He had won the first round. Sebastian knew that he himself had just lost a little piece of something precious and irreplaceable, and that he was about to lose more. And he knew that he was helpless to prevent it. Perhaps he had within him the power to shake the earth, to shatter the heavens, to unleash the pent-up forces of the cosmos. But he did not have the power to protect his personal dignity against the routine verbal assaults of this minor agent of government.

"Now tell me this," Dysell said, coming back to the attack. "Looking back, do you consider it was a mistake for you to have engaged in all these left-wing activities?" He made a gesture again with his hand toward the pile of folders.

Sebastian saw the trap, but there was no avoiding it.

"To the best of my knowledge then and now," he said, "nothing that I did in that line was, in intent or in fact, detrimental to the interests of the United States. I—"

"Dr. Bloch, let me ask you this," Dysell broke in, and his manner now was that of a teacher trying with a patience bordering on exasperation to extract the correct answers from a particularly obtuse pupil. "Would you agree that the Communist Party has played an important role in the whole movement of the Left?"

"Yes, but—"

"Wouldn't you agree that the Communist Party has played a *most* important, in fact a *dominant* role in the whole movement of the Left, and wouldn't you agree that it has played a particularly important role in those very organizations of which you were a member?"

"I'm not in a position to answer that either in the affirmative or in the negative. I should be inclined to doubt it."

"Dr. Bloch, you've belonged to quite a few left-wing organizations, wouldn't you say?"

"Yes, I think that would be a fair statement."

"You've attended a good many left-wing meetings?"

"Yes."

"Did you ever go to any such meetings where there were not communists present?"

"I don't know. I couldn't say."

"Do you think it likely?"

"No, I suppose not."

"So that you would say that there were always communists present?"

"That would be a fair guess."

"Isn't it also a fact that communists consider it their duty to assume the leadership in any workers' or progressive movement?"

"So I've been told."

"So you've been told." There was an edge of sarcasm in Dysell's voice. "And is it your impression that they've been on the whole successful or unsuccessful in this policy?"

Sebastian was in great pain. He braced his hands against the seat of his straight-backed chair to relieve the excruciating strain on his back. His mind seemed to be in a kind of fog. Yet worse than the physical pain was the agony of being reduced to a kind of idiot role in which he was inexorably being pushed into giving just the answers that his tormentor wanted. He must be co-operative. To the last ignominious syllable.

"You probably have the answer to that," he said in a desperate effort to salvage what dignity he could. "I don't think my impression would be worth much."

"But you do have an impression?"

"It's only an impression."

"Well, what is your impression?"

"I suppose it would have to be that they've been fairly successful."

"So that you agree that those organizations we've been talking about have been communist-dominated."

"That might be putting it too strongly."

"Shall we say strongly influenced?"

"That would seem to me more accurate."

"All right. So you've admitted that for years you belonged to a large number of political or semipolitical organizations which you had reason to believe were strongly influenced by the communists. Now, Dr. Bloch, I want to ask you this: are you or are you not aware that the Communist Party, by its own admission, professes loyalty first and foremost to the Soviet Union, and advocates the overthrow of the Government of the United States by force and violence?"

Through the floating haze that surrounded the island of pain that he had become, Sebastian recognized that here was one of the most dangerous hurdles he would have to meet. He could not show up this distortion of the truth for what it was. At best he could try to dodge it.

"That I cannot answer. There is a good deal to be said. I have read, I think, the relevant literature and I think it is not so simple as that. I can merely say that in all the activity that I and others like myself engaged in, in these organizations, there was never the slightest question about our primary loyalty to the United States; nor was the thought of abolishing our laws and institutions ever entertained."

"We're talking about the Communist Party now. Have you read the *Communist Manifesto?*"

"Yes."

"Do you remember what it says there about workers giving up their loyalty to country and substituting for it loyalty to class?"

"Yes, but it's in a context—"

But he was powerless to argue. He had reached the depth of indignity.

"All right. Now let me ask you this: if the United States were to find itself at war with Russia tomorrow, do you think a communist could be regarded as a very reliable citizen?"

"No, probably not in such a case."

"But you think he might in another case?" Dysell looked at him sharply. "Take the present time, for instance, when we're allies of Russia. Do you think the communists' all-out support of the war is motivated by loyalty to America or by loyalty to Russia?"

"I suppose it could be both."

"A double loyalty, in other words. Do you consider that good citizenship?"

"No." He was caught again.

"So you admit that a communist makes a poor citizen?"

"Yes."

"And is therefore dangerous?"

"And is therefore dangerous."

"And yet for years you played an active role in any number of organizations which you admit were strongly influenced by an organized group of people whom you now admit are dangerous. Now let me ask you again: looking back, do you consider it was a mistake for you to have engaged in all those left-wing activities?"

Sebastian could feel his pulse racing, with hammer beats straining the fragile envelope of vessels and arteries. His temperature must be considerably over a hundred.

"Yes," he said weakly, "it was a mistake."

"In other words, you used bad judgment?"

"Yes."

Dysell got up and disappeared into the inner office. Barber stretched his legs in front of him, put his hands in his trouser pockets and yawned. He looked at Sebastian with an air of commiseration, seemed about to say something, but remained silent. Sebastian felt as if he would collapse at any moment.

Dysell came in again and sat down. He looked at Sebastian and said, "You don't look very good. Is anything wrong?"

Sebastian made a superhuman effort to control himself.

"I've been laid up recently. I'm not quite up to par. Could we shorten this?"

Dysell studied him coldly for a moment, then looked again at the pile of folders.

"We've got a lot of ground to cover," he said. "I just want to take up one more item today."

He reached for the top folder, thumbed through several sheets of paper, apparently found the one he was looking for. He again gave Sebastian his inquisitor's look.

"On September 24th, 1939," he said, "you wrote a letter to Professor Phineas Deakin, chairman of the Physics department

of Northern Plains University, recommending a certain Bruce
Patterson for a position in that department. Do you remember
that?"

"Yes, very well."

"Did he get the appointment?"

"No. It went to a man from Columbia."

"Did you know at the time that this Bruce Patterson was a
communist?"

Sebastian remembered his conversation with Bruce and Fritz
only two months before. How far away it seemed! "Never let
yourself be dragged into a discussion about other people,"
Bruce had said. "If you do, you're lost."

"Yes, I knew it," he said in answer to Dysell's question.

"And you still recommended him?"

"He was the best man for the job."

"Did you at least mention in your letter that he was a communist?"

"No."

"Do you think that was the right thing to do?"

"I thought so at the time."

"What do you think now?"

Sebastian did not answer. How far, and how long, was this
sadist going to make him crawl?

"Do you still think it was the right thing to do?" Dysell insisted.

"No." The word was all-but-inaudible. But he had said it.

"You admit it was wrong?"

In another moment he would scream. "Yes," he said.

"In other words, you used bad judgment?"

"Yes. I used bad judgment," Sebastian said, savoring the bitterness of the words.

"You wouldn't use that kind of bad judgment today, would
you?"

"No," said Sebastian. Then he fainted.

There were several more interviews with Dysell and Barber
in the course of the following weeks. Meanwhile the Crossroads
project was moving forward. Sebastian's days were spent cal-

culating, supervising research, visiting plants and laboratories, conferring with representatives of the industries to which contracts were beginning to be let, with engineers, technicians, physicists, chemists.

He sought out Gröndahl one day.

"Your bloodhounds are giving me a pretty rough time," he told him.

"I can imagine," Gröndahl said. "But it's something you just have to go through. Once it's over, you'll be able to forget all about it."

"I wonder," Sebastian said. Within himself he knew that the humiliation that had been inflicted on him would remain an open sore for the rest of his life. He had been made to violate his own code of honor. He had betrayed some of his closest comrades.

He had gone into this with open eyes. But the price was more terrible than he could possibly have foreseen. And what if, in the end, the sacrifice should turn out to be vain?

"Is it going to go through, at least?" he asked tonelessly.

Gröndahl did not immediately answer. "It's *got* to go through," he said gruffly. "I hope you're doing your part."

It seemed to Sebastian that every day removed him a little farther from the ordinary, familiar reality of men and women living their lives, working, playing, having relations of trust and friendship and love. He was being inexorably carried toward a cold, high region to which all this was alien.

"There's another worry," he said. "We need hundreds of people for our project. We need every capable man we can get. A lot of our most valuable people, especially the younger ones, are going to have difficulty with the security people. How are we going to handle that?"

"We'll have to fight for them, that's all. Once we get you cleared, everything's going to be easier."

The recent years were coming into focus in a new perspective. It had been a time of innocence. But the innocence had carried within it the seeds of an almost criminal heedlessness. The insurgent Left had seemed to all of them at the very heart of the great American tradition. Yet in the course of these years the Left had increasingly isolated itself from the main current of American life. How had that happened? Was the gradual corruption of the Left leadership enough to explain it? The political coming to consciousness had occurred as a result of the Depression—and the rise of fascism abroad had helped, though it had not been decisive. The withering away of this political consciousness had occurred with the Recovery. It seemed as if, in America at least, political insurgency was a function of economic breakdown. All this would have to be thought out afresh. But there was not time for it now.

The fact that he had admitted to Dysell that those years had been a mistake and that he had used bad judgment weighed on his conscience. Because in doing so he had condemned not only himself but the hundreds whom he had influenced, the thousands, the tens of thousands, who had been similarly motivated. He had made the admissions without sincerity, through *force majeure*. At the same time he could no longer look back upon that past with the pride he had once felt. How much time and effort spent, for such negligible results! They had not saved Spanish democracy. They had not stopped Hitler or Mussolini. They had not even been able to prevent the Roosevelt government from giving sanction to the policy of big business to support the Japanese in their campaign to destroy the Chinese communists. How futile in the end had been all the passion that had gone into the campaign to boycott Japanese silk stockings, in which Tanya had been so active, or the attempt to stop the shipment of scrap iron to Japan! And at home, along with great successes like the growth of the labor movement and the putting through of progressive social legislation, how many failures, how many setbacks! How many mistakes had been made, how many once-militant leaders had sold out, how many betrayals and defections there had been!

And in the Communist Party itself, things were far from healthy. It had not grown, as it should have grown, it had not brought forth the leaders that it needed. Above all, it had not won the hearts of the American people. It remained something alien and unassimilated. Its members were dedicated, brave and hard-working, they had undoubtedly made an enormous contribution to the social progress registered in the country in the thirties; but they were shrill, cocksure, they carried a chip on their shoulders, they spoke a strange language, they were rigid, argumentative, devoid of a sense of humor. People might sometimes agree with them; they did not love them.

Looking back, Sebastian could recognize how exceptional were the communists he had known best—Bill Parrish, Vorontov, Baum, to say nothing of the members of his unit. And there was Hal Norberg, who though extraordinarily enough he seemed never to have been an actual member, was a model of what a communist labor leader should be—wise, keen, flexible, warm, sparkling, fearless, incorruptible, loved by his men, respected by his enemies the plant owners . . . Sebastian brushed his image aside. They had all been above the common run, and Sebastian's experience had been atypical.

In any case, if he had regarded himself as a communist— which was rather in the perspective of history than in the context of a specific time and place—he had not been a communist in the commonly accepted sense, and technically had in fact not been a communist at all. Only the other members of his unit supposed him to be an actual member like themselves (a cheap deception, it seemed to him now), and he knew that he could count on each and every one of them to keep that presumed knowledge absolutely secret. His position was, besides, a little special in that he had never paid any real dues, as had the others. The sums that he had handed over—to Bill Parrish, to Vorontov, sometimes to Baum, never to Bruce Patterson or anyone in the unit; sums too large, in any case, to be considered dues—had been by way of special contributions, and there was, he believed, no record of them of any kind. So far as his actual involvement with the party was concerned, therefore, he could consider himself reasonably safe.

Chapter 13

ONE afternoon in late spring a small group of men met in Washington. They sat around a large oval table in a big oval room, and the magnolia trees outside were reflected in the tall wall mirrors across from the French windows.

The Justice Department official had been making a report for over an hour, reading copious extracts from a voluminous sheaf of documents in a harsh, monotonous voice. His close-shaved beard gave a blue-black cast to his cleft chin and glossy cheeks, and his piercing eyes shone from under a deep shadow.

"Our conclusion," he said, "after carefully weighing all this evidence, and after giving full consideration to all the arguments in the subject's favor, is that we cannot approve the clearance of Dr. Sebastian Bloch."

There was a silence. Dr. Gröndahl held a whispered consultation with Dr. Smithson, in which presently Dr. Harnden joined.

At last Gröndahl turned to the Justice Department official. "You realize, Mr. Wilbur, that this is pretty serious?"

Wilbur looked at him disapprovingly. "I think you can take that for granted, Dr. Gröndahl," he said tersely.

"I wonder."

With studied informality Gröndahl reached a huge arm into the air and began scratching the back of his neck, unperturbed by Wilbur's severe stare.

"I wonder if you realize how serious it is," he said.

Wilbur raised his eyebrows slightly. "Exactly what do you mean, sir?"

"I'll tell you what I mean." Gröndahl's was a big voice, and now there was an edge of anger in it. "The project on which Dr. Bloch is working is a top priority war project. I've been ordered by the President to go full-speed ahead and to *let nothing stand in the way of achieving our objective.*"

He leaned forward across the table toward Wilbur.

"The seriousness of your decision is just this: without Dr. Bloch *there is no project!*"

He pushed back his chair and stood up, his bulk massive above the table top.

"I'm going back to the President and tell him his project is being sabotaged by the Justice Department."

"Wait a minute, Dr. Gröndahl, please sit down."

Wilbur, suddenly becoming ingratiating, half rose in his seat and held out his arms in a deprecatory gesture.

"Let's talk this over calmly and see just where we stand."

"Yes, Hjalmar, sit down," Smithson said placatingly. "Let's see what we can figure out."

Gröndahl grumblingly sat down again and went back into a huddle with his fellow scientists. And now Philip Mitchell, president of Continental Exchange, who was sitting at the far end of the table, spoke up for the first time.

"I'd like to hear a little more about this," he said. "I wasn't aware of the fact that this Dr. Bloch was so indispensable that the project couldn't go ahead without him. I personally would be highly disturbed—what am I saying?—I should regard it as a major calamity for this country to be in the position of having to depend on an out-and-out communist to save its skin. There must be something fundamentally wrong with our whole system if we have to depend on one single man. What's the matter with our other scientists? What about all the people we've got at M.I.T., Yale, Harvard, Princeton, Columbia, Chicago and other places? Who is this Dr. Bloch anyway? I never heard of him—I mean until this came up, of course."

"Hear, hear!" approved Samuel Wainbridge, chairman of the Steel Board. His eyes were slits between folds of flesh, enlarged by his shell-rimmed glasses.

"I'd like to say a few words in answer to that, if I may," Smithson said in a meek voice. "I don't happen to be a personal friend of Bloch's, like Gröndahl here, so what I say will be less open to the charge of being special pleading . . ."

He made a careful statement, describing Bloch's rather special position in the scientific community.

"Of course, Mr. Mitchell, I think we all agree with your unexpressed thought, that no man is indispensable."

Under the circumstances, however, it would be absolutely disastrous to eliminate Bloch. His standing was such that if he were to be ruled off the project, there would be so many defections that it would completely cripple it. His special value lay in the fact that while he might not be the best man in every single branch of the many that were involved, there was no one who knew so much about *all* of them and who could carry the over-all picture of the whole problem in his head as he could. Without Dr. Bloch the project could lose months, perhaps years, and this could spell the difference between victory and defeat.

As for Dr. Bloch's communism, Smithson was not inclined to take that too seriously.

"You can be sure," he went on, "that he wasn't a communist as we usually understand it, with the doctrine and all that, but he was a humanitarian and for the underdog and opposed to Nazism. Once he has entered government service, and he has put all that behind him, you can absolutely count on him. In fact there's no one I would trust more completely."

There followed a general discussion, in the course of which everyone around the table expressed his views. The scientists and university men pleaded for Sebastian Bloch's clearance, the representatives of government and of industry expressed varying degrees of reluctance.

"Gentlemen," Wilbur said finally, after the others had mostly talked themselves out, "we seem to have reached an impasse. Let me try to summarize the position." He waited a moment for heightened attention. "Those of you who are closest to, and who know most about the project itself seem to consider that the success of the project would be seriously jeopardized if Dr. Bloch were ruled out. Those of you who carry political responsibility, and those who have some responsibility for the underwriting of the project, don't see their way clear to setting their seal of approval on a man so markedly identified with the communist cause."

Gröndahl, who had remained silent during the whole discussion that he had launched, now looked up.

"As a matter of fact," he broke in, "exactly what does this identification with the communist cause actually come down to?"

Wilbur's hand went to his pile of documents. "It's all here," he said, "and I read you some of the most essential parts of the evidence, though by no means all: his marriage to an avowed communist, his own membership in the party, his extensive activity—"

"About his membership," Gröndahl interrupted. "That's in that long report, isn't it?"

"Yes, sir."

"Well, I'd like to ask some questions about that report, and also about the man who prepared it."

Wilbur deliberated for a moment. His eyes lost their intensity and seemed to withdraw into the shadow of his brow. "In that case," he said finally, "I shall have to call in Mr. Gregg, the man in charge of this particular investigation, who happens to be in Washington."

A recess was called until Mr. Gregg could arrive.

Groups conferred in low voices. The first news of the battle of Midway had begun to come in during the morning, and Mitchell, Wainbridge and the other industrialists talked about that, and about the battle of Coral Sea and the surrender of Corregidor, still fresh in the memory. The shadow of the magnolia trees deepened in the room.

Wilbur reappeared, accompanied by a tall gray figure. Mr. J. W. Gregg was introduced, and sat down at Wilbur's left. Good-looking, rugged, square-cut, he radiated an aura of authority as Gröndahl proceeded to question him.

"Mr. Gregg, I understand that you are responsible for this report."

"That's right, sir."

"If I understand correctly, you assigned one man to spend his full time investigating Dr. Sebastian Bloch; that he devoted three years to this work, and that during this time he succeeded in getting himself admitted to the intimacy of Dr. Bloch and his family and friends. Is that right?"

"Yes, sir. It should be added, though, that while the report deals mainly with Dr. Bloch it also covers several hundred other persons in the community, and constitutes from that point of view alone an extremely valuable report."

"Isn't this a rather unusual procedure?"

"To the best of my knowledge, sir, there has been no other instance of it. It is probably unique. It was, in fact, conceived as something of an experiment."

Gröndahl looked slowly round the table.

"I don't know how the rest of you feel about this, gentlemen," he said, "but personally I am moved to say that I regard such police methods as peculiarly revolting. To subject a private person against whom there is no charge or even suspicion of crime or illegality whatever to this kind of investigation seems to me a gross infringement of his democratic rights under the Constitution and a fundamental violation of the sanctity of a man's privacy and home, and I find it shocking that such practice has been resorted to. I should like to know, first of all, whether this has official sanction."

There were murmurs around the table, but no one challenged Gröndahl's position.

Gregg did not flinch as Gröndahl spoke, but his eyes moved from face to face before finally returning to Gröndahl.

"I'm sorry, Dr. Gröndahl," he said evenly, "but I'm not at liberty to divulge the background of this investigation. I can tell you that it was motivated by a number of things: by the international crisis, which was reaching an acute stage at the time this action was initiated; by the importance assumed by science in modern warfare; and finally by the fact that Dr. Bloch was recognized in well-informed circles as being possibly the most brilliant and promising of the younger scientists. The fact that he had the kind of personality that could powerfully influence a large number of people, and the fact that he had already begun to attract attention as a leftist, determined the decision to put him under a discreet form of observation. It was of course never intended, nor is it now intended, that any of the material gathered should be made public. Apart from this I can merely say that this was not, strictly speaking, an official undertaking, and that it was not paid for out of public funds."

"That at least," Gröndahl said, "is reassuring. The question remains whether we shall not lay ourselves open to serious criticism by taking official cognizance of such a document."

This was debated with considerable animation, and Gröndahl was invited to pursue his questioning.

"This investigator whom you put on the assignment, Mr. Gregg—what is his name?"

"Mark Ampter."

"Could you tell us a little about him?"

Gregg pondered for a moment.

"He was one of the best of our younger men," he said. "Well-trained, bright, enthusiastic. He had been with us for two years. I considered him thoroughly reliable. He got a job as a teaching assistant in the Economics department as a cover, and went on to get a Doctor's degree. He finished up last fall and is now in the army."

"From the passages that Mr. Wilbur read us, and from his summary, I had the impression that the investigation was left rather up in the air. Is that the case, or did the investigator come to some kind of conclusion and wind up the case in a formal way?"

Gregg gave Gröndahl an odd look, in which incredulity contended with deference.

"I may as well tell you," he said at last, "that we parted on rather strained terms." He hesitated for a moment, then went on. "In the course of carrying out his assignment, I'm sorry to say, this investigator fell down on the job and became guilty of disloyalty to the service."

"And yet you're asking us to give credence to his report?"

"Only that part of it, sir, which was prepared before he had completely fallen under the influence—"

"Under the influence . . . ?" Gröndahl prompted.

"Under the influence of Dr. Bloch. You see, the shocking thing is that before he was through, Dr. Bloch had completely won him over to his way of thinking, and Mark Ampter had ceased to be a reliable agent. As you can gather, there are many angles to this thing, and this is one of the reasons I consider this report so important. It may help you to understand, among other things, why I continue to regard Dr. Bloch as a very dangerous man."

There followed an embarrassed silence.

Samuel Wainbridge cleared his throat noisily. "From what I can see," he said, "we've got a much bigger job on our hands than we thought we had when we came here, and we're not going to settle it this afternoon. I would suggest that we will need at least one more meeting, and that before we come together again we all be given a chance carefully to examine this report and any other relevant documents."

I shouldn't have let it surprise me so, Gregg told himself, looking up from his newspaper. The battle of Midway was still going on. He wanted another cup of coffee. It wasn't yet eight o'clock, and the dining room was already crowded with intense, worried-looking breakfasters. Almost all men—businessmen from all over the country, in a mad scramble for war contracts. The Washington hotels were full to overflowing.

He had come prepared for a battle on the Ampter report, though not anticipating too great difficulty. Now he was being faced with the insistence that Bloch be cleared, and with the threat to carry the issue before the President. He had always known that Bloch was strong. But not that strong.

I should have known it, he kept telling himself. Yet deep down he *had* known it. He had always known it. Sebastian Bloch. All these years, and he had never yet laid eyes on him. But how well he knew him nevertheless! Murdock had expected he would show fight under Dysell's grilling. But the transcripts proved he had behaved just as Gregg had said he would. "He's after something bigger," Gregg had told Murdock.

Barber appeared as Gregg was finishing his second cup of coffee.

"Let's go," Gregg said.

For Gregg, as for all the men in the far-flung network of the service, Murdock was a magic name that floated over Washington and a signature at the bottom of endless documents. Presidents and Congresses came and went, but Murdock was a permanent institution.

Again, as on previous occasions, Gregg was struck by the fact that Murdock had nothing about him of the soldier or the man of action. He had, rather, all the earmarks of a businessman, of a desk executive. Few people had, in fact, ever seen him away from his desk. Here he transacted all his business, held his interviews, from here he telephoned all over the country, from here he issued his orders, here he wrote his famous directives and the innumerable magazine articles and pamphlets on the menace of communist subversion. Although Gregg was not excessively sensitive to the refinements of literary style, it was a constant source of embarrassment to him that the vituperative violence of the top chief's outbursts against the ideological enemy should be marred by inadequacy of language. The people in the office were able to fix up the spelling and do something about the punctuation, but there was nothing to be done about the grammar or the words that didn't say what they were meant to say. He was an effective administrator, and displayed positive genius in obtaining ever larger appropriations for the service. In fact, Gregg mused, perhaps the very ineptitude of his communications served as a powerful argument, giving the appropriations committees the impression that he was understaffed and overworked, fighting a gallant but hopeless battle against overwhelming odds. But Gregg increasingly had the feeling that he lacked psychological insight and the kind of imagination that the responsibilities of his high office would seem to call for. Was it not possible, in the light of the parlous times that lay ahead, that he might be moved up to some more exalted and less demanding post?

Gregg sat down and faced Murdock across a tangled no man's land of telephones and cords and desk paraphernalia.

"How are we goin' to handle this?" Murdock asked, a limp cigar butt hanging from a corner of his mouth.

"In the first place, hold off clearance as long as possible."

"Yes." Murdock considered it for a moment. "But we got to be careful not to let it get to the President."

"We can stall. Keep the thing dangling."

"You goin' to put up a fight for the report?"

"No, we'd probably better drop it. We might lose. Keep it in reserve; it'll come in handy at some future time. I suggest we drop the issue of membership too. It would embarrass the policy group unnecessarily. We can save that for later as well. But we've got to get some other kind of hold on him—before clearance, if possible."

"You have an idea?"

"Yes, sir."

"Good."

"Another thing. We mustn't let him out of our sight."

"That's goin' to be hard. This is where the army takes over."

"I know. That's why I'm thinking of going back into the army. I'm a reserve officer, you know."

"Fine, fine! We could probably work you into the job of chief security officer on the project . . ."

"That would be the idea."

There were many things for Gregg to clean up in his office before he could get into uniform, but the necessary arrangements were made before he left Washington. He was given a major's commission and assigned to take charge of security on the Crossroads project.

He called in Zelinski as soon as he got back to town.

"Have you seen Ampter recently?" he asked him.

"He's in training camp," Zelinski said. "I haven't seen him for months."

"He hasn't gone overseas yet, has he?"

"Not that I know of. I'll see what I can find out."

"I want you to get in touch with him. It's most important. Meanwhile I'll see to it that he doesn't get away."

Gregg had Ampter traced at once, and had orders issued that he was not to leave the U.S. mainland until further notice. It was several weeks, however, before Zelinski could report to him that Mark Ampter was in training at Fort Minden, on the West Coast. He came home on a three-day furlough just at the time Rommel was capturing Tobruk and beginning his push toward Alexandria. But Zelinski found out about it too late, and missed him. Meanwhile Gregg, having wound up his business in town, left the office in charge of his deputy and went east to take over his duties as chief security officer for Crossroads.

Chapter 14

THE matter of Bloch's clearance was becoming pressing. "Still investigating," became Murdock's office's stock answer when Gröndahl or some other member of the policy group pressed for a decision. The project was growing. Bloch was traveling all over the country recruiting personnel. New laboratories were being built and equipped, giant processing plants were going up, and the many scattered research projects were moving forward.

The summer passed as the vast movement of building ships and planes, of manufacturing arms and munitions, grew in momentum. The flow of men and supplies across the Atlantic and the Pacific was constantly increasing. The British fought Rommel to a standstill before Alexandria, pushed him back and

smashed him at El Alamein. The Nazi steam roller reached
Stalingrad and stalled there. The Japanese, blocked in their
drive south at the Solomons, were consolidating their vast new
continental and island empire.

One week in late October, after several unsuccessful maneuvers, Zelinski managed to run into Mark Ampter "casually"
outside Krylenko's bookshop.

"How about lunch someday?" Zelinski proposed, after the
initial greetings.

"Thanks," Ampter said, "but I really won't have the time. I
only have a few days' furlough, and I want to spend every minute with my family."

"A quick lunch, say tomorrow," Zelinski insisted. "I have to
talk to you. It's rather important."

"What's it about?"

Zelinski hesitated. This time he must not fail. "It has to do
with Sebastian Bloch," he said.

"Couldn't you tell me now?"

"It will take a little time."

Ampter finally agreed, and they met the following day in a
quiet downtown restaurant.

Zelinski tried to make some small talk before launching into
the main business of the occasion.

"How do you like army life?" he asked, when they had ordered.

"It's O.K.," Ampter said.

"I'm afraid I'd find it too strenuous," Zelinski said. "I guess
I've gotten soft."

"It would do you good," Ampter said. "It's done me a lot of
good. It gives you a fresh outlook. You're thrown in with people you would never have believed existed. You have time to do
a lot of thinking. And you discover that a lot of the ideas you
used to swear by were ideas you had never thought out very
thoroughly."

"That's what our civilization needs," Zelinski said senten-
tiously. "Time to think. Tell me, when do you expect to be sent
overseas?"

"God only knows. It might be in a week, it might be in a year."

"And where do you expect to go?"

"Probably the Pacific. By the way, what did you want to talk to me about?" Ampter asked abruptly. The waitress had just brought two steaming plates piled with roast beef, mashed potatoes and canned peas.

"Yes, I was coming to that." Zelinski waited until the waitress was out of earshot. "But first I have to ask you something. Do you have any idea what Bloch is working on?"

Ampter looked at him suspiciously. "No, why?"

"It doesn't matter. I don't either, except that it's a government project. It's something important connected with the war effort, probably a new weapon."

Zelinski lowered his voice further, and brought his face a little nearer to Ampter's across the table.

"This is the point. I'm an engineer myself, and though I don't actually know, I have a rough idea of what this thing might be. The possibilities are rather terrifying. It's not even certain that the thing can be done. It will cost a staggering amount of money, will require thousands of scientists and technicians, and it may take years before it's actually made and can be used. The only reason our people are going ahead—and they *are* going ahead—is that they believe the Germans are working on the same idea and may be even more advanced than we are. Are you following me?"

"Yes," Ampter said, "but I don't see—"

"Just a moment. Our intelligence has had reports that the Germans are going ahead on this. Men like Otto Hahn, Strassman, Heisenberg—" Zelinski looked at Ampter probingly. "Do those names mean anything to you?"

"Yes."

"All right. Before going on with the rest of the story, I have to tell you how I come in on this. I am, as you know, what you might call a progressive-minded liberal. Some people even consider me something of a left-winger, though I've never gone in much for politics. Oh, I've engaged in some minor activities like helping to organize the scientists' and technicians' union, and especially I've always had strong feelings about the Nazis. That's how I've come to know quite a few anti-Nazis, including one or two important ones—I mean members of the underground, who go in and out of Germany, and who have high connections there. I can tell you that there are some consular and embassy people of invaded and neutral countries—I could mention Holland and Sweden—there's a network, and we have contact with what goes on inside Germany. Now here's the rest of the story . . ."

Ampter was sitting with his fork half-raised above his plate, all attention.

"We have just heard," Zelinski continued, "that the German scientists are *not* going ahead with the project. We have this from the scientists themselves. They've sent a message that they want to get in touch with Bloch, whom they know personally. They say that if he will communicate with them, through channels that I will indicate, they can convince him that they are not going ahead, and this will make it unnecessary for us to go ahead, and thus save an untold amount of destruction and loss of life."

A frown had darkened Ampter's face as Zelinski spoke.

"I'm not quite sure what you're driving at," he said, "but whatever it is, you can count me out."

"Wait a minute," Zelinski said. "Don't you see? This is terribly important. This can change the whole course of history. All you're asked to do is to mention it to Bloch. If it means nothing to him, well, that's that. But how do you know that this isn't exactly what he's been hoping for, praying for? Can't you put yourself in his place? I don't know Bloch, and I understand you know him well, but from everything I've heard he's a very humane kind of person and has strong feelings about human brotherhood. I can imagine him lying awake nights thinking about this new weapon which he feels it is his duty to bring out because he believes the Germans might get it before we do. But just think what might happen if he found out, and really could convince himself, that the Germans *are not* working on it! On the other hand, suppose you refuse to let him know, suppose he goes ahead. And then suppose, after the war, and after all the damage is done, you tell him that you knew long ago that the Germans weren't working on it . . . I can hear him saying, 'My God, why, *why* didn't you tell me?' "

Ampter did not answer immediately. Zelinski felt he had made an impression.

"I'm going to assume that you're speaking in good faith," Ampter said finally, "and that your information is reliable. If that is the case, there's a very simple thing for you to do, and that is to go to any official government agency, to any federal office, and tell them enough of your story so that they can direct you to the right person or persons. You're sure to get a hearing. Your story is too important to be sidetracked."

Zelinski shook his head. "I've thought of that, but it won't work. You know that Bloch has the reputation of being a Red. He's under strong suspicion, and he still hasn't been cleared. This message is addressed to Bloch. If I were to go to some official with the story, it would make them even more suspicious of Bloch, and they wouldn't believe it. It would just get him in more trouble. No, the only way is to take the thing direct to Bloch, and he'll know what to do with it—whether to drop it or pursue it."

Ampter was finishing the last scraps of food on his plate. Zelinski had eaten very little. He wasn't hungry.

"It's your headache," Ampter said. "I'm in the army now. I no longer make any decisions or take independent action. I just obey the orders of my superior officers."

"I know you're a close friend of Bloch's," Zelinski said. "I understand you both see eye to eye politically. As a matter of fact, I fully share your views. I've heard some of Bloch's lectures on science. You know how strongly he feels about science as a force binding men together, rather than separating them, about scientists working to create a better life for the common man, rather than for the destruction of life and property. As a friend of his, don't you think it's your duty at least to bring this to his attention, knowing that it might completely change everything?"

Ampter shook his head.

"Sorry, but I can't do it. In fact it would be highly improper for me to have anything to do with it. But there's nothing to prevent you from seeing him yourself. You know him, after all."

"I wouldn't be able to get to him, in the first place. Not these days. And anyway he wouldn't listen to me. No, it's got to be someone who's a close friend, whom he trusts. It's got to be you."

"And besides," Ampter said, "he isn't around, and I won't be seeing him. I haven't seen him for months, and I probably won't see him again before the war's over."

"His wife is still here," Zelinski protested.

"Yes."

"You'll be seeing her, you can tell her."

Ampter said nothing.

"Will you tell her?" Zelinski urged.

Ampter looked at him. His face was completely deadpan.

"If I were you, it's the last thing I'd count on," he said.

Zelinski was again overcome by his sense of being misunderstood, rejected, trampled upon. Even when he was going out of his way to help people! He must have been born under an unlucky star.

"Think it over," he said, concealing his desperation. "It's one of those things"—he was tossing about a little wildly—"a chance to do some good . . . otherwise regret all your life . . ."

The luncheon with Zelinski had upset Mark more than he liked to admit to himself. Eight months in the army had been a wonderful therapy. He had begun to possess his own soul again. Many things were still unresolved, but he was getting back to a basis of health. The hard physical life seemed to act like a purge, eliminating all the poison of duplicity and guilt from his system; its routine and its discipline imposed upon his spirit and his organism a rhythm that cut across the solipsism in which he had been in danger of foundering; and his new associates, raw recruits from all over the country of every background and character, having in common only a certain minimum of health, plunged him into a world that had practically nothing in common with the one over which his life had cast such a sinister shadow of ambiguity. Talking with Zelinski had brought back many associations that he had happily forgotten during all these months.

He felt there was something fishy about Zelinski's story. Yet he wasn't absolutely sure. And the uncertainty was very disturbing. Most disturbing of all, however, was the mention Zelinski had made of Sebastian's not having been cleared. This undoubtedly meant that Gregg was using his report, and having his way. For weeks Mark's mind had been free of that whole dark embroilment. Now his sense of guilt again overwhelmed him, and he realized that a few months of army camp life, of training, of toughening up, were not enough. It would take a lot more: action, combat, danger. Again he considered going to Sebastian and making a clean breast of everything. And once again he decided against it. It would deeply upset Sebastian now. And it would do no good. After the war . . .

Tanya came for dinner on the second evening of Mark's leave. But after the first effervescence of joy at their reunion, she fell into a state of listlessness. Her face had an unusual pallor in which her eyes, by contrast, shone with a strange blue fire. She answered one or two questions about Sebastian, but seemed reluctant to speak of him. She did not see him for weeks on end, she said. He was nervous, and slept only two or three hours a night. He was wearing himself out. She did not know how long he could stand up under the ordeal. He had never been very strong.

It was a rather sad reunion, but there was sweetness in it. It was perhaps the only time Mark had ever seen Tanya without Sebastian, and he was struck, in a new way, by her beauty. She looked ravishing in a pearl-gray tight-bodiced, full-skirted wool dress, with a lot of lapis lazuli jewelry, including a huge

stone set in each of the silver buckles of her kid shoes of matching blue.

Mark kept thinking of Sebastian, trying to remember his
face, of which he had never been able to manage a mental image. He could remember his lips, and the subtle smile that
would play over them, and also his eyes, with their brooding
depths. He had often thought about their last conversation
when they had walked together in the night. There had been
an almost despairing note in Sebastian's voice. What had he
wanted to tell him—or to ask him?

Several times in the course of the evening he was on the
point of bringing up the conversation he had had with Zelinski and each time, without any precise reason, he held back.
Tanya left early, and he escorted her out to her car. As he held
open the door to her Cord, and she was about to step in (looking, Mark did not quite know why, like a lost princess: the pallor of her fine features, against the sable jacket, accentuated
by the ghostly light from the arc lamp, the slim grace of her
movements . . .) he suddenly asked her:

"Sebastian *is* all right, isn't he?"

She looked at him questioningly for a moment. "I don't
know," she said finally. She got into the car and started the
motor. "I don't know," she repeated, almost to herself.

As the car leaped forward, he heard her faint good-by.

His conversation with Zelinski kept prodding him in the
course of the following weeks. What if the story, unlikely
though it seemed, was bona fide? Zelinski was obviously somewhat informed as to the project Sebastian was working on,
and what he had said about it had reminded Mark of information he had picked up in the course of preparing his early reports to the Chief. Perhaps, after all, Zelinski's proposition
might be of crucial importance. He didn't believe it, but he
was in no position to judge. Didn't Sebastian at least have a
right to be told? Day after day Mark debated the problem to
himself.

At the end of November his outfit was alerted and sent overseas, but he himself was pulled out at the last moment, without explanation, and put into a unit of recruits who had freshly arrived in camp. Although he had already had considerable training in beachhead landing and jungle fighting, he was made to take basic training all over again. Perhaps by way of compensation he was given another five-day furlough.

Traveling by train and bus, coming again into contact with civilians in everyday life, Mark immediately sensed how the mood of the country had further evolved as it was increasingly committed to the war. American troops, together with the British, had landed in North Africa under the command of General Eisenhower. German troops had invested unoccupied France and moved into Italy. The air was full of rumors of impending large-scale action in the Pacific. An endless flow of ships, planes, tanks, supplies of all kinds, was pouring from the production lines, and American troops in increasing numbers were moving up to the battle fronts.

Mark kept worrying about why he had been lifted out of his outfit. His record, so far as he knew, had been perfect, and he had earned a Pfc. rating. He had no idea what the action meant. Had Gregg had a hand in it? Had he been branded as a communist?

Again when he arrived home Sebastian was away, although Tanya was expecting him any day. Mark waited until the last moment, and then decided to talk to her. He reported his conversation with Zelinski as accurately as he could remember it.

"My own feeling was just to forget it," he explained. "For some reason I don't set much stock by this Zelinski, and the very fact of his making this kind of indirect, secretive approach to something that could be so important looks suspicious to me. I don't know whether you should tell Sebastian or not. Maybe it'll just disturb him and make him lose more sleep. Or maybe it's terribly important and he should be told. I don't know."

Tanya was greatly upset.

"Oh, dear, I wish you hadn't told me," she said. "Now I just don't know what to do, and I'm sure whatever I do will be wrong."

"Has Sebastian—if it isn't indiscreet—has he been cleared?"

Tanya hesitated a moment. "No," she said. "And that of course makes him nervous too."

Mark told about his own experience of being separated from his outfit.

"It's a time of bitterness," Tanya said. "We *should* be brave allies. And of course right now we *are* giving the Russians a lot of help. After all, they're getting killed, and they're saving American lives. But nevertheless there is one emotion that dominates the thinking in high policy circles, and that is fear of Russia. The moment we defeat Hitler I'm convinced we'll have trouble with the Russians."

They were sitting in the Blochs' vast living room, which had a bleak, empty look in the late sunless afternoon.

"Is that what Sebastian thinks?" Mark asked.

"He doesn't say."

Mark looked at her, puzzled.

"We—we don't discuss politics any more," she said simply. "Not that kind. We talk about the war, yes," she went on hurriedly. "And—and events, things that happen, what people say and what the papers say. But no political analysis . . ."

She looked, a little wistfully Mark thought, into space, and again he was overcome by her beauty. She wore a billowing white dress with a low neckline that showed the surging curves of her breasts when the bright blue wool shawl swung free from her shoulders. She had found a half bottle of Jack Daniels in the drink cabinet, and they were sipping it out of pony glasses.

Suddenly, as Mark's glance moved up from Tanya's face to the bookshelves behind her next to the window, he realized why the room looked so empty.

"All your books—" he said.

"Yes. Sebastian gave them to the University. They were part of his father's library." After a silence she said, "We'll probably be leaving here fairly soon. I don't know where we're going." Her hands were clasped in front of her, and she looked up at Mark disarmingly. "My impression is that we're going" —she unclasped her hands and opened them outward—"to be living—nowhere."

Chapter 15

LATELY Tanya's thoughts had been reverting more and more to her childhood. Sometimes she would wake up, almost always alone now in her bed, and for a moment or two she was a little girl again and the world was reduced to the scale it had had then: so small an area well-defined and familiar, and everything beyond it dim, fabulous, full of wonder, containing elements of delight and elements of terror.

A violent urge came over her one day to reread Andersen's fairy tales, and she got hold of a copy in a Russian translation in her father's bookshop and read it from cover to cover. How real much of it still seemed to her, and how much of its imagery had remained with her!

And now Sebastian—so often away on distant, mysterious missions, hardly ever home longer than the magic one night, three nights, sometimes five or seven nights accorded to the princes in the fairy tales—Sebastian was becoming for her more and more a fabulous being endowed with strange powers and attributes. In her fantasies, each time he left her in the symbolic dawn before sunrise he would turn into a wild swan, to assume his human shape again only when he returned to her.

On the morning of December 3rd there was a telephone call from Chicago—she was still in bed—and it was Sebastian. He sounded positively exuberant, as she had not heard him sound for years now, it seemed, and this made her happy.

"When are you coming home?" she asked.

"In two or three days. I'll send you a wire. I just wanted to say hello."

"Hello!" Tanya laughed.

They had a few bantering exchanges, and said good-by.

When she met him at the airport four days later she was in a holiday mood. Her wild swan was coming home; he would be restored to his human shape.

It was nearly midnight by the time they got back to the house where Tanya had prepared a cold supper. Sebastian was in a radiant mood. He had brought her a fantastically beautiful antique necklace of wrought silver, composed of hundreds of intricately worked parts assembled with wonderful artistry. His eyes sparkled as he opened the bottle of Montrachet that she had chilled to just the right temperature, and they sat down to the little midnight feast.

There were all the weeks of their separate lives to weave together. She had to tell him about Gino and about her music and about the social fabric of the community that the war was rapidly unraveling; he had to tell her about how everything looked in other parts of the country, how various scientist friends were faring, about the high officials he had been seeing.

Sebastian was so voluble and ate with such zest that it was not until they had finished the lobster and the Montrachet and she had brought on a bottle of his favorite Nuits St.-Georges 1927 to drink with the Camembert that she noticed how pale he was, and how drawn his features. Yet he did give the impression of being relaxed and free of anxiety. He acted as though a great weight had been lifted from his shoulders.

"You sounded so happy over the phone the other day," Tanya said as they sat down to their coffee in the living room in front of the fire. "I got the feeling that something wonderful had just happened."

"You were right." Though his face had a studied impassiveness, Tanya felt that he was beaming inwardly. "Something wonderful *had* happened."

He was obviously not going to tell her. It occurred to her to wonder if perhaps the project had been suspended, had somehow been made unnecessary, and that Sebastian was again free. Perhaps even—was it possible?—he had found out from some other source that the Germans were indeed *not* working on the dreadful weapon, and America had accordingly decided to abandon the program.

The dreadful weapon . . . Until Mark had told her the other day, obviously assuming that she already knew all about it, she had had no idea what kind of thing Sebastian was working on. And it was this that had upset her, more than anything else Mark had told her. She understood now, as she had not before, the weight of responsibility that Sebastian carried on his shoulders, she could accept more readily the change that had come over him since he had become involved in the project. Knowing his gentleness, his humaneness, she could imagine what a nightmare it must be for him.

"The most wonderful thing that could happen," she ventured, "would be—wouldn't it?—if you, if all of you, decided to call off the whole project."

Sebastian looked at her rather oddly. "No chance of that," he said.

He was shutting her out again, and in spite of herself she felt a little nettled.

"But what if you were to learn, authoritatively, that the Germans are not going ahead with it, that they have definitely decided not to make the Weapon?"

Sebastian gave her a startled look. "What are you talking about?"

The question seemed pointless.

He got up and put his coffee cup on the mantelpiece. There was thunder in his look. "Who said anything about a weapon? And what is this about the Germans? Whom have you been talking to?"

Some demon impelled her to recklessness. "Why don't you answer me first? *Would* it make a difference to you?"

For the first time since she had known him she saw an ugly expression come over his face; but he controlled it almost immediately.

"Come, now, tell me," he said in an expressionless voice.

Now she suddenly felt distressed. She should never have brought this up. A feeling of panic came over her. Ever since Sebastian had become involved in this fearful thing she had had a sense of being increasingly separated from him, of becoming more and more a stranger. Each time she was to see him she looked forward to it more passionately, and each time they were together something happened that seemed to separate them more. And now it was happening again, and she was helpless.

"I'm sorry," she said, knowing it was useless, "let's just forget about it."

Sebastian came and sat down next to her on the couch. "Whom have you been talking to?"

"To Mark."

"Mark?"

"Yes."

"What does he know?"

"He doesn't know anything. He wanted to see you. He was worried about something. He waited until the last moment. He didn't know whether to tell you or not. It wasn't really anything . . ."

"You're holding back something—something I should probably know."

"Look, darling, I think it's much better if we drop it. I shouldn't have mentioned anything to you. I only did it because—because I thought it might have something to do with why you were so elated over the phone the other day. But I see it didn't. So let's forget it."

Sebastian's eyes were boring into her.

"I want to know," he said in a hard, metallic voice she had never heard before. "What did Mark tell you?"

She felt powerless. She told him what Mark had told her about his conversation with Zelinski.

As she spoke his face darkened. He got up and began to pace.

"Fool! Idiot!" he muttered several times under his breath, but she had no idea to whom he was referring. After she had finished he continued to pace back and forth from the fireplace to the opposite wall for some time in silence. Then he stopped in front of her.

"This is nonsense," he said. "I want you to forget all about it—everything that's been said. Do you hear?" But immediately he added, in a softer voice, "Will you?"

"Yes," she said.

He stood in front of the fireplace looking down into the flames. The distortion of lights and shadows flickering in his face gave him a demoniac look. He squeezed his lower lip between thumb and forefinger.

"This is terribly serious," he half whispered.

"I don't see what's so serious," Tanya said. "Or do you intend to do something about it?"

"No, certainly not."

"Well, then, there's nothing to worry about. Nothing has happened. Nobody has done anything. No one need even have said anything, so far as you're concerned. Mark didn't talk to you. He only mentioned it to me, more or less by chance, because it puzzled him. He didn't know what to do about it."

"But you said he wanted to talk to me."

"Well—but maybe he wouldn't have. He was all confused. Zelinski had asked him to convey the message to you . . ."

"What message?"

"From the German scientists."

"You didn't tell me there was a message from the German scientists."

"Not a message exactly, although I guess maybe you could call it that. Anyway, Mark wouldn't have anything to do with it, but Zelinski tried to tell him something about these scientists wanting to get in touch with you . . ."

Sebastian's face was tight with rage.

"Now tell me again precisely what Mark told you!"

Tanya felt like crying. She controlled herself, and repeated her whole conversation with Mark as accurately as she could remember it.

"But I just don't see why you're so upset about it," she added when she had finished. "Why can't you just forget about it? As you said, it's all just nonsense."

"You don't understand."

"Oh, all right, I'm stupid!" She was suddenly exasperated. This was something he would never have said to her in the old days. Even in those days his inner world had been enveloped in mystery, had been in large part inaccessible to her, but he had always sought to communicate with her on the highest level possible. He had made her feel more important, more intelligent, than she really was. Now he was withdrawing more and more into his world, and perhaps that world too was changing, was becoming more forbidding. Was he trying to protect her? In any case, he was no longer shoring her up.

Unexpectedly he had put his arms around her. "I'm sorry," he said. "I didn't mean that." His face was frighteningly close to hers. It was as if she were looking at a stranger. They had been away from each other too much.

He was looking into her eyes now, and his expression was full of gentleness, of kindness.

"I don't know how to tell you," he said.

His voice was soft, but high-keyed as it used to be, sometimes, in bed when they would talk, in the dark, after making love.

"It isn't that I don't trust you," he said. "I trust you more than I trust myself." He shook his head. "But this is a fearsome business that I've become involved in, and I don't want you involved in it in any way."

"But maybe I could help you," she said hopefully. "Remember? You used to say that just talking to me, even about things I didn't understand, helped you to make right decisions." She put her hand on his cheek.

He looked at her and shook his head again, with her hand still on his cheek. "Believe me, it hurts me more than I can tell you to shut you out as I'm doing. I know it isn't any good, but the other would be worse."

One of the flaming logs in the hearth tumbled forward against the andiron guard and released a shower of sparks. Sebastian got up to poke the fire and sweep up the hearth floor.

"I think I'd like some brandy," Tanya said.

They sipped the cognac in silence. She could sense his worry, the vicious circle turning upon itself. And she had her own worry. And neither of them could talk about the sources of their distress, which thus became a screen separating them. He knows, he surely knows what he must do, she told herself. But the burden of his responsibility must be appalling. If only she could help him!

At last he broke the silence.

"Would you—" he said, "would you play a little?"

She kissed him softly on the forehead and went over to the piano and began to improvise. There was at least this. And perhaps this was a great deal. This was something no one else could give him.

She could improvise for hours on end, easily and without repeating herself or falling into monotonous patterns. She had no great creative gift, and the elements of the music that flowed so freely from her fingers were distilled, she knew, from many sources. Yet she had absorbed Corelli and Scarlatti and Bach and Haydn and Mozart and her other masters so thoroughly that what she gave back in her improvisations was not specifically what any of them had contributed, and was in fact her own.

She remembered the first time she had ever played for him. It had been that first day—after the first night she had spent with him—when he had driven her back to Mrs. Baxter's boardinghouse in the late mid-August afternoon. She had asked him in, and they had sat in the Baxter parlor. They were both a little dazed—at least she was—by everything that had happened in the last twenty-four hours, and she had been quite swept off her feet by him and felt as if she were walking on clouds. In the parlor, with its flowered carpet, its overstuffed furniture upholstered in olive-green cut velvet and its lace curtains and group pictures on the walls, Sebastian had immediately noticed the piano and asked her to play. She had acquiesced without the slightest hesitation and had proceeded to improvise.

Always when she played, even now, she would shut the

immediate world completely out of her consciousness and immerse herself in the music. But on that occasion Sebastian was sitting in full sight of her, a little to her right where she could look or not look at him without strain, and she had suddenly realized that for the first time she was bringing another person into the private world of her own music and that the very character of her playing was changed, seemed to take on a new dimension. As she had played she had sensed a response in him, and this response became a part of the pattern elaborated in her music: so that the world of sound in which she moved was no longer hers alone, but his as well.

So it had been ever since. When she played for him alone, something happened that never happened otherwise, that made it for her as for him an adventure and a revelation, an encounter in which their two beings fused in a rapture that had no name and no face, but that was perhaps more real than any thought, perhaps more real than their love.

The memory of that August afternoon cast its glow over her now and it seemed to her, though she could not be sure, that the same thread of melody that she had hit on then ran through what she was playing. Sebastian glanced up, his face an abstract mask, but she thought she detected a glimmer of recognition in his eyes.

She felt him returning to her as he listened—perhaps not even listening, merely existing, in a realm in which he belonged wholly to her.

Chapter 16

ONCE again, late that winter, Mark was pulled out of his unit as it was being shipped overseas, and for a second time was put back into a raw unit and made to repeat basic training. It was over a year since he had enlisted, and he was still right where he had started. He tried to get some kind of explanation, but the only answer he was able to elicit was "orders." Whose orders? The one person he could think of who might be behind it was Gregg. But why should Gregg want to prevent him from going overseas? And what kind of pull would enable him to get such an order through the whole administrative machinery of the army?

He found himself thinking about Sebastian almost incessantly, to the point of obsession. Would he be cleared? And if not, what would happen? And did he know yet that it was he, Mark, who had built up the record against him? Had he been shown any part of those reports? Mark had seen neither Sebastian nor Tanya again. Eve had written that they had closed their house at the end of February and left, with Gino, for an undisclosed destination . . . without any forwarding address.

When he had first read Eve's letter that had come in the morning mail he had simply registered the fact that the Blochs had left for the "nowhere" that Tanya had spoken of. It was only when he stood in the long mess line that noon that the implications of this piece of news had suddenly struck him. He had immediately had a strange hollow feeling inside, had stepped out of line and gone back to his barracks and lain down on his bunk. He had shut his eyes tight and dug his head into the bedding and tried to calm himself and sort out his emotions.

He was staggered to discover how much Sebastian meant to him. He had of course been aware, to a certain extent, of the bonds of friendship that had gradually attached him to Sebastian, but they had grown so insidiously in the shadow of the fierce conflict of emotions stirred by that other relation of secret agent and suspect that he had never really sounded the depth of the affection that he had come to feel for him. Now it struck him, with the impact of fresh discovery, that this friendship was his most precious possession, and at the same time he was overwhelmed with a sense of irrevocable loss at the news of his departure.

The weeks that followed were a stretch of utter barrenness. He was a desert no longer even visited by an occasional rain. Drill, fatigue duty, K.P. and all the trivial routine of military life filled the days, which wore on in monotonous aridity. The only live thing in him was his love of Eve burning in his heart with a steady flame. And then at last in late May his unit was alerted for overseas duty, and he was told that this time he would be going along. He was given a week's furlough before the date of embarkation.

Eve greeted him with the news that she had run into Tanya downtown the week before. Tanya had come just for overnight to attend to some business formalities. She had been traveling incognita and was not supposed to see anyone in town whom she knew, but she had been delighted to meet Eve by chance on the street, and they had gone into a drugstore for a cup of coffee and had a chat.

"Guess what!" Eve said when she reached this part of her story as Mark was driving the old Chevrolet back from the airport, spotting the familiar landmarks out of the corner of his eye. "Sebastian's been cleared!"

"No!" He had to make a controlled effort to keep his hands on the wheel. "Is that definite?"

"So she says. The clearance came just recently. He must have gone through hell. He was grilled for hours on end over a period of months, and that kind of thing. Apparently the security people continued to hold out against clearance, and it was finally forced through by some higher-up, probably the President."

"Thank God!" Mark exclaimed. An enormous load had been lifted from his conscience. During all these months he had been nagged by the thought, absurd and incredible though it sometimes seemed, that because of him Sebastian might not be cleared, and that because of this America, and the Allies, might lose the war. After his last interview with the Chief, he had written his final report on Sebastian and a carefully worded letter of resignation and had sent notarized copies to the chairman of the Policy Group of the Emergency Research and Development Office, Dr. Hjalmar Gröndahl, as well as to a number of other strategically placed persons. His own lawyer had a copy of each locked away in his safe. He wondered now whether these, or at least one set of them, had got into the right hands and been instrumental in counteracting the effect of his earlier reports. It seemed inevitable that those two documents must have had some weight. Perhaps he was deluding himself, but it was a comforting delusion; and he was in need of some moral comfort, and he clung to it.

But quite apart from the relief to his conscience, Mark was elated by the news of Sebastian's clearance. It was a further victory—for the Left, most immediately, but for the country as well, and for the world.

"I suppose," he said, as they were approaching the University, "that I know as much about Sebastian Bloch, from the outside at least, as any man living. And I give my unqualified blessing to his clearance."

Home, now that he was about to leave it without knowing when—if ever—he would return, was home for him this time in a deeper sense than it had ever been. Yet it was still the ugly, impossible flat that he had picked out as a makeshift while he was in the throes of cramming for his Ph.D. When he had enlisted, he and Eve had decided that she and Jimmy should go back to her mother's for the duration, but that they would stay on here in the flat until he went overseas so that they would still have a home of their own for him to come back to on furloughs. At that time they had imagined that it would be merely a matter of a few months. It had now been nearly a year and a half, and Eve had given her little personal touches to the place which with new curtains, their own pictures, books and objects, had acquired a pleasant, comfortable atmosphere. Mark, during those too-few days, looked avidly at each object, at each scene in relation to Eve and Jimmy, to imprint them indelibly on his memory.

And at night, in bed, making love to Eve with insatiable appetite, he had to make up not only for all the good times they had missed in the past but for the long lean months ahead.

There was a memory of the mind, and there was a memory of the heart. But there was also a memory of the lips, of the hands, of the limbs and the loins, of all the organs, and all these memories he had to store up for a long time to come.

Besides which, he and Eve had so much to talk about! For nearly three years now they had seen very little of each other. And talk they did, for hours on end.

"Something just occurred to me," Eve said one evening. "Do you think it's just a coincidence that you're being allowed to go overseas such a short time after Sebastian has finally been cleared?"

Mark stared at her for a moment.

"My God, you're right! But what do you suppose . . . ?"

For some reason, he had not thought of relating the two things, but now that Eve had mentioned it it seemed obvious that there must be a connection.

"Gregg must have wanted to keep you available," Eve surmised, "in case he needed you as a witness."

"But certainly he was one of the people holding out against Sebastian's clearance," Mark said slowly, trying to think the problem through. "And he knew I was for Sebastian and that I wouldn't help the case against him. It must have been one of the others who was *for* Sebastian's clearance who wanted to keep me where he could get hold of me. And it must have been someone who read my final report. Probably Gröndahl."

"Do you suppose we'll ever know?"

It was appalling to think of all the intrigues, the plots and counterplots, the play of forces constantly at work behind and underneath all the happenings that actually got into the news.

He spent an afternoon on the campus for a last glimpse of the place, and to say hello and good-by to those he knew who were still around. Many professors were on leave (Anderson, among others, was in Washington, working with the Price Control Board) , and a considerable number of the students he saw were in uniform. Everything about the University seemed so different: many of the familiar faces gone, so many new faces, the whole atmosphere of the place unrecognizable, a grimness

and a pressure that did not belong to an institution of learning; but also something furtive and fake. Mark was glad he was
out of it right now.

The wrench of parting was acutest at the moment of separation from Eve and Jimmy. But it had the seal of finality only
when his troopship left its moorings in the Port of Embarkation and headed due west into the Pacific. It was only then that
the impulse that had made him enlist assumed its full weight
and meaning. Up to that moment, despite the sincerity of his
intention, there had always existed the possibility of a change
of heart, of compromise, of turning back. Now he was irrevo-
cably committed.

Chapter 17

GREGG watched Murdock behind the barrage of telephones and
the litter of papers and objects on the vast glass-top desk. There
were even more telephones than there had been the last time
he had been in this office. He could count a dozen. A mania
of Murdock's. Something about security. Apparently what he
had learned about the uses to which wire tapping could be put
had made him nervous. He was talking to Seattle.

"I'll be with you in a minute," he tossed to Gregg from Puget
Sound.

Dr. Bloch's clearance had just been forced through over
Murdock's head, and he had sent out an urgent call for Gregg
to come for a consultation. Gregg was becoming increasingly
aware that Murdock was no longer the cool, bold, resourceful
executive whom he had first known in the early depression
years. He looked the same outwardly, but something was miss-
ing.

Now he was talking to New Orleans.

In his time Gregg had seen quite a few high-powered executives go to pieces. Depending on the character of the individual concerned and on circumstances, there were two kinds of symptoms, quite different in nature, either of which was a forerunner to disaster. One was the impression a man gave of being progressively snowed under by the gathering momentum of events, of losing control of the means to cope with them, his subordinates, and finally himself; the other was the illusion that he created, amid an accumulation of unanticipated hazards and reverses heading toward crisis, of completely dominating the situation—appearing calm and self-possessed, displaying a prodigious resourcefulness in multiplying countermoves, always just short of adequate, to meet emergencies that were in fact submerging him. Murdock seemed to Gregg to be showing some of the latter symptoms. Those telephones looked bad. And that new electronic filing system being installed downstairs that was going to be able to handle up to twenty million names. Why not a hundred and fifty million?

"Now," said Murdock, after having issued a set of instructions, mostly in code, to Tampa, Florida, "let's see where we stand." His face assumed a momentary worried look. "Well, we might as well face the fact that *he* has stolen a march on us again."

Gregg was thinking that if *he* had been President he would very likely have done the same thing. There was a kind of pressure that was not so much a pressure of the men who exerted it as of events, and statesmanship had to reckon with it.

"It was inevitable," he said.

"This is goin' to make our job ten times tougher," said Murdock.

"I'm not so sure. In one way it may make it easier for us."

"How do you figure that?"

"I think we can get Bloch to play ball with us."

"I wouldn't trust him."

"Not with a lot of things. But with security, yes."

"I wouldn't take a chance. You still have no hold on him?"

"Not yet. My little scheme may take some time to work out, but I'm sure it will."

Murdock shook his head. "You amaze me, Gregg." One of the telephones rang. San Francisco.

Actually Gregg felt none of the assurance that he expressed. It was five months now since Zelinski had reported on his meeting with Ampter. He claimed he had been successful in planting the story about the German scientists, but there had been no further trace of it. Had Mark reported the conversation to Mrs. Bloch, and if so had she relayed it to her husband? Gregg was still completely in the dark.

There were moments, like the present, when Gregg was overcome by doubt and self-reproach. This was so exceptional for him that it quite unnerved him. The Bloch case represented the greatest challenge of his career. It challenged him not just professionally but deep down, in some dark intimate region of his being where strange things stirred that he could not always identify but that were at the very core of what had meaning for him. He had been working on the case for nearly five years now. He had still not laid eyes on Sebastian Bloch. Yet in a sense he knew him more intimately than he had ever known any human being. And he knew, absolutely now, that there was in this man, in spite of—or perhaps partly because of —his many virtues, his almost godlike gifts, something negative, something destructive, something *against nature,* which it was his duty to fight. But the character of that dangerous force eluded him.

Now he had staked everything on one daring stroke. Never before had he taken such a long shot. Four things had to happen, and the success of the scheme was predicated on his accurate sizing up of four characters—Zelinski, Mark Ampter, Tanya Krylenko and Sebastian Bloch. Zelinski had been relatively simple. Ampter, he had calculated, would not believe the story, would be suspicious of Zelinski, would be torn as to whether or not to communicate his disbelief and his suspicions to Tanya Bloch, and would in the end tell her. And Tanya would tell her husband because, no matter what her particular rationalization might be, it was the kind of thing no woman was capable of keeping from her husband. Although he had as yet absolutely no proof, all Gregg's instincts told him that the story had reached Bloch. On the strength of that hunch he had passed on word that Ampter could be released for overseas duty. (Maybe the censors could pick up some information from his correspondence with his wife—had he, for example, told *her* about Zelinski's approach?) And he had given Zelinski a mild dressing down—enough to indicate his dissatisfaction with his inability to follow the thing through, but not enough to make him realize that Gregg considered him to be of no further use.

The problem now was the next move. Bloch, although he would like to believe the story, would give no credence to it, but it would torture him. Gregg could picture the havoc it must be creating with his peace of mind. And the irony was that the story was probably substantially true. Gregg had based it on ultrasecret reports of attempts by some of the top German physicists to make contact with their western opposite numbers through the University of Copenhagen. It would be possible to check it only at the end of the war, but it seemed pretty reliable.

It was the next step that was going to be the most difficult; and about it Gregg had periodic misgivings. Bloch would make no move on his own. He would have to be helped. He would have to be helped to tangle himself up so inextricably that he would deliver himself right into Gregg's hands.

"Comin' back to Bloch," said Murdock, returning the receiver to its cradle, "what I'm worried about is the precedent that's been set. We sweat and stew over security, we break our backs ferretin' out communists and gettin' rid of them, and here they go and let one right in through the front door and hand him a top post on a silver platter. How we goin' to do our job when that sort of thing happens?"

"We're going to have plenty of trouble," Gregg said, "with all these people with bad records whom we're not going to be able to keep out because they're specialists and are considered essential. But Bloch doesn't fit into the same category as these others."

"How do you mean?"

"He's not a security problem—not in the same sense."

"Why not? He's a communist, ain't he?"

"Not any more."

Gregg hesitated. Would Murdock get the point?

"He used to be," he explained. "But now this other thing has come into the picture. Now his past is a liability that he'll be only too anxious to try to liquidate. What worries me is something else."

Gregg had recently been rereading Ampter's reports.

"He wants to save the world," he said. "He's big, and he wants to be bigger. Too big for his own good, and certainly for this country's good. That's why he's dangerous."

"Sure you aren't lettin' your imagination run away with you?" Murdock opened a box of cigars that he had picked up from his desk and offered Gregg one, forgetting that Gregg did not smoke.

"I've been studying this case for five years," Gregg said, declining the proffered cigars, "and I think I know what I'm talking about."

"Maybe so," Murdock said, cutting off the end of a cigar, "and maybe we'll have to keep an eye on that. But our immediate problem is security. We're bein' infiltrated by hundreds of Soviet agents. And a lot of these foreign scientists we don't know nothin' about. Whatever he may be now, your Bloch by his past activities, associations and personal commitments has made himself a focal point for attempts at subversion and sabotage. Let's not kid ourselves."

"There'll be no relaxing of vigilance," Gregg said. Murdock was obviously unable or unwilling to depart from the conventional approach to the problems of security. But Gregg at least had done his duty by reporting what he considered to be the heart of the problem.

"Now then," Murdock said, "we've got to figure out ways and means of tightening up our security system all the way up and down the line. No matter what it takes, we've got to see to it that there are no leaks to the Russians."

Gregg was on the point of adding, "—or to the enemy," but stopped himself in time. It went without saying that every effort would be made to track down the agents of the Axis powers and to negate their activities. But these enemies of to-day would be the allies of tomorrow, and a leakage to them of technical or scientific secrets, except for such as could be im-mediately utilized, would not have far-reaching consequences; whereas any leak to the Russians could be disastrous. For the purposes of security, at least, Soviet Russia was the enemy.

Chapter 18

IN THE secret womb of the Crossroads project the embryo of the Thing, as many outside the inner circle of scientists re-ferred to it, was now in full growth.

To feed it, mountains of ore were being extracted from the bowels of the earth, purified in vast, specially designed new plants, whence the product was sent on to undergo a succession of processings, up to the ultimate stage at which it would be available for the new entity that was coming into being. Scores of factories, hundreds of laboratories and offices, thousands of men were working night and day, as they would continue to work for months, perhaps years, in a race of which the object, apart from the assurance that it involved the winning of the war, was known only to a very few. Through the revolving sea-sons, through the evolving pattern of the war on many fronts, they pursued their task, each contributing an infinitesimal share toward bringing into existence a phenomenon that had no precedent in the world's history: a freak that would spawn cataclysm or millennium, a sport that would swallow yesterday and rip the heavens open for doom or eternity.

There was fumbling still, and hesitancy; there were pitfalls and blind alleys; a few millions spent here on a process that proved unrewarding, a few millions spent there on an idea that had to be discarded. Many problems remained, many questions, all leading up to the biggest, the last and the essential question, to which only the full-grown Thing would be able to give the answer: Would it work? But the direction was now clear, the path fairly well marked out, and every passing week brought the project a little closer to its goal.

As the army of scientists, technicians and workers of every category grew, lines of order and direction began to define their activities. The complexity of the undertaking was such that at the beginning there had been constant duplication of effort and endless wasted motion in the scattered laboratories and research institutes. Now the work was becoming increasingly co-ordinated. For this there had to be organization of superlative efficiency and flexibility, divisions and services with highly qualified heads, facilities for all essential contacts and exchanges among all levels, and at the same time a strict observance of the rules of secrecy and compartmentalization imposed by the security requirements.

For the vast and intricate machinery to work it was essential that there be one brain to encompass both the whole and all the parts, to conceive all the relations in the constantly evolving structure, in the large and in the small, in time and in space, in terms of the materials, the physical laws, the concrete possibilities, the available means, the human factor, and finally to guide and direct its operation and to co-ordinate all efforts for the most rapid possible achievement of the objective. The brain upon which this devolved, by high decision unanimously approved both within the inner circle of possible candidates and in the wider community of scientists, was Sebastian Bloch's.

As dumb animals, when they sense that their hour has come, look for a dark hole to die in, so man, in those supreme moments when he must face his destiny and make ultimate choices for good or evil, seeks out the high places. A mountaintop was selected as the birthplace of the Thing. The blunted 8,000-foot peak of Mount Arron, on which had stood a lone forest-ranger station with an abandoned amateur observatory, was renamed Valhalla. The first comers shivered in improvised shacks buried under snowdrifts. But shortly the bulldozers appeared, and endless caravans of tractors and heavy-duty trucks began moving up building materials, equipment and supplies. Streets, water mains, sewers and power lines were laid out. A great power plant, transmission stations, laboratories, shops, stores, office buildings, a school, garages, dwelling units, were built, and construction continued uninterruptedly to expand accommodation for materials and equipment and for the increasing hundreds of scientists, research workers, engineers, technicians and ancillary personnel and the families of all of these, for whom this was to be home "for the duration." Here, almost completely isolated from the world, all access guarded, all communication surveyed, the basic research and experimental work and all the stages, the chemistry, the metallurgy, the ordnance, up to advanced development, could be carried on with relative freedom and a minimum of compartmentalization.

Sebastian had brought Tanya and Gino here late in February. Bruce and Genia Patterson joined them soon after, as did Fritz and Hannah Leutner, the Webers, Ed MacAvoy and dozens of his other former students. Foreign scientists—theoretical and experimental physicists, chemists, ordnance and explosives experts, mathematicians—individually and in teams, from Britain, France, Scandinavia, Germany, Italy and other countries, came to swell the ranks of the leading American specialists. Their numbers grew as the work advanced and as new necessities arose. The lives of the whole community—the scientists and the auxiliary workers and their families, the army personnel—were geared to the stirrings of the embryo as it approached maturity.

Over-all chief of Valhalla was a high army officer, General Ephraim Sproncke. Under him, Major J. W. Gregg had charge of security, having under his orders several subordinate officers and an army of agents all over the country. The Valhalla area was enclosed by barbed wire charged with high-voltage current, and guarded day and night. No one was allowed in without a careful security check. Sebastian alone, and Tanya, had not yet been cleared.

Tanya was interrogated by Captain Sanders, Major Gregg's immediate subordinate, before she was admitted. The questioning took place in Gregg's former office in town.

CAPTAIN SANDERS. Mrs. Bloch—you married Dr. Bloch November 17, 1938?

MRS. BLOCH. Right.

Q. Had you been intimate with Dr. Bloch before that?

A. What do you mean, sir?

Q. I mean . . . a . . . a . . . well: physically intimate.

A. That, Captain, is none of your business.

Q. I beg pardon?

A. I said it was none of your business.

Q. Mrs. Bloch—you understand, of course, why you are now being interrogated?

A. I believe I do.

Q. You realize, then, that there is a great deal at stake?

A. Yes. For all of us.

Q. And that a decision regarding your husband may depend on your giving responsive answers?

A. I think you can assume that I'm moderately intelligent.

Q. Very well. Then you will understand that I have a right to ask you any question that I consider relevant to the purpose at hand.

A. All right. But I reserve the right to refuse to answer any question that *I* do *not* consider relevant to that purpose.

Q. You are taking a very arbitrary attitude, Mrs. Bloch.

A. I'm sorry you feel that way.

Q. You refuse to answer my question?

A. Yes.

Q. Very well, in that case—[Interruption. Captain Sanders

makes a telephone call. Resuming interrogation.] Mrs. Bloch—your son Eugene was born May 13, 1939, is that right?

A. Yes.

Q. The inference, then, is that you *did*—

A. You may infer whatever you please, Captain.

Q. Yes. Now, Mrs. Bloch, have you ever been a member of the Communist Party?

A. Yes.

Q. When did you join the party?

A. I can't remember exactly. I think it must have been some time in 1935.

Q. Here is a photostatic copy of a Communist Party membership card bearing the name of Tanya Feodorovna Krylenko, dated March 11, 1935. Do you recognize this?

A. Yes. That is a copy of my membership card.

Q. Is this your signature?

A. Yes.

Q. Were you an active, militant member of the Communist Party?

A. Yes.

Q. Did you, while you were a member, actively proselytize and attempt to gain converts to the communist cause?

A. Yes.

Q. Were you successful?

A. Yes, to a certain extent.

Q. You made converts?

A. We did not call them converts.

Q. You persuaded a certain number of people to become members of the Communist Party?

A. Yes.

Q. How many?

A. I can't say. I guess quite a few.

Q. Will you mention the names of some of those you converted—I beg your pardon, whom you persuaded?

A. No.

Q. You refuse?

A. Yes. I will answer no questions that could involve other people in any kind of difficulty.

Q. We'll come back to that. Will you tell me, now, who originally recruited you for the party?

A. No one did. Or rather, quite a few did. But I decided myself. And that's the only thing that matters.

Q. No one persuaded you?

A. I didn't say that. I said quite a few did.

Q. For instance?

A. I won't give any names. I told you that.

Q. Do you know William Parrish?

A. Yes.

Q. How well?

A. Quite well. I've known him since 1935.

Q. Did you ever have intimate relations with him?

A. That again is none of your business.

Q. Mrs. Bloch, the fact that William Parrish is a top party functionary *does* make it our business to know whether or not you were at one time close enough to him to have had physical relations with him. And unless you deny it I shall assume that you did have such relations.

A. If you are going to assume the answers to the questions you are asking me I see no point in your asking them.

Q. Mrs. Bloch, I feel obliged to remind you that your husband's clearance is at stake.

A. I'm quite aware of it. But I know he would not want his clearance to be bought at the price of indignity.

Q. So you refuse to answer this question?

A. Yes!

Q. All right. Now let's come to your husband. When did you first meet him?

A. In August of 1938, so far as I can remember.

Q. Were you then still a communist?

A. Yes.

Q. Did you influence, or attempt to influence, Dr. Bloch in order to persuade him to become a communist?

A. Captain, I can see from your line of questioning that I shall have to make a brief statement. It will save both yourself and me a good deal of time.

Q. I'm sorry, Mrs. Bloch, but I have to carry out my interrogation according to instructions. Any statement of yours would be uncalled for.

A. Then you may as well call an end to this interrogation right now, for I shall refuse to answer any further questions.

Q. Mrs. Bloch, I'm sure you don't realize that you are jeopardizing your husband's position.

A. I know perfectly well what I'm doing.

Q. All right. [Interruption. Captain Sanders makes a telephone call. Resuming interrogation.] Very well, Mrs. Bloch, you may make your statement.

A. Then this is it. I have come to this office on a voluntary basis at the request of the security service of the Crossroads project in order to answer questions. I understand quite clearly that my answers to these questions will serve in part as a basis for the decision whether or not to grant a clearance to enable my husband to continue to work on the project, and incidentally to enable me to accompany him to the Center. I regard this as a wholly proper procedure. I believe that the security officials have a right to know the public activities, associations and written or spoken public statements, both past and present, of employees on such a project. I am prepared to answer fully any such questions that pertain to myself. I do not, on the other hand, consider that the security service has any right to inquire into the beliefs, opinions or attitudes of its employees, and I shall refuse to answer any questions so aimed. Also, I refuse to answer any questions involving other people, except in so far as I may have had public or social, rather than purely private, relations with them.

Q. You are making things very difficult for yourself, Mrs. Bloch.

A. I'm sorry, but that is how it is.

Q. You will not tell me whether you influenced Dr. Bloch in communistic thinking?

A. No.

Q. Then tell me this: Dr. Bloch did, shortly after he met you, and particularly after he married you, become interested in left-wing ideas, didn't he?

A. My husband can answer that question much more pertinently than I can.

Q. You refuse to answer that too?

A. It's the same kind of question.

Q. Then I shall ask you this: are you still a member of the Communist Party?

A. No.

Q. When did you cease to be a member?

A. Some time in November or December of 1938, to the best of my recollection.

Q. In other words, shortly after your marriage?

A. Yes.

Q. Why did you leave the Communist Party?

A. For personal reasons.

Q. What were they?

A. I'm sorry, but I have already said that I would not answer questions pertaining to opinion or belief and which I regard, moreover, as purely personal.

Q. Do you at the present time hold communist beliefs?

A. I have told you repeatedly that I would not answer such questions.

Q. Mrs. Bloch, this is most serious. I can sympathize, at least theoretically, with your position that an individual citizen has a right to his private beliefs. But this is a most special case. You are intelligent enough to understand that it would be impossible to tolerate the presence of a communist sympathizer on a secret government project.

A. I haven't said that I was a communist sympathizer.

Q. Well, are you, or aren't you?

A. Again I must repeat that I will not answer such questions.

Q. Then I must assume that you are.

A. Then I must repeat what I said about assuming the answers to the questions you are asking me. If you're going to do that, this whole interrogation becomes pointless.

Q. Mrs. Bloch, I'm afraid you are doing your husband a great disservice. This interrogation is going to look very bad on the record.

A. What did you expect?

Q. I'm not sure, Mrs. Bloch, that you aren't taking advantage of the fact that you're a woman and that because of that I can't press you quite so hard as if you were a man. But I can assure you that on paper nobody is going to make allowances for your sex. You are privileged to have your own ideas as to your right to hold your private opinions. But it is my duty to tell you that our security system regards suspicion of communism most seriously. You have admitted that you were once a full-fledged, militant communist. You have said that you left the party a little over four years ago, very obviously for tactical reasons. Nobody is going to believe that you aren't still at heart a communist, in the absence of positive proof to the contrary. I want to tell you now that the specific purpose of my interview with you today is to obtain such positive proof from you.

A. Then it looks very much as if you're going to have to go away empty-handed.

Q. Once again, Mrs. Bloch—

A. I believe, Captain, that we have already said all we had to say to each other.

Q. Mrs. Bloch—

A. Captain, you'll have to excuse me . . . [End of interrogation.]

On a memo slip attached to the transcript from the tape recording of the interrogation Major Gregg, over his signature, merely made the notation *O.K.*

The Blochs left for Valhalla two weeks later.

When his clearance had at last come through in early May Sebastian had hoped that it would mean an end to the constant harassment to which he had been subjected. General Sproncke had introduced him to Major Gregg, whom he had not yet run into during the brief stays he had so far made at Valhalla.

"Major Gregg is in charge of security," Sproncke had said in introducing him.

They had shaken hands. Sebastian had had the impression of touching an automaton.

"I shall be depending very much on you, Dr. Bloch. This is a tough assignment they've given me." The whole face was wooden, but the eyes had human, if not very reassuring, depths.

It was only two days after he had received his official clearance that Sebastian ran into Lieutenant Kidd in the main corridor of the old observatory which had been converted into offices and seminar rooms. The lieutenant was one of Major Gregg's subordinates. He had a long, thin, humorless face.

"I wonder if I could speak with you a moment, Dr. Bloch," he said, stepping forward. He had evidently been waiting for him.

"Here? Or do you want it to be more private?" A snag had just been encountered in connection with the capture cross section, and Sebastian, after a long conference, was under considerable tension.

"Perhaps we'd better go into some office, sir," Kidd said. A number of Sebastian's colleagues were standing or moving about.

They found a small empty office. Lieutenant Kidd pulled some papers out of a briefcase.

"Doctor," he said, "you remember we had a conversation some weeks back on the train coming from the University and I asked you about certain persons who you thought should be watched and who might be dangerous?"

"You will have to refresh my memory," Sebastian said. "There have been so many things . . ."

He felt a great inner exhaustion. There had been *too* many things. He had hoped that he could now give his mind wholly to the problems of the Monster. Were the security police going to plague him forever? He had already reached the depth of ignominy. What did they want further? They had come to him again and again, at all times of the day and night—with warning and without, when he was fresh and alert, when he felt relaxed and off his guard, and when he was exhausted and oppressed; when he was in good physical shape and when he was on the verge of collapse. They had asked him so many thousands of questions, about so many hundreds of people. What had he said about X, Y and Z last week, a month ago, a year ago? He had always tried to tell the truth. But there were times when it was not possible. Times when he did not know the truth, but must seem to; times when the truth might jeopardize his work; times when the truth might hurt someone he was trying to help or protect. He would not betray a friend. But friends had been foolish. And there were friends who were no longer friends. And friends about whom one no longer knew. So much had happened. So much had changed. He had been questioned so many times. So many times when he had been in pain, when his nerves had been so on edge that he hardly knew what he had answered. Now there was so much that he could not remember.

"We talked about Jerry Matthias, Curtis Needham and Bertram Musing. I asked you which you considered the most dangerous of those three, and you said Musing."

"I certainly have no recollection of that."

"We have a record of it, Doctor."

"I shall have to take your word for it."

"It's not just my word, Doctor."

"All right." So they had hidden microphones even on a train. But how could he have said Bert Musing was dangerous? He remembered the times Bert had come to the house, when he had played four-handed pieces with Tanya; he remembered in particular some Brahms variations (was it Opus 23?) on a theme by Schumann . . . Tanya admired his musicianship.

"Now," Kidd said, "we have your request for his clearance to enable him to accept an appointment here on the project. Would you care to say anything about that?"

So it was not ended, after all. It would go on and on. He was having to pay the price for being allowed to make the Monster, which had to be made in order to save the Kidds and the Greggs and the Spronckes, among others, from the threat of a fascist victory.

The constant nagging of Major Gregg's security men, over the weeks and the months, would have been unendurable if he had not been able to escape into an altogether different *ambiance* of confidence, respect, and a deference bordering on reverence that he found among a class of men who were relatively new to him. All his old associations were cut off from him now; his students, his liberal or left-wing colleagues, the politically conscious professionals and middle-class people he used to meet at parties, the union men and party people with whom he used to have engrossing discussions. More than this, he had completely severed contact (it had never been physically very real, but it had nourished his spirit) with the working class, with the people of the land, with the *people,* in short, in whom he had come to recognize the spring and the source of the vitality, the fertility that constituted a nation's wealth.

But now he was brought constantly into contact with people about whom he had formerly held rather set views, even though he had never really known them. Men in government —the President, cabinet heads, secretaries and undersecretaries, chairmen of congressional or senatorial committees, career diplomats; military men—chiefs of staff in the three services, staff officers in the higher echelons, ballistics and logistics experts, strategists; men of the business world—lords of empire about whom he had so often speculated and spoken and whose role in the political picture he knew so well, as a Marxist; presidents of investment trusts, of the biggest banking corporations, men who controlled the power, communications and transportations networks, the steel, nonferrous metals, chemical and other basic industries, chairmen of this board and that, public relations counsels, owners of newspapers and press syndicates, radio, motion pictures, representatives of America's greatest fortunes . . . Whichever compartment they specialized in—government, the armed services, industry—they were all recognizably of the same breed. Whether they were born to it, or had acquired it, they had the same stamp on their brows; they were the rulers. All of them, knowing little or nothing that was certain, were attracted, like flies to a piece of carrion, by the smell of the Monster.

The Thing was the focal point on which Valhalla's energies converged, but not the exclusive one. For the Thing would have progeny. It would have children conceived for war, but also children conceived for peace. And much of the research that proved tangential to the main project was pursued, when it did not divert energies from the central project, in the exploration of other fields. Limitless possibilities were opening up. The higher circles of industry close to the Government were alert. American business had always given proof of vision. It was not too early to lay the foundations for the postwar era. Industry was co-operating generously with government, placing its fabulous resources and plant facilities at the nation's disposal in this time of emergency. Sebastian Bloch was beg'nning to be talked about. Some of the country's top leaders in business, industry and banking were discreetly seeking him out.

As he traveled about the country to attend innumerable conferences of scientists, technicians, industrialists, government and army people, he would be invited, now and again, to spend the night at the city or country houses of various business magnates. In these informal, relaxing and cordial encounters he developed friendships and associations among these people in whom he was coming to discern virtues and gifts that he had not suspected. They were urbane, and they had their fingertips on the pulse of the world. Besides being movers and shapers of events on a large scale, they were art collectors, sponsors of young talents, philanthropists, generously endowing the arts and the sciences, founding and maintaining hospitals, medical research centers and institutions dedicated to human welfare. The brightest stars of the stage and screen and concert hall were at their beck and call. Their women were often exquisite. In their presence all life's values were heightened. Their minds, like the houses they lived in and the air they moved in, were spacious. He came to know presidents of billion-dollar corporations, full generals and cabinet heads by their first names. He would send their wives or daughters gifts of flowers or art objects on appropriate occasions, and would in turn be remembered lavishly by firms who hired specialists to select gifts for their most favored clients and contacts—an occupation that they had developed into a fine art.

In the beginning he was very wary in his contacts with these people. They were the people whom, as a Marxist, he had always regarded as the enemy. They were undoubtedly laying traps for him, they knew his left-wing reputation, they were out to destroy him. But as he was increasingly thrown in with them, nothing seemed to confirm these fears. High army officers, government officials and business tycoons alike treated him with the utmost deference, hung on his every word, sought his advice. He came to the realization that the men—and they must include some of the higher-ups in each of the key categories: government, army, business and science—who were privy to his unconventional past were making a point of keeping it to themselves, and that while they might discuss it in private or in the committees or boards called upon to deal with these things, and might even divulge it to an initiated few, it would remain a carefully guarded secret, a kind of state secret.

He had been afraid at first of the awkwardness of continued and repeated contacts with these people. Whenever, outside of purely technical matters, ideas were expressed, class prejudices were bound to assert themselves, and he would be in difficulty. As it turned out, he ran into no real trouble. These people were so intelligent and reasonable that, once one granted their premises, it was difficult to quarrel with them. And he hardly felt called upon to assail their premises. Occasionally someone would launch into a virulent attack against the Soviet Union that would lead to a prolonged discussion. But he was never pressed to give his views. And he could listen to their sometimes intemperate outbursts with all the greater tolerance as he recognized that these were the people who obviously stood to lose most by Revolution, by any upheaval initiating an order of which the Soviet Union could be regarded as a prefiguration. Lords of empire, masters of immense wealth, wielders of untold power, however enlightened and humane, they were certainly the first who would be liquidated under any socialist order. They embodied a value of civilization and were understandably committed to defending at all costs the existing order that allowed them to remain on their high pinnacles.

Sebastian's excursions into this world of privilege were dictated less by choice than by necessity, though there was a little of both. But sometimes, in the face of the almost embarrassing respect with which he was treated, he would reflect upon his role. I deserve none of this homage, he would tell himself, but they see in me the instrument that will bring the Monster into being. And this in itself was good. In this primitive, almost fetishistic way, they were paying tribute to science. And this it was legitimate for him to take advantage of.

It was impossible for him not to be conscious of the fact that he had a certain power over men. He had known it before, with his peers in the field of science, with his students, with women, and also with everyday people. But it was a revelation to him to find it operating with these men who lived only to command. And this too was good. For while he knew, as they did not, that their power though great was limited and running out, it was still a power to be reckoned with and one that might at some future moment serve him if he should happen to be entrusted with it. So he quite consciously set out to cultivate these people and to win them.

The war was going ahead. From Germany came horror tales of the wholesale extermination of Jews, of special gas chambers into which men, women and children were herded by the thousands. From the Pacific theatre came other horror tales of the torture of war prisoners and captured civilians by the Japanese military. But it looked now for the first time, when one viewed the war picture as a whole, as if the turning point had been reached. The Axis countries had attained the limit of their offensive powers. The Nazis had been in steady retreat since

Stalingrad. The Germans and Italians had been swept off th
African continent, and the landing in Sicily in July was fo
lowed by the landing on the Italian mainland in September, I
the resignation of Mussolini and the surrender of Italy. In th
Pacific the Japanese had been on the defensive since the Sol
mons and New Guinea, and the strategy laid down in the Tr
dent conference in May and the Quadrant conference in A
gust was beginning to bear fruit. A long and bitter struggle sti
lay ahead which could take a further ghastly toll of human lif
But the Allied High Command was no longer haunted by th
specter of possible defeat.

Unless—

For there were persisting rumors of "new weapons" comir
out of Germany. Some of these were in the rocket and guide
missile category, which could be devastating enough if succes
fully developed and turned out in quantity. But were they no
also working on the Thing? There was no room for compl
cency. Any day might bring the shattering news and the cata
trophic proof that the Germans had been successful in develo
ing it. The very thought sent cold shudders down the spines
the few who were in on the secret of the Valhalla effort an
who thus had some knowledge as to what was to be feared.

Chapter 1

EVER since the night when Tanya had told him of Mark's co
versation with Zelinski—he remembered that it had thrown
wet blanket on his elation over the success of the first self-su
taining chain reaction, initiated only a few days before—S
bastian had been tortured by the endless implications of th
fantastic story.

Of course it wasn't true. But then, why was he so terribly disturbed by it? Over the months it kept festering in his mind. *If*
the German scientists had really decided not to go ahead with
the Monster, then— But each time this thought lifted its head
he would knock it down. The Germans, at the outset at least, in
'38 and '39, had been farther advanced theoretically than the
Americans. It was inconceivable that they would not go ahead.
Of course there was the appalling cost. The terrific drain on
scientific and technical manpower. And the uncertainty. The
big question mark: Would it work? And would it work *in time?*

He thought of Hahn, Heisenberg, all the German colleagues.
Unless Hitler himself somehow had got wind of the possibility
of the Monster, which was most unlikely, the scientists were
quite capable of keeping such knowledge from him. They
would work on rockets, on all sorts of new gadgets that German
ingenuity could contrive. But of course they would very much
hope that the other side would also refrain from developing
what they knew with certainty to be the master weapon: the
absolute weapon. It would be an international conspiracy of
scientists to curb the destructive mania of the rulers on both
sides.

He remembered the revelations that had come after the First
World War—how all through those four years, while hundreds
of thousands of men were being killed and maimed, leading
German and French bankers and industrialists had been in
constant contact, through personal meetings and agents and
correspondence, making arrangements for the supply of this
or that raw material or product that one or the other side
needed, to enable the profitable war to continue; how an agreement was made not to damage the Longwy mines, in the very
heart of the battle zone, because the steel that they produced
was needed by both sides. And he wondered what revelations
would come to light after the present war.

This was sick thinking, and he refused to pursue it. But the
thought of Zelinski's approach would not be dispelled. Who
was Zelinski? What were his connections? A Russian. A White
Russian. But Sebastian seemed to remember something about

his being active in the left-wing scientists' and technicians' union. If there were really a serious anti-Nazi network, if a bona fide effort had been made by the German scientists to get a message through to the Americans, it was most unlikely that they would have chosen Zelinski. And it was inconceivable that they should have stopped with that one approach, through Mark, through Tanya. If it had been serious they would have multiplied their approaches, gone to Gröndahl, to Smithson, to any one of a dozen scientists, even to government agencies.

No. It was obviously a concocted story. But for what purpose? Someone was playing on his well-known humanitarian feelings. But surely no one would suppose him to be so naïve as to give any credence to such a story. Was someone feeling him out? Testing him, to see whether he could be tempted to relax his efforts in the relentless drive to bring the Monster to birth? Or perhaps to lure him into some kind of trap?

He expected that another attempt would be made to approach him through some other channel. Mark was gone, but there was still Tanya. Why had they chosen Tanya? Or was it true, as Tanya had said, that Mark had waited till the last moment for him, and then had told her just before he had to leave? It sounded plausible, but still . . . It wasn't that he didn't believe Tanya, but the Monster had created a gulf between them. There was so much now that he could not tell her, and therefore there was by now so much in her that he no longer understood. And there was nothing he could do about it.

The weeks passed, but they brought no easing of his anxieties. The security people were constantly after him. What did he know about so-and-so? They had just learned that X had been a Communist Party member in Germany—had he known that? . . . Always very polite.

But now Major Gregg's men were beginning to be worried about Soviet espionage. They had had several leads. A British research assistant had left the project area without authorization and had vanished without trace. And at the University, where certain research projects relating to the Monster were going on, involving observations and long-term calculations, there had been irregularities in the employment, movements and activities of some of the personnel. The security people were concerned over attempts being made to unionize research assistants and technical workers. Gregg's people were coming to him more and more frequently. They would pop up unexpectedly, in Schenectady, Cleveland, Pittsburgh, Milwaukee, to drop some item of information, ask for a lead, or simply to pass the time of day.

Sebastian was becoming jittery. In a way it was natural that they should be reporting to him and checking with him. But it was too regular and too insistent. He would steal precious moments from his responsibilities to speculate about the work of these security people who were nowhere and everywhere. When he was traveling, in his long hours on the plane, in the train, riding by car to some new plant located in an out-of-the-way spot, his mind would drift away from the calculation, the report, the pressing problem that it was tackling, and he would wonder what they were after. Zelinski, Zelinski, Zelinski . . . the soft, slippery sibilance of the name was becoming obsessive, sometimes only a faint rhythmic tickling of the mind's ear like the remote *tzig-tzig* of a cicada, at other times a formidable *hiss-click-spit* like the endless pounding echoes of voices heard when going under ether.

Perhaps they knew about Zelinski. Or perhaps they knew about the plot in which Zelinski was involved, without knowing about Zelinski. Perhaps Zelinski was somehow connected not with an anti-Nazi but with a Soviet network, and perhaps, having failed in his approach through Mark, he was, even successfully, making other approaches. If so, was it not Sebastian's duty to report him to the security officers? But if he did, what about Mark? Mark had nothing to do with this, Mark was wholly innocent. Come what might, he must not involve Mark's name in any of this.

One of Gregg's henchmen, a Lieutenant Siracusa, ran into Sebastian late one afternoon in the hallway outside the offices that served as a kind of clearinghouse for some of the administrative business of the Crossroads project in New York, and shuffled his way behind Sebastian into the latter's office.

"Have a seat," Sebastian said. The young lieutenant had given no indication that he had any business to discuss with him.

"Thanks, sir," the lieutenant said, and sat down in one of the leather-upholstered armchairs.

"Cigarette?" Sebastian shook a cigarette forward in the package he held out, lit it for the lieutenant and lit one for himself.

Lieutenant Siracusa had a gentle, sad face and a soft Italian voice, and his feet were bad: fallen arches, or something of the sort. He seemed glad to be sitting down, and he puffed at his cigarette and made no immediate overture.

It was, for Sebastian, one of the rare moments when he could feel almost as satisfied with the work already accomplished as he was overwhelmed by what still lay ahead. Many exciting new things had developed in the last few months, a number of important pieces of research had led to converging results. Parts of the puzzle were beginning to fit together.

"How are things?" he asked, to break the silence.

"Oh, all right, sir. Pretty good. Can't complain." Lieutenant Siracusa gave a shy smile, and his face resumed its look of sadness.

"I suppose you have your busy spells and your slack spells," Sebastian said, to make conversation.

"I guess you could say that, sir, though we usually manage to keep pretty busy. There's always something or other."

"Yes, I know."

Sebastian felt a little foolish. It was perhaps the one thing he really did not know anything about. The police and their ways constituted one mystery that he had no urge to explore.

But what did the lieutenant want? Or did he want anything? Why didn't he talk? Why had he come?

"Is there anything I can do for you?" he asked lamely.

Lieutenant Siracusa slowly blew out a breathful of cigarette smoke through his nose.

"Not unless you have any ideas."

"What kind of ideas?"

"Frankly, Dr. Bloch, we're worried."

Yes, Sebastian said to himself, instantly alert. They've heard something. Perhaps Zelinski has made other approaches, and has mentioned that attempts were being made to get to me.

"Is there anything new?" he asked.

"Nothing that we can put our finger on," said Siracusa. "And that's part of the trouble."

He fell silent again, but then apparently made up his mind that the time had come to speak.

"I'd like to be perfectly frank with you, Dr. Bloch, because I think you can help us. Can help us a lot. The situation, actually, in spite of what I said a moment ago—I wasn't being quite frank with you—is pretty bad. We know for a fact that information about the project is being transmitted to the Soviet Government, is probably being transmitted right now. It's got us really worried."

"I had no idea," said Sebastian.

He did not believe it. It was possible, of course, but it seemed to him unlikely. The security people took it for granted that an American communist's, like any communist's, first loyalty was to the Soviet Union, and that if an opportunity were offered him to transmit information to the Soviet Union he would do it as a matter of course, out of what he would regard as a higher loyalty. There were on the Crossroads project dozens of communists—technically *ex*-communists (since, as a matter of party policy, all members were told to sever official connection with the party on going into the army or war work)—most of them brought in by Sebastian himself, because these were men he himself had trained, and the project needed them. But Sebastian was certain that no communist he knew would, however strong his feeling for the Soviet Union might be, ever entertain the thought of acting as a spy even for the Soviet Union, and even though he might feel it would be a good idea for the Soviet Union to be given access to any scientific information that could benefit the country and help win the war. Political loyalty was one thing, and individual integrity was another. And while the two were perhaps equally important, integrity was the more basic, and without it political loyalty was a mere counter—something that could be assumed or discarded, exchanged or even sold, like a commodity. He might be mistaken about some of the people for whom he had vouched, but he honestly believed them all to be individuals of integrity and had no misgivings about any of them. But Major Gregg's men were worried.

"You can understand our position," the lieutenant went on. "We are responsible for security on this project, which is perhaps the most important single venture our country has ever engaged in. If there is any leak in security, we are responsible. Well, now we know that someone on this project—maybe it's just one person, maybe it's several—is transmitting vital material which is reaching the Soviet Government by one or several channels. You can see how serious the situation is, and why we don't feel very happy about it."

"What have you in mind? Have you anybody in mind? I mean are you doing anything—"

Lieutenant Siracusa's face was still sad and gentle. But Sebastian was thinking that somewhere in this office a microphone was working, and of course the lieutenant knew it.

"We are working along certain lines," Siracusa said. "And this is where we think you can be of some help to us."

All Sebastian's doubts and suspicions of the past weeks and months now became certainties: they knew about Zelinski. They also probably knew that he had tried to approach him. In any case they knew something. He was faced with the choice between voluntarily reporting information that could be of vital importance and seeming to withhold it.

"I don't know that I can be of much help to you," he said.

For the first time in his life he felt himself mentally floundering. Not just caught off his guard as on numerous previous occasions. Not bludgeoned as in those first interviews with Dysell, where he had merely tried—unsuccessfully—to dodge the blows. Now he barely knew what he was doing or saying.

"I've heard about some of these things, of course," he said.

"Yes?" It was merely a polite encouragement to continue.

"I mean some of these attempts or approaches." What was he trying to say? "Let me put it this way: I've heard, it's come to my notice, that someone, perhaps there were several, I'm not sure, but anyway trying to establish—would contacts be the word?—to get information for some anti-Nazi outfit or whatever, but that isn't very clear to me."

"That's the kind of thing," Siracusa said, brightening. "Could you tell me a little more?"

"Not much," Sebastian said. "Perhaps it's not even worth mentioning. But I've heard people have come, both at Valhalla and at several of the scattered laboratories, to sound out some of our people. But nothing has come of it as far as I know, and I should very much doubt—"

"Could you be a little more precise?" The lieutenant's face registered no other emotion than its natural gentle sadness.

"The reason I hesitated to mention it in the first place . . . there is, you see, so little really to go on . . ." He thought of something that would probably do. "I can't mention any names, you will understand, because in the instances that came to my attention nothing came of it, and it would be putting innocent people on the spot, but perhaps it would be helpful for you to know that there were definitely a number of approaches . . ."

"But Dr. Bloch—"

"I can say this, though, and it's the only reason I'm mentioning the thing at all, because it could be a source of trouble. You've heard of a man named Zelinski?"

"Zelinski? I don't seem to recognize it."

"Alexander Zelinski. At least I believe his first name is Alexander. He's an electronics engineer—on a government project too. Radar. I think you would do well to keep an eye on him. He's the source of the trouble. He's been active in organizing the research workers' union that's been making trouble for us. He might be dangerous."

"Zelinski has been making the approaches that you mention?"

"Not directly, no. Through intermediaries."

"Could you give me the names of those intermediaries?"

"I don't think I should."

"But how many were there? Or perhaps I should say *are* there?"

" 'Were' I think is the right word, because this was quite a few months ago, and I haven't heard of anything since."

"How many months ago?"

"I can't be too precise. Perhaps six."

"Six months ago! I wish you had told us at the time."

"Oh, I didn't hear anything about it myself at that time."

"You only heard of it recently?"

"Well, fairly recently."

Lieutenant Siracusa got up, walked with a slow shuffle over to the window, from which a stretch of the Hudson could be seen between two blocks of buildings and through which the thin September sunshine slanted in. He came back slowly to where Sebastian was sitting and rather cavalierly perched himself with one buttock on the corner of the wide oak desk.

"Let's get back to this Zelinski. You said something about an anti-Nazi outfit. Is that his connection? And what kind of an outfit is that?"

"As I have told you, I don't have any of this directly. I don't know. Anti-Nazi is what I was told, but that doesn't seem to make too much sense. You'll probably find Soviet agents behind it."

Lieutenant Siracusa lifted himself from the corner of the desk and went back to the armchair.

"Now what kind of an approach was this? What did they want to find out?"

"That's something—"

I'm not thinking very clearly, Sebastian told himself.

"The reason I didn't take it seriously at first. But I see now I was probably wrong. They didn't actually seem to be looking for anything. They were trying to get people on the project to slow down the work, maybe sabotage it."

Lieutenant Siracusa half rose to his feet, then sat down again.

"That sounds serious as hell. Let's get this straight now. You say these people are trying to sabotage the project?"

"Well, let's not exaggerate anything. This is all pretty vague and indirect. But I think you ought to go after Zelinski."

"I'm trying to get a picture—"

"As I say, I didn't take it seriously at first. But now this seems to me a possibility. We know Soviet agents are working. I've heard about that. They know about the project, and they know something about our commitment. Well, they're using two approaches which may be quite separate. One is to try to get information. The other is to try to slow down our work, so we won't get too far ahead of them. And so they've thought up this idea of spreading word that the German scientists are not working on the Bolt. I must say there's a possibility that this could make some headway, because a lot of our people, you know, for humanitarian reasons and various kinds of scruples, aren't too keen anyway about this thing that we're doing. But these are just thoughts, and I wouldn't—"

"Now let me just try to get this straight. According to your story, there is this man Zelinski, who claims to represent an anti-Nazi group but who is probably a Soviet agent, who is making approaches through intermediaries to people on the project with the aim to slow down and/or sabotage work on the project, and this might be co-ordinated with other approaches to get technical information . . ."

"This all makes it sound more important than it probably is, and I wouldn't—"

"You're damned right it's important, if you'll excuse my language, and I want to know now all you can tell me about these intermediaries. How many are there?"

Sebastian was frantically trying to feel his way out of a maze that did not exist.

"Well, I don't know, there's just one whose name I heard, though there might be others."

"And what is his name?"

"I don't think I should give it to you. I happen to know that his approaches were unsuccessful, and I am quite sure that they were not repeated. I regard him as quite innocent, and he certainly doesn't know anything, so that nothing would be gained by your having his name."

"None of this sounds very innocent to me, and I think you should give us his name."

"I feel very strongly that I shouldn't."

"Do you know this man?"

"He's an acquaintance. I know him well enough to feel pretty sure—"

"Is he a scientist?"

"No. But he's a university man, a teacher, and he has no connection with any of this."

"And where were these approaches made? At Valhalla?"

"No, these that I am speaking about were made at the University laboratory."

"But to project people?"

"To project people."

"Who are now at Valhalla?"

"Yes."

"And how many of your people were approached?"

"I can't say exactly. Three, four, possibly five—not more."

"If you don't know how many there were, how can you be sure they were unsuccessful?"

"Well, of course I can't be absolutely sure, but I think, knowing the man—"

"I do think, Doctor, that it's rather important for you to give us his name . . ."

When the lieutenant finally shuffled out of the office, more than an hour later, Sebastian had still given no other name than Zelinski's. But he was left limp, emptied of all his substance. What had he done?

He tried to reconstruct what had happened. He had woven an elaborate tale out of whole cloth. But why? He continued to sit at his desk, quite still, smoking cigarette after cigarette. The only certain fact in this whole tangle was that Zelinski had tried to get at him. Mark's role was of no consequence. But Zelinski was not acting independently. There was someone behind him. And this "someone" had a malevolent purpose, aimed either at himself or at the project. He had been right to warn Siracusa against Zelinski. Except that he should have done it long ago. Why hadn't he? It hadn't seemed urgent or dangerous, for one thing. And it hadn't occurred to him that the security people might somehow have wind of it. Nor did he want to involve Mark. But perhaps more fundamental was the tormenting thought that the German scientists *might* not be working on the Monster.

Inside, he felt a weariness that was beyond any fatigue of the body, of the mind, beyond anything he had ever experienced or imagined possible: an utter weariness of the soul.

But perhaps this would be the end of the matter. And he had, at least, been able to keep Mark's name out of it.

Chapter 20

INSIDE the cafeteria on the corner of Thales and Lucretius, facing the one square of some spaciousness up here on the windswept peak of Valhalla, Bruce Patterson and Fritz Leutner were having coffee. The temperature, even now in October, was subzero. There had been a flurry of snow during the night and the frozen flakes, like tiny fluffed-up hailstones, were being blown against the windowpanes. It was the afternoon hour when all the Britishers, from the laboratories, from the offices, from the shops, were having their tea, but there were many others too, civilians and officers.

"So this afternoon we saved about 1,478 years of work for

some twenty expert mathematicians," Bruce said. "That is, assuming none of them made any errors." They were discussing a new computing machine into which Sebastian had introduced a feature that made it adaptable for some of the essential calculations that they were making.

"They might of c-c-course d-d-die, t-too," Fritz suggested, "somewhere along the way."

"Let's not talk about that."

They were sitting next to one of the windows which were all fogged up from condensation, and they both mechanically kept swiping clean with their hands an area through which they could look out. The scene, at best, was uninviting to the eye. One expert Valhalla had never had was a city planner. Dark figures huddled against the weather moved briskly along the walks.

"We still won't make it," Fritz said.

"No," said Bruce.

"There is of c-c-course the P-P-Pacific."

"Yes." Bruce was working at the moment on the weight of *mu* mesons, and he thought of Yukawa, marveling again at the insight that had made him posit mesons to explain the binding force between nucleons and the process of *beta* radioactivity. "Germany will certainly be knocked out a good bit before we pin his first diapers on the Bolt baby."

Through his thick glasses Fritz's drooping eyes gave Bruce a mute look of agreement.

Bruce cast a quick glance about him and lowered his voice. "And very possibly Japan too. Then what?"

This was not defeatist but realistic talk among the scientists, but it was indulged in only cautiously, among those who knew one another well. The "Monster," as Sebastian called it, was a monstrosity, and, they had been told, the only excuse for making it was to win the war. But what if the war were won without it?

Fritz shrugged his shoulders. "My hunch," he said, "is that the Germans haven't g-g-got it, and haven't even b-been working on it."

"That's the way it looks to me. Otherwise—"

"There g-g-g-goes Sebastian," Fritz broke in, pointing toward the window.

The tall, hunched figure was unmistakable, though the hat was pulled almost down to the turned-up overcoat collar, hiding the face. The characteristic angularity of his movements was accentuated, perhaps by the effort to keep his balance in the wind. Bruce and Fritz's frantic gestures against the two clear spaces in the window apparently caught his eye, and he changed his course to head into the cafeteria entrance.

There was a perceptible change of pitch in the hum that rose from the conversations of the several dozen people in the big room as Sebastian approached the table at which Fritz and Bruce were sitting.

"I was just looking for you," he said to Fritz immediately upon greeting the two of them, and proceeded to pump Fritz on a problem he was working on.

"Sit down," Bruce said after a few moments.

"No, I have to be moving along," Sebastian replied. But he paused for a moment to look at his two favorite students, and his haggard face shone with a glint of his old affection.

"We hardly ever see you," Bruce said.

"I know." Sebastian shook his head. "It isn't what I would wish. But this is not a time when we could meet as we should like to meet, and say what is in our minds—or even what is in our hearts." He shook his head again, and a sad smile came over his face. "I think it's better this way."

"I don't agree," Bruce said. His tone was vehement, though he kept his voice low. "This more than ever is a time when there should be a full exchange of views on basic questions of principle."

"You have your discussion groups—"

"It's not enough, and it isn't what I mean. I'm talking about fundamentals. Major decisions have to be made, and no one— *no one*—is qualified to make them alone."

Sebastian's face darkened. "The major decisions are out of our hands."

"Not those in which we are directly involved. This is a crucial moment. What the scientists, *as* scientists, do today will be decisive for the role of science for a long time to come."

"We are making the Monster. There is no other immediate issue."

"If we win the war without it, if we find that the Germans—"

"This is political talk," Sebastian said hotly, "and we've ruled that out!"

"Man," Bruce answered gently, "is a political animal."

Sebastian's face went white with anger.

"We're not men!" he said, and left.

Bruce and Fritz looked at each other. They did not need words to communicate to each other what they felt.

Chapter 21

INSTEAD of being the end of the matter, it had been only the beginning. Lieutenant Siracusa had buttonholed Sebastian the very next day, in a half-lighted corridor in Washington, between two conferences.

"I'm sorry, Doctor," he had said, without preliminaries— he was short and he had to bend his head back to look straight at him—"I had to report our little conversation of yesterday to headquarters—line of duty, you understand—and I've been ordered to get the name of that intermediary you mentioned from you."

Sebastian had managed to shake him off, but they had been after him ever since. Week after week, sometimes at intervals of only two or three days, one of Gregg's men would turn up— in Chicago, in town, at the University, in New York, in San Francisco, at Valhalla, sometimes at an out-of-the-way railroad station (Sebastian had been ordered now to travel only by train). Always polite, always deferential, they did not ask him for the name of the intermediary most of the time, but he would be harried by questions on this, that or the other of his former students or associates. Was so-and-so a communist? Had he been a communist? What were, and had been, his associations? Did he know such and such a one? The agent would sigh, and explain the tremendous difficulty the service was having in tracking down this unknown man, would speak in veiled terms of the threats to the security of the project, of the constant fear of sabotage, of suspicions of leaks, of how enormously useful it would be if Sebastian could see his way clear . . . Surveillance was redoubled. Instead of spot-checking correspondence and telephone calls in and out of Valhalla, all wire communication was now monitored, all missives censored. An increasing nervousness made itself felt, accentuated by the fact that some essential aspects of the Bolt research had just been successfully completed, and that plans were moving ahead to begin practical production within six months' time.

Sebastian was becoming alarmed at the proportions the whole thing was assuming. He kept harping back to Zelinski, but none of them seemed interested in discussing Zelinski. Zelinski, if he were questioned, would no doubt make no difficulty about mentioning Mark's name, especially as Zelinski knew that he had got nowhere with him. The fact that they showed no interest in Zelinski was very puzzling. He was, after all, the key man through whom all the channels might lead. But while Sebastian continued to mention him, he never asked them whether they had checked on him. Some instinct told him to leave it alone. Was it because he was afraid it might show too great interest, or suggest to them that he knew more than he was admitting?

Gone now was all peace of mind. There was never a moment when he could feel free and relaxed, when he could forget the menacing cloud hanging over him. Perhaps this afternoon, perhaps tomorrow morning, he would run into one of them again, and this time they would have something on him, something they would be able to pressure him with. The molehill of his innocent little invention—he had merely wanted, on the one hand, to co-operate with the security police, and on the other to protect his friend Mark—had by now become a mountain. If he had simply reported the incident, exactly as it had happened, immediately after it had happened, no one would have been hurt—except possibly Zelinski, but he in any case *should* be under observation. Now dozens, scores of agents all over the country were tracking down every clue in a desperate effort to ascertain the identity of a mysterious intermediary who actually did not exist. For if the three or four or five scientists who had allegedly been approached did not exist, neither did the one who had allegedly approached them. Zelinski, on the other hand, and Mark Ampter and Sebastian himself undeniably did exist. And between the fiction and the reality there was a certain connection that was sheer invention, the product of his imagination. The problem now was to keep them apart, to prevent their ever blending and becoming inseparable and indistinguishable. And for this reason, if for none other, he must not mention Mark's name. What would originally have been so easy had by now become impossible. For if he were now to mention Mark's name he would also have to reveal his whole invention, and this would strain their already strong suspicion of him beyond the tolerance point.

When his thinking brought him back again and again to this realization, he would feel himself being invaded by an icy sweat, and seized with a trembling of his knees and elbows. He had taken upon himself the responsibility of becoming the Monster's keeper, because once unleashed, it could devastate the world, it could annihilate mankind; and he felt compelled, as a scientist and as a man, to sacrifice himself if necessary—and it *would* be necessary—in order to safeguard it against misuse. Already he had paid fearfully, told lies without number, betrayed friends, comrades, even people he hardly knew.

But Mark at least he must not touch—Mark, whom he had come to love like a brother, who was as close to him in his way as Tanya and Gino were in theirs. And the very thought of the menace in all this left him weak and greensick.

The secret vice of his position was that in spite of all the sacrifices of principle that he had been forced into, they still did not trust him. The more than generous co-operativeness he had shown all these months was now all but wiped out by this Zelinski complication: a matter, he was convinced, that was absolutely trivial and without consequence. And it was essential that they should trust him. He would have to give them more assurances. But how? And at the same time he must keep his objectivity, as well as his idealism.

Yet even in the midst of this soul torment, new perspectives were being opened to him. From his present point of vantage many things, though they were surely not changed in themselves, had a different appearance and assumed different proportions. Before the war he had been with the "little people," he had been one of them, working with them, united with them in their effort to shape events. What had been the harvest of those years? The vast movement of millions of people throughout the world who had worked and suffered and bled in the struggle against fascism and war had produced only bitterness and failure.

His heart remained with the people. But he saw now that the effective means of realizing their aspirations lay not in the futile attempt to bring their numbers to bear on a program of reform or revolution, but in the manipulation of the men at the controls.

It had been borne in upon him, again and again, in his conversations with industrial leaders, that it was not too early to think about the shape of the postwar world. The problem to which more and more of them were giving their attention was put sharply one evening in an after-dinner discussion among the guests of his host, Samuel Wainbridge, the steel magnate, at whose house in Harrisburg he was spending the night. The small group gathered around the fire in the library included an Air Force general, a bishop, a high State Department official, the president of one of New York's largest investment trusts, a utility corporation executive, and one or two others. It was Wainbridge himself who stated the problem in its acutest form.

"I sometimes shudder," he said, "when I think of what the

postwar situation is going to be like. All these years we've been living rather comfortably behind the ramparts of Germany and Italy in Europe, and Japan in Asia. They were countries we could do business with. Hitler and Mussolini and Hirohito formed a powerful barrier to hold Stalin and world communism in check. And here we are in the process of destroying our most effective defenses against communism. We could have got along with them. Something went wrong with our calculations. Now we're going to have to think up something that will be absolutely foolproof. And I have a feeling that our friend Sebastian, whom I once, I am sorry to say, seriously misjudged, may be able to come up with the answer."

It was shortly after this that Sebastian was visited, by appointment in his office, by Captain Sanders and Lieutenant Siracusa.

Something about their expression, their manner, told him instantly that this was not a usual visit. When they left, nearly three hours later, he had not given them the name they were after, and his impression was that in the course of the interview he had not dropped much additional ballast; nevertheless, when they walked out after observing all the civilities and making many apologies for inconveniencing him, he somehow had the conviction that it had been a fateful interview—that, had he been willing or able, he might have turned the tide, salvaged something precious and irreplaceable; but that, having done nothing, this thing was now irretrievably lost.

Chapter 22

TANYA was studying herself—as much of herself as she could see—in the mirror above the washstand in the bathroom, by the light of the bare bulb in the wall socket above it, trying to decide whether she looked as worn as she felt, or whether she felt as worn as she looked. "You're thirty-one," she told her reflection. Her reflection frowned, proffering no consoling rejoinder. The dark mass of her hair, which she now washed herself, had become unruly and was a little lusterless, and her skin was dry, perhaps from the mountain water and the air at this altitude. There *was* a beauty parlor up here on the Knoll, but you had to make appointments several days ahead, and she really had no time for it. With her three hours of nursery school supervising every morning and four hours of volunteer office work every afternoon, taking care of Gino, cooking meals, keeping the house clean and tidy, she had her hands full. There was no piano on Valhalla, and even if she had had one she would have had little opportunity to play. But it was the thing she missed most, of all the things that had composed the furniture of her life.

However, it wasn't the hard work, she reflected as she began brushing her hair, nor the harsh climate, that accounted for the dullness, the impression of lifelessness that her face seemed to her to convey. Sometimes she had the idea that it actually showed in her face when she hadn't been made love to for weeks—months it was even, sometimes. Some women seemed to be able to get along without it indefinitely, but she was the kind that needed it—not just the physical thing, but the warmth, the tenderness, the climate of love. It was this that she missed so terribly. This, and a sense of security in the being on whom she leaned.

She proceeded to brush her teeth, to cream her face and to perform the other little rituals preparatory to going to bed. But tonight at least she must banish all somber thoughts from her mind. For tonight she had coaxed Sebastian into promising to come to her bed. Where there was love there was life, and where there was life there was hope.

He had been sleeping so little in the last months that he now almost always spent the night in the other room. He had been for so long distant and aloof—unapproachable. She understood how his terrible responsibilities must weigh on him. But she felt that it was essential that he get some relief from the inhuman pressure. For months she had been thinking that if she could only come close to him once more as she had in the beginning, perhaps a miracle might happen again, as it had then. When they had met it had been love of a sort, and it had been fun, but it had not been a thing fated to last. It had only been when he discovered, when she told him, that she was pregnant that the miracle had happened. It had to do with creating life, with her becoming a mother, with probably other things besides. But it had transformed him, his love had blossomed into something deep and rich, his whole approach to life and to people had undergone a metamorphosis. Couldn't something like it happen again?

So, among the preparations that she would ordinarily make for such an occasion, there was one that she was careful to omit.

He came to her in the dark, after she had turned out the light, and she first became aware of him as a shivering presence in the bed. She reached her hand over and felt an icy chest, an icy shoulder. The contact with hard bone covered with cold, clammy skin bristling with hairs was, for a second, repulsive; but just as suddenly her whole being overflowed with an aching tenderness for this frail, vulnerable being—a mere skeleton covered with skin and hair, yet possessing a heart and a sensibility more precious to her than all the universe, and a mind whose scope was infinitely beyond her measure. She pressed herself against him, enveloped him with her woman-flesh, ashamed of the fullness and the firmness of the matter that composed her body, of the sheath of muscle and tissue that clothed her bones, and at the same time happy to have the curves and the hollows, the softness and the smoothness to cushion and to blanket him.

He was taller than she, but though he had once been forty pounds heavier he now weighed considerably less than she did, and here in bed, in the dark, in the cocoon of the sheets and blankets, he felt to her so small and frail and insubstantial that it was almost like clasping a naked, undernourished little waif to her bosom.

Gradually the heat of her body communicated itself to him, and she felt his hands on her, exploring her. He had a way of running them over her contours as though, out of shapeless clay, he were molding her into a divinely beautiful woman. He made her *feel* her own beauty and invested it with a value that enabled her to enjoy it without vanity. His hands, big and ungainly to look at, had authority and knew exactly what to do with her.

He had taken over now and she merely had to let herself be done to. In a kind of half swoon she found herself carried by him into that realm of enchantment that was in so many ways akin to music. But this time, for the first time, in and out of the pattern of movement, of tactile thrill, of the outwardly radiating pulsations of desire and assuagement, she was conscious of the motif of a little life asserting itself, making its bid for recognition. And that little being, trembling on the threshold of existence, invested this moment with a gravity and a joy that she had never yet experienced.

In a great surge of emotion into which her whole being seemed to fling itself, her youth, her beauty, her tenderness, her hope, her faith, all fused into one burning offering, she felt herself being lifted to the very peak of surrender, not only of the flesh but of the spirit; undergoing the ultimate transfiguration in which the death of two individuals is but the prelude to the resurrection of the couple.

And just at that moment something happened.

"No," he whispered, gasping, spent, his too-light, bony, clammy weight upon her. "This wouldn't be a good time."

He fell back on the bed and she felt him shivering again, but not from cold this time.

There would not be a new life. There would be no miracle.

Chapter 23

GREGG, sitting at his desk in his office at security headquarters, glanced at his watch. Four o'clock. Bloch would be arriving shortly.

In his capacity as chief security officer of Valhalla, he had sent a message to Dr. Sebastian Bloch early in December—just when the invasion of the Gilbert Islands in the Pacific was assuming the proportions of a large-scale operation—requesting that he come to see him in his office at his earliest convenience. In so doing he was, strictly speaking, overstepping his authority, for, among the military personnel, only General Sproncke had the right to invite the Chief Co-ordinator to displace himself for official purposes. But he knew that Bloch would come, that he would not make an issue of the minor breach.

This was Gregg's show, even though it was in a sense dictated by pressure from above. Dr. Gröndahl had hinted several times in the past few months that he didn't want Bloch to be unnecessarily annoyed. Now he had virtually ordered Gregg to lay off him. "The harassment you're subjecting him to is interfering with his work," he had said sternly. "It's got to stop." And Gregg had decided that the time had come for him to take Bloch in hand personally.

He felt a kind of excitement. He had been looking forward to this moment for a long time. Five years. Now it had come.

He was not nervous. He knew how it would go. The hard work had already been done; this was just the finishing touch. Dr. Bloch would walk out of this office a free man, all right. But he wouldn't be the same man who had walked in. He would have given away something that he would later discover it was disastrous not to have kept.

Dr. Bloch was announced. The door was opened by an orderly, and the Wizard of Valhalla, as he was often called by the military detachment, came into the office.

Although Gregg had not specifically planned his manner of reception, he found himself rising to his feet as Bloch entered and going around his desk to meet him. Bloch did not take his proffered hand, but the sequence of their movements was such that Gregg could not tell whether the slight was deliberate or accidental.

"Please sit down, Dr. Bloch," he said, pointing to a folding steel-frame and canvas armchair.

Over the past five years Gregg had spent many hours looking at photographs of Sebastian Bloch, trying to probe the mystery of the personality that they represented, wondering what the man himself really looked like in the flesh. Now, though he had had several brief glimpses of him in the past few months, he had him before him really for the first time.

His first impression was not what he had expected. Every feature was exactly as it had engraved itself in his memory, but life gave it a value that completely altered it. He was sure now that he would not have recognized him in a crowd. And if he had met him in a crowd he would have been drawn to him. But that would have been wrong, he told himself.

He had heard much about the power that this man's personality exerted, and he had laughed at it. But now already he himself felt it and had to steel himself against it.

"I'm sorry to have disturbed you, Dr. Bloch," he said, "and to have taken you away from the invaluable work you're doing, but it seemed rather important at this time that you and I have a heart-to-heart talk."

Bloch reached into his pocket and pulled out a package of cigarettes. Gregg pushed an ash tray on his desk in his direction, and declined the cigarette Bloch offered him.

He watched him pull out a cigarette, put it between his lips, light it deftly with a battered but efficient silver lighter. He noticed the brown tips of his fingers, particularly of the right hand. Between two and three packs a day, probably. The man was terribly emaciated. Living entirely on his nerves. He was forty-three, forty-four; but he looked sixty. Hair almost white, face deeply seamed, dark hollows around the eyes, and a generally ravaged look, like a piece of sculpture dug up after many centuries and showing the mark of time—but not only of time.

He looked up at Gregg and smiled, a disarming smile. "I'm afraid I've given your people a pretty bad time," he said.

"On the contrary, Doctor," Gregg said. "I must express my regrets for all the trouble we've put you to." He gave a smile that he meant to be reassuring. "Your own orders, you know. And the protection of the project. But," he went on, straightening in his chair, "I must also apologize for my men, who haven't always treated you with the consideration you have a right to expect. They're rather new at this, most of them, I hope you realize and—well, I guess they take their work pretty seriously, and I'm sure they mean well."

"Yes, I'm quite sure of that."

"This whole problem of security," Gregg said. "I'd like to just give my views on the matter, and perhaps you might have some ideas—"

"I'm at your disposal," Bloch said. "I understand the importance of the work you're doing, and I'd like to be of whatever help I can."

"That's just the way I hoped you'd feel about it, Doctor. I feel that if we have your confidence, as you have ours, it will make everything easier all round. Now here's the thing. I have the responsibility for the good behavior—from the security point of view, you understand—of several thousand, I don't even know how many, anyway several thousand, individuals; not just here, but scattered all over the country. Statistically, only a tiny percentage of these could conceivably give us any real trouble. But because we have to assume the people on the other side are at least as smart as we are, chances are that trouble will start in the most unlikely places. That is one thing, and it explains why, from a statistical point of view, any security organization is necessarily top-heavy. You have ten men to do the job that one man could—*if* you knew exactly what the job was."

Gregg knew he was doing a lot of talking, and that it was way off the point, but he knew exactly what he was doing. He was watching for Bloch's reactions. But Bloch wasn't showing any reactions. He had good control. And he probably knew that this conversation might somehow be decisive.

"Now the other thing is this," Gregg continued. "Important as security is, it isn't *the* most important thing . . ."

"I'm not sure I'd agree with that," put in Bloch.

"Wait a minute. What I was going on to say is this. The *most* important thing is, after all, for you to carry out your assignment and produce the thing you're working on. As a matter of fact, our point of view now on the situation is that if getting the job done by a certain date meant the leakage of vital information to a foreign power, and preventing such leakage meant an appreciable delay in getting the job done, our directive is to choose the former course."

For the first time Bloch registered a reaction, a strong one. His sharp features became sharper, and his eyes shone with an increased intensity.

"That I think is very wrong," he said with feeling. "You are mixing up two things that should be kept absolutely separate. The project must go ahead full steam. That is one thing. And security must be one hundred per cent. That is the other. And neither must be sacrificed to the slightest extent because of the other."

"I'm glad to hear you say that. But while I agree with you theoretically, there are unfortunately practical difficulties. This is one of the things I want to discuss with you. Our point of view is that since our primary objective is to get the project completed, if this involves taking some risks—well, we have to take those risks. We've given this matter a good deal of thought and we've come to the decision that these people who are essential to the project, we can't keep them off it even if we know they're communists or pro-Nazis or no matter what, as long as they're valuable to the project."

"I don't agree with that," said Bloch. "I think it's leaving the door too wide open."

"Would you say that because a man was once a communist he would necessarily be dangerous or unreliable today?"

"Not necessarily. But you would want to make pretty sure that he no longer had any commitments or attachments, and that he had thoroughly revised his thinking."

"Well, that is of course the way we'd like it, but we don't after all have much choice."

"The way I look at it, if a man is a communist he is bound to have a divided loyalty. He thereby becomes unreliable, and therefore dangerous."

"Yes," said Gregg.

Everything was going very smoothly. Even more smoothly than he had anticipated. Bloch was bright. He had learned fast. He knew what he was doing, too, and he was playing for high stakes. But he had made one tiny slip, and it was going to trip him up. Gregg felt sorry for him. It wasn't pleasant to see a man of his stature reduced to his present role. But Gregg had his duty to perform.

"What we're faced with," he said, "is this enormous sprawling project with thousands of people we don't know much about. Of these we know, or have a pretty fair guess, that several hundred are or were communists. We can't, we don't want to, weed most of them out. We need them. But we want to know who they are and where they are, and we want to watch them. This is only part of our problem, but it is the acutest one and the one that I'm interested in today. And I want to accentuate the gravity of this problem by telling you that we know that information is going from here to the Soviet Union via a regular channel right now, and that we're making desperate efforts to track it down."

Gregg had raised his voice somewhat and assumed a note of mild intimidation, but he felt that this was all that would be necessary. He passed his forefinger between his neck and his olive-drab shirt collar which were quite dry. "Excuse me, Doc-

tor, for getting all hot and bothered. But I think you can understand our concern."

"Of course, Major." It was the first time Bloch had addressed
him by his rank. He could of course not know that his promotion to lieutenant colonel had just been approved, though it
would become official only in another ten days.

"Now, Doctor, I hate to bother you with this sort of thing,
and I know you've already given us some of this, but I wonder
if we can't have, first of all, the names of all the people you have
known more or less closely whom you know to have been or believe to have been members of the Communist Party."

Bloch, who was chain-smoking and was now lighting his
fifth, looked pained, but made no protest.

"Well," he said, "there is of course my wife."

"All right, let's leave her aside."

Bloch went through a dozen names. Gregg had them all.

"That is incomplete," Bloch said, after thinking of one or
two more. "You can suggest some names."

Gregg ran off a score or more of names. Bloch's answers
seemed pretty straight, though they didn't always tally with
statements he had made about the same people before. Gregg
went through the names of Baum, Vorontov, Daisy Radcliffe,
William Parrish, Jane Middleton, and other party officials.
Bloch admitted having met them, at more or less public gatherings, but of course made no mention of discussing party problems with them in the closed unit meetings that Ampter had
described in his reports.

Then Gregg went down the list of Bloch's students: Fritz
Leutner ("Yes") . . . "And what about Mrs. Leutner?" "I
would imagine so." . . . Bruce Patterson ("Yes"), Hans
Weber, Ed MacAvoy, Hsueh Ling, Bert Musing, Roos, Levitt,
Breuer, Hendrickson . . . faculty members . . .

"How about Mark Ampter?"

"Is he a member of the party?"

"I don't know," said Gregg. "I'm asking you."

"He's an economist, and he's in the army now. I know him

well. He's quite a left-winger, he could very well be a member."

Gregg continued probing. There was a lot of ground to cover, and he wanted to cover it all—all the main points. Dr. Gröndahl or no Dr. Gröndahl, this would probably be the last interrogation of Dr. Bloch for some time to come. Once he had what he wanted, Gregg was going to leave him alone.

"Now what about yourself, Dr. Bloch, were you ever a member of the Communist Party?"

"No."

A year ago, or even six months ago, Gregg would not have dared to ask this question. He would have been afraid of getting a truthful answer which might have created complications. He had given his men strict orders not to raise it. But now he had the right answer, the useful answer. He might not ever use it, but it was there for him to use.

"You were pretty close to it, would you say?"

"I suppose you could say that." Bloch gave a kind of inward smile. "I've always put a lot of passion into the things I went in for. I guess I put quite a bit of passion into that too, during the short time I was interested."

"And this interest of yours lasted—how long, would you say?"

"Oh, it was quite short. The Nazi-Soviet pact brought me back to my senses."

"That was August 1939. And after that your interest cooled?"

"Definitely."

"Coming back to what we were talking about earlier—our main worry is all these people on the project who *might* be members and whom we really don't know anything about. They're of course the people whom we regard as most vulnerable to the kind of approaches that are giving us trouble. Now I want to know if you are close enough to members of the party to be able to get any information from them?"

"What kind of information?"

"We want to know about the people on the project who are or were party members."

Here Gregg anticipated that he would run into trouble. This was asking for more than he had a right to expect.

Bloch hesitated only a moment.

"It would have to be on a quite informal basis."

"Naturally, we wouldn't want to embarrass you."

"This sort of thing isn't exactly up my alley."

"I understand that," Gregg said. "But you would be willing to give us such information?"

"I don't know that I could find out much. I could get a certain amount of information."

"I hate to bother you with this sort of thing . . ."

Gregg pursued his probing for another hour or so. This was a moment he had looked forward to for so long, he was savoring it, and he was reluctant to let go of it. This man who was playing into his hands, who had walked into the carefully prepared trap, was one of the world's great geniuses. The gods had endowed him with all the gifts that it was theirs to bestow. He was one of the elect. In intelligence, in imagination, in sensibility, he was supreme. And with this he was gentle, selfless, inspired by a deep love of mankind. The stuff that saints and martyrs were made of.

Yet he was dangerous.

Why? "He's big, and he wants to be bigger," Gregg had said to Murdock. But what was the secret of that compulsion? Gregg was no nearer to an answer. With all his policeman's instincts, his knowledge of human nature, he knew that he was right. But the mystery still eluded him.

He looked at Sebastian Bloch sitting there within a few feet of him. He was really quite extraordinary to look at; he looked both unreal and more real than life. He could be a reincarnation of some holy man out of a remote century. All his features seemed to be endowed with a more than human quality; the eyes were the eyes of a creature who saw *more* than mortals could see, the lips were those of one whose words had a deeper meaning than any spoken by men. And who could tell what visions haunted the brain within that nobly proportioned skull? In the whole cast of the features there was a brooding tenderness, a compassion, an invitation to grace that even Gregg found hard to resist. Now, at least, he understood how Ampter had succumbed to the man's influence. He understood the love, the devotion, he inspired in his students, his sway over men, the authority he commanded.

Gregg glanced at his watch.

It was time to move in for the kill.

"We have our troubles," he said. "And I wouldn't be bothering you with them except for the fact that you seem to know something which it is our business to know and which you're keeping from us."

Bloch looked up nervously. "What do you mean?"

"Let me come back to what we've been talking about, essentially, right along. Espionage. It exists. We're trying to track down the channels. We have reason to believe that you yourself were felt out, not actually about passing information but about making some sort of contacts."

"You've heard this?"

"I'm not going to make it any more precise. Is it true or isn't it?"

"If such an approach was made, I certainly wasn't aware of it."

"All right." Gregg folded his hands and leaned forward with his elbows on his desk. "Dr. Bloch, you've been most co-operative, and I want to thank you for your understanding of our problems, and for the good will you've shown in meeting us more than halfway. Now I have just one last question to ask you, and you will realize in the light of all we've been saying that it's the most important of all."

He looked straight at Bloch, his face expressionless.

"I want you to give me the name of that intermediary. You know who I mean."

The hand holding the cigarette began to tremble slightly. But by a great effort Bloch controlled himself, brought the cigarette to his lips and took a drag.

From all the island bases, including Mark's, army and marine troops were being embarked. Their destination was Okinawa, 350 miles south of Tokyo. The sea swarmed with hundreds of ships, all converging on the Ryukyus, and clouds of planes formed a protective umbrella overhead. For over a week the Fast Carrier Force had carried out a systematic pre-assault bombing of the seventy-mile-long island. The isles of Kerama Retto, just to the west, were seized in late March, and the landing on the west coast of Okinawa began on April 1st.

By now, Mark was what was called a "seasoned fighter." It was nearly two years since he had fought his first campaign, in New Guinea. That time he had merely come down with dengue fever in the jungle swamps of Lae. But in Makin, in November of '43, he had suffered a deep knife wound in the shoulder in the hand-to-hand fighting. He had come through Eniwetok unscathed the following spring. Then on July 4th of that year, in the fighting on Saipan, he had been hit in the head by a revetment beam flung up by an exploding land mine, and been laid up for months with a brain concussion. On Palau, last fall, he had had his left thigh ripped open by a shell fragment.

But the seasoning of a soldier meant more than just accumulating wounds. It meant, Mark had come to think in the rare moments when it was still possible for him to think, a kind of dehumanization, the transforming of a man into a machine: a machine for killing. The mind and the emotions were anesthetized. The body obeyed the orders that were given to it, and everything beyond the immediate present was blotted out.

His outfit was put ashore several days after the initial landings on Okinawa. A solid beachhead had been established against little opposition, and the airfields at Yontan and Kadena had been captured. Day after day tens of thousands of troops were put ashore. Soon they numbered between two and three hundred thousand. Marine fighters, based on Yontan airfield, gave air support to the ground forces while offshore the fleet was subjected to devastating raids as wave upon wave of kamikaze planes from Home Island bases came over in an attempt to break the vital life line supplying the invasion forces. Bakas carrying more than a ton of explosive in their warheads, slung beneath medium bombers and directed in their rocket-assisted dive to the target by suicide pilots, struck ship after ship.

From the landing beaches the Marines swung north while the major force, including Mark's division, drove south toward Naha. Here after a short advance they encountered heavy opposition, and the battle settled down to a slow and deadly slugging contest.

During a break when fresh replacements were being brought up, the news came of the German surrender in Europe.

It was good news. It was wonderful news. It meant that the war was half won. But it was the other half, and it didn't immediately affect the half that was being fought desperately here in Okinawa.

The news, however, struck Mark in an odd way. He had the impression that it ought to remind him of something. What was it?

He ransacked his memory. What could it be? Germany. Surrender. End of war in Europe. Then it came to him. Zelinski: his story about the German scientists having decided not to make the Weapon.

It certainly seemed that the Germans hadn't used the Weapon, whatever it was. Perhaps they hadn't even tried to make it. Perhaps Zelinski's story had been true! But then it was also possible that Sebastian, if he had heard the story from Tanya or from some other source, had believed it, and that the Americans also had decided not to make the Weapon.

How many times, during this seemingly endless season of carnage, he had thought about the "gadget" that he knew Sebastian was working on! When he felt most desperate, when everything looked blackest, when death was right at his shoulder, he would suddenly remember that Sebastian, together with the country's top scientists, was devoting every ounce of his energies, dedicating all his genius, to the turning out of an invention that would bring the war to an end. Perhaps to-morrow? The very thought of this had tided him over his worst moments.

Now suddenly the idea that the "gadget" would *not* be forthcoming after all struck him like a blow, and produced in him a creepy feeling of panic. Like all soldiers, he had become superstitious. He realized that the knowledge that Sebastian was working away at his "gadget" had been for him, all these months, a talisman. Deep in his guts there came over him now a fear of a new kind which quite unnerved him. He became aware, as he had never been before, of the terrible fragility of flesh, blood, bone and nerve, of the substance that composed his being.

His company was ordered up to the front again. He was put in charge of his squad as acting sergeant—their sergeant had been wounded.

The terrain in which the assault troops were now hacking their way forward was rugged, with many cliffs and natural and man-made limestone and coral caves that were well de-fended and full of traps. The enemy had good fire power and plenty of ammunition, and knew how to use it. Backed up against the Shuri stronghold, they poured a steady rain of death on the invaders from Spigot mortars and 250-mm. mor-tars, and fired aerial bombs and large-sized rockets.

Just a week after the end of the war in Europe, he was war-ily leading his men into a shallow cave that they thought had been cleaned out. Nothing stirred in the semidarkness. Three dead Japs lay crumpled beyond their knocked-out machine gun.

He took a step forward. There was a violent flash and a deaf-ening explosion, and for a fraction of a second he was conscious of a sharp, unbearable wrench in his belly. And then every-thing went blank.

By the time Acting Sgt. Ampter was brought back to the field hospital he was more dead than alive. He had lost a tre-mendous amount of blood from an ugly abdominal wound, and he had bad body and leg burns. One of the doctors lifted his hands with a look of helplessness. The other said, "Let's try anyway."

He was given an emergency blood transfusion and a temporary patch job. The response of the organism was sufficiently positive to warrant flying the patient back to Hawaii. It was that or curtains.

The medical officer in charge of the ambulance plane glanced at Acting Sgt. Ampter's chart. "Any chance of his pulling through?" he said.

The doctor who had come with the hospital truck shook his head.

"One in ten," he said.

Chapter 25

Sebastian's gaze, moving down the length of the highly polished conference table, was caught by the big round steel ash trays placed at regular intervals on its surface. They were precision-tooled machine parts, made to micron specifications to serve a vital function in a complicated assembly. Some fairy decorator, in an access of virile inspiration, had had the idea that they would make cute ash trays. One of the peripheral mice that were always gnawing at the outer fringes of his mind now worried the idea that a dominant trend in contemporary interior decorating, which the war seemed particularly to have accentuated, was to make things look like what they were not, to manipulate the data of space, color, texture and light for purposes of deception, to use elements to ends for which they were not intended or appropriate.

He shifted his position. The pain in his spine had become almost unremitting in the past months. Was that what they were all doing? He thought of the Monster. Was it inevitable that the energy that constituted its fabulous secret should manifest itself first for the purpose of destruction rather than as a force tamed for the constructive uses of man?

Each flanged steel disk was piled high with ashes and butts: an image of futility and desolation. The smoke that at the beginning of the conference had risen buoyantly to the high paneled ceiling had now settled heavily, oppressively, like a tule fog, around the generals and technical advisers and secretarial assistants.

"Let me summarize the position this way," said General Van Nuys, addressing himself to Sebastian. He was a man of big bones, on which the old flesh hung loosely. "Our directive up to this point has been a double one: A, to deliver the Bolt at the earliest possible date in order to win the race against the German scientists; B, to deliver the Bolt at the earliest possible date in order to assure our victory. It appears now that whatever progress the Germans may have made on the thing, they aren't going to get it in time. And, barring the unlikely possibility of a surprise" (Sebastian smiled to himself.) "—and we'll know about that in a matter of weeks—our victory is no longer in doubt. Our present directive therefore is to deliver the Bolt at the earliest possible date, in order to shorten the war in the Pacific and to save lives. In our view, this directive is no less compelling than the first. Now, Dr. Bloch, in the light of all that has been said around this table, what are the prospects for early delivery?"

General Sproncke stirred in his chair. Ephraim Sproncke— Eph, he was called by his intimates—had a full, fleshy face with pouting lips, pale blue watery eyes and wavy silver-gray hair.

"I'd like to answer that in part, if I may," he said. When he spoke, one had the impression that he was at the same time tending a brood of invisible chicks on the table in front of him, over which his big soft hands hovered like the wings of a worried mother hen.

He went on to describe at great length, but in safely general terms, the many difficulties that the Crossroads project had

had to surmount in the two years "since we moved up on the Mountain." No one who had not been there could have any conception of the nature and the size of the obstacles that had constantly arisen "to bedevil us." This was a completely new and uncharted field. "The whole time, we've had to grope in the dark, grappling with elusive and terrifying forces." He paid tribute to the hundreds of scientists, engineers and technicians, to the thousands of workers of all categories, who had worked tirelessly, without respite, goaded by a stern sense of duty and a consciousness of the fateful urgency of their mission.

When Eph turned to him and waved his arm in his direction, Sebastian winced but tried to conceal his sense of discomfort behind a self-effacing smile.

"As for Dr. Bloch," said the general, "all you have to do is look at him: he's become a shadow of his former self."

More true even than appears, Sebastian reflected, with a perverse feeling that verged on gratification. The brain was still there, and the heart. The feeling heart. But of the rest, what remained? They looked to him to create the Monster. But even before the Monster existed, he was being consumed by it.

While he had been listening to the generals here this afternoon, he had at the same time been hearing other voices: the voices of his colleagues, the other scientists. They had said little so far. But he knew they had plenty to say, and that before long they would say it. And he would agree with what they would say. He moved again in the armchair designed for a general's comfort. Sleep, he thought. Three hours of sleep.

The war in Europe was as good as over. The Russians had taken Warsaw and had reached the Oder. On the western front the American, British and French forces were making fast headway against the crumbling and demoralized remnants of the German Wehrmacht. It was a matter of weeks. And that would leave Japan. But the fanatical Tojo and his cabinet had been forced from office more than eight months before. Once Japan stood isolated and alone against the world, faced with the threat of strangulation, the Japanese war party would fall like a rotten fruit and peace—an equitable peace—could be won, practically without the firing of another shot. Well, not quite. An air and sea blockade would have to be established. Saipan, last July, had been the decisive battle. It was as a result of the loss of that strategic island that Tojo's cabinet had been replaced by a government charged with giving fundamental reconsideration to the problem of continuing the war. The peace faction had been putting out feelers to Russia to initiate negotiations for a cessation of hostilities. This would merely need a little tactful encouragement. And of course the Emperor would have to be assured that he would be maintained in his position.

But the generals were thinking in terms of a fight to the finish, of unconditional surrender. They were bent on wiping out the outrage of Pearl Harbor. The grand strategy had been worked out in detail, with no reliance on the Bolt. The timetable called for the invasion and capture of the Japanese Home Islands by the spring or early summer of 1946. With the Bolt it would take—how long?

"All the theoretical problems have been solved," he said in support of Eph's statement, as General Van Nuys again turned to him. "There are still a number of kinks to straighten out, one or two rather ticklish details that need working on. But mainly, now, it's a problem of production. I should judge we might be ready in about six months."

The moment the meeting broke up General Van Nuys took him by the arm and, nodding to Eph, led the two of them into a tiny office, bare except for a desk and two straight-backed chairs. He made the other two sit down in the chairs and squarely seated himself on the desk. Sebastian found the hard chairs easier to sit in than the upholstered armchairs in the other room.

"I have something particularly important to tell you in connection with all this that we've been discussing," said the general. He kept his voice low. "I couldn't bring it up at the general meeting. This is top secret." He looked earnestly at Sebastian and at Eph in turn. "Just tuck this away on a back shelf of your minds, and don't ever discuss it with anyone." He paused again as if trying to decide from which angle to tackle a difficult subject, then peered up at the ceiling. "As you know, there are differences in views in the top echelons of government when it comes to national policy, as there are on the lower levels. A crucial instance concerns our relation to our ally, the Soviet Union. So far the Russians have more than had their hands full holding and pushing back the Germans on their western front. Now that will be over in a few weeks, and the Russians are going to have a tremendous reserve of armed forces available. This is a matter that has been discussed in the inner circles of government and the high command for a long time. On this, as on other questions, we haven't always seen eye to eye with our Chief."

General Van Nuys got up, took a few steps, then turned around, folding his arms, to face the other two.

"As you know," he said, "a conference has just been held in Yalta between the President, Prime Minister Churchill and Stalin. You've read the official report of that conference. Now we've just received the text of the secret clauses written into the agreement that was reached by the three chiefs of government. One of these frankly has us worried. As you may know, the President has for some time been very anxious to get the Russians in on the war against Japan. This we consider a big mistake. We've just learned that not only has he got the Russians to agree to declare war on Japan within two to three months after the German surrender—which they are most anxious to do anyway—but in addition he has offered them a lot of concessions, like the return of the southern part of Sakhalin, the Kurile Islands, the maintenance of the status quo in Outer Mongolia, and so forth."

He frowned and, unfolding his arms, clenched his fists.

"There's one thing we don't want, and that is a Russian Red Army in Japan or a Russian Red Army in China. And that means," he said, looking sharply at Sebastian, "that within at most three months of the date of the German surrender, the war against Japan must be brought to an end."

He looked evenly at the two of them.

"You heard in the other room what our timetable will have to be if we rely on conventional weapons. You will therefore understand the importance of delivering the Bolt within the shortest possible time. Every day, every hour, counts."

Most of the buildings of Valhalla had been knocked together in a hurry under the pressure of the urgent job to be done, and after two years many of them were beginning to show signs of deterioration. But in the past year a number of solid, permanent structures of steel and concrete had begun to be built, including the recently completed administration building with its big auditorium in which some six hundred-odd scientists were now meeting.

Bruce Patterson, while the routine business of the Association meeting was being concluded, had been watching with fascination the pool of water formed by the melting snow from the galosh across the aisle from him. The galosh encased the left foot of Dr. Ehrlich. Bruce found himself thinking that the fact that Sebastian was not here to attend the meeting was going to make it easier for these people to say how they felt about the question that was on all their minds, but that it was very strange that this should be so.

"Any further discussion?" asked the chairman, Professor Baker. No one spoke. It was the last item on the agenda. Bruce could feel the tension in the room becoming almost palpable.

"Any new business?"

A general commotion spread through the hall, people shifting position, shuffling their feet, crossing and recrossing their legs, clearing their throats, holding whispered exchanges. In the back of the room a voice was heard. Heads turned around, there were shouts of "Up front!"

"You'd better come up here on the platform, Dr. Keller," said the chairman, "where we can all hear you."

Dr. Keller, known as T.N.T. to his colleagues, was one of the leading explosives experts, a slightly stooped and fragile-looking man whose skin had a gray cast. Bruce was surprised to see him coming forward. He was a thoroughly unobtrusive man, and a lone wolf—belonging, so far as Bruce knew, to none of the numerous cliques up here on the Knoll.

"There is one item of new business, Mr. Chairman," he said in a dry voice. "I was hoping someone else would bring it up first. It has been on my mind for several months now."

He paused and looked defiantly over the audience. Bruce sensed that he was steeling himself.

"The Bolt," he said. "What are we going to do about it?"

He paused again, and there was a frightened look on his face. But the sky did not fall, and no one interrupted him. He went on.

"Personally, this is the way I feel. We contracted to do this job—most of us, I am convinced, against our better judgment —because there seemed good reason to believe the Germans were working on the idea, and it was a question of our survival. And there was also, apart from this, the possibility that the Bolt might spell the difference between defeat and victory. Now we know that the Germans haven't got it—at least we're going to know it very soon. And once Germany is out of the running, there will no longer be any doubt as to the outcome in the Pacific. There is therefore no longer any justification for making the Bolt."

Everyone was listening intently. There was not a sound or a stir in the vast auditorium.

"I think we, as scientists, and even more as members of the human community, have the duty to discuss this question thoroughly and to take a position as a body with regard to it. The Bolt is now in the final stages of design and production. But it is not yet completed, and it cannot be completed without us. If we go ahead with it now, whether or not we formulate our views as to the implications this will have for the future of humanity we shall be committing ourselves to all the consequences, and we shall bear the responsibility for them. I personally do not feel that we should go ahead without a clear understanding of where we are going."

A burst of applause from the majority of the assembly greeted this brief speech, while Dr. Keller, pale and frightened, awkwardly made his way back to his seat.

"Is it your wish, then," said Professor Baker after the flurry had subsided, "that our association take up the discussion of this subject here and now?"

A chorus of responses indicated approval as Dr. Emmett Martin, dean of the scientists of the first rank here in Valhalla, was making his way to the platform with short, springy steps. He was close to seventy, short and round, bald with a fringe of white hair behind spanning the space between his ears, and his crinkled face shone with good humor.

"I have listened very carefully," he began, when the noise had died down, "to what Dr. Keller had to say. But I cannot agree with him. If we embark on a discussion of this kind we shall be stepping on dangerous ground. It is not our business to decide if, when, or how the Bolt is to be used. It *is* our business to make it available to the Government to use or not to use as it sees fit. To air our views on these matters, which lie entirely outside our province, would be to imply a lack of confidence in our Government and to undermine public faith in our institutions. Who are we to set ourselves up against the constituted authorities as self-appointed arbiters in matters ranging from global warfare to the future of humanity? We are scientists, gentlemen. Do you not consider science a sufficiently vast field? Let us leave questions of state to statesmen, and military questions to military men. I would urge, Mr. Chairman, that we drop the subject entirely."

The suggestion was greeted by an uproar. One speaker after another came forward, and it became a full-scale debate from which it clearly emerged that all of them, whatever their views as to the appropriateness of the discussion or of possible action, regarded the prospect of using the Bolt at this juncture with a concern that in many cases verged on anguish.

Bruce had been listening with eager attention. He and Fritz

and a couple of others, in spite of their reluctance to embarrass Sebastian, had been seriously thinking about promoting just some such discussion as this. They had discovered that it wasn't necessary. The discussion had practically arranged itself. Dr. Ehrlich, an old mathematician from Göttingen, and for many years at Yale, had simply said one day, some weeks ago, to two or three of his close associates, "Ve vill talk about it at the next Association meeting." And the word had gone around.

Bruce himself was surprised to see how strong the feelings were. He was glad now that Sebastian wasn't here, for people were expressing themselves as they would never have dared to in his presence. This of course was completely crazy. What had happened to make them react to him in this way? He was the last man to discourage his colleagues—or anyone, for that matter—from expressing themselves freely. He and Fritz had attempted, for hours on end, to analyze the change that had come over him. They recognized that he was in a hellishly difficult spot—mistrusted, watched, followed; assigned to let loose upon the world a force that had no parallel in history and that could, if mishandled, bring immeasurable disaster to mankind; worked on by a whole new environment that was bent, consciously or unconsciously, on weaning him away from his former views, his cherished beliefs, his sense of man and society; and at the same time exposed to the most insidious and destructive of all temptations: the temptation not of power but of infinite power. No one else, Bruce and Fritz agreed, could possibly have stood up against the combined pressure. But Sebastian should be able to. "I wish I knew, though," Fritz had said on one occasion, "that there was even *one* p-p-person whom he felt he c-c-c-could talk to."

The galosh across the aisle from Bruce moved. It had lost the last trace of snow. Dr. Ehrlich shambled up to the platform, leaving wet tracks on the new linoleum.

"I vass able," he said without any preliminaries, "to make a smoll calculation." The words, which came forth harshly from beneath the bristling, untidy mustache, were somehow moving. "It vass nossing. But it hass gone into the Bolt and it iss a part of it. I do not vant my smoll calculation to help to destroy unnecessary lives."

No one laughed at the misused adjective. In fact, for those who knew Dr. Ehrlich—and most of the people here did—it was not a misused adjective at all, but an image full of solemn meaning and at the same time tinged with irony. Dr. Ehrlich returned to his seat.

Bruce, who had had long experience with meetings, sensed that the moment had come to crystallize all the scattered emotions and ideas into some concrete proposal. He asked for the floor and went up to the platform.

"Our laws," he said, "make a distinction between killing in the heat of passion and killing in cold blood. All of us, whatever our qualms, felt justified in using the Bolt—or accepted the idea that it might be used—when it seemed as if it might be our one hope of survival. Using it in such a case would have been killing in the heat of passion. Now it turns out that the situation is quite different from what we had feared. By no stretch of the imagination can we regard our survival as a nation as being in any way threatened. There can no longer be any doubt as to the outcome either in Europe or in the Pacific. It is simply a question of how to end the war. Using the Bolt now would be killing in cold blood.

"I have heard the army advance the argument that using the Bolt will save lives by limiting the destruction and shortening the war. They say that the massive raids now being carried out strategically by hundreds of planes dropping incendiary and explosive bombs over industrial centers are much more destructive of life and property than one or two Bolts, which would at the same time be more effective and end the war. There are several things wrong with this argument. In the first place, the time factor. Those strategic bombings have already begun and will continue. The Bolt will not be ready for several months. We don't know what the situation will be at that time, but it will certainly have evolved even further in our favor. The second thing wrong with the argument is this:

we know what conventional weapons will do. We *don't* know
what the Bolt will do. It will have an impact and a radius of immediate destructiveness that will presumably be measurable if
and when it is actually tried out. But unlike any other weapon,
the Bolt will have a long-distance and a long-term effect that it
may not be possible to measure for generations, if ever. The
far-reaching effects will extend to living organisms over an
area and for a period of time that it is altogether impossible
for us to calculate on the basis of data now available to us.

"These are things that we know. The Bolt is a horror
weapon, a weapon of desperation. Now, providentially, circumstances make recourse to it unnecessary, and even
uncalled for. The question is what can we do about it? As I
see it, we have several possibilities of action. One extreme
would be to refuse to continue production. At the other extreme—and this would seem to me the very least we should
consider doing—we could pass a resolution expressing our
view that resort to the Bolt as a weapon at the present juncture
cannot be justified. Between these extremes there are a number of choices. I think it is important that any action that we
take should be endorsed by the largest possible majority, and
preferably by the whole association as a body."

The six hundred scientists had listened to Bruce's words in
absorbed silence, and the silence continued as he regained his
seat. Dr. Ehrlich nodded to him gravely as he sat down.
All at once a number of hands went up and voices rose in various parts of the auditorium. "I move we stop production!"
shouted a young voice. "Let's appoint a committee," said another. In the midst of the confusion Dr. Martin was moving
forward to the platform.

"Mr. Chairman," he said. "Gentlemen." His face now was
flushed, and he lowered forbiddingly. "I'm sorry this discussion ever began. I think it was quite unnecessary. We all know
how we feel, and we have accomplished nothing by airing our
feelings. There are things that are better left unsaid. Now we
are being asked to take action. All I want to say is that if we
make any move behind Sebastian Bloch's back we shall be

guilty of the worst kind of disloyalty, and I for one shall dissociate myself from it with all the energy at my command."

He went back to his seat. Bruce waited for someone else to take the floor, but as he looked around he felt that the eyes of the group were upon him. Everyone knew of his close friendship with Sebastian. They were looking to him now to give them an idea as to how he might feel about their taking some kind of action. He raised his hand and was recognized, and went up to the platform.

"As you know," he began, trying to keep his tone informal, "no one can speak for Dr. Bloch. I don't know any better than the rest of you how he feels about this, what he would or will do, how he would react to any move that we might make here and now . . ."

He was thinking as he spoke that this, which was true today, would have been inconceivable two years ago. Then he would have known exactly what Sebastian would do. At the same time he *did* know, deep down, that he hadn't changed, that he was still, as he had always been, a man for whom human life was invested with a value beyond any other, and that if he seemed to have detached himself from the passions and the problems of the common man it was simply because, during these years of the Bolt, he had had to rule out everything that was tangential to his overriding task. The strain of his responsibility had told on him terribly. He had become distant, unapproachable. Perhaps he was consumed by a feeling that in dedicating himself to the inhuman task, even though its purpose was to save mankind from a return to barbarism, he was estranging himself from humanity. But now? Bruce could only guess that Sebastian too was hoping to destroy the "Monster," as he always termed it, before it was born. But his position was a delicate one.

". . . We all know Dr. Bloch's views on science and its function, and on the role of the scientist. I think we can take it for granted that he feels even more strongly about the problem we've been discussing than we do. But at the same time, because of his responsibilities, he is in a difficult position. He isn't as free to take certain initiatives as we are. My own feeling is that if we take a stand on this question—the strongest stand on which we can reach a broad agreement—it will strengthen Dr. Bloch's hand for any action he wants to take. But quite apart from this," he added earnestly, "quite apart from Dr. Bloch and the loyalty we owe him, this is a matter that challenges us as scientists and that we cannot ignore. I think we should be failing in our most elementary responsibility if we simply let matters take their course, if we refused to take a position, if we were to lose the battle of science by default."

He sat down. But even as he sat down and sensed the stir of excitement around him, sensed the eagerness, particularly of the younger men, for a clear and unequivocal stand against the Bolt, he realized that the case was lost. In spite of himself, he could feel no conviction as to what Sebastian's position might be. He had not been able to communicate any such conviction. And, by whatever mysterious waves such moods were transmitted, he knew that the mere evocation of Sebastian's name had produced an inertia that nothing would now overcome.

The discussion continued animatedly for some time. "Let's do *something*," said those who seemed to speak for the majority. "We must not embarrass the Government," said others. If they were to go on record as being opposed to the use of the Bolt, they pointed out, it would be bound to leak out and it would reflect unfavorably on the Government, especially in the eyes of the rest of the world. "This," Fritz Leutner replied, getting up to speak for the first time, "is a risk the Government has to take." Fritz suffered agonies whenever he addressed any kind of audience, though curiously his speeches and lectures were unmarred by stuttering. "The Government has to base its decisions on the advice of experts. It can ignore this advice if it wishes. But the only guarantee that it will make right decisions is that the experts should give their advice honestly and fearlessly."

When the meeting finally adjourned, the only decision that

had been reached was to do nothing without previously consulting Sebastian.

It was late at night when Sebastian returned, this time, to Valhalla. The Cadillac with the G.I. chauffeur that the army had put at his disposal had met him at the station, and as the car climbed, ever higher, up the thirty-mile stretch of winding mountain road, as he breathed the increasingly rarefied air, he felt a growing exhilaration. He had always loved the mountains.

Tanya was waiting up for him when he got home—though he had at last made her understand that he had resolved to forego all sexual indulgence during this difficult period when the embryo of the Monster was coming to maturity. She had contrived to seduce him several times in the last year and a half, and as he found her not less but rather more desirable than ever, he had had to harden himself against her. This was at least a beginning of renunciation.

When she told him of last week's meeting of the Association, as Bruce and others had reported it to her, he became prey to an extraordinary excitement. He would have liked to retire immediately to his room to think things out since it was too late to call anyone, but he owed it to Tanya to spend a little time with her. She had prepared one of her fine midnight collations to celebrate his return. But he had absolutely no appetite. He took the large drink of Irish whisky that she poured for him.

"I wish I knew what thoughts were working in that brain of yours!" she exclaimed at one point.

"It's much better that you don't."

The fact that, because of Mark—because of Zelinski, really —she knew about the Monster and that she therefore understood the import of the Association meeting, made it no easier to communicate with her than it would have been otherwise. She was obviously hoping now that he would tell her he was overjoyed by the news, and that the long nightmare was at last over. But he couldn't.

He thought about her remark later when he was finally alone in his room. He sensed her rebellion, contained but explosive, at their estrangement. But he was finding it harder and harder to think about her now, to accept her in the orbit of his life. The resentment that he had felt that time when she had announced to him that she was pregnant again rose vigorously to the surface. She—or rather nature, through her—had tricked him, and in tricking him had lessened him, had reduced the intensity of the pure flame of his being. "Consumed by my own flame!" The thought, and the image, sparkled and beckoned in the depth of his mind.

What Tanya had reported to him of the meeting of the Association had stirred him to a pitch that he could hardly contain. He glimpsed possibilities that he had not dared dream of since his first involvement with the Monster. To stifle it before it was born! There *was* a way out! A way out for humanity, a way out for himself.

He paced back and forth in the small room for hours. The scientists, all of them—most of them certainly—were waiting merely for him to say the word. And he had heard that Hans Viereck and several other research directors and institute heads at M Lab were drafting a letter that Viereck was going to present personally to the President. Yet Viereck and his colleagues alone couldn't do it, even if supported by a handful of the men on Valhalla who might take independent action. But if he, Sebastian, were to lead the movement it was certain to succeed.

The thought of what would happen was dizzying. Work would of course continue. Not on the Monster, however, but on the Monster's children. Their uses for peaceful ends were infinite. The war would cease. The frontiers of knowledge would be opened again, and the men of Valhalla would be able to communicate once more with their German colleagues, with the Russians and the Japanese, with all their other colleagues. And they could say: "Look! This is how far we went. We could have made the Thing. We knew—we know—how to make it. We were within a few months of turning it out.

But we abandoned the project. We knew that to have made it would have been unnecessary, and would have been wrong. Because if we had made it, we knew others would make it. We would have exposed humanity to unpredictable horrors. We felt that this thing was evil. And evil engenders evil. And horror engenders horror."

He had been smoking cigarette after cigarette, and from time to time he was seized with a convulsive fit of coughing. He opened the window for a moment to let out the smoke, and the cool mountain air enveloped him. The night was clear and the sky, pricked with the scintillation of its myriad stars, was as still, as serene, as it had no doubt been in ages past when men had looked up to the vault of heaven in the belief that it was the divine abode of beings solely concerned with the fate of earth's creatures. The chill air sent shivers through the thin sheath of flesh that covered his bones though he was perspiring, and he shut the window again, putting to flight the beckoning phantoms of the night.

He had let himself be carried away, for just a lightning second, by an unhinging thought: *the fate of the Monster was now in his hands—in his hands alone.* He had only to say the word, and all the scientists would follow him. He immediately took hold of himself. He rubbed his forehead and a shudder shook his whole frame. That was an odd, a frightening sensation he had just had. As though he had been standing on an edge, and— No.

He sat down on the bed. In all the crises that he had faced he had made an instant and unwavering decision. He did not waver now. The Monster would be born. The Monster would be unleashed for its lethal destiny. But his whole being rebelled. If he had the power to stop the Monster, why couldn't he use that power? He knew what he wanted to do. But in the unfolding of his fate he sensed that he was in the grip of a necessity that transcended his own will.

The next day, and in the course of the following days and weeks, he had many encounters with his colleagues, and in the warmth engendered by their contact he was calm again.

There was no irremediable night, no stalking evil, no soul-searing dilemma concealed beneath the smooth surface of a problem that was in part technical and in part political—and in so far as it was political, beyond the purview of the scientist. He listened, discussed, reassured, made vague promises. He spoke of the solidarity of scientists, of the need to make right decisions based on a full knowledge of the facts, of the gravity of political responsibility, of the besetting difficulties.

As a background to these discussions, and to his own inner dialogue, there was another factor. For several months—since the turn of the year, perhaps—he had again become vaguely aware of Gregg and his men. They had left him alone for over a year, ever since that fateful interview with the security chief which he had tried to blot out of his memory, when he had revealed Mark's name. But now he had begun to encounter them again.

He had hardly noticed it at first. They had of course been around Valhalla ever since the beginning. But normally their paths did not cross his, and he had nothing to do with them. And then one day, perhaps sometime in February, as he crossed Lieutenant Siracusa in a hallway of the administration building, it occurred to him that for some weeks he had caught sight of or run into several of them in just that way. Sometimes they did not even see him, or if they recognized him on a street or along a path, merely nodded a greeting.

He was at first inclined to think these encounters were a matter of pure chance. But then he began to run into them also in Washington and New York and elsewhere. Always in the same way: coming in or out of a hotel, in the corridors of an official building, in a station, on a street. Sometimes an easy "How do you do, Doctor," more often a friendly nod. One morning on his way to his office in Valhalla he met Gregg himself. A few days later, at the same time and place, he met him again. Gregg stopped to shake hands.

"Everything going well?" he asked.

And that was all.

Inevitably he was led to conclude that all these encounters

were not accidental but deliberate. They had a purpose. But what purpose? More and more he found himself thinking back over all the interviews he had had with the security people. He could not feel very happy about them. Particularly that last interview with Gregg. When he had finally been pressured into giving Mark's name, he had meant at once to explain that the whole story he had told had been a fabrication, and to tell exactly what had actually happened. Had he, or hadn't he? The intention had been clear in his mind. He couldn't remember with certainty.

It came to him now that this new maneuver of Gregg's must be a warning. They weren't talking to him, weren't asking him any more questions. They didn't need to. They had what they wanted. They were just reminding him.

What have I done? he asked himself again and again.

The discussion of what to do with the Monster continued among the scientists at Valhalla and at the other centers.

"You do agree, don't you," Bruce said to him one day with his characteristic annoying persistence, "that no matter what, we must—as scientists—go on record against the use of the Bolt except as a measure of desperate necessity?"

"We are certainly committed to support whatever course will be most sparing of human life," he replied. "But who is to be judge of how desperate the necessity is? We have to recognize that the decision is not ours, and while we want to give the Government the benefit of any constructive advice that we have to offer, we must be careful to do it in the way that is most likely to be effective."

There were so many elements in the situation that the others could not know about. For one thing, there was the commitment to the Monster. He knew, as they did not, the temper of the men in power; knew that if he were to thwart them now—and it *would* be he—not only would they never forgive him, but he would be destroyed. This he could accept; this he had already accepted in contracting his unnatural alliance with the Monster. But what would happen then? He had lost all faith in humanity's ability to cure its mania for self-destruction unaided. The Monster, once created, would constitute a new, a wholly new, element in the world situation. Its potentialities were awesome and terrifying, but they could be used in a decisive way for good. If the Monster were still-born, the world would revert to the very situation that had bred the present conflict. Except that it would be even worse, even more explosive.

For there was Soviet Russia. And already it was apparent that several of the overrun and devastated states would go communist: Poland, Yugoslavia, Rumania, Bulgaria . . . and China certainly. He had once looked upon the spread of communism with hope. He no longer found in it anything resembling hope. He faintly remembered some idea he had once had about the residual wisdom of the masses. He had been guilty—he was ashamed of it now—of sentimentality. He remembered a phrase of Lenin's: the "god-builders," applied to leaders who sentimentalized over the peasants and workers and so misinterpreted Marxism as to assume that, because they were workers and peasants, they were necessarily always right. If the ultimate goal to which the socialist effort led was one in which he still believed, it was, in the perspective of contemporary stresses, an infinitely remote and well-nigh chimerical one, threatened by a thousand hazards—by increasingly desperate resistance without, by factionalism and corruption within.

The Monster had become the vehicle of a new hope.

During these weeks of torment, while on the one hand he struggled to elude a decision that he had already accepted and on the other tried to justify it as though it were a decision that he had freely chosen, and while, day after day, work on the Monster proceeded under maximum pressure, events on the various war fronts were moving toward finality. The capture of Iwo Jima after nearly a month of the most savage fighting that the war had witnessed was followed by the British recapture of Mandalay. Five days after the American Third Army marched into Frankfurt, American forces, in the biggest amphibian attack ever staged, landed in Okinawa and proceeded to set ashore several hundred thousand assault troops. Every day brought news of fresh victories. On the German west front the combined Allied forces completed a double envelopment of the Ruhr, while on the east front, a few days later, the Russians took Vienna. On April 11th American forces reached the Elbe. And the following day brought the black announcement of the death of President Roosevelt.

Sebastian knew that Viereck's letter, co-signed by several of his colleagues, had reached Roosevelt a short time before. Had the President even read it? Had he discussed it with any of his advisers? He had in any case taken no action. It was in fact extremely unlikely that, even had he been willing, even if he had asserted all his authority, he could have put through a decision that would have gone directly counter to the wishes of the High Command. The army, of course, wanted the new weapon that it had been promised. But more telling, even, than this among the higher councils was the argument that the Bolt had cost a hell of a lot of money and had to be delivered.

There was mounting excitement, not only on Valhalla and in government and army circles but throughout the country, as April wore into May and the collapse of Germany became daily more imminent. The Americans took Nuremberg, and five days later the Red Army was fighting its way into Berlin. Five days after this, the United Nations Conference opened in San Francisco, and the American and Russian forces effected a junction at Torgau. It was all over now. May 1st brought the report of Hitler's death. The following day Berlin fell, and less than a week later Germany surrendered.

Sebastian noted the date of V-E day: May 8th. He remembered what General Van Nuys had told him. The Russians therefore could be expected to declare war on Japan not later than August 8th. By that date the Monster must be ready. It would be ready.

The swinging door that led into the bar swung noiselessly and was soft to the touch, as if made of plush. Inside, it was so dark that for a moment Hjalmar Gröndahl could see nothing.

The place was air-conditioned, but he was nevertheless aware of a faint cool aroma in which lemon and bitters seemed to predominate. A muted radio was whining a popular melody of long ago that he recognized, because of an association, as "There Ain't No Maybe in My Baby's Eyes."

His eyes growing accustomed to the half-light, he was able to make out, in the glow cast by the indirectly lighted ceiling, the bar with its glitter of glass and chromium, the many empty tables in the small room, and over there in the corner, General Forester: ruddy face, close-cropped gray hair and mustache, four stars on his shoulders, several rows of ribbons.

They shook hands, and Gröndahl sat down.

"What'll you have?" said the general. He was working on an old-fashioned.

Gröndahl asked the bartender if he had any Linje akvavit. He did. "The officers' bar has everything."

They talked about the war. The battle of Okinawa was in its second month.

"It's deadly," General Forester said. He gave figures from the last reports of Allied ships sunk and damaged, the Japanese plane losses, the casualties.

They clinked glasses when the bartender had poured out the akvavit.

"Skaal!" Hjalmar said.

General Forester went on to talk about mopping-up operations in Europe.

"Well, now we know that the Germans didn't have the Bolt," Gröndahl said. "They weren't even working on it."

"Lucky for us," said the general. "They might have beat us to it."

Hjalmar shook his head. "I doubt that they could have done any better than we have."

"That's what I want to talk to you about." The general signaled the bartender and ordered another old-fashioned. "Are those boys of yours going to give us trouble?"

"How do you mean?"

"I mean all the talk that's going on among them. I've read

the security reports. You know: now that we've won the war, there's no need to use the Bolt. It would be bad politics. It would be a crime against humanity. That kind of thing."

"Yes," Hjalmar said. "I don't think you have anything to worry about."

"I don't like some of the things I've heard."

"You mustn't pay too much attention to the talk," Hjalmar said. "Naturally they have their own ideas and their feelings."

"I think it's pretty serious when they all get together and discuss it in a general meeting the way they did recently."

"But as you know, they decided not to do anything."

"For the time being only."

"They won't do anything. Bloch will keep them in hand."

"I want to talk about him, too. I don't trust him, you know."

Gröndahl ordered another akvavit. Since the acute crisis of the war had passed, he himself was far from keen on carrying on with the Bolt. He saw in it nothing but danger. He had assumed that Sebastian would be all for putting a stop to its development. To his amazement he had given no indication that he was opposed to the army plan. Expecting to get a rise out of him Gröndahl had asked him to head a study group which the army had requested to make recommendations regarding the objective to which the Bolt was to be directed. The group was asked to consider three possibilities: directing the Bolt to a desert area, to a purely military objective, or to a military objective situated in a densely built-up urban area. Sebastian not only had not refused, but his group had come out for the last of these choices, which was exactly the one the army wanted.

"You saw the recommendation his study group brought in?" Gröndahl said.

"Yes," said Forester. "But I always have the feeling with him that he's playing a game."

"We can be glad we have him. No one else could have accomplished what he has, in the first place. And in the second place—well, I wouldn't answer for the delivery of the Bolt if he weren't on the spot."

General Forester looked at Gröndahl.

"Is it that bad?"

"Well, I don't want to exaggerate. It's idle, of course, to speculate as to what the situation might have been if Bloch had never been in the picture. But he *is* in the picture, and what has happened is that he has crystallized in the scientists, on the level of the group, something that surely existed individually in them before—namely a conscience. They don't like the Bolt. They never have. And if he were to come out against it —or even if he were suddenly to vanish from the picture— they wouldn't go through with it. That's why I say—"

"You mean he's *that* important?"

"I'm telling you. They look upon him as God."

"That's what I mean," Forester said. "I don't trust him. I don't know what he's going to do."

"You're wrong," Gröndahl said. "He has to the highest degree the basic, the indispensable qualification of an administrator: a sense of responsibility. He's been given a job to do, and he'll do it. And he'll make all those people toe the line."

"I hope to hell you're right," said the general. "But it won't make me change my mind. It's an unhealthy situation." He took a swallow of his drink. "One man," he said musingly. He looked at Gröndahl. "Do you realize the position we're in? You tell me he'll do the job. You tell me he has a sense of responsibility, that he'll keep the others in line. But I shouldn't have to just take your word for it. I should *know* it. And I don't know it."

"What makes you so skeptical?"

Gröndahl too had been worrying about Sebastian in recent months, but for quite different reasons. First of all his health. The physical change that had come over him was frightening. His black eyes had become enormous and shone with a feverish fire in the dark hollows of their orbits. He had become terribly emaciated, and the parchmentlike skin stretched tight across the sharp bones of his face. Yet he was as alert as ever in his movements, and his mind had lost none of its agility and power of penetration. But what worried Gröndahl more than his health was the change that had come over his character. He

was no longer the warm, life-loving, versatile-minded human-
ist that he had been before the war. His whole being seemed
to be wrapped up in the Bolt—to be devoured by it. Remembering the conversations he had had with him when he had
had to resort to every kind of intellectual and moral pressure
to persuade him to work on the project, Gröndahl could not
now understand that he showed no qualms about going ahead
with it, when there were serious grounds for hesitancy and
when none of the arguments that had originally induced him
to join it were any longer valid. At the present moment, Gröndahl was deeply disturbed by Forester's words.

The general held out his pack of cigarettes, and took one
himself. "You've got a very good man up there on the Knoll,"
he said. "Your chief security officer, Lieutenant Colonel Gregg.
I've had several long talks with him."

He gave Gröndahl a light and lit his own cigarette.

"This Bloch, you know," he said, "has quite a record."

"I know. But that's all in the past."

"He used to be a communist."

"I didn't know that for a fact originally, though I had
strongly suspected it. But in any case he's definitely put all
that behind him."

"Yes. That's one of the things I don't like. He's put it behind him—much too quickly and easily. From one day to the
next. He's lied about it. About himself and about others. Tangled himself up in a maze of fabrications. Why would he do
that?"

Gröndahl shook his head. He was stunned.

"I don't know," he said.

"All this would be less serious," Forester said, "if he were
one of those disreputable characters like so many we've seen
who make a career of being ex-communists and whom the
Government uses as informers and witnesses against their
former associates—which incidentally I regard as a terrible
mistake. Bloch's case is much more serious because he's a man
of the highest caliber, a man . . . quite exceptional . . . in
fact, perhaps unique."

He looked at Gröndahl squarely, his gray eyes sharp beneath black brows.

"He's after something," he said, a huskiness in his voice. "And what I'm afraid of is—he'd stop at nothing."

Gröndahl remained silent. He had never thought of Sebastian in this light, yet what Forester was saying, shocking though it was, did not sound absurd. He remembered the conversations he had had with Sebastian in Paris, more than ten years before—his exaltation, the cosmic scale of his concepts.

"Well, anyway," the general pursued in a more matter-of-fact tone, "there's nothing we can do about him right now. We still need him, and we're more or less at his mercy. We must redouble our vigilance. And take certain precautions."

He went on to outline the plan for setting up a special provisional committee to advise the new President on both immediate and postwar problems involving the Bolt. This body, which would include two or three research institute heads along with representatives of the branches of government concerned, would make the final recommendation as to the fate of the Bolt.

"It will need a group of experts from Valhalla to assist it," Gröndahl said.

"Yes," Forester agreed. "Three or four of the top men. And I guess Bloch had better head it."

He pondered for a moment.

"I wish I could think of somebody who would do as well, but I can't."

Chapter 26

IT was late afternoon when Sebastian let himself into the house with the key that Tanya had left under the door mat.

She was still at the office, and six-year-old Gino was at the Brandons'.

He had been gone since before noon. He had taken a long hike over the rough mountain trails, the first since he had come here, and he was dead tired. But the sheer physical fatigue that was superimposed on the long-accumulated mental, emotional and nervous exhaustion was healthy, almost comforting, and he had an idea that tonight he might be able to sleep.

He went straight to his room, got out of his clothes—the Windbreaker, plaid shirt, jeans and hiking boots that he hardly ever had a chance to wear any more—and went into the bathroom to take a shower.

The magic of the mountain country was still upon him. He had climbed part way up the slope across from Mount Arron. The outlines of Valhalla's installations, the only sign of man in the timeless landscape, had been ever so faintly blurred by an impalpable mountain mist, and he had tried to imagine the peak in its virgin state. It had stood here, unchanged and inviolate, for thousands of years, a granite giant on whose crags hawks and eagles had always built their nests. Soon its name would become a synonym of wholesale death and destruction.

The Provisional Committee had decided in favor of the use of the Monster on a combined military and civilian objective. The machinery had been set in motion. A number of appropriate targets had previously been selected, which had been spared in the systematic strategic bombing raids of the past few months so that the destruction inflicted by the Monster might afterward be more accurately assessed. Those cities, thought Sebastian, seeing themselves unmolested amid the surrounding havoc and thereby encouraged to regard themselves as benefiting by some special dispensation, were perhaps an image of the world of tomorrow.

It had been hurry and pressure all the way. And for good measure, his particular Calvary. And now the time was drawing short. Weeks. Days. Adjustments, final tests, checks, synchronization, time schedule, all the final arrangements. Statements were being drafted for release once the Monster had been unleashed.

The hot jets of the shower spray pierced into his flesh like arrows, but the pain was almost pleasurable. His body had caused him so much suffering, had tricked him so often, that he liked to punish it. He splashed and gasped and blew in the steady down-slanting stream which sent twisting rivulets of hot water cascading over his bony frame. Clouds of steam rose and enveloped him. What a wretched thing the body was! And the mind, how glorious! What did the body of Socrates matter, or of Buddha, or Dante, or Bach? Yet it was alas necessary, he recognized, as he gradually turned off the hot water and turned on the cold, to have some kind of body, no matter how miserable, to attach a mind to. Bodies . . .

He was turning off both taps when there was a knock, and the door opened.

"May I come in? . . . Do you mind?" It was Tanya, and she was out of breath. "I've got some news."

"Wait," he said, but she was already in. "Hand me that towel." He didn't like her to see him, especially since he had grown so thin; he looked like a scarecrow. He dried himself hurriedly in the shower.

"I've just had a letter from Eve," Tanya said.

His heart made a leap. "Hand me my bathrobe."

"Mark's been wounded," Tanya said, passing him the robe. "Badly. They're not sure they can save him."

They went into the bedroom, where Sebastian sat down on the bed and read the letter.

He read it through again.

"We've got to do something," Tanya said.

"Wait a minute," he said.

Mark was in a bad way. A serious abdominal wound, with complications. He had had several blood transfusions and one initial operation. He would need two, possibly three more, if he could stand them. The prognosis was not reassuring. Meanwhile he was in Hawaii and could not be moved, and Eve was at home and could not get to her husband. She was asking that

Sebastian intercede with the military authorities, if he could, to get her permission to go to Hawaii.

One part of his mind immediately began working on it. Nothing would be easier. He could even arrange to have her put aboard an army plane within twenty-four hours, and tomorrow, or the next day, she would be there. He could visualize the joy in Mark's face.

But another part of his mind—the censor—was also at work. The joy that shone in Mark's pain-distorted face faded before Gregg's grim features. He imagined the report flashed to the various intelligence offices: *Dr. Sebastian Bloch, Valhalla Coordinator, arranges flight to Hawaii of wife of Mark Ampter, notorious spy . . .*

"What are we going to do?" Tanya asked.

Sebastian stood up and walked to the window. The sun had set behind the range of mountains to the west, and their black outlines stood out sharp against the pink sky. He would gladly have given his right arm, even both arms, to provide Mark with some little comfort in what might be his last moments.

He felt a funny pulling of the muscles around his eyes. His throat was dry.

"Nothing," he said, and choked.

Chapter 27

THE four members of the advisory group to the Provisional Committee were all pacing the large office, each following his own pattern, each seemingly oblivious of the others. Sebastian paced the length of the room, as did Roy Menander Porter, but they moved in opposite directions so that they kept crossing each other in the center. Dr. Baker's course was across the width of the office, and he moved with short shuffling steps. Dr. Goodrich confined himself to half circles around one of the wide desks that stood away from the wall on the window side.

They had been at it since midmorning, and it was now nearing lunchtime. The report on which they had to make a recommendation lay on the desk around which Professor Goodrich was circling. The opening phrase kept running through Sebastian's mind: *At this grave moment of history we feel it our solemn duty to warn our Government* . . . He could see the group at Lab V sitting down to write that report. Schultz had probably drafted it. They were all men who weighed their words carefully.

They had addressed the report to the War Department, and the committee was referring it to Sebastian and his group. They warned that the use of the Bolt at this juncture, especially against a civilian population, would have incalculably disastrous consequences for the future of mankind, and in particular for America's position in the world. They made a detailed recommendation that the Bolt be simply demonstrated in a desert area before representatives of the United Nations.

"What a day!" exclaimed Dr. Baker, stopping before the window at the end of his path.

The July sun spread a shining coat on every surface that it touched, the light air sang with summer, the blue sky etched the ridge of the distant mountains.

Dr. Goodrich stopped to look out through the window nearest him. "So peaceful!" he said.

They all stopped their pacing then and looked out, in silence. There had been all the years of war, of violence, of suffering and death, when no one could in good conscience even look out upon a lovely day with unqualified pleasure. But now it was almost over. The United Nations charter had been signed in San Francisco. The battle of Okinawa had been fought and won. Every day brought news of new surrenders by Japanese forces on the Pacific islands or on the Asiatic mainland. There was no major engagement anywhere in the world at the present moment.

Porter, his hands in his trouser pockets, walked over to the desk on which the Lab V report lay, and stood staring at it.

"I'd be in favor," he said, "of our simply endorsing that report."

They all looked at Sebastian.

He shook his head. "You know how I feel," he said. "I know how you feel. I think we'd all be in favor of doing just that. But can we, honestly?"

He repeated the arguments that had been made many times. The Lab V group's proposal had been carefully considered and rejected because there was no assurance, before an actual trial, that the Bolt would work, that it wouldn't prove a dud, in which case the effect would be disastrous to American prestige. That was why it had to be used without warning. As to the objective, that had already been thoroughly gone into and decided, and the group's recommendation would not alter the decision but would, on the other hand, only diminish the scientific community's authority in future recommendations that it might be called upon to make. The main question—whether or not the Bolt should be used at this juncture—was one on which they as a group were not honestly in a position to advise. That decision must be made on the basis of data that were not available to the group.

He would have liked to mention what was for an important group among high policy circles the most compelling reason of all for having recourse to the Bolt at the earliest possible moment: the fact that Russia would be entering the war by August 8th at the latest, and it was considered imperative to bring the war with Japan to an end before the Red Army could be brought into the picture. But this he was pledged not to reveal. And perhaps it would not have struck his colleagues as being decisive.

He presented the arguments as effectively as he could, feeling no conviction about them. And when the others finally acquiesced with great reluctance, he sensed that they had not been convinced, but that they had understood that he had taken a position from which he would not be shaken.

The last words as the meeting broke up were spoken by Dr. Baker, the oldest and most conservative of the group, the first to walk out of the office, who said, as he opened the door without looking behind:

"God help us!"

One day in early August there was an unusual stir on and about the air base on one of the islands of the Marianas group. It was several hours before dawn and a B-29 and a heavy escort were being given a final check before the take-off. There had been a last-minute modification in the flight orders, and the mission was taking off one hour later than originally scheduled.

In addition to the contingent of officers and enlisted men who regularly turned out for these take-offs there was a small group of civilians. They had recently arrived on the island and had been very busy about the airport for the past few weeks. Now they were all here in a body, brought in person by the colonel commanding the airport who was acting as their host.

There was an unwonted excitement about the occasion. The plane had been specially fitted out. It did not carry the usual bomb load, but instead one single object that had been transported here and put into place by a team brought for the purpose. The civilians, who were said to be scientists, acted very nervous. Two of them ran after the bomber's crew as they went aboard, disappeared inside the plane for several minutes, and then came back.

The motors were started, one by one. After the warming up and testing of the controls the B-29 slowly taxied to the southeast end of the field while the escort planes got ready.

Some minutes later the B-29 was racing down the take-off runway. It lifted off the ground and slowly rose, higher and higher, growing smaller, and was soon joined by its escort and sped in a northwesterly direction into the predawn.

From the conning tower the scientists watched the formation, straining their eyes until the last speck had vanished from view.

When one by one they stopped looking out into space and

again became aware of one another as a group, no one spoke. There was nothing to say. One and all had the feeling that the next few hours would be longer than all the months it had taken them to build the contraption that was now being borne toward its destiny.

PART III: *Man of Destiny*

Chapter 28

SEBASTIAN had been unable to sleep for even an hour that night. He had picked up a guidebook of the place some weeks before in a secondhand bookshop in New York, and he had spent most of the night reading it, absorbing the history, familiarizing himself with the landmarks, the districts, the principal streets, studying the photographs, taking in all the statistical data, his mind intent on registering every detail that it could of the reality of the doomed city on this last day of its existence.

He had got dressed unusually early, hoping to sneak out of the house before anyone else was up. But Tanya had already prepared coffee and she made him sit down to the breakfast table. It was too early for the papers.

Tomorrow, he thought. Would he dare to open the papers?

They sat facing each other, but neither said anything. He drank two cups of black coffee and ate a piece of toast, though he wasn't hungry.

He did not see Tanya. At this hour (there was a ten-hour differential) night was just descending on the city ten thousand miles away. For its citizens it was a night like any other night, the end of a day like any other day. Most of them had probably finished the evening meal. Most of the children had probably been put to bed. There too it was probably one of those hot August nights that bring people out on their doorsteps, into their gardens, or on the street for a cool breath of evening air. He thought of the youngsters who would have spent the day playing, growing, learning to live; of the factory workers; of the people who ran the offices and the stores and the hundred services that kept a city going; of the women, lovers, families, the old and ailing people; of all the thoughts and emotions and memories and plans and hopes that were woven into the infinitely intricate fabric of relations of a city's social life.

When he left the house no word had been spoken between him and Tanya. He spent the morning in his office; there were many matters to attend to. He did not go home for lunch.

There was silence in the offices, silence in the laboratories. The traffic and the bustle that usually rose from the outside areas seemed to be muted. People went about their work mechanically, avoiding rather than seeking opportunities to communicate.

Zero hour had been scheduled for 1702 local time. Early in the afternoon, word came that it had been delayed one hour.

He felt his mouth suddenly go dry. He realized instantly the difference that that one hour would make. A large part of the working population of the target city lived outside the city limits. The new zero hour would give them all time to report for work and be in the heart of the zone of destruction. His hands went to his throat, and for a moment he thought he was going to vomit. His stomach seemed to harden into a tight knot. There were three—no, three and a half—hours left. There was yet time. Perhaps something could be done to stop it!

The minutes ticked by. Time was running out. But not only for that distant city: for the whole span of man's history. Throughout the millennia man had lived in a certain relation to the forces of nature that was governed by his knowledge and his control of those forces. Now he had broken through to a new dimension of knowledge, and his first use of that knowledge was going to be the perpetration of the most spectacular massacre in all history. For what? He sat rooted to his chair, gripped by a kind of panic. Should he do something? Was there anything he *could* do? The earth was whirling through space along an orbit that it had followed for millions of years. In a little over two hours an event would occur upon its surface that could initiate a chain of disasters whose consequences, though impossible to foresee, were fraught with horror.

The plane at this moment was roaring its way over the ocean toward its target. There was no way of stopping it now. It was of course in radio communication with its base, but no message of his to deflect it from its mission would even be allowed to reach it.

He sat at his desk as that point of the earth swung away from the sun, bringing the city beyond the ocean nearer to the dawn. All these things had been worked out in anguish and in hope through many months, through many seasons, and now they were reaching their fulfillment. What was good? What was evil? He had been willing to trust no one else. He had stored the conscience of humanity within himself for safekeeping. Would he be equal to his trust? And could he bear the weight?

The minute hand on the small clock on his desk had begun its slow ascent toward the hour of six. He got up. He could no longer bear to be alone.

He went into the big general office where all the instruments were. A score or more of his colleagues, perhaps prompted by the same impulse, had already gathered. The big clock on the south wall ticked out the seconds. The telephone and telegraph and radio operators were at their posts and all the office staff was present, but the big room was quiet except for the ticking of the instruments. There were windows along the whole length of the west wall, and Sebastian went over and took his post in front of one of them. The day had been hot, but already the mountain chill was returning and most of the windows had been closed.

5:45 . . . 5:50 . . . 5:55 . . . Seven minutes more . . .

More colleagues kept drifting in, and most of them came and stood in front of the windows looking to the west. The sun was moving down toward the ridge of mountains. It was bright, but not blinding, and as it sank it slowly turned orange.

5:58 . . . 5:59 . . . 6:00 . . . Sebastian desperately tried to fix his mind on other things, but in spite of himself he kept visualizing the last buses and trains that were at this moment bringing their loads of victims to the city in the rising sun. He could see them, hear them—the men and women sitting, standing, crowded together, jostling, gesticulating, talking, laughing. The beginning of another day . . .

6:01 . . .

Something passed in front of his line of vision, brushed against his face, startling him—too close for him to identify, with his eyes focused on the distance. As he looked directly at the glass he noticed a faint streak of golden dust, and following the movement that had caught his eye he saw that it was a miller moth that was fluttering on the surface of the window, its head repeatedly beating against the glass. The man next to him raised his hand and was about to crush it, but he thrust out his arm, gently enveloped the moth with his hand and caught it.

It was 6:02. Zero hour.

All this time the scientists—over fifty of them by now—had not said a word. Now Sebastian was aware, in the stillness, of a suffocating tension as though everyone was holding his breath, and the signal to breathe again might never come.

In his hand he felt the trembling of the tiny wings, the palpitation of a little life. With a sudden sense of outrage, feeling the sweat run down his face, he wrenched the window in front of him open. He flung out his arm, unclenched his fist, palm upward, spread his fingers wide and set the moth free. It fluttered away in halting, clumsy flight toward the sun.

As if it was the signal, the whole group stirred into motion, let out a collective deep breath and began to talk.

When the official announcement finally came over the wires, there was another dead silence.

Now it was done.

Outside, in the street, a group of people standing in a doorway suddenly displayed great excitement. Through the window that he had opened a young voice was heard.

"Whoopee!" rose the shout, in a piercing falsetto.

Chapter 29

"WE'VE got to get away!" Tanya exploded. "Otherwise you'll go mad, I'll go mad, we'll all go mad!"

It was a week after the Bolt had burst upon a stunned world. The surrender of the enemy was imminent.

Sebastian had come home that evening, and had fallen into a dead faint the moment he was inside the door. She had immediately sent for Dr. Wirin, who had diagnosed his ailment as an acute case of nervous exhaustion. "How he's stood it this far is nothing short of a miracle," he had said. "He needs absolute rest. A complete change. Otherwise I won't answer for him. He's none too strong to begin with, and he's incredibly run down."

Sebastian had slept uninterruptedly for forty-eight hours, had awakened only to take some pills that the doctor had prescribed and a little bouillon, and had slept again till the following morning a deathlike, absolute sleep.

The doctor had come again.

"Keep him in bed for a few more days. Don't let him see anyone. And then get him away," he had said.

During these days Tanya had been at her wit's end. The telephone had rung so constantly that she had had to have it disconnected. In a relaxation of security measures, prompted by the tremendous public pressure, a number of newspapermen and photographers had been admitted to Valhalla for the first time, and they had been so annoyingly persistent that she had had to get guards to keep them at a distance from the house. From the papers she learned that Sebastian had suddenly become world-famous. They were full of him—almost everything inaccurate—and all of them carried blown-up reproductions of two or three pictures of him dating back to a time before she had known him.

Her first experience with the press had given her a dreadful fright. When she had come into the living room on the morning after Sebastian had had his collapse, a moronic face had popped up from behind the sofa standing in the corner. The man had emerged—a short, ungainly figure bristling with photographic equipment, pockets bulging.

"Hi, chicken!" he had greeted her. "How about a little cooperation?"

She had tried to tell him that her husband was sick, that he had to be kept absolutely quiet.

The oaf's face had simply broadened in an expression of triumph.

"Hot diggedy dig!" he had exclaimed. "That's perfect! 'Valhalla Wizard Victim of Own Monster'! Sensational! Lemme get a picture of him just like he is, sleepin'. I won't wake him up, honest. It'll be—"

It was after that that she had asked Colonel Gregg's office for the guards.

Now Sebastian was awake and alert. He was still in bed, but restive, and he didn't want to believe that he had been asleep for sixty hours, that he had collapsed on the floor the moment he got inside the front door the day of the Monster.

"I've got too much to do," he replied, to her suggestion that they get away.

But Tanya got Dr. Wirin to talk to him, and when Sebastian got up and realized how weak he was, he finally consented to take a couple of weeks off—as soon as he had wound up some urgent matters.

Tanya, while she was careful not to broach any subject that Sebastian himself did not bring up, had a hunch that seeing Mark again—if he was still alive (she had had no word from Eve since she had written that Sebastian could do nothing to help her) —might be good therapy. She proposed, with great trepidation, that they take a trip to Hawaii: they could go to one of the small islands, lie around on beaches, take dips in the ocean . . .

Sebastian's face hardened, but he merely said, "We can't go that far away."

They settled on Florida.

But a monumental pile of things had accumulated on Sebastian's desk. There were endless telegrams and long-distance calls. He had to attend this and that urgent conference, make statements. Newspapermen and photographers were constantly on his heels. At last, after a few days of this, Tanya realized that the situation was hopeless. She made arrangements, gave Gino over to the care of the Brandons, chartered a plane, and got Sebastian aboard by practically kidnaping him.

In Miami they again ran into a swarm of press people. At dinner that first evening (tacitly they had both preferred the big hotel dining room to the silence of their suite) Sebastian by a movement of his eyes drew her attention to a man sitting a few tables away.

"That's one of Gregg's men," he said.

"I know. He came with us on the plane. He's been helpful."

"It's not going to be a vacation for me with him around—and the press to boot."

The following day, by a complicated series of maneuvers that Sebastian worked out, they managed to elude all surveillance and flew off to Key West, which had the advantage of being on an island. They rented a luxurious secluded cottage, with every service provided, and registered under assumed names.

"Maybe they'll leave us in peace for a few days," he said.

It was an idyllic setting. The weather was hot, but with a caressing breeze brought by the sea. The roomy, comfortable cottage with its wide terrace sat on a spur of land overlooking the sea, and a path led by a gentle slope down to the beach. For three days they slept and idled and let themselves get unwound. Tanya had been marooned on Valhalla for two and a half years, and being waited on hand and foot, for a change, was heavenly.

They played games in the sand with sticks and shells. They watched the boats that came and went, identified birds and insects and plants, recited poetry and at night, before going to sleep, read mysteries. There was a radio, but they never turned it on, and they saw no newspapers, received no mail and did not go into the town.

Tanya herself was near the breaking point. The cumulative strain of the past three years, sharpened almost beyond endurance in these last weeks, had drained all her reserves of strength. She had become a mere bundle of nerves. And yet she could not really relax, could not let herself go or yield to a healing passivity, so long as the agonizing questions remained unanswered, so long as all the foundations of her life remained insecure.

For Sebastian had become an almost total stranger to her. There was no longer any flow of emotion or of mind between them. There was a blank wall. He would not even talk about Mark and Eve. He had not made love to her since that humiliating night when he had somehow had an intimation of her plotting to have a child. In the last six months—since the moment when it had become apparent, even to her, that the war situation no longer necessitated resort to the Bolt—the wall that separated them had become impenetrable.

The whole situation was aggravated for her by the fact that throughout all these agonizing months, without being able to bring herself to face the question in an objective, cold-blooded way, she found the question—the crucial question—constantly prodding her, sneaking into her consciousness, from which she would expel it whenever she recognized its pitiless, uncompromising features. It went, in the words of the revolutionary song that they used to sing back in the thirties: *"Which side are you on? Which side are you on?"* The melody itself *(d d f g a—a a g e d)* had haunted her obsessively all these months. Had he remained faithful to the revolutionary ideal that was the very cornerstone of their union, of their love, or had he abandoned it? It was the question that, despite everything she could do, rose to her mind every time she saw Sebastian, every time she thought of him, that she tried to suppress from her mind, with the desperation of Midas in his efforts to bury the whispered words "Midas has ass's ears . . . Midas has ass's ears." But, like the taunting words that plagued Midas, the haunting question would not be stilled.

She had said to herself, The minute the dreadful job is done, he will resign, dissociate himself from any further activity connected with the Thing. He will be a free man again, be able to voice his views and devote himself to his ideals. He will become open and forthright as he used to be, and we shall be able to look back on all this as on a bad dream.

But now Sebastian had had a physical breakdown, and she herself felt too exhausted in mind and body to face any kind of showdown. Like survivors from a shipwreck lying panting on a beach that they have reached by dint of superhuman exertions, they had no strength left to talk about what had happened or about what they were going to do next.

She supposed that Sebastian was in the same state of numbness as herself. But she knew his extraordinary gift for sensing people's moods, especially hers, his almost abnormal solicitude for the well-being of those around him. And her uncertainty grew ever more agonizing. Surely he would say *something*, if only just a word.

The first day passed, and the second. There were spells, sometimes fairly long ones, when he was aware of her, and at such times he would be sweet, solicitous, would talk and even have moments of playfulness. But most of the time he was absent, and she felt that she existed for him only as a presence without any identity except perhaps a faint aura of femininity. At no time did he communicate his sense of her as Tanya, the woman to whom he was attached, the mother of his child, a being with whom he was emotionally involved, with whom he shared passions, experiences, aspirations, a segment of his life. Not once did he mention Gino.

By the end of the third day Tanya was beside herself. They had been dining out on the terrace. The air was balmy, and she was wearing only a thin short-sleeved blouse, a pair of shorts and sandals. A slim crescent of a moon hung in the deepening pink sky, and the light out on Sandy Key had begun to flash. They had been talking about fish, about deep-sea fishing, and Sebastian had said that someday they would come down here and rent a boat and try their luck. The boy had brought coffee, and Sebastian had lit a cigarette.

Now, thought Tanya. But Sebastian was silent. Three pelicans, flying low, passed just offshore. She could stand the uncertainty no longer.

"Maybe it's a little early . . ."

She hesitated, uncertain how to broach the subject.

". . . But I guess soon we'll want to start thinking about what we're going to do now that all this is over . . ."

Sebastian looked at her. His face was enigmatic. "It isn't quite over yet," he said.

"But I thought—"

"We'll see when the time comes."

"But you promised me—"

"I still have responsibilities. In fact, greater than ever."

She had understood the danger when they thought the Germans were working on the Bolt. But then they had gone ahead and used it anyway. Why hadn't he tried to stop it? And what was it now?

"There are so many things," she said. "I'm all at sea."

"Someday we'll be able to talk about it."

"But the war's over, isn't it?"

Sebastian shook his head. "In a sense. But there's a lot of unfinished business." He picked up the coffeepot.

"No, let me do it."

She poured the coffee into the two cups.

"We've let this thing loose," said Sebastian. "Now we've got to see that it isn't misused. That it doesn't get out of hand. The danger is greater now than ever."

"But you're in no shape to take on anything like that."

"I'll be all right. And I have no choice."

"Darling— I'm afraid. I keep wondering about you. I just don't know—"

"You mustn't worry."

"Oh, darling, if only you'd talk to me. I can't help worrying. I can't help wondering . . . You're up so high there in your inaccessible thoughts. No one can talk to you, no one can reach you. . . . Isn't there *anyone* you can trust, whom you can talk things over with? Can't you—"

"What are you talking about?" An angry look had come over his face.

What she was saying was based on intuition. But she was remembering some conversations of a long time ago, when he had still hesitated about committing himself; and recently, some of his colleagues, or their wives, had dropped hints that confirmed her hunch.

"Am I wrong?"

"You're talking nonsense. But I can't go into any of this now. Please try to understand."

She knew he was eluding her. But she needed something she could hang on to.

"You must tell me one thing at least," she said, with a sense of desperation. "You remember all the things we used to talk about, the way we felt, the people we loved—all that hasn't changed, has it?"

Sebastian looked at her and quickly smiled, reached his hand out and with it covered hers that was clutching the arm of her chair.

"*I* haven't changed, darling," he said. "But a lot of things *have* changed."

He gave a thin smile.

"The world has moved a long way since the time of our innocence."

The following morning they had their first visitor. They were out on the terrace when the boy came to announce him. Tanya went into the parlor, but Sebastian followed on her heels. It was Lieutenant Gillespie, one of Gregg's officers.

He grinned from ear to ear. "You sure gave us a run for our money, Doctor," he said. "We've had fifty people out looking for you." He mopped his brow with a big white linen handkerchief. "Whew! Did you have us scared!"

Chapter 30

MARK heard the news of the unleashing of the Bolt from his hospital bed in Pearl Harbor. It swept through the ward like wildfire. Several scattered radios were tuned in to different stations. Someone shouted, "Hey, d'ye hear that?"—and the mounting roar of voices created a bedlam that brought the nurses and the medical officers running. Out of the din came the word "Bolt" repeated again and again, and Mark finally gathered that Sebastian had at last produced his "gadget." He was weak and could hardly move, and he let the noise and excitement roll over him. He thought of all his dead comrades. "Too late," he said in a half whisper. "Too late."

The account of what had happened came to Mark in crazy, broken fragments that made little sense, that added up to something that sounded utterly fantastic. The Thing had been released over a city of a third of a million inhabitants and had completely blotted out an area of some four square miles right in the center. There were an estimated two hundred thousand dead. But the damage had extended far beyond this central area of total destruction caused by the blast, the heat, the blinding light. There was talk of emanations, rays that traveled long distances, contaminating everything they touched, penetrating and destroying living tissue.

The prevailing reaction was one of awe. These men were fighters. They had all been badly hurt in battle. They knew what every kind of known weapon could do. The Bolt was worse than the worst multiplied by at least five figures.

"Well, that's the end of soldiering, boys!" was one cheerful comment. "This is where the civilians take over! Hurrah for the civilians!"

The weeks that followed brought more and more details, and along with them an unending flow of commentary, speculation, and reports of policy discussions on high government, military and scientific levels. Events moved so fast that it was hard to keep up with them. A few days after the Bolt had been unleashed the enemy surrendered unconditionally. Russia had meanwhile declared war (an item tucked away in the middle of a paragraph on an inside page that had rather surprised Mark); for Russia, however, hostilities had virtually ended on this front before they began.

Meanwhile accounts of the havoc wrought by the Bolt had

been coming from the source. The details were ghastly. Most disquieting was the fact that weeks after the event hundreds of people who had merely been exposed to the Thing's breath were dying daily. Others were blinded, from looking at it. There were agonizing new diseases for which there was no known treatment. What would be the effect on future generations?

On one thing, if on nothing else, all those who flooded the channels of communication with their views agreed: the devastating new weapon that had just been invented and used with such telling effect had opened a new age—the Age of the Bolt.

Mark had been in the hospital for nearly three months. Three months. It was an unreal span of time. During most of it he had been unconscious, or hovering between consciousness and unconsciousness, between life and death, shot full of drugs. Time had lost all reality. The minutes, the hours, the days, had no meaning in the state he had been in. All this time, he vaguely gathered, he had been teetering on the ragged edge. And it was still touch and go. He had had two major operations —or was it three? He didn't know exactly what he had. His guts, a big part of his guts, shot away. All he knew was that he hadn't eaten all this time. He was fed intravenously, by injections, rectally. He was an exhibit, a guinea pig. Doctors from every which-where, specialists, dozens of them, were constantly hovering around him.

Most of the time he had been too weak to care about anything, to think about anything. Most of the time everything was blank. And then there was the pain. And it was only when he had the pain that he had memories, and sometimes thoughts. Some things were clear, but most things were foggy. And he could never hold on to anything long. He had a vivid memory of stepping into some kind of cave, out of the light into the dark, and then a violent shock that hurled him back into the world of pain, a pain that would have doubled him up if he could have moved, but that he had to take lying out flat, his whole middle convulsing and tearing him apart.

It was only in the last couple of weeks that he had begun to regain a sense of his own identity. "You're going to be all right, if you'll behave," the head surgeon had told him after the last operation. But the bastards would never let you know exactly what was wrong with you. "I don't mind telling you now," he had said, in a rare expansive mood, "for a long time I didn't think you'd make it." He had manipulated some tube that was stuck into him, and checked various contraptions that were rigged all over his middle. "You'll make it all right." He had shaken his head. "Too bad. It's always the no-good characters that seem to pull through."

When several weeks later he was able to take food by mouth, exclusively liquids at first, then thin purées that were gradually thickened, he began at last to have a certain faith that perhaps he was not going to die or be a permanent invalid, that perhaps he would live and be able to walk and work and make love, and that he might see Eve and Jimmy again . . . And then of course there was Sebastian.

The papers were full of Sebastian these days. The story of how the Bolt had been built was still wrapped in mystery, but there was a lot about Valhalla, the mountain where most of the work had been done, a lot of facts about the project, its vastness, the tens of thousands of people who had been involved in the work in its final stages, stories about the top scientists, many of whose names Mark already knew. But the focus of all this attention was on Sebastian himself, who was being more and more frequently referred to as the Begetter of the Bolt, and sometimes even, by the more smart-alecky news commentators, as Thor or Jupiter.

Mark recalled the days when he had first made contact with Sebastian Bloch—seven years had gone by!—and Sebastian's total obscurity then. He had been known only to a small circle of specialists, then gradually to a somewhat larger circle of friends, colleagues, students. This had been so, right up to the present time. Now suddenly he was receiving fantastic publicity. He had become the man of the hour—more famous than the President, than any political or military leader, even Mac-Arthur, than any other scientist except Einstein.

There were hundreds of photographs of him. (Mark remembered Gregg's wondering if he was camera-shy, the impossibility of getting a single good picture.) He seemed to be everywhere at the same time—in Washington, New York, Valhalla and elsewhere, conferring with other scientists, high government officials, military commanders, lecturing, talking on the radio, appearing in newsreels. There were family pictures of him with Tanya and Gino, and with Tanya alone, in a variety of settings, looking like lovebirds, and in some with Gino alone: father and son—Gino (now six and a half) looking very important.

There were picture stories in the pictorial weeklies, articles in all the periodicals covering current events. His daily movements were reported and commented upon: where he went, whom he saw, what he said and did. Honors were being heaped on him: medals, degrees, memberships in a great assortment of exclusive societies, honorary offices. He was made chairman of a score or more of scientific, academic, government and financial boards, committees, commissions, councils and panels. All over the country civic bodies and women's groups were putting on special events in his honor.

In the beginning Mark had merely a kind of passive identification with Sebastian, over the great distance that separated them. It was almost four years since he had seen him. Mark was wonder-struck. He knew that in his weakened state he was not able to react and judge as he ordinarily would. But the idea of Sebastian having fathered an awesome thing like the Bolt was unsettling. He didn't know what to think, how to feel. He fell back simply on his familiar sense of identification with Sebastian, who was after all his closest friend. He was proud of him, delighted by his success, his fame. He followed his activities through the periodicals he could get hold of. Seeing his picture in all sorts of poses, after the long separation, was almost like seeing him again in the flesh—especially as he could supply from memory, even though he had always been unable to visualize him, characteristic fleeting expressions that could not be caught by a still camera.

He was careful not to mention to anyone in the hospital that he was a friend of the famous Sebastian Bloch. He had in any case been too sick to establish much contact with other patients. But since he was condemned to passivity it gave him a kind of pleasure to hear occasional discussions on the subject of Bloch and the Bolt. As the talk went back and forth between beds ("Wonder if they're gonna make any more of them damn things?" . . . "Suppose the Russians start turning them out!" . . .) Mark would remember the many discussions, particularly in the unit meetings, when Sebastian, with his piercing mind, would launch upon some political analysis. Mark would slyly treasure within himself the knowledge that in the inner councils of government, at the very top of the structure of the state, was a man, his friend, who was a Marxist, a great humanitarian, a genius possessing an uncanny political insight, who would surely contrive to direct events of state along the road of peace and progress. Each time he read of a new honor, a new distinction, conferred upon Sebastian, he rejoiced and saw in it a confirmation of Sebastian's moral authority and a widening of the allegiance extended to him by the forces of enlightenment.

Mark had several more operations to look forward to, and there would have to be quite a bit of plastic surgery done on him to patch up the surface after the inner organs had been repaired. It was heartening to think of the miracles that were being achieved by surgery, and to reflect that, with all its horrors, war had enabled medicine to make enormous forward strides. Which reminded him that in all the talk about the Bolt and the menace that it represented for the future of mankind, attention was also being given to the possibility of taming it and making it serve man's needs.

As his strength slowly returned, his mind became more alert and his emotions more demanding. He began to notice that there was something unsatisfactory about Eve's letters. They overflowed with love and every kind of attention that could be communicated through letters—to say nothing of the packages. But she hardly ever mentioned Sebastian, and again and again failed to answer questions that he would ask. He could not help remembering, of course, the negative feeling she had always had about Sebastian, her mistrust of him; but surely she could not go on feeling that way forever!

He had been hoping that Eve could come to the islands, especially some months back when he had been convinced that his days were numbered. But he knew what the state of the travel priorities was, and he had resigned himself to not seeing her for many months to come. The doctors talked hopefully about the possibility of discharging him sometime late next spring—"if everything goes well," they always added. So he and Eve were reduced to communicating by correspondence for many long months more. It was two and a half years since he had last seen her. And how long since they had had a really stable life together? He thought back: he was appalled. He remembered the first quarrel he and Eve had had, that Thanksgiving—it was just two days before they had met Sebastian at the party for Spain—seven years!

Now for the first time as the year was drawing to a close, Mark was able, and dared, to think about going back, to wonder what it was going to be like. A lot of course would depend on the shape he was in. But there was one resolve which had been born in him probably in that first battle experience he had had on Makin, the first time he had ever killed a man, which had grown in him through the interminable nightmare of the war, through all the grim battles he had fought, and which had by now become embodied in his flesh and in his spirit: he would dedicate the rest of his life to peace, he would work and fight to build a world from which war would be forever outlawed. This, he knew, was a task not for one man, not for a thousand men, but for a million, ten million, a hundred million men, women and children. Peace—a true peace, a lasting peace—would be won not by governments, not by the men at the top, but by the people. And he would be one of them. Sebastian too would be one of them. Sebastian would have plenty of ideas as to how the movement should be organized. Perhaps he would be willing to participate in a less self-effacing way than he had done in the Teachers' Union.

Mark began to think about their reunion, what it would be like. The first thing he was going to do, of course, was to confess the wrong he had done him. That was going to be all the easier now, as he knew that his reports, whatever had happened to them, had not stood in the way of Sebastian's carrying out his war assignment. He had been able to overcome his sense of guilt at having approached Sebastian in the role of an informer. For one thing, the influence of Sebastian himself had changed his whole outlook. And any lingering sense of guilt that he might have felt about anything connected with his role as a special agent had been thoroughly knocked out of him by the punishment he had taken in this war. He had paid—he had paid plenty; and Sebastian in his wisdom and compassion would forgive him.

As his strength slowly revived, and he began to regain weight and was allowed to make certain cautious movements, he became increasingly impatient to return home. He knew that he had changed profoundly. But it occurred to him one day that others would have changed too. The country would have changed, and the people—in themselves, and in relation to the world. And those who had borne most would have changed most.

None perhaps had borne more than Sebastian. At the beginning Mark had not been so struck by the difference in him, but as he studied the pictures now he saw that the face showed ravage. Perhaps it was the fault of the photographer, but in some of the pictures he had a positively satanic look. The eyes gleaming in the great dark hollows, the bones sharp under the thin flesh, the mouth piercing the face like a wound, had an almost sinister suggestion. But in other pictures Mark recognized his warm, encompassing smile.

He too must have gone through a kind of hell, must have fought many desperate battles along the way. And lost some of them as well, Mark imagined—like the unleashing of the Bolt when it was no longer needed.

Yes, there was going to be plenty for them to talk about.

Chapter 31

AT FIRST Sebastian had been startled and dazed by the tidal wave of publicity that had lifted him immediately after Victory Day to the very crest of fame. He felt no pride, no sense of achievement, and no ease of conscience. The frenzy of victory and the glad shouts had a false ring. When, without irony, he was tagged as the "Begetter of the Bolt," this attribution of paternity made him wince; both because it was monstrous and because, even taking it as a well-meant tribute to a task accomplished, this had been outstandingly a collective effort, in which the collaboration of hundreds of scientists and thousands of workers had been indispensable, and in which the contributions of insight, imagination, knowledge and genius, to say nothing of hard work, were too numerous to make it possible for any one man to claim more than a modest share in the final victory.

But once the shock of unexpectedness had been assimilated, the recognition, the honor, the adulation, acted as a powerful tonic to his exhausted system and a balm to his spirit. He saw himself as a symbol of science. In him the world was paying homage to science.

With bewilderment he found himself confronted by the headlines featuring his name, by the endless articles and editorials, by his own picture looking back at him from all the newsstands. He remembered how for years he had refused to have any pictures taken of himself. But how many things had changed!

He had to get used to meeting the press after every conference, after his interviews with political and military leaders, get used to the newsreel cameras, the flashing of bulbs at meetings, banquets and every kind of gathering, to requests for autographs. Honorary degrees, medals, election to membership in the most distinguished societies and clubs, appointments to committees and commissions and boards—every mail brought new evidence of universal recognition.

The general public was of course avid, among other things, for the "human angle" on the great man. It took the photographers no time at all to discover that Tanya was an exceptionally beautiful woman. They would insist on her getting into the pictures. And then there was Gino. Did he inherit his father's genius? Gino had a rather bad school record. He wasn't, in fact, overbright. But he was a good kid. Family pictures. A happy family. An American family. Tanya was besieged by all sorts of public relations people. Cosmetics, food and soap manufacturers, garment and household appliance firms . . . She was offered contracts to lecture to women's clubs, and even a movie contract. Then it was discovered that she was a pianist, and all the concert tour managers were after her.

It came to his attention that a shady national weekly had got hold of a number of pictures of Tanya in the nude, taken in her student days when she had been working as a model, and that it had used them for a "sensation" story.

He was abruptly brought back to the realization that he too had a past. It was a sobering reminder of the vulnerability of his position. He remembered that Vincent Carter, the columnist, who now had a radio program with a national hookup in addition to his syndicated column, had at the time run a story, without mentioning names, which was a transparent version of his affair with Estrellita and the suicide of Leo Hirschberg. And Carter had had wind of at least one of his other affairs. He would certainly have a good filing system. But what he had most to fear from was his political past. And the higher he rose in public esteem, the harder he would fall.

He had moments of panic. There were things in his past that could be terribly damaging. What if they came out? It was a rhetorical question; they were bound to come out. And because of this the fruits of triumph had a taste of ashes, and a sense of defeat hovered over the achievement of victory.

Very quickly the glare of publicity that was focused on him became a source of anxiety and menace—an effect aggravated by the fact that he had to "play the game," that he could not run away from it and show it up for the cynical mockery that it was. He was being hailed as a hero who had saved countless lives, whereas he was, he felt, in fact the agent and the instrument of a cold-blooded mass murder. He was being lauded as the architect of victory, whereas in fact the Bolt had come too late in the day to affect the issue of the battle. He was being given academic honors for his contribution to science, whereas the building of the Bolt, though an impressive technical achievement, had not advanced fundamental science by a single step.

The war was ended. And peace—the peace that millions had yearned for through years of anguish—had come. But how had the war ended? And what kind of peace had been won?

An answer to these questions was provided him by a general at a conference, shortly after his return from Key West, called to discuss the future control of the Bolt. The army was anxious to maintain its grip on this decisive weapon that made all other means and implements of warfare obsolete, and Sebastian had indicated, without committing himself, that he would support this position.

The general had come to him after the meeting had broken up, had grasped his hand and shaken it fervently. "I want to congratulate you!" he had said. "We owe you the greatest of debts. Thanks to you we've won the first round in the war that has now at last begun, the war against Russia. We've got the edge on them. Now we've got to see to it that we keep it."

Sebastian had too great a familiarity with the thinking of the circles in whose hands the country's power was vested to be shocked by such a statement. Yet he was deeply disturbed to hear it now reasserted in this brutal way. It was a harsh reminder that objectively he himself, by consenting to the unleashing of the Bolt, had contributed to transforming the antifascist war into an anticommunist war. But more fundamentally, it underscored the fact that the peace was not yet won, and that a far deeper conflict lay ahead.

He was face to face with his final task which must justify every sacrifice that he had made. The destiny of humanity was in his hands. But now that detailed news was arriving daily of the terrible and growing toll of human lives taken by the Bolt, he was visited by occasional misgivings: had he been wrong to allow the Bolt to be unleashed? If he had stopped it, he would have saved suffering and bitterness. He might have made it possible to reach an international agreement never to resort to the Bolt. But nothing would have been solved—humanity would simply have returned to its old murderous ways, the conflict between the East and the West would not have been averted; whereas the Bolt constituted a wholly new factor in the world situation that could be used decisively to break through the vicious circle of endless wars. The way to permanent peace, the saving of humanity from itself, was fraught with infinite hazards. But the goal was worth every risk.

Would he have the strength to carry out his task to the end? He was conscious of his own fragility. And periodically the thought that the fate of the world was dependent upon this flimsy, faulty organism that he carried about with him would appall him. He must not fail through a physical breakdown. At the same time he knew that his responsibility was consuming him.

Amid the hosannas of victory, he was pressed by an urgency even greater than that which had presided over the building of the Bolt. Everything compelled haste: his own fragility, the precariousness of his status, the imminence of danger abroad, the threats in the situation at home.

He had been receiving reports of the rapid advances being made by the Soviet scientists. Perhaps they already had a Bolt? He alerted General Pendleton of the Air Force and set in motion a plan for round-the-clock reconnaissance flights on the periphery of Soviet territory by planes equipped with newly developed instruments of extreme sensitivity to register any Bolt tests. With Gröndahl, Porter, Baker and Benelli he began, immediately after his return from Key West, to work out a plan for equipping the army with Bolt weapons. He needed the Monster. A bigger and more effective Monster. A Monster of overwhelming power.

Now that the war was over, the people in Valhalla and on the other projects had only one thought in mind, to get back to civilian life and resume their familiar pursuits. Yet despite many defections he was able to maintain, and even to expand, the program of production. There were signs of growing turbulence in the postwar climate. Pressures were mounting. Government leaders and military chiefs anxiously scanned the horizon to the east. There were endless conferences. Many of his fellow scientists wanted to scrap the Bolt, develop Bolt power for peaceful purposes and bring the whole project under civilian control. The army wanted to keep control of the Bolt and continue to produce it. The Government was studying the problem of international control.

He had not forgotten Mark. When he received a letter from him from the Pearl Harbor hospital two months after the unleashing of the Bolt all his old affection welled up in him anew. He was overjoyed to learn that Mark was well on the mend, though his recovery would be slow and he would not be able to leave the hospital for several months. Perhaps by then —though it seemed unlikely—he would have achieved his goal and he would feel free to tell Mark about the little fabrication that he had built up at his expense. However, although it had originally weighed on his conscience as an act of disloyalty to his friend, it now appeared, in the light of all the things that had happened both to Mark and to himself, as a trivial matter—especially as he had, he was quite sure, told the true story at the time that he had given Mark's name. And in any case, Mark would never find out about it. It was buried away in some file gathering dust. By this time it had been completely forgotten.

Chapter 32

"I THOUGHT you and I might just have a little talk, Bill, before going in to the staff meeting," General Forester said, getting up to meet General Van Nuys who had just come into his office. "Have a seat."

He went back to his desk and they both sat down.

"About this Dr. Bloch," he said. "Sebastian Bloch."

"Oh," said General Van Nuys. "Yes. I'm interested."

"You're friendly with him, from what I can gather?"

"You might say that. I have a great admiration for him."

"I suppose we all have. He's quite a remarkable man."

H. Granville Forester (Harry officially, Granville to his friends) again made a mental note of the fact that Bill Van Nuys didn't carry his age very well. He was only five years older than himself, but he looked ten.

"Quite a remarkable man," he repeated. "In fact"—he watched Van Nuys sharply for his reaction—"a little *too* remarkable."

Van Nuys registered the expected surprise. "What do you mean?"

"I'll tell you what's on my mind."

He found himself straining his mental capacities to the utmost. What he had to say was difficult. Especially as there were elements that eluded him. All this was in a world of thought that was unfamiliar to him.

"This Bloch is, I guess, the closest thing to a genius that we shall see in our lifetime. Though perhaps Einstein tops him in some respects; I don't know. I don't think anybody else could have done what he's done. We couldn't have got along without him. What we owe him is tremendous. I'm not forgetting that. But now we've got to look at the future."

He paused to consider his next words.

"Don't jump," he said finally, "when you hear what I'm going to say."

He paused again, but this time it was for effect.

"Bloch has done his job. He's served his purpose. Now we've got to scrap him."

Van Nuys did jump. "Look here, Granville! Don't talk nonsense!" He was on his feet and he came over to the desk and leaned over him, resting his knuckles on the green steel surface. "Bloch is more indispensable now than he ever was! Don't you realize that we've got this control bill coming up, and that our only chance—"

"Keep your shirt on, Bill—" Forester noticed how the veins stuck out blue on the backs of Van Nuys's hands. "Sit down and let me explain to you."

Van Nuys straightened up and looked at Forester defiantly. They were friends from way back and had often worked closely together. But they had always scrapped.

"They call you Hardhead Harry," Van Nuys said. "Well, I believe in being hardheaded too. And I don't think this is a good time to let your inferiority complex get the better of you." (Forester felt himself puffing with indignation, but restrained himself.) "Bloch is smarter than you. He's smarter than me too. So what? That's no reason we can't use him. Especially as he asks nothing better than to do what we want him to."

"Sit down, Bill," Forester said. "You don't understand what I'm getting at."

Van Nuys stood uncertainly in the middle of the room, but made no move to sit down. "I don't think you know what you're talking about," he said.

"Listen, Bill," Forester said. "Do me a favor and sit down."

Bill Van Nuys sat down.

"Now let me tell you about Bloch—"

"I know all about his record."

"No, you don't. But that's beside the point. The point is this: he's becoming too powerful. Pretty soon we won't be able to handle him. That's what's worrying me."

Van Nuys looked genuinely bewildered. "What you're saying doesn't make any sense to me," he said. "Everything I know about the man seems to contradict it."

"I know," said Forester. "It isn't what you'd expect. But let's look at the thing a little closer."

Although, in order to convince his older colleague, he spoke with a certain persuasiveness, what he had to say troubled him.

"Here's a man who was a communist. Not an ordinary, run-of-the-mill guy, but the exceptional, phenomenally intelligent, highly sensitive man we know. His tie-up with communism wasn't just a hit-and-run affair. It was a genuine commitment. He believed in it, and he made others—many others—believe in it. He was an important member of the movement. And he had no illusions. He knew the worst about Russia. He was thoroughly aware of the weakness of the party in this country. He knew the going was rough. Yet he believed in it. He believed in it strongly enough to be willing, when the time came, to work on the Bolt—yes," he said, seeing Van Nuys's expression of incredulity, "I'm pretty certain of that."

Van Nuys shook his head. "I find it hard to believe."

"Why is it hard to believe? He isn't the kind of man to go in for making weapons of wholesale destruction. He's a man of peace, if ever there was one. And his field is theory, not practical development. This just wasn't his meat. But he was a communist. This was the war against fascism that they had been advocating for so long. And there was good reason to believe the Germans were working on the Bolt. Draw your own conclusions."

"There were other scientists," said Van Nuys. "They were just as anxious to work on the Bolt as he was."

"Yes," said Forester. "Most of them even more so. Because they didn't have his humanitarian reservations, they weren't so sensitive. And he was a communist: his reasons would necessarily be different from theirs. The others, all of them, went into the thing for mixed motives. Bloch, I am sure, went into it out of pure idealism."

"He claims—I've looked through the file—that he lost all interest in communism long before the war."

"It's not true. He was a member right up to the time he began working on the Bolt. Right now I don't know what he thinks. I doubt if anybody does."

Van Nuys pondered for a long moment.

"All right," he said.

"Now then. He went to work on the Bolt. The minute he did, he made a complete about-face: disavowed all his former beliefs, lied about his past, turned informer and not only told on his old friends and comrades but even invented highly compromising stories about some of them—one in particular."

Forester could tell from Van Nuys's expression that this was mostly new to him.

"Now you may say," he went on, "that a man could honestly change his mind, and having changed his mind would repudiate his former associates. And as for the lies—well, perhaps these people were more or less disreputable, and one or two details more or less . . . Personally I don't subscribe to that, mind you, but you might make a case. What disturbs me far more, however, is this. A man may change his ideas; he can't change his character. And since he has been involved with the Bolt, Bloch's character *seems* to have undergone a profound change."

Van Nuys rubbed his face with both hands. "I find all this very disturbing," he said.

"So do I."

What disturbed Forester most was that he was unable to make an absolutely clear case against Bloch, and yet he knew that he had to be got rid of.

"Take our decision to use the Bolt. We had our reasons for it. But most of the scientists were against it. Not Bloch. Why not? If there is one thing that is outstanding about his character it is his gentleness, his sensitiveness, his humaneness. Yet he didn't make a move, not a gesture."

Van Nuys's face was a mask, but Forester knew it so well that he could tell that he was taking in every word.

"What terrifies me is this: *if* he had been against our using the Bolt he could have stopped us. He could have mobilized all the scientists, appealed to public opinion, and stopped us cold. He didn't. Why not?"

"I see what you mean. But where does this leave us?"

"It leaves us—"

Forester shook his head.

"I don't know what to say. I just know we've got to get rid of him."

They both fell silent. Outside could be heard voices and the shuffling of steps past the door.

An idealist, Forester was thinking. But one who would use any means to achieve his ends. Bloch must have been tempted to stop the Bolt. What would have happened? He would have succeeded, of course. But he would have been through as an influence in government. And he knew the counts against him which would have been used to ruin him. Those were still there.

Bill Van Nuys looked at Forester. "It would be very awkward right now. He's a national hero. And we need him. We're going to have a fight on our hands over that bill."

Forester got up. "I know. We'll have to move slowly. We've got to plan it very carefully." After a moment he added, "But I guess Gregg will be able to take care of it."

There was a knock at the door, and General Sproncke appeared, looking jovial. The three exchanged boisterous greetings against the background of the movement in the hall in the direction of the conference room. They had not seen Sproncke since before B-Day, the Day of the Bolt.

"—a moth," they heard Sproncke say, grinning above the stir and babble, some of his words drowned out by the other voices, "—one of our men . . ." There was a volley of laughter out in the hall. "I want to tell you a story about a moth . . ."

Chapter 33

"OH, DARLING!"

Eve had only just stepped inside the cottage entrance when she was overcome with emotion. She dropped the things she was carrying on the floor and threw her arms around Mark's neck.

"Oh, darling!" she repeated, and she felt big tears rolling down her cheeks.

As Mark, having put down his various bundles more gingerly, took her in his arms, there was a plaintive "Aw, come on, Ma!" from Jimmy.

Eve slowly unwound her arms from around Mark's neck and, clutching his lapels, smiled through her tears. But seeing Jimmy, and Mark in his prewar suit that was now too big for him, and the front door that they had just come in by, and the key, still in the lock, that Mark had opened it with, and this front entrance and the double door opening into the living room, she was overwhelmed again. Something caught in her throat and she let herself collapse on Mark's chest.

"Darling, you're *home!*" she sobbed.

A few hours later she had the flutter inside her under better control. The van had come, bringing the rest of their things— the china and kitchenware and books and linen and odds and ends. She had made the beds and cooked their first meal and tucked Jimmy away for the night, and she and Mark were sitting on two straight-backed chairs in the curtainless and carpetless living room, surrounded by crates and cases and burlap-wrapped rolls and bulging shapes.

"Darling, do you realize that this is the first time we'll have had a real *home*—I mean with all our own things and not other people's—since—" She had already figured it out many times, but each time it seemed incredible. "—Well, it's been nearly eight years . . . since you took on that job that . . ." She had a sudden feeling of awkwardness. ". . . that first brought us here to the University."

There had been too many things in the past few weeks, and she was too happy and excited and tired to think. She could only *feel*, and what she felt right now was that for the first time in the ten days since she had been with Mark she was sure that it was he and that he was back and that it was really true.

But she jumped up and had to go over and touch him once more.

"I know just how you feel," Mark said softly, stroking her hand. "I can hardly believe it either."

When she had seen him first at Letterman Hospital in San Francisco where she had gone to meet him, they had been utterly unable to say anything to each other. There had been three frustrating days of formalities before he could get his discharge and they could be together. And then there had been those four days in San Francisco—wonderful, but not quite real. During the two-day train trip and the day and night they had spent in town, at her parents' home, seeing both his and her family, the world had crowded in on them too much to allow her to feel that Mark was *hers*.

Now at last they were together, just the two of them and Jimmy, in their own home.

"So you really like it?" she asked for the tenth time, as Mark looked around at the bare white walls.

"It's wonderful!" he said.

It had been her idea to rent a place for them to live before he arrived, and to get all their things out of storage. Fond as she was of their respective parents, she could not have stood sharing Mark with either family for an indefinite period of weeks after he got home. Mark had approved of the idea, and she had found this small house with its nice garden, only a five-minute walk from the University, and Mark seemed pleased.

And now began a kind of postwar honeymoon for the two

of them, in which of course ten-year-old Jimmy had his share.

"Let's give ourselves a week or so of complete irresponsibility," Mark had suggested. "After that we'll begin to think of serious things."

A good part of their irresponsibility turned out to be composed of unpacking and arranging and putting things in order. After his nine months in the hospital Mark was not yet strong: he could not exert himself too much, or lift heavy weights. But he was perfectly capable of doing most of the things that needed to be done. And before long, the doctors had assured him, he would be "almost as good as new."

Jimmy was put into school, and things gradually assumed a degree of order. Eve was thrilled to rediscover her electric stove, her big refrigerator and her washing machine. The piano and the sofa and all the other pieces of furniture found their place, the carpets were laid and Eve busied herself with the curtains. There was the delight of seeing again pictures and books and knickknacks, many of which they had forgotten they had.

But along with all this, and more than anything else, they had to talk. They had so much to catch up on. It wasn't just the nearly three years he had been in the war and all he had gone through: it was all the other times they had been separated. Now they had found each other again—both battle-scarred, both older and wiser. "Wiser," said Mark, "we *hope!*"

It was hard for Eve, getting used to Mark again. Because, while he was of course still the wonderful Mark she had always known—more wonderful than ever, if anything—he was also different. He was a Mark who had been through dreadful battles, who had faced death many times, and who now had been on the edge of it for months and was just slowly pulling away from it. Everyday life was so false! It was posited on the assumption that one lived forever. Yet that assumption, balanced against the fragility of human life, falsified all values.

"There's something wrong with our whole approach to existence!" she exploded one day. "There's something wrong with our civilization!"

They talked for hours. The thing that was wrong, they decided, was the whole pattern of relations—of human, social, economic, political relations—which generated distrust, envy, hate, leading to conflict, leading to war.

Mark told her that in his very first battle he had made a solemn vow that if by some miracle he were to survive, he would dedicate the rest of his life to working for peace. Now that he had come through, he meant to keep that pledge.

There was about Mark now a gravity, a depth, that she had not known before. Although it was something she rarely thought about, she kept remembering that she was two years older than he was. Yet for the first time in their lives he seemed to her older than herself—older, especially, in the best sense of having more experience and having digested it, and being thereby wiser and nearer to the truth, or at least to such truth as was available to man. Not forbidding, not solemn—quite the contrary. But self-possessed, having his center in himself. And at the same time not the least self-centered.

Eve understood and approved Mark's resolve, and much of their talk was concerned with future plans. The first and most immediate concern was earning a living and acquiring a status. In their exchange of letters they had agreed that the first move should be for Mark to take up his deferred teaching job at the University. As a professor he would have a position of influence that would be valuable. It was a point of vantage from which he could survey the situation and determine how he could be most effective.

"But before I take the next step, I want to talk to Sebastian," Mark would say. "He'll have ideas as to how I can best serve the cause of peace."

Every time Mark mentioned Sebastian's name Eve felt herself stiffen. It was the only subject that she could not discuss with Mark without embarrassment. She had never told him how she had written Tanya to ask if Sebastian could help her get to Hawaii to visit Mark in the hospital when it seemed possible that she might otherwise never see him again. Reading between the lines of Tanya's answer she had gathered that

Sebastian had refused. But even apart from this, Eve had acquired the certainty, ever since the unleashing of the Bolt, that Sebastian had "sold out." Otherwise why was he accepting all the honors that were being heaped on him for having made it? Why had he not protested against its use, as so many other eminent scientists had? Why wasn't his name ever mentioned among those of his colleagues who were demanding the outlawing of the Bolt as a weapon, and an effective international control of its power? Why was he so high in the councils of government and army?—a government and an army which, after all, were responsible for the horrors inflicted by the Bolt. Every day new deaths were reported, resulting from aftereffects of the Bolt. An undetermined number of people who had been thought to be unharmed by the Bolt were developing belated symptoms of a dread new disease which they had named Bolt sickness.

She did not have the heart to convey any of this to Mark. If she was wrong, she did not want to upset him. And if she was right, he would find out soon enough. But meanwhile Sebastian remained a touchy subject. She found it impossible to discuss him. Fortunately Mark did not press her. But she felt he could not help noticing her reticence and resenting it, and this distressed her.

By the end of their week of "irresponsibility" they were both ready for more serious things. Mark made an appointment to see Anderson. They would begin looking up colleagues and old friends. Mark presumably would not be able to begin teaching before the fall session, but Eve could already see herself as a faculty wife.

"Somehow, though," she said, on the morning of the day Mark had his appointment with his former professor, "I don't think we can expect that things are going to be exactly the same as they were before the war, that we'll be able to go back to the same kind of life."

"No," Mark agreed. "I'm sure everything is going to be very different. What I'm not sure about is whether it's going to be better or—worse."

He thought, as Tom Anderson gave him an account of how the war had looked from the office of an administrator in the Price Control Board in Washington, that his former teacher had changed very little. Perhaps his hair was just a little grayer, the look in his face a little more stern and disapproving.

"Well, it wasn't very pretty," Anderson concluded, "but we managed somehow to do a job that wasn't too discreditable."

He leaned forward on his desk. "As for what's going on in the country today—"

He looked at Mark and shook his head.

"I'm afraid you'll be pretty shocked. A wave of Red hysteria such as we have never witnessed—not as blatant as in 1919, in the time of the Palmer raids, but much more insidious and sinister."

Mark remembered that Anderson was always given to strong, uncompromising statements. All this was quite new to him. He had gone through the whole war in a kind of ideological vacuum.

A diabolical glint came into Anderson's eyes.

"Remember how I warned you against Sebastian Bloch?"

Mark looked at him questioningly. "Yes . . . But what's that got to do with—"

"The Bolt," said Anderson. "Why do you suppose it was used? It was used against the Russians. And Bloch knew it. He could have stopped it, but he didn't. Why not? Let me tell you something: America is moving into a period that the future —if there *is* a future—will look back upon as the Dark Ages. And one of the men who will be recognized as chiefly responsible for it will be none other than your friend Sebastian Bloch."

Mark could not help taking this as an almost personal attack, but Anderson skillfully parried his objections, and then abruptly switched to the object of Mark's visit.

"I'm afraid," he said, "that you may find yourself to be one of the early victims of this wave of reaction."

Mark became suddenly alert.

Anderson continued: "I spoke to the chairman the other day about your coming back. It seems there's some difficulty."

Mark was taken completely off his guard. He had been assured when he had left to go into the army that his post would be kept open for him. It had never occurred to him that he might run into trouble here.

"I don't know what the difficulty is," Anderson went on. "I'll see what I can find out. Of course I'll help in any way I can. I'd like to see you on our staff."

Over a solitary cup of coffee at a drugstore counter, Mark tried to imagine what obstacle could have arisen. He could only think of Gregg. Gregg had threatened him with trouble. He had threatened him with trouble in the army too. Mark hadn't taken it seriously, but now, in the light of all that had happened, it had some plausibility. Gregg had kept him from being sent overseas for over a year, though he had no idea why. And something had bolloxed him up while in active service too. He had been an acting sergeant when he was wounded in Okinawa, but in his discharge he was given only a corporal's rating, and his pension was accordingly less than it should have been. Moreover, in spite of his unusual battle record and his many wounds, he had not received a single citation, apart from the Purple Heart. Someone certainly had it in for him.

And now they were trying to take his job away!

Eve agreed, when he told her, that it must be Gregg who was behind all this. "But let's just wait and see what happens."

Anderson called him in to his office some ten days later.

"Bad news," he said.

He looked at Mark with genuine sorrow.

"They've got something unbelievable cooked up against you," he said.

His voice, even, sounded unnatural.

"I couldn't get any information from the president's office, naturally. But a friend of mine in the provost's office has access to the files."

He smiled at Mark grimly.

"Hold on tight to your seat while I tell you. You're alleged to be implicated in an attempted spy plot."

He saw Mark's expression of incredulity.

"Yes," he nodded, "it's unbelievable. But it's symptomatic of the times."

He looked at Mark and shook his head.

"You might as well face the situation squarely: unless you can find some way of clearing this thing up, I'd say your goose is cooked so far as an academic career is concerned. With that infamy on your record, there isn't a university or college in the country that would touch you."

In the weeks that followed, Mark tried to get his bearings. He had had his fill of army life in the past four years. How many times he had thought back longingly to the blessings of civilian life—its security, its freedom, its avoidance of the arbitrary! Now he was discovering that civilian life had its own hazards and uncertainties—less lethal than those of battle but no less demoralizing. What he was discovering, in fact, was that by getting out of the army he had not escaped from the world of war to the safety of the world of peace, but had simply been caught up in a different kind of conflict.

Now he was more anxious than ever to talk to Sebastian. There were so many problems that positively clamored for his insight. But in the affectionate answer that Sebastian had written to Mark's letter from the hospital, there had been no indication of when, if ever, he planned to return to the University.

Mark went to call on Professor Cummings one day. Through the formality of his manner Mark had no difficulty in recognizing the warmth of the old Latin professor's feelings, and his genuine pleasure at seeing him again. Cummings's wife, a chronic invalid whom Mark had never met, had died during the war, and Cummings had just moved into a jewel of a modern house that an architect friend of his had designed for him. It was in a new real estate development. A postwar building boom was under way.

They had a lot of ground to cover, and Cummings, who drank well, had brought out a bottle of Irish whisky. Mark told of his war experiences, and Cummings reported on the changes that had come over the University. There were ever-increasing army and navy subsidies for research, for specialized technical training, and the very character of the academic life was rapidly changing. The hand of the military was everywhere in evidence. There was talk of requiring all the faculty to submit to a loyalty oath.

Cummings never directly brought up the subject of the Communist Party, or the unit to which he and Mark had belonged, and Mark did not feel that he should initiate it. But they spoke of all the people who had been in the unit. Cummings had seen Leutner recently—a rather bitter and disillusioned Leutner. He was coming back to teach in the fall. Hsueh Ling was editing a left-wing Chinese-language newspaper in New York. Philip Jones had been eased out of his job in the Spanish department, but had found a post in a private college in Oregon. As for Lou Goldstein and Hans Weber, who had both been at Valhalla, they had recently had their contracts canceled for security reasons, and had been refused reinstatement in their posts here at the University.

Sebastian was now the only member of the unit who had not yet been mentioned. Cummings filled Mark's glass and took a stiff drink. He looked at Mark and Mark looked at him.

"What about Sebastian?" Mark said finally, finding the suspense unbearable.

Cummings lowered his eyes and looked at his fingernails.

"I don't know," he said.

Mark felt a mounting anger. This was exactly the kind of reticence that Eve was always displaying. What was behind it?

"I've been in the army for four years," he said. "I've been out of circulation. I don't know what's been going on."

Cummings looked at him quizzically. "You've heard about the Bolt?"

Mark smiled reproachfully. "Yes, of course. But that—"

"I'm not drawing any conclusions," Cummings interrupted. "We'll know all about that someday. But there are a lot of other indications: articles Bloch has published, statements he's made, and things I've heard from colleagues and former students—Fritz Leutner, for instance. Well, I don't want to gossip. But I think you should be prepared for at least the possibility of a fundamental change in our friend. I hope I'm wrong."

A few days later Mark ran into Bruce Patterson on the campus, and again he found the same reluctance to talk about Sebastian. Bruce was here only for a short time, to catch up on some research work being done at the University laboratory. He merely shook his head when Mark asked him about Sebastian.

"He'll be here in a few weeks for a short conference, and you'll be able to see him and judge for yourself," he said.

Mark felt increasingly dejected. Then one day as he was walking home a taxi pulled up along the curb and the driver called out:

"Hi, Mark!"

Mark looked at the face under the yellow-visored cap with the license number and couldn't quite place it for a moment, though it was familiar. Then suddenly he recognized the man. "Bert Musing! What the hell you doing in that cab?" He remembered Musing as one of the small circle of Sebastian's most brilliant students.

"I'm driving, can't you see?"

They shook hands and exchanged greetings. Bert excused himself for being in a hurry; he had to pick up a fare.

"But why aren't you in your laboratory, where you belong?" Mark asked, as Bert released his brake.

Bert's taxi was already in motion.

"Ask Sebastian Bloch!" he called back as he raced off.

Mark could not bring himself to talk about any of this to Eve. He felt ashamed about keeping it from her, since he had resolved to share everything with her. But all this touched him too closely, hurt him too much, and knowing her to be already unfavorably disposed toward Sebastian, he did not want to give her any more grounds without full knowledge.

It was shortly after this that the two agents appeared.

Chapter 34

Eve and Jimmy and Mark were about to sit down to lunch when the doorbell rang.

There were two men. They showed their credentials. Mark's old outfit.

It gave him a funny feeling. It was the first time he had been on the receiving end of their attentions.

"How's Gregg?" Mark said.

"Fine, I guess," said one of the agents, whose name was Durant.

"Where is he now?" Mark asked.

"I dunno. More than likely he's in Washington."

"I mean what is he doing?" Mark persisted.

"What's the matter, don't you read the papers?"

"I've just got out of the army. I'm not up on what's happening."

"Oh," said the agent nodding, with an air of incredulity. "Well, he's the top chief."

Mark gave a start. "What do you mean? What about Murdock?"

"Oh, he's been kicked upstairs. Gregg's the boss now."

Mark had an impulse to let out a whistle, but restrained it. He had always known that the Chief was headed for the Big Leagues.

"Well, what do you know?" he said.

"That isn't why we're here," Durant said. He looked at Eve, then back at Mark. "Would you mind coming along to the office? We'd like a little information from you."

This was undoubtedly some more of Gregg's doing. What could they be after? Familiar as he was with the psychology of the hunter, he now had completely the psychology of the hunted. It wasn't what you knew, it was the situation, that made all the difference. Realizing that it was pointless, he nevertheless decided to try to stall.

"It isn't convenient today," he said. "I'll drop in at your office tomorrow afternoon."

"It's rather urgent," said Durant. "We'd appreciate it if you could come with us."

Mark had been in Durant's shoes many times, and knew exactly what the score was.

"We were just about to sit down to lunch," he said.

"Go ahead," said Durant in a feigned access of polite solicitude. "Go right ahead and have your lunch, we'll just sit down here and wait."

Mark decided that there was nothing to be gained by putting it off. He ate a hurried lunch which was rather disturbing to his newly repaired digestive organs.

Eve was worried. Mark could only recommend that she keep calm. "They probably want to pump me on some of our friends. But I know how to handle them," he said.

There was nothing but polite small talk on the long ride to town in the black Pontiac sedan. It was odd to be back in the old offices that had once been the center of his own activities, where he had begun what he had planned as his life's career.

"Now, then," Durant said after they had settled in one of the offices. The service had taken over a whole extra floor, and this was one of the new ones on the twenty-third floor. There had been some unnecessary commotion, going in and out of offices, fetching of documents, shuffling among papers. Russell, the other man, had hardly opened his mouth the whole time.

Durant leaned forward on his desk, folded his hands, and assumed a stern air. He had a long dark face, with a broken nose and a straight harsh mouth.

"As you may have come to realize," he began, "this is a time when it's becoming very popular to be a good American."

Mark interrupted him. "You can cut out the lecture," he said. "Let's get down to what you want to know."

Durant glared. "I'd advise you," he said sharply, "to try to be a little more co-operative. Otherwise—"

"Oh, get off it!" Mark felt anger taking hold of him. "I know this racket. I'm here on a voluntary basis. I'm here to answer questions, not to listen to your crap. If you have any questions to ask, let's have them, otherwise I'm getting out." He had risen to his feet and started backing toward the door. He could sense Durant's rage, but knew he couldn't do anything.

"All right, sit down," Durant said.

"You could be polite about it." Mark remained standing by the door.

Durant's exasperation broke.

"You won't be so cocky," he said, "when you find out what we've got on you."

"You have nothing on me."

Mark caught an almost imperceptible signal that passed from Russell to Durant.

"If you wouldn't mind taking a seat again," Durant said with exaggerated politeness, "we could get down to business."

"The sooner the better, so far as I'm concerned," Mark agreed, and sat down.

Durant began going through the ritual of a routine interrogation: name, age, place of birth, and so forth.

"You'll find all that in my record right here in the office," Mark protested.

"I know," Durant replied, and went right on.

There followed a series of questions on associations. The list began with names like Max Baum, Bill Parrish, Leo Vorontov . . . Mark saw what was coming.

"You've got a detailed report of all this," he said, "that I wrote for this office several years ago. There you'll find much more accurate answers to your questions than anything I could give you now."

"Yes," said Durant, and went right on with his questions.

He came to Sebastian Bloch.

"Why don't you skip all this rigmarole," Mark said, "and come to what you're really interested in?"

"*I'm* asking the questions here, you just answer them."

"Suit yourself," said Mark. "You're wasting your time and mine."

There were a number of harmless questions.

Then:

"Is Sebastian Bloch, to your knowledge, a communist?"

Mark had known it was coming.

"If I ever knew, I've forgotten," he said.

Durant, realizing he was blocked along that line of questioning, could not conceal his fury. But he would try once or twice more.

"When did you last see Bloch?"

Mark thought back. "It must have been about four years ago."

"Can you be more precise?"

"I'm afraid that's the best I can do."

"Was he a communist at that time?"

"If I ever knew, I've forgotten."

After a few more tries, Durant bit his lip and looked at Mark hatefully.

"Smart, aren't you?"

Mark was not reassured.

Durant asked a series of questions about miscellaneous people, including Professor Ronald Outland, Mrs. de Rivas, Erasmo Alvarez . . . Mark could feel the key question coming.

"How well do you know Alexander Zelinski?"

That was it. Through the casual tone of voice Mark sensed

the suppressed eagerness of the hound who had just come upon the scent.

Mark gave careful, truthful answers, saying no more than he had to. Now he knew that Gregg was behind this and that he had something serious to deal with. The questions became more insistent and more detailed. When had he met Zelinski the first time? In what connection? And subsequently? They were obviously feeling their way toward that last conversation he had had with Zelinski. How much did they know?

He was sure now that they were trying to get something on Sebastian. Zelinski's conversation with him and his subsequent conversation with Tanya had nothing in themselves that could get Sebastian into trouble. But they might be tied up with something else—possibly some other attempt of Zelinski's to get at Sebastian. And Mark did not rule out the possibility that Gregg had put Zelinski up to this, and was manipulating him. He decided to say nothing about that last lunch with Zelinski until he had more to go on.

Durant tackled him from every angle, and got nowhere.

"You're keeping something from us," he said at last in exasperation.

Mark, from experience, could appreciate his predicament, but he couldn't feel sorry for him.

"Work some more," he taunted. "Give a little. That's what the book says."

Durant went white, and Mark knew that he had called his next move. Durant had never been up against one of Gregg's ex-agents. Mark leaned forward.

"All right, what have you got? Let's have it."

Russell tapped his foot nervously. Mark realized that he hadn't been aware of him for a long time.

"Stop that!" Durant snapped, too loudly. He turned to Mark. "You talk a good line, but it's not getting you anywhere."

Mark sat back. Perhaps now Durant would come out with it.

Durant was turning over sheets of paper in a file he had in front of him.

"We have here," he said, after a long pause, "four—five affidavits, from scientists on the Crossroads project. Each of them testifies that you approached him, on one or more occasions, in order to persuade him to sabotage the work on the Bolt; that you claimed to be acting in the name of German anti-Nazi scientists, but that you were actually an agent for a Soviet network."

This was serious. It was absurd, it was laughable, in that it had no reality, that it was a farfetched invention. But it was serious in that someone had gone out of his way to invent it, with intent to do him harm. Mark had steeled himself for an unpleasant surprise, but this went considerably beyond what he was prepared for.

"Tell me more," he said, to give himself time.

"I'm listening," said Durant.

"I'll tell you what," Mark said. He didn't feel much like joking, but he hated Durant's guts. "It seems to me you've got a pretty good case there. Why don't you take those affidavits and hand them over to a federal grand jury? You ought to be able to get an indictment. Just to clinch it, you might add that this character, in order to cover up his tracks, went and enlisted, fought for two years in the Pacific and was four times severely wounded on the battle front, the last time almost fatally."

Durant had no sense of humor, or if he did he wasn't letting on.

"This is on record against you," he said. "It's bad. If you have anything to say, I'd advise you to say it now."

Mark reflected a moment. Yes, he had to think of himself too. The story was terribly damaging. The fact that it was untrue was irrelevant: it was on record. But who could have invented it? He thought of Gregg. He would never have thought of him as vindictive; he was too big for that—at least that was Mark's guess. But in any case this didn't sound like Gregg. Yet on the other hand, Gregg was the only one who could possibly have it in for him.

Mark tried another tack. It seemed unlikely that the story

had been invented to hurt *him*. Whom, then? Sebastian? But the story did not mention Sebastian—or was Sebastian one of the four or five scientists?

"I'll make a bargain with you," he said to Durant. "You give me the names of those four or five scientists, and I'll give you a word-for-word account of everything that was said—where we met, what we did, what was decided: the whole works."

Durant gave a look of exasperation. "This is no joking matter," he said.

"No," said Mark. "But there's a joker somewhere. And I think you've got it either up your sleeve or there among your papers."

"Coming back to Zelinski," said Durant. "Did he ever make you any kind of proposition?"

Mark had been weighing the matter for some minutes. They must have heard of Zelinski's approach through some other channel—probably Zelinski himself or else another who had it from Zelinski. Someone had built the story of the four or five approaches on that flimsy foundation. Someone, not several people. Because it was inconceivable that more than one person should have invented the identical story independently. Yes, they certainly had the story of Zelinski's approach, although perhaps even that was twisted or embroidered. Mark decided that the straight story, since it was in fact harmless, could not possibly harm Sebastian and might even be helpful in unscrambling things. So far as his own situation was concerned, it was important that he tell the truth about the only element in this whole affair that had any foundation.

"I've just remembered something that had slipped my mind," he said, giving Durant a knowing look. And he told, in circumstantial detail, the story of his luncheon conversation with Zelinski and his brief conversation with Tanya.

But after many questions on this Durant again came back to his original charge.

"I still want to know about your approaches to these five scientists," he said.

So it was clear that Sebastian was not one of the alleged scientists. Mark was more puzzled than ever.

Durant kept plying him with questions for quite some time, but there was nothing more to be got out of him. Durant made no secret of the fact that he did not believe him.

Chapter 35

WHEN, a couple of weeks later, Eve announced that Tanya had phoned, Mark was overjoyed. But she went on to explain that the only time Sebastian would have to see them would be at a large cocktail party that they were giving the following Friday afternoon, to which a lot of faculty people were invited. He was in town for a three-day conference and was leaving that same evening. Eve and Mark were to come early, so that the four of them could have a good hour together before the others arrived.

Mark was beset by a strange excitement as they drove up to the Bloch house. It was four years since he had last been here, and even longer since he had seen Sebastian. But it was more than a span of time that had separated them. There had been their divergent lives, there had been war and upheaval, there had been the wind of chaos that had swept over the world. And there was a question mark: the Bolt—Sebastian's Monster. Sebastian had made it. What had it done to him?

Sebastian's smile, when he greeted him, was like a benediction. Mark's immediate reaction was one of complete recognition, instantly followed by an impression of strangeness. Sebastian's face had been marked, as though by some searing vision, by some soul-shaking revelation. Fatigue and pain had bitten into it, and with this, inexplicably, there was a stonelike serenity.

Mark immediately recaptured in his presence that cherished

feeling of being admitted to a privileged world. In the enchantment of this paradise regained in which, besides his own Eve,
there was that other seductive Eve whose name was Tanya—
in a lovely pale-green shantung dress, with a spray of small
green orchids pinned over her left breast—he quite forgot all
the questions and doubts that had troubled him recently.

Both Sebastian and Tanya had much to tell about the years
of the war, about life on Valhalla, about the spirit of dedication and adventure that had animated the scientists and workers on the project, and about the annoying concomitants of
fame—all spiced with lively anecdotes. Mark had to tell about
his war experiences and his wounds, and while Eve, turning to
Tanya, told about Jimmy and how everything had worked out,
Sebastian inquired with concern about Mark's present health,
wanted details about his operations, the treatment he had been
receiving, his diet.

"And now what are your plans?" Sebastian asked.

Mark told how he had intended to go back into teaching,
and how he had then learned of the highly compromising
charge that had somehow got into his file.

"And then shortly after that," Mark went on, "just a couple
of weeks or so ago, I was called in by the security police and
had a long session with them."

Sebastian took Mark by the arm.

"Let's go out in the garden," he said.

Sebastian led the way out, across the lawn and into the cop-
pice, where a path wound among the trees and shrubs.

"Now tell me about it," he said.

Mark gave a detailed account of his interview with Durant.
Sebastian's face became somber.

"By the way," Mark asked, "did Tanya ever tell you about
that conversation I had with Zelinski?"

"Yes," said Sebastian.

"I hesitated for a long time about telling them," said Mark.
"I finally decided that they already knew about it, and that a
truthful account of it wouldn't hurt anybody."

"I think you did right," said Sebastian.

"I wonder how they found out, though."

They were walking back and forth slowly, from one end of the winding path to the other.

"I had to tell them," Sebastian said.

Mark looked at him with surprise.

"It wasn't something that could be completely ignored," Sebastian explained. "There were things about it that were a little worrisome: that about a message from the German scientists, a channel through neutral embassies . . . I was duty-bound to report it."

"Yes, I suppose so . . ." said Mark. He was plunged back into the bewilderment induced by the accusation of spy activities. "But who do you suppose could have cooked up that story . . ."

At that moment Mark caught sight of Tanya coming across the lawn.

"Darling, the guests are arriving," she called to Sebastian. "You'd better come in."

"We'll be there in a minute," said Sebastian, and continued to pace.

Tanya remained standing on the edge of the lawn. She looked lovely, and appealing, and somehow a little forlorn. Mark's heart went out to her.

"I think you should come right away," she said.

Sebastian continued to pace.

"Leave us alone," he said.

But Tanya stood her ground. "Everyone's coming at once," she said. "It isn't polite—"

Abruptly Sebastian exploded.

He stopped in his tracks and glared at her.

"Shut up, you bitch, and get the hell away from here!" he shouted. "We'll come when we're goddam ready!"

Tanya stood for a moment as if paralyzed, then spun around and ran back to the house.

Mark was stunned. He had never seen Sebastian behave rudely, and more particularly he had never heard him address Tanya otherwise than with loving deference. Sebastian resumed his pacing, and Mark, his neck burning hot, fell into step beside him.

"I can't imagine how that story got started," Sebastian said. His face was distorted by some obscure emotion. He looked at Mark.

"You yourself have no idea?"

"Not the slightest idea."

"Let's hope it dies a quick natural death."

"Not likely. Those things have a way of sticking. And meanwhile it's ruined me for a teaching job—and perhaps any other kind of job."

"I don't know if there is anything I can do. I wish I could help you. You must let me know. Keep in touch with me . . ."

Mark remembered his resolve to confess the role he had played when he had originally met Sebastian. But there was no time now. It was not a subject that could be disposed of in a hurry. And besides, Sebastian's generous solicitude, the concern that he obviously felt over Mark's predicament, made the avowal of what he still regarded as an infamy almost unbearably painful.

"When do you think we can get together again?" he asked.

Sebastian shook his head, and they began walking slowly toward the house.

"I don't know," he said.

He continued to shake his head slowly.

"There are so many things that I don't know."

Chapter 36

ON HIS next passage through Washington Sebastian was visited in his hotel early one morning by two agents of the security police and invited to go with them to their headquarters.

"I have an important meeting," Sebastian objected. "Army business."

"That isn't until ten thirty," said the agent who did the talking.

Sebastian was startled. "But I have to prepare for it," he said.

"We won't keep you long."

He assumed, as he was being whisked up in the elevator of the tall building, that he would be seeing J. W. Gregg, who had recently succeeded Murdock as head of the agency. But Murphy, the vocal member of the tandem that was bringing him here, led him into a small empty office and asked him to sit down. Murphy took up his post behind the desk, a secretary brought in a stack of folders, and Sargent, the second agent, sat down in the extra chair.

"I hate to take up any of your precious time, Dr. Bloch," Murphy said, "but we think you have some information that could be valuable to us, and we should appreciate your co-operation."

Sebastian smiled uncomfortably. "I think by now I must have given you all the information that could possibly be of value to you."

"Perhaps not quite," Murphy said. "We'd like to ask you a few questions about Mark Ampter."

"Oh, yes."

So he was going to be able to help Mark out after all. He was being given the opportunity at last to straighten out that crazy tangle of fabrication that he had created in an unguarded moment. Now he could squelch that ugly story once and for all.

"What we are interested in," Murphy said, "is the role Ampter played in the Soviet spy network."

"Perhaps," said Sebastian, "the simplest would be for me to give you a complete account of what I actually know."

"I see no objection to that," said Murphy. "Go ahead."

For weeks his mind had been absorbed by problems of world scope, and it took a moment of concentration to narrow his attention to the scale of Mark's personal predicament. Other men in his position would probably have considered such a private matter too trivial. But Mark's situation was a very human one, and Sebastian was quite incapable of simply washing his hands of it.

"You can correct me on details," he said, "and I'm not too sure about dates. But this is the story in substance. Some time in the fall of—of 1942—it could have been in October or November—this Alexander Zelinski went out of his way to effect a casual meeting with Mark Ampter, and persuaded him to make a luncheon date with him, on the pretext that he had something important to tell him in connection with me. Ampter knew Zelinski only slightly, and had no great liking for him. In the course of the luncheon Zelinski told Ampter that he was connected with an anti-Nazi apparatus; that they had found out through a network leading to Germany that the German scientists whom we assumed at that time to be far advanced on the development of the secret weapon that we were also working on, had decided not to pursue the work; and that these scientists, several of whom I knew personally, were anxious to establish contact with me in order to convince me that they were sincere and, presumably, to persuade me—and the American Government through me—not to make the Bolt. Zelinski claimed to have access to the channel through which messages could be sent back and forth. Ampter at that time was enlisted in the army, and was on furlough. He told Zelinski he would have nothing to do with his proposition, and advised him, if the matter was bona fide, to get in touch with me directly. But he was disturbed by it. He didn't trust Zelinski, and suspected that some trickery was concealed. Yet he wasn't sure. He thought perhaps this was something I should know about. After long hesitation he decided to report his conversation to me. But we did not see each other again. In the end he told my wife, but left it up to her whether I should be told or not. It was she who told me. That is the whole story."

There was silence for a moment. Sebastian relit his cigarette, which had gone out.

Murphy looked at Sebastian probingly. "There was nothing more to it?"

"There was nothing more."

"You are quite sure?"

"Positive."

"What about his approaches to those other scientists?"

"To the best of my knowledge," said Sebastian, "there were no other approaches."

Murphy raised his eyebrows and glanced at some papers that were lying on the desk before him.

"What about these four—or is it five?—scientists you said were approached by Ampter? And what about the tie-up with a Soviet spy ring?"

Sebastian curiously felt no emotion. He shook his head and smiled sadly.

"I'm afraid there were no other scientists, nor any spy ring. I'm afraid that was all an invention on my part."

"You made it all up?"

"Yes."

Murphy leaned forward, and in a voice that was infinitely gentle asked:

"What made you invent such a story, Doctor?"

Sebastian still felt no emotion.

"I must have had a good reason at the time," he said, "but whatever it was, I have forgotten it."

"You can think of no reason why you fabricated such a story?"

"I'm afraid I cannot think now of any good reason."

"Mark Ampter was your friend?"

"Yes."

"And do you still regard him as your friend?"

Sebastian did not immediately answer. In the realm to which he was being swept by destiny, terms like friendship no longer had any meaning. Yet in the world in which personal attachments still had validity, Mark had a special place.

"Yes," he said in a low voice.

"Did you realize that this story that you told seriously compromised your friend?"

"I realize it now, and I am glad to have this opportunity to retract my original story and get the true story into the record."

"I see."

Sebastian thought he saw Murphy exchange a lightning glance with Sargent, but could not be sure.

"Tell me, Doctor," Murphy continued. "You said Ampter was in the army. Is he still in the army?"

"No, he was wounded and discharged. He's back home with his family now."

"I see. Have you happened to run into him since he was back?" The tone was easy and conversational.

Sebastian was on his guard. Possibly they already knew that Mark was back, and that he had seen him, and exactly when and where. But if not, it would look better if he could have seen him before Mark had been questioned by Gregg's agents— which he had calculated must have been about May 15th.

"Yes, I saw him when I was back at the University not so long ago. At a cocktail party."

"Can you remember when that was?"

"It was a number of weeks ago. I should say around the end of April, or the first days of May."

"Could it have been a little later than that?" Murphy's voice was smooth as honey.

"I shouldn't put it *much* later," Sebastian said cautiously.

"Could it have been, say—May 29th?"

It was the exact date, but Sebastian had himself under control.

"It's possible," he said in a casual tone, "though I should have put it considerably earlier."

"Can we agree then, that it *was* on May 29th last that you saw Mark Ampter?"

"If that is what your records say."

"Your answer is yes?"

"Yes."

He had lost again.

"I think that's really all we wanted to ask you, Doctor," Murphy said cheerfully, standing up. "And please excuse us . . ."

By the time Sebastian was back in his hotel room he still had not been able to overcome the intolerable impression that his story had not been believed, and that by telling the truth he had fallen into a trap that he had himself contrived.

Chapter 37

MARK had seen posters all over town announcing that Dr. Bruce Patterson was giving a public lecture on "The Bolt and the Future" in the Veterans' Memorial Auditorium the following Thursday night. He decided to attend it, and Eve went too.

There was a big turnout. It was the first crowd Mark had been in since he had been in the army. Bruce was introduced by Professor Roy Menander Porter.

Since his return Mark had read in the papers about the considerable agitation among the scientists, particularly among those who had worked on the Bolt, over the future fate of the weapon of mass destruction. Should America go on making more such weapons, or should the Bolt be outlawed? The newspaper stories were confusing, and Mark had been too much involved in his personal problems to give it his serious attention. Now that he heard Bruce give a lucid and detailed picture of the whole situation he became terribly excited. What Bruce was talking about was crucial. The outcome of the battle in which he and his fellow scientists were engaged would be decisive for the future of all humanity.

The immediate issue was the Kerner-Price Bill, on which a

congressional committee was now holding public hearings. This bill, if passed, would put the Bolt wholly in the control of the army. This would mean that all the material for producing energy would be earmarked for making Bolts; the energy, which could revolutionize human life if turned to constructive ends, would not be made available for such peacetime uses; science would continue to be confined behind walls of secrecy; wartime regimentation would continue, the army would extend its control over higher education, and progressively invade every field of activity. The New Science Association, which Bruce represented, was agitating to have the Bolt placed under civilian control, which would promote the constructive application of Bolt energy and pave the way to international action to outlaw the Bolt.

Bruce, who on the platform had the same earnestness, the same homely persuasiveness as among friends, gave an account of the formation and growth of the young association. The scientists were awakening to a sense of social responsibility. They had created the Bolt. They now felt it their duty to see to its safekeeping, to prevent its misuse, to divert it from destructive to constructive ends. The association had come into being for the purpose of alerting public opinion. The young scientists, conscious of the immeasurable danger inherent in the new force that they had created, alarmed by the atmosphere of silence and mystery that was being created around the Bolt and its future fate, had felt impelled to act. They were now conducting a campaign to inform public opinion of the issues.

After the long and animated discussion period Mark and Eve went up and said hello to Bruce; and although Bruce was obviously exhausted he gladly accepted an invitation to go home with them for a chat and a drink.

There was first a lot of personal data to catch up on. But by the time Mark had served a second round of drinks the conversation turned to other topics. Mark had so many questions that he wanted to ask that he had to make an effort to hold them back—questions mainly about Sebastian: how he had obtained his clearance, how it had been made possible for him to do his work, how all the left-wing physicists had fared; who had been responsible for the belated unleashing of the Bolt, and why Sebastian had been unable to use his influence to stop it. . . . But he was so gripped by the current situation Bruce had described that it was this that was uppermost in his mind.

"You mentioned in your lecture," he said, "quite a number of outstanding scientists who are working with you in your campaign, but you never once mentioned Sebastian. What about him?"

Bruce's bright, ruddy face clouded over.

"I wish I could be as positive about him as I should like to be." He shook his head. "He's become something of a mystery to us. We don't know exactly where he stands."

He fell silent again. He was obviously embarrassed.

"He's done some pretty bad things that we know of: got people in trouble. And we've been surprised and very much disappointed by the stand—or lack of stand—that he's taken on a number of crucial questions. At the same time he's in a hellishly difficult position. I guess none of us will ever know what he's gone through. He's a tortured soul. And it's beginning to show. But the trouble is, we don't really know. Maybe he's planning something big that's going to surprise us all that will justify all the compromises he's made."

He wrinkled up his face and shook his head again.

"It doesn't look good to me."

Mark felt a deep distress. If Sebastian had made sacrifices of principle—though this seemed inconceivable, and obviously Bruce could be wrong—it was certainly for a higher reason that would completely vindicate him.

"But in this campaign of yours to defeat the Kerner-Price Bill," he said, "surely he has taken some kind of stand?"

Bruce was still shaking his head, his whole face a picture of dejection.

"He's been trying to soft-pedal us. He says we are putting the scientists in a bad light in the eyes of the public just at a time when popular support is needed for the acceptance of the principle of international control of the Bolt. Sebastian is working now on a small commission that is drafting a plan that, if the authorities accept it, this country will submit before the international conference that meets next month. He says that it's much more important to set up a sound system of international control than to take the Bolt out of the hands of the army here at home. He claims that the army will largely control it in any case, no matter what the setup is, because it will have priority on the material for making it. I don't agree with that at all. I think that if we can defeat this bill we shall have won an important round, though only a first round, in the battle for world peace. The Russians will be much more ready to listen to us if they know that we have been able to wrest the Bolt out of the clutches of the army. And then, if the plan is a fair one, and an acceptable one, our position will be all the stronger."

"Maybe it's that plan that Sebastian is counting so much on," Mark suggested.

"It's in the picture, at any rate. All I can say is his plan had better be a good one!"

Bruce emptied his glass.

"Well, I think I have to be getting back to my hotel and hit the hay."

"Have just another drink," Mark urged. "There's so much more to talk about."

A wistfulness came over all of them. Memories crowded in upon Mark. The Teachers' Union, the Report to the Faculty bulletins, the Spanish parties, the Russian War Relief parties, the parties for Tom Mooney, for Hal Norberg, all the labor defense and civil liberties battles . . . and in the center of all of them was Sebastian! No problem was ever settled, no decision was ever made, without consulting him. Mark remembered the radiance that seemed to be within him, how it shone through in his eyes, that young-old face with the enigmatic, melancholy smile, the lightning intensity that came into it when he untangled a knotty problem and proceeded to communicate it with his inimitable persuasive power.

" 'The time of our innocence'!" Bruce mused, with an inward smile. "That's a phrase of Sebastian's. The time before the Bolt."

He became somber.

"The Bolt has done more than destroy innocent lives. It's done something to people's characters; it's corrupted science; it's poisoned human relations, and relations among nations. And it's only begun!"

He got up, holding his half-finished drink, and began walking, angrily, then turned around.

"The time is short," he said grimly. "If a race develops between us and the Soviet Union, God help us!"

He threw up his hands in a gesture of despair, and at the same moment broke into a grin over his own outburst of emotion, having managed to hold on to his drink without spilling it.

"You must excuse me, I'm sort of worn out," he said apologetically, looking at his watch. "Tomorrow I have to be in Minneapolis. And when I think of the mess back in Washington . . ."

He gave a despairing picture of the way the association was conducting its campaign from two tiny borrowed office rooms in downtown Washington, with practically no furniture or equipment. The campaigners were all volunteers, of every rank from Nobel Prize winner to graduate student, contributing time and money, drafting endless manifestos, bulletins, leaflets, broadsides, press releases, writing thousands of letters, running a duplicating machine, addressing envelopes and licking stamps, or touring the country to lecture before every kind of audience, buttonholing people at cocktail parties, pestering legislators in their offices or in the lobbies of Congress, besieging the State Department and the White House.

"If we only had *one* full-time levelheaded man to take charge of the office for a few weeks and put a little order into things," Bruce sighed, "it might spell the difference between defeat and victory."

Suddenly Mark had an idea. He remembered the Santuro strike.

"What about me?"

It was a full hour later before Bruce finally got away and Mark drove him back to his hotel. But by then it had been decided that Mark would go to Washington right away and assume the duties of executive secretary of the association until the end of the campaign. Eve was to follow with Jimmy as soon as Mark found a place for them to live.

It was strange being back in the world of physicists, which he had originally come to know only thanks to Sebastian. But now there was no Sebastian. From all over the country, from the far-flung universities and research institutes, scientists, including the most eminent, would turn up unannounced in the little office. But never Sebastian. Many of the young scientists whom he saw almost daily, such as Fritz Leutner, Hans Weber, Ed MacAvoy and others, were the same whom he had seen in Sebastian's entourage at the University. And this crusade of the scientists was precisely the kind of movement of which Sebastian would have been the soul and the mainspring in the old days. But Sebastian these days was moving in more exalted spheres. He had a voice in the highest councils of the nation. Mark had the impression that these young crusaders no longer considered Sebastian to be one of them. When they spoke of him it was with a mingling of dismay and formal deference. The old worshipful affection was gone.

Into the sweltering heat of early July the feverish activity of the association continued and became even more intensified. Holding a telephone in one hand and the speaking tube of a dictating machine in the other, Mark negotiated, discussed, pleaded, arranged interviews and meetings, dictated press releases, memoranda, letters. More and more volunteers came in to carry the battle to Congress, to the press, to the radio, and in the evenings Bolt physics courses were given to classes of congressmen, government officials and the more serious-minded members of Washington society.

The Kerner-Price Bill was killed. But no sooner had this battle been won than Senator Wollenstein managed to slip in a rider to their own bill, sponsored by Senator Morris, that would in effect have thrown control of the Bolt back into the hands of the military. The rider was killed by an avalanche of letters.

Now, catching their breaths, as the International Conference was about to meet, all the scientists eagerly awaited the publication of the plan drafted by the commission of which Sebastian Bloch was the most articulate and persuasive member.

Chapter 38

SEBASTIAN had the impression, as he listened to the secretary reading the long document in a clear but colorless voice, that what was happening here was something from which he himself was completely detached.

Yet it was essentially his document, though none of the members of the commission knew it. In the long weeks of its elaboration, as they had met day after day to piece the thing together, idea by idea, word by word, organizing it, giving it substance and form, envisioning as they did so, the world of tomorrow shaped in conformity to its design—a daring, a breath-taking dream!—he had managed, by a trick that he had learned to use with his students, unobtrusively to plant one idea after another into the mind of this or that member, who would then propose it thinking it was his own. Sometimes, when the idea was proffered timidly, without conviction, Sebastian would challenge it, raise objections; and then the member would think up arguments to strengthen his case, arguments which would at the same time buttress his own faith in its soundness. Consequently when the Draft Proposal for International Bolt Control at last reached its final form, each member of the commission was conscious of having contributed an important share to it, but none of them could have said exactly what Sebastian's contribution had been.

Here, however, before the Joint Policy Group composed of representatives of government, the military, industry and international jurists, the commission looked mainly to Sebastian to defend the Plan against the considerable opposition that was expected; and yet he himself felt detached from what was going on, and when in a moment he began to speak he would be detached still.

He had attended so many conferences in the last few years that he was no longer "present" in them in the true sense of the word. The long table, the pads and paper and pencils, the ash trays, the five, ten or twenty faces around it, the conventions of conference exchanges . . . His mind would function swiftly and accurately, but he himself would be absent. Not elsewhere—still here; yet in another realm. His own realm, which claimed him more and more, in which anguish was the other face of ecstasy, in which the soaring imagination was yet captive to the wretched flesh. The problem was metamorphosis: to transcend reality, and in transcending it refine it, intensify it, infuse it with a vital principle as miraculously luminous and free in relation to the gross matter of fleshly life from which it sprang as was the butterfly emerging from its larva . . .

"Well!" General Pendleton exclaimed, breaking the silence after the secretary had sat down.

A general hubbub arose as the meeting broke into a number of small groups that began discussing excitedly. Printed copies of the proposal had been distributed before the meeting opened and some of the members proceeded to study the text and to take notes.

The buzz created by the various small huddles was beginning to subside when Percy Simmons got up to speak.

"Mr. Chairman," he said, addressing Warren Pollock, "I should like to say a few words about this proposal, if I may, by way of opening up the general discussion."

Percy Simmons was president of Continental Standard Corporation. He was sovereignly self-possessed, as only a very rich man in high executive position can be.

"I should like to say first of all," he began, as silence fell, "that I consider this a remarkable document. And I think that before we venture upon a discussion of its various aspects and parts we should pause to pay tribute to its drafters . . ."

He named the members of the commission, made a special mention of the three members, including Sebastian, who were present . . .

"This document was written by men of vision, by men who set the welfare of humanity as a whole above the interests even of their country, which is perhaps the truest and noblest kind of patriotism. Just as a man who accepts the blessings of freedom that a democracy like ours offers him must be ready to lay down his life for his country, so a nation, as a member of the community of nations, must be prepared to sacrifice for mankind as a whole, if not its life, at least a considerable measure of the power that it could otherwise use for purposes of self-aggrandisement. I don't know whether we shall be able to reach an agreement to adopt this Plan, as a whole or in part. But I think we shall be making a negative and sterile approach to the problems which this Plan has been drafted to meet, if we do not at the outset pay tribute to the lofty spirit that has inspired it and to the deep humanity that informs it. If it is adopted it may very well be looked upon by future generations as the most generous gesture ever made by a great nation at a crucial turning point of its history . . ."

Simmons proceeded to discuss the Plan as a whole. There was, he said, in addition to what might be called the theoretical or idealistic aspect of the question, a practical aspect. Would the Plan work? Could America afford the risk involved in relinquishing its possession of the Bolt? Would the Plan be acceptable to the other countries, and particularly to Russia? He foresaw enormous difficulties in the way of setting up plants at strategic points, of allocating the amount of energy that would be made available to this or that country.

The speakers followed one another—the generals, the government officials, the international jurists, the industrialists. All expressed varying degrees of skepticism or opposition. The generals were the most vehement. They were dead set against giving up the Bolt, which they were already beginning to incorporate into their strategic plans. "We appreciate the high motives that lie back of this proposal," they said. "But we have a responsibility for the defense of the country, and we regret to have to say that we regard the whole scheme as unrealistic, and in fact dangerous for the security of our nation."

"Perhaps Dr. Bloch might have something to say by way of answer to these objections," said Chairman Pollock, after the various points of view had been expressed.

Sebastian had to make an effort to pull himself back to this stage of the battle. He had done what could and had to be done. He foresaw now that it wouldn't work, and his mind was already grappling with the problems of the next and even more difficult phase of his task. But he could help make the position clear, since there was after all a chance.

"Yes," he said, his voice barely above a whisper, and shook his head. He looked up, above the heads of the tensely silent group.

"I don't want," he began, "to say that this is a perfect plan. It is far from being that. It is only a sketch—a first approximation. I don't want to say that it can't be vastly improved in many of its detailed provisions before it is submitted to the International Conference. But I do want to say that in its main outlines it is the *only* plan that we can submit, that we *have* to submit it and that once its implications are fully understood it is likely to have your unanimous support."

His words caused something of a commotion around the table, particularly among the generals.

"I have listened carefully," he went on, "to the objections you have raised. They are all, in my opinion, to a greater or lesser degree valid. But there are other, fundamental, overriding considerations. First of all, I think it is necessary to warn you that while we have the monopoly of the Bolt today, we are not likely to keep it for very long. Some of you seem to think

we can keep it for twenty or even fifty years. That is a dangerous illusion. My guess is that the Russians will have it within
five years at the latest, and it is not impossible that they may
already be sufficiently close to it to be able to go into production within a matter of months.

"The question, then, that arose before the commission was
whether there is any way of avoiding a Bolt armament race—
in other words, of preventing the Russians from developing the
Bolt. The Plan that you have before you is first and foremost
an answer to that question. *And it is the only answer.* If the
Russians accept it they will thereby be abandoning whatever
plans they may have for making the Bolt, whatever stage of development they may have reached, because the necessary raw
material will immediately come under the control of the International Authority and will not be made available for the making of the Bolt. If the Russians reject it, we shall be headed for
an armament race that we are by no means sure of winning.

"Now you will say that for this very reason the Russians are
not likely to accept the Plan. I personally think they are almost
certain to turn it down. What then is the point of proposing it
at all? There are two points:

"The first is that while the chances are practically ten to one
against the Russians' accepting it, there is perhaps one chance
in ten that they will, and the chance is worth taking. The second point is linked to one of the fundamental considerations
that moved us in drawing up this plan."

Everyone, including the generals, was listening intently.

"More important even than our economic or military position in the world," he went on, speaking softly, "is our moral
position. We have to face the fact that our moral position as a
nation at the present juncture is very weak. We must not allow
ourselves to forget—most particularly when we are dealing
with other countries—that we have come off in this war incalculably better than any of our allies, that we have emerged
from it immensely richer than when we went into it, and that
we have suffered far less than the other countries. In addition
—and this has to be said—history will not allow us to forget

that we resorted to the use of the Bolt, against a civilian population, in the last hour of the war when there was no longer any military necessity to justify it. And finally there is the fact that we hold the Bolt, and that by virtue of this we find ourselves to be the most powerful nation on earth. The world fears us.

"But at the same time the world looks to us with hope. We cannot disappoint that hope."

He then drove home the need for a message from America, for which the world was waiting, which would appeal to the imagination, which would restore the faith of mankind in the abiding values of civilization and point the way to lasting peace. This message, embodied in the Plan, would be heard throughout the world. The whole success of the plan was predicated on faith in America, in its dedication to humane values, its sense of justice, its determination to achieve world peace. The other nations must be willing, during the transitional period, to relinquish some of their traditional suspicions and fears. The new situation in which the world found itself called for a new approach. And if the Russians accepted the Plan, this would be an immense step forward. And if the Russians refused to accept it, the world would hold them responsible for rejecting what all would recognize to be a creative and generous solution to the problem that now haunted every mind—the problem of the Bolt.

As he went into the details of the Plan, assent relaxed the features of his audience little by little. Basic to the Plan was the rejection of the principle of unanimity. Decisions must be adopted by majority vote. And the United States would control a majority in any conceivable combination of members of the International Authority in the foreseeable future. In cases of violation of an agreement, the Plan called for the application of sanctions. Moreover, there was no time limit set for the expiration of the various stages by which the Plan would come into operation. Meanwhile the United States would be free to continue making the Bolt until such time as it became clear that there no longer existed any threat to the peace of the world. At that point the Plan would begin to operate fully as it was intended that it should, on a basis of equality for all nations, great and small.

Sebastian knew that the one chance the Plan had of acceptance by this Joint Policy Group lay in the fact that it would appeal to their consummate cynicism. The combination of a toughly realistic core and an attractive altruistic envelope was calculated to elicit their highest approval.

In his own mind, he did not consider that there was even one chance in ten of the Russians' accepting it. They would go along only if they saw in it the possibility of trickery. If they did, it would immensely simplify the great task that lay before him, for he was confident that he could outtrick them—especially because there were factors involved in the situation that were helpful to an understanding of the problems involved and that, for reasons of security, would not be divulged to the Russians. But he was discounting their acceptance, and already his mind was absorbed by the problems that lay beyond.

As the discussion progressed, and his interest in it dwindled, he thought of a remark he had come across recently, attributed to Mao Tse Tung. When asked what he thought about the Bolt, and the fearful menace that it represented for the future of humanity, the Chinese leader was supposed to have answered, "The Bolt will not destroy the people. It is the people who will destroy the Bolt." Mao still had illusions about the people. But Sebastian knew that there was only one answer: it was the Monster that must destroy the Monster.

Chapter 39

WHEN the Plan was published it was received with tremendous enthusiasm and hailed as an epoch-making document. It was printed in tens of thousands of copies. The newspapers throughout the country reprinted copious extracts from it. It was analyzed and commented on by all the radio commentators. Its loftier passages rang forth from platform and pulpit.

The scientists, who for weeks had been awaiting it with anxiety, read it with relief and satisfaction. The Bolt had been marked too long and too deeply in the public mind with associations of wholesale death and destruction; here at last it was linked with man's future health and well-being, here it was projected as the servant of man, destined to liberate the generations of tomorrow for self-realization and creative achievement, the whole couched in language that was stirring, that nourished hope in the hearts of the war-weary, of the survivors of battles, bombing, siege, invasion, enemy occupation and concentration camps. But the Russians rejected the Plan, and gloom spread everywhere.

A small group of the young stalwarts of the New Science Association who had borne the brunt of the campaign for the repeal of the Kerner-Price Bill and the adoption of the Morris Bill met in the tiny downtown office two days after the end of the International Conference. They were closing the office, and there were tedious tag ends of business that had to be wound up. Mark would stay on for another week or so to take care of the last-minute details, finish up the correspondence and ship the files to Chicago headquarters.

The heat was stifling and the soft approach of dusk brought no relief. They were all in shirt sleeves. Someone had brought a bottle of rye, and they were now draped around the two wide-open windows looking out on the dreary courtyard where the gathering shadows gradually effaced the shabbiness of the buildings backed up against it.

For some moments the group had let the outer scene take over, and in the silence Mark had watched the brightness fade in the patch of sky above the rooftops from a washed-out blue to a deepening gray.

"For Christ's sake, Bruce, say something!" a voice suddenly broke out next to Mark. It belonged to Hank Everest—a brilliant young astrophysicist from Columbia.

Ever since the publication of the Plan, Bruce—usually so

outspoken and articulate—had withdrawn into his shell. Amid the excitement of all the people around him he had merely nodded and smiled, refusing to discuss anything connected with the international control of the Bolt.

"What do you want me to say?"

They were drinking out of odds and ends of tumblers— mostly water, with just enough whisky to take away the nasty taste of the water and to make up for the absence of ice.

"Why did the Russians turn down the Plan?"

Of the six in the group Hank was the youngest. And while he was easily the most brilliant, he had had no political experience. He was sitting with one leg over the window sill, opposite Mark, with Bruce hunched on a canvas campstool between them. The other three—Fritz Leutner, Hans Weber, and a young mathematician from Chicago named Jay Johnson —were at the other window.

Bruce crinkled up his sharp, tough face and looked at Hank. Mark had been watching him for days, not daring to question him. But he knew something was churning inside him, and now he had a hunch that Bruce might let it all out. The details of the windup of the International Conference had just come out that day in the papers. He knew that Bruce did not like to express an opinion on a subject until he had the full available information on it.

"Did you read the Plan?" he asked.

"Of course!"

"Would you have accepted it, if you had been a member of the Russian delegation?"

Hank looked at Bruce. His face was almost feminine in the delicacy of its features, and it now expressed a candid eagerness. "All right," he said, "you tell me why I shouldn't have."

"Because it's a trap." Mark could still make out Bruce's face distinctly enough to see that there was no twinkle in it, as there usually was when he tackled a subject that passionately interested him. "It looks beautiful from the outside. But when you examine it closely it becomes clear that if the Russians accepted it they would put themselves completely at the mercy of the American military. They would be deprived, from the word go, of the possibility on the one hand of making the Bolt, or on the other, of creating Bolt energy on a scale that would enable them to overcome their economic backwardness . . ."

"Wait a minute," said Hank. "We've got the Bolt. The Russians haven't. So we already have a great advantage over them, which will increase as time goes on. Why isn't it a generous gesture to offer to relinquish this advantage, even if it is only at the end of an unspecified period?"

Bruce's eyes flashed in the semidarkness. "It might have been a generous gesture, if we had known that the Russians would never be able to make a Bolt of their own, or that they would be able to make one only after many years—say thirty or forty years. But if we had known that, we wouldn't have proposed the Plan in the first place—and the Russians *would* have accepted it." He made a grimace. "The offer was made because we know the Russians may have a Bolt in a very short time, and the whole idea of the Plan is to prevent them from getting one."

"That's taking a pretty hard-boiled attitude," said Hank, shaking his head.

"In politics," said Bruce, "you've got to look for the hard-boiledest motive you can possibly think up. And then the chances are that the *real* motive of the statesman or diplomat in question will be twice again as hard-boiled. The minds of the men who shape our policies are sly, calculating and ruthless beyond anything that we poor bastards are capable of conceiving." His face suddenly brightened for the first time. "Which doesn't mean," he added, "that they're necessarily very clever."

"On the other hand," Jay Johnson broke in from the other window after a moment's silence, "the Plan was not offered as a finished product. It's a basis for negotiation."

"That's true," Bruce granted. "You noticed, however, that the American delegation refused to budge from the basically unacceptable features—first of all, America's refusal to destroy the Bolt before the final stage of the putting of the Plan into operation has been completed: in other words, before Russia and any possible other rival to the United States has been rendered impotent and subservient. During the interim, to which no time limit is set, the United States is to go on holding the Bolt over the world's head. The other main unacceptable feature is the setting aside of the unanimity principle. That means that from the very outset the cards are stacked against Russia, because the United States would be assured of a majority in the International Authority. You can see what that would mean in the case of the application of sanctions."

All were listening with their minds working. Mark was thinking that this was the way such a group would have listened to Sebastian in the old days, and that this was the sort of analysis that Sebastian would have made. In the discussion of the Plan among members of the association during the past two weeks there had been criticisms of various aspects of it, but nothing so fundamental as what Bruce was giving now.

Jay Johnson was refilling the tumblers. "But if one of the major powers were to violate the agreement," he said, "the other great powers could hardly be deterred by the vote of the responsible power. I don't see that the veto, which is largely a question of legality, makes very much difference."

"It could make a big difference," said Bruce. "In the absence of the veto, the International Organization, by a two-thirds majority, could *oblige* member states to participate in military sanctions against the country in question, whereas if a unanimous vote were necessary, each country would be free to determine its own attitude. . . ."

Bruce had got up to stretch. The twilight had deepened, and in the windows of the surrounding buildings the lights were going on, one luminous rectangle after another puncturing the oncoming dark. Even the features of Hank, sitting next to Mark, were growing indistinct.

"None of the men on the commission that drafted the Plan," he went on, "is exactly stupid. Sebastian in particular, who certainly had a big hand in drafting it, isn't stupid. They knew the Russians wouldn't—couldn't—accept it. In other words, it wasn't an honest proposal, offered in good faith. It was a disguised hostile act, which would put Russia at a disadvantage, whether she accepted or not."

Mark had never seen Bruce so wrought up.

"We were fools," Bruce continued, "ever to believe that a government like ours, even in the euphoric moment of victory, would of its own free will make a proposal that would actually lead to the outlawing of war." After a pause, he added: "But that isn't all"—and Mark thought he heard a catch in his voice. "Now we know where Sebastian stands."

For a second Mark thought he had misheard. Then he knew that he had heard right, and he let it sink in and tried to grasp the implications.

"And where do we g-g-go from here?" In Fritz Leutner's voice there was an unfathomable note of sadness.

Bruce did not reply immediately. Mark felt that this was for all of them a crucial moment.

"Next week," said Bruce at last, "we're beginning a new series of Bolt tests. As you know, they were scheduled earlier, but were delayed until after the meeting of the International Conference, because it was thought that they might not strike everyone as an appropriate accompaniment to the offer of a Plan ostensibly designed to establish peace on earth . . ."

He swallowed his saliva.

"Peace," he said. "There is only one power in the world capable of building it. The people. Only the combined strength of the people will be able to establish and to enforce a lasting peace. We've got to work from the bottom. It's going to be a long, tough battle. But it's the only way."

Chapter 40

IT WAS a year, almost to the day, since Sebastian had had his first collapse. Then it had immediately followed the letting loose of the Bolt. Now suddenly he had had another breakdown

—in the course of a diplomatic dinner, this time, as he was sitting next to the Soviet ambassador. He had had to be taken to the hospital in an ambulance.

New and even more terrible Bolts were being unleashed just now, but they were being used in tests, and not immediately for death. To the world Sebastian's breakdown was obviously the result of overwork and strain in connection with the preparation and presentation of the plan for international control.

The attack, whatever it was—for the doctors didn't seem able to diagnose it too well—was more severe than the last one had been, and it took him longer to recover. He was out for most of five days—not unconscious, but in a kind of stupor from which he could not be roused. Tanya was nearly frantic.

"Absolute rest," said the doctors, when he was finally allowed to leave the hospital.

Tanya knew they must get out of Washington. The clammy heat was unbearable. She hated the vulgarly luxurious apartment they were living in, she hated the city and its atmosphere. But all this was secondary to the fact that Sebastian *had* to get away from the pressure that he was bound to be subjected to here. He had resigned from Valhalla six months before, thank God, but more and more things had piled up on him since.

On his desk among the stack of papers that she had somehow to sort and attend to was an appointment to go back to teaching at the University. She had a sudden nostalgia for the academic life, for the lovely house and garden, and especially for her piano, untouched during all these years—an intense, almost desperate longing for the old days before the war, before the Bolt. She was conscious, too, of an obscure need to be close to her parents again. And perhaps the place where she and Sebastian had been happy together, the familiar scene and the familiar faces, would help to speed his recovery. She decided, since he was in no condition to decide anything, that they would go back to the University. She made him sign the contract, which he did without protest, and made all the necessary arrangements. Gino came back from the summer camp in

the Adirondacks where he had spent the past two months, and
they all flew west to the University.

Sebastian convalesced slowly. Most of the time he was submerged in a deep, trancelike sleep. He would spend long afternoons stretched out in a chaise longue on the terrace, not sleeping, but looking fixedly into the distance, without blinking,
without changing his expression. He was very docile. He did
whatever Tanya told him. He did not smoke, he did not drink.
He ate whatever was put before him. He never asked for anything.

When he was awake he seemed to live only in the immediate, and to enjoy each passing moment. When he spoke he
never referred to the past or to the future or to the world beyond the limits of the garden. He would spend long hours with
Gino, telling him stories, explaining to him some of the mysteries of plant and animal life, of matter and motion, sometimes playing dominos or checkers with him, or simple children's games. With her he would occasionally converse, de-
lightfully and at length, about simple everyday things—food,
the weather, the way the garden grew, the minor mechanics of
domesticity—and at other times would hold forth on the poets
of the Greek *Anthology*, or else on Ovid, Catullus, or Virgil's
Eclogues, quoting long passages in Greek and Latin.

At the doctor's orders she guarded him against the outside
world, in the form of visitors, mail, or the telephone. This became increasingly difficult after the first week. She had had the
foresight to instruct Sebastian's secretary to follow them to the
University and had put her up in a downtown hotel, and to her
she forwarded all but his personal mail. She had had the telephone disconnected for all incoming calls. To protect the
house against unannounced callers she had found it necessary
to call upon a private detective agency. But the man who
turned up immediately after to take charge of guarding the
house proved to be one of Gregg's agents.

"Just leave it to us," he said soothingly, when she tried to
protest. "We'll take care of the situation as long as necessary.
No reason why you should go to any expense."

The whole situation was difficult and strained, and she knew that it could not continue indefinitely. Even here where all her ties were, she could not satisfy her longing to see old friends except for rare glimpses. She saw her parents only surreptitiously. She did not dare to leave the house except for the briefest of errands. Her prime concern was to see Sebastian regain his full health.

It was a new, wholly unfamiliar Sebastian that she was confronted with now. There was no trace of the fire and intensity that she had come to think of as an inseparable part of his nature, no restlessness or nervousness, no impatience, no curiosity. He did not ask to see a newspaper or try to turn on the radio. He was gentle and calm. Not unhappy, but surely not happy either. She simply had no clue to what was going on inside him. From time to time she was haunted by some phrase that she had once heard or read—like "burning oneself out." Had Sebastian burned himself out? Had the fire gone out of him, had the light of that exceptional intelligence failed? But when he did talk he was so coherent that she could not believe that anything was wrong with his mind. Dr. Dennis was not very helpful. He spoke of traumatism, of cumulative fatigue, of psychosomatic syndromes, and on the whole managed to make himself perfectly incomprehensible. But what she did seem to understand was that Dr. Dennis was quite satisfied with Sebastian's progress, that his passivity was a healthy concomitant of the healing process and that he would snap out of his condition as suddenly as it had come upon him.

The very first evening after things had become a little settled—Sebastian was already in bed—Tanya had sat down to her piano. *Her* piano, which Sebastian had given her so debonairly almost exactly eight years before. She had had it tuned, but in the first hours of playing it had the stiffness, the soullessness of all instruments that have been left long unused. And there was something wooden and lifeless about her playing, too. She did scales and exercises all the way up and down the keyboard, despaired repeatedly when she found how much her technique had fallen off. Her fingers no longer danced on the keys with the intoxicating spontaneity she had once delighted in, and she had lost much of that virtuosity of phrasing that had been a fundamental part of her musicianship. But after a few days she was able to convince herself that she was improving and she ceased to be overwhelmed by the impossibility of regaining her former skill.

"I've been listening to your playing," Sebastian said to her one day. "It has made me realize how much you must have missed a piano over all those months up on Valhalla. You must never be separated from your music again."

It was the first time since his breakdown that he had referred either to the past or to the future. It suddenly occurred to her that her playing might be good therapy, that it could conceivably hasten Sebastian's recovery. She began to play in the daytime when she knew he was awake—a little at a time at first, to make sure it did not disturb him. But it seemed to stimulate him, to stir his inner world to life, and this encouraged her to play at greater length. At mealtimes he would launch into discussions of music, and something of his old enthusiasm would come into his face and into his voice.

Soon Tanya's anxiety yielded to a beguiling charm that developed in her relation to Sebastian. He became more animated and more attentive to her. He slept less, moved about more freely in the house and in the garden. One night he came into her bed. He did not attempt to make love to her, but lay close against her all night. And after that he came every night.

They were close together again, on a basis of free give and take. But it was still confined to things immediate, bounded by the house and garden, though extending to the sky and also embracing the arts, especially music. Tanya hoped that as he gradually got better, and he *was* getting better, their sphere of mutual confidence would widen correspondingly until it became all-embracing. For the time being they intimately shared little enjoyments that carried them from morning and the breakfast coffee through the day and into the chaste but tender embraces of the night. And every afternoon, and sometimes in the evening, she would play for him while he sat where she could see him, and she could watch the magic operating in him—the music placing its healing hands upon him, gradually making him whole again.

Yet with all this she had a feeling of precariousness. Dr. Dennis was highly pleased with his patient's progress, but Tanya was beginning to dread the moment, which was bound to come, when Sebastian would again confront the outside world. Daily the pressure was becoming more difficult to resist. The government agents were having greater trouble holding the newspapermen at bay. Tanya had more and more frequent sessions with Sebastian's secretary, who was receiving ever more pressing calls from Washington and other parts of the country urgently requiring Sebastian's services. Dr. Dennis, who for weeks had been besieged by people demanding reports on Sebastian's health, was visited by an eminent colleague from the east with a mandate from the highest source to examine the distinguished patient personally. Dr. Dennis could not very well refuse.

After Dr. Matzger and Dr. Dennis had left, Tanya noticed a new look on Sebastian's face—a crafty and at the same time frightened look.

"What did he want?" Sebastian asked.

"He's a doctor," said Tanya. "Dr. Dennis just wanted him to have a look at you, to see how you were getting along."

Sebastian said nothing more, but she could see that something was working on his mind. Had the appearance of the strange doctor, or something he had said, given Sebastian for the first time an inkling that something was wrong with him?

"Play for me," he said a little later.

She had got out the score of Beethoven's Fourth Piano Concerto—the one she had played that evening long ago when Mark and Eve had come for dinner and Sebastian had sounded Mark out as a possible recruit for his unit. Perhaps some happy association from that time had spanned the years and would stir a strengthening emotion.

"Do you know, I think I'd like a martini," he said suddenly, after she had played for half an hour. It was the first time he had asked for a drink. She guessed that he must have remembered that other occasion.

Dr. Dennis had said that his reasonable wishes should be humored. He went himself to the drink cabinet in the dining room that he had not been near all these weeks, and got out the gin and the vermouth. He mixed the drink with his old skill, and they looked into each other's eyes over the rims of their full glasses. Sebastian looked almost happy.

There followed several pleasant, uneventful days. If only this could last forever, thought Tanya. Classes would begin in less than two weeks. She had put the announcement of the fall courses on the living-room table, not too conspicuously, but so far as she knew, Sebastian had not looked at it. Was he planning to teach? Would he be able to? She did not dare ask him. She only hoped their happy intimacy, circumscribed though it was, would last.

One morning at the breakfast table, unexpectedly, he looked at her.

"Where are the newspapers?" he asked.

She herself, during all this time, had seen no newspapers and was almost as much out of touch with the world as he was.

The next day they began to receive the papers regularly. Sebastian read them avidly the first day, then fell back into a kind of apathy and for several days looked through them only perfunctorily. She was aware of some struggle going on within him. Her playing calmed him, and there were more days of intimacy and peace. His movements were quicker, his responses sharper, his eyes more lively and more probing.

There came a day when he asked her if there wasn't any mail. She gave him a few of the hundreds of letters that had accumulated—she had not dared to open them herself.

"There must be a lot of other things," he said.

She could tell that his mind was now actively working to penetrate the fog in which it had been submerged all this time, and that the fog was beginning to lift. She was able to put him off for a few days longer, but finally had to send for Miss Riley, his secretary.

At the same time that Sebastian was visibly improving, his nervousness, his angular movements, returned, and a kind of anxiety appeared in the depths of his look. He was spending time at his desk, calculating and making notes for longer and longer spells, and he would pace back and forth the length of the living room. He had begun to smoke again.

He had long sessions with Miss Riley, dictating to her for an hour or more at a stretch. And then one day he announced that he was going to the University the following day, that he had made several appointments.

"Don't you think it's a little too soon for you to go out?" Tanya asked.

"I'm all right now," Sebastian replied. "I've already wasted too much time."

That evening he again mixed a martini, and they had wine with their dinner. He was sparkling, almost jovial, but under the bright surface there was an indefinable tenseness that troubled her.

When they went into the living room after dinner, and Gino had gone to bed, Sebastian became absent and uncommunicative. Tanya went to the piano and began to improvise. For the first time since they were back, since she had taken up playing again, she felt the music flow through her irresistibly, felt herself a part of it, and it was as it had been in the old days. Sebastian was not where she could see him, but she knew that he was there, and this music that was her language, that was their language, their secret language, must, she was sure, be flowing through him too, and he must be responding to it, must be in communion with her.

Everything was so uncertain, so difficult and so dangerous. There was so much that she did not understand. There were the fearful things that had happened. But although she had had doubts, she had never despaired. Sebastian had always been—one part of him at least—a stranger, a mysterious being, half man, half—half what? . . . She was tempted to say half god, but of course that was silly. A wild swan. The image had haunted her through the years. Into her music she wove all these threads, and among all these threads, constantly reappearing, forming a part of every pattern, ran one unbroken thread, pure gold, which was her love.

As she played on, carried as on great wings in a realm half dream, half reality, she suddenly and for no reason had the impression that she was in a void. Her playing faltered, and a chill came over her.

"Stop!"

It was Sebastian's voice; yet it did not sound like his voice. He appeared before her, his face livid.

"You must stop!" he said, and she could tell that he was controlling himself with difficulty.

He was looking at her, but it was as though he did not see her.

After a silence he said slowly, and his voice sounded far away:

"I don't want you ever to play for me again."

He did not come into her bed that night.

Chapter 41

THE papers were full of accounts of the new Bolt tests. Bigger and more powerful Bolts. The intensity of effect and the area of devastation were much greater than those of the first one. Improved techniques had made them much more economical, and they were now beginning to be turned out on a mass-production basis.

"Let's get the hell out of here!" Eve exploded, throwing on the floor the newspaper she had been reading. She had detested Washington from the first day, and each day she liked it less.

Mark had just come home at the end of the day after his last visit to the New Science Association office. Everything had been shipped off or otherwise disposed of, he had settled the final accounts and turned over the keys to the building manager. Now there was nothing to keep him here any longer, and Eve had been trying for over a week to get him to set a date for their departure.

But he had one more thing to do before he left Washington. Ever since his session with security agents Durant and Russell he had brooded over the story of alleged sabotage and spy activities that someone had inexplicably introduced into his file. The more he thought about it the more he was convinced that Gregg had something to do with it and that in any case he certainly knew something about it. Mark knew the story would block him in almost any kind of job he might try to find, and he was determined to get to the bottom of it if he could. He decided that while he was in Washington he would tackle Gregg. Gregg might not come through with everything he knew, but he must certainly have the answer to at least part of the riddle.

Gregg as top chief was harder to reach, however, than when he had been Mark's direct boss. Mark had to try for days to get through to him before he was finally able to arrange an interview.

He had bought no new clothes since he had got out of the army, and since he had not yet regained enough weight to fill his clothes properly, he constantly felt rather as though he were wearing a big brother's hand-me-downs. Besides which, his lightest suit was still too warm for Washington summer weather. Even before he reached the agency's headquarters his underwear and shirt were soaked through, he felt acutely uncomfortable, unpresentable, and somehow disreputable. Fortunately the building was air-conditioned, and by the time he was ushered into Gregg's office after a wait of only five minutes he had recovered some of his self-assurance.

Gregg greeted him quite cordially.

"Glad to see you, Ampter," he said, getting up and coming forward to shake hands. He looked at Mark appraisingly. "You took something of a beating out there in the Pacific, didn't you?"

They sat down and talked for a bit about the war.

"And what can I do for you?" Gregg asked presently. He had never been much given to chitchat.

Mark looked at him. There was nothing in Gregg's attitude to indicate that he carried any kind of grudge. But the Chief had always been an enigma to him. Mark had been struck, on entering, to note how much this office resembled his old office back in town; though it was more than twice as big, and here the walls were white, the all-over carpeting battleship-gray, and the furniture black. There was the same bareness: not a picture on the walls, not an object on the huge shiny black desk except a gray blotter in a black blotter pad. Nothing to give anyone a clue to the character of the man, his tastes, his interests—except that the very absence of paraphernalia of any kind might suggest an almost pathological reluctance to reveal anything more of himself than he could possibly help. Mark knew that Gregg would never do anything he didn't want to do, and that he would never let himself be caught off guard.

He took a long shot.

"Zelinski still working for you?"

Gregg eyed him cannily. He shrugged his shoulders ever so slightly, reminding Mark of an old lion watching a cub make a bid for attention.

"Don't jump so fast."

He kept Mark waiting. He was relaxed. Mark suddenly felt a little tingle at the top of his spine, realizing—as one does sometimes in rushing headlong into something, and it is too late to turn back—the man he was up against. He controlled the tingling with an effort, and had, for the first time in months, the reflex of reaching for a cigarette. He hadn't smoked for well over a year—since he was wounded in Okinawa.

"I know Zelinski," Gregg said easily, and let the silence fall again.

"Alexander Zelinski," he said.

Another silence.

"Funny sort of a guy, they tell me."

Gregg looked at Mark then, as though he had for a moment forgotten he was there.

"But he never worked for me."

Perhaps the Chief had trained him too well. Mark knew now the Chief was lying. His mind was working overtime. The Chief was not given to lying: he was far above that. Why was he lying now?

He looked at Gregg evenly across the polished top of his desk.

"You wanted to pin something on Bloch," he said slowly. "You got hold of Zelinski. You cooked up that story about the German scientists and got him to pass it on to me so that I would put it up to Bloch as a business proposition."

Gregg's face was completely deadpan. All this had come to Mark on the spur of the moment. But it could be right. Maybe it was right.

"I knew it was a phony," Mark went on. "But I wanted to warn Bloch. I told his wife."

Mark had the impression that Gregg was nodding, though his head didn't seem to move.

"This is all very interesting," Gregg said. "What do you want me to do with it?"

"Someone," said Mark, weighing his words, "someone who knew this—about Zelinski's approach to me, and my conversation with Mrs. Bloch—has invented a very damaging story about me—"

"I know," Gregg said. "It's in our records. But there's one thing I don't go along with. I'm not at all convinced that it's an invented story."

"What do you mean?"

Gregg gave Mark a long, measured look. "I mean that it looks to me to be true."

Mark gasped. "Look here!"

Gregg waited.

"It's sheer fabrication," Mark said. "It's a vicious lie, invented by someone who had it in for me."

After another silence Gregg said, in a matter-of-fact voice, "We have it from the best possible source."

Mark felt himself shaking his head.

Gregg's eyes were boring into him. "You know whom I mean," he said.

Mark was shaking his head more and more violently. "No!" He could hardly get his breath. "No! It's not true!"

Gregg reached for a telephone receiver concealed in his desk, gave a brief order, and got up.

"Come with me," he said.

He led the way out to the elevator. They got out several floors below and walked down a long corridor and into a kind of large laboratory with a variety of instruments and machinery.

"Right in here, sir," said a young man in a white blouse, and led them into a smaller room where a dozen or so chairs faced a long table with a tape recorder and other instruments.

"I know you wouldn't take my word for it, and I wouldn't expect you to," Gregg said as he made Mark sit down.

Mark was in a daze. He could hardly control his movements. He half fell into the oak armchair. The technician was tinkering with the recorder and putting in a reel of tape. There was a faint hum as the motor was turned on, and the tape was reeled through without registering the sound.

"It's close to the end," Gregg said to the technician. He watched the reels spin. "There. Try it there to see where we are."

There was a whisper that rose to a roar, and then as the technician adjusted the volume and the pitch Mark recognized Gregg's voice, clear, unmistakable.

"That's just the way I hoped you'd feel about it, Doctor," Gregg's voice was saying. "I feel that if we have your confidence, as you have ours, it'll make everything . . ."

"Yes, that's it," Gregg broke in, "but a little farther on."

A moment later the sound was turned on again and Mark heard:

". . . want to make pretty sure that he no longer had any commitments or attachments . . ."

And he knew that this was Sebastian. He would have recognized his voice among a million.

"Well, that is of course the way we'd like it," Gregg's voice said, "but we don't after all have much choice."

"The way I look at it is this . . ." and Sebastian's voice was now speaking, "if a man is a communist he is bound to have a divided loyalty. He thereby becomes unreliable, and therefore dangerous."

The voice was Sebastian's. But it was not Sebastian speaking. Mark felt dizzy. He wanted to get outside.

"I don't want to hear any more," he said, feeling himself choking.

"Take it easy," said Gregg. "You've got to hear it."

The tape continued to give forth the voices, and there was something inexorable about it. Sebastian was giving names, revealing the party or left-wing affiliations of one after another of all his friends, colleagues, students.

"How about Mark Ampter?" he heard Gregg's voice say.

Mark jumped up.

"No, no! I'm getting out of here!"

He felt indecent.

Gregg seized his arm with a powerful hand, and as he heard Sebastian's voice say "He could very well be a member" he collapsed on the chair.

It went on. Mark was feeling more and more sick.

"We're nearly at the end now," Gregg said, and he held his hand on Mark's forearm. There was something both cruel and calming about that grasp.

"Now I have just one last question to ask you," he heard Gregg's voice say over the tape, "and you will realize, in the light of all we've been saying, that it's the most important of all." There was a silence. "I want you to give me the name of that intermediary. You know who I mean."

Mark held his breath. He was all tight inside, and he felt his newly repaired organs straining.

"I don't think I should tell you," Sebastian's voice said.

"I understand your reasons," said Gregg's voice. "But we want to know."

Mark began to tremble in all his limbs.

"Steady," said Gregg, and his hand gave a little pressure on Mark's arm.

"This man is innocent," Mark heard Sebastian's voice say. "He was not really involved. His approaches, I am sure, were not repeated. And he is now in the army, overseas, where it is certainly impossible for him to have any activity so far as the project is concerned."

Mark was still trembling.

"If you will not tell me his name," said Gregg's voice, and it had an implacable quality, "General Sproncke will order you tomorrow to give it to him. That, as you know, will look bad in the record. I'm not ordering you. I have no authority to. I'm merely asking you."

In the silence that followed Mark was aware of the noiseless turning of the motor, the tiny thread of light on the passing tape. He had stopped breathing.

"Well," he heard Sebastian's voice say, followed by another silence which was almost unendurable. And then, low but clear: "It was Mark Ampter."

Mark was shaken by a kind of sob which he tried in vain to hold back.

"He was a friend of yours?" he heard Gregg's voice say.

"Yes."

"Let me go!" Mark cried, and tried to wrench his arm free. But Gregg held it in an iron grip.

"Just one moment," he said. "It's almost over."

Gregg's voice said, "He made those approaches you told Lieutenant Siracusa about?"

"Yes," said Sebastian's voice.

"Is that all?"

"That's all."

Gregg let go of Mark's arm. The tape had wound itself out, and the young technician turned off the motor.

"Let's go back to my office," Gregg said.

"No," Mark said. The tears in his eyes blurred his vision, but he made no effort to wipe them away. He was struggling with all his might to keep from being sucked down into the pit of humiliation that he felt yawning beneath him. A sullen rage began to form and mount in him slowly, like a tide, steadying him.

"No," he said, making an effort to keep his voice even. "There is nothing more I want to know."

Chapter 42

GENERAL FORESTER was thinking, as O.S.P. Director Gregg sat down, that he was one of the most intelligent men he had occasion to deal with. With him you didn't have to waste any words. He knew what you wanted to say almost before you spoke, and he nearly always came up with an answer.

"I suppose your file on Bloch is pretty complete," Forester said by way of opening the discussion.

"Quite complete, sir."

"And I take it you yourself are pretty familiar with it?"

"I've been working on the case for eight years," said Gregg. "I'm tempted to say that I know more about Sebastian Bloch than I do about myself."

Forester laughed good-humoredly. It was a pleasure to work with a man like Gregg. A sleuth to the fingertips. A cool precision instrument of a mind. Yet easy on the give-and-take, and human enough in his way.

Forester got up from his swivel chair and began to walk slowly along the window wall of the big office, toward the potted rubber tree.

"As you know," he said, "we're getting ready to move in on Bloch any day now." He started pacing back. "He's becoming too much of a risk. Too powerful. And we'll never know where we stand with him. Besides, he's no longer indispensable.

There's a whole new crop of young men coming up—very good ones, too, with no carry-over."

He stopped at his desk and rested his fingers lightly on its surface.

"What I called you in for today," he said. "We'll be sending some people from our legal staff over to your office in the next few days. What I'd like to know from you—partly for my own information, but not only that. We have of course this mass of derogatory information against Bloch extending over a period of years, and there's no real problem about that. But in your opinion, looking at the whole picture—what is the one thing, the outstanding thing that the case, so to say, ought to focus on. What I mean, if there is any incident that in your mind gives the crux of the man's character, and that—"

"Character," Gregg broke in. "Character is the most important thing."

"You know what I mean?" Forester said, warming to the other's understanding.

"Yes," Gregg said.

Forester looked at him expectantly.

"There's this very remarkable man," Gregg continued. "He's tops in his field, and all that. He has everything in his favor. Likable, too. But he has a character weakness. It ruins everything."

"Yes," Forester said. It was what he felt, too. "Could you put your finger on it?—the weakness, I mean. The character weakness."

Gregg sat back and folded his hands. A mellow look came over him.

"I never went to school when I was a youngster," he said. "Until I went to law school. And even then I just did my own reading and took examinations. I always did a lot of reading. There was an old man I used to know. Was sort of a father to me. He taught me a lot."

Forester listened patiently. All this seemed to be beside the point, but he knew Gregg and he listened.

"He made me read some of the Greek tragedies," Gregg

went on. "Aeschylus and Sophocles. There was a play about Oedipus. He was a king and a wonderful man. He was wise and just and humane. But he murdered his father and went to bed with his mother and did a lot of mischief and came to a bad end. Not really any of his own doing. There was a kind of curse on him. The gods, when he was born, gave a little twist to his character, and it spoiled everything for him."

"Yes," Forester said eagerly. "And Bloch? What is the twist, the weakness?"

Gregg shook his head. "I guess we'll never really know. But to my mind it's pride. A pride of the mind that is measureless. He's intelligent, all right. Maybe he's more intelligent than anybody else. But even so. One man's intelligence. There's something else that's much more important. But he doesn't know it. He thinks he has it all in his head."

Forester nodded. "You know, I've felt that. Maybe that's what's always bothered me."

"Coming back to your question," Gregg said. Forester suddenly realized that he himself had for a moment forgotten it, and that Gregg had let himself go as he never remembered him doing. "The best bet is the mess he got himself into over his friend Mark Ampter."

"Ah, yes! That would have been my guess too."

"It's got everything," said Gregg. "Blatant disregard of security regulations, withholding of critically important information, setting up of his own judgment against the combined judgment of the authorities, reluctant compliance with the decisions of superiors, and finally—this sort of caps it—attempting to dismiss the whole thing by a barefaced lie, and thereby putting loyalty to a friend above loyalty to country."

Forester had followed him until he got to the last point, and there he lost his bearings.

"Let me get it straight," he said. "There was this incident that happened way back there, some four years ago or so. This Russian fellow Zelinski got Ampter to approach his friend Bloch and try to get him to co-operate—"

"No," said Gregg. "That isn't quite the way it was." He

leaned forward in his seat, resting one elbow on one knee. "You'll see it all in the documents, but let me go over it with you. Mark Ampter made these five approaches that you've read about in the file—"

"But I thought—"

"Wait a minute, let me go on. He made these five approaches. Bloch got wind of it. But he didn't say anything about it. He didn't want to get his friend in trouble. So for months there was this danger that he should have warned us about but didn't. Meanwhile he was worried about it. Then we got a clue on the thing, and we went after Bloch, and he finally broke down and told us about it. But by then it was too late for us to do anything. The trail was cold. Ampter got away to the Pacific war. And we were never able to pin anything definite on Zelinski. All that was some four years ago. Now we come to the present time. Ampter is demobilized. We send out our men to interrogate him. He denies the whole thing. He invents an innocent story about Zelinski's having asked him to approach Bloch in order to have him get in touch with some German scientists. Ampter claims he took no stock in Zelinski, and simply reported his conversation to Bloch—through his wife—just in order to warn him."

Gregg edged farther forward on his chair, resting both elbows on his knees. "Now listen to this: shortly after our men interviewed Ampter, he and Bloch got together. We have no record of what they said to each other; they did their talking in the garden. But only a couple of weeks or so after that, we had Bloch come in to our Washington office. We asked him about Ampter and the Zelinski matter. Well, believe it or not, he then gave us substantially the same story that Ampter had given us just a short while before—and incidentally tried to make us believe he had seen Ampter *before* Ampter had been interrogated, so as to make his testimony look spontaneous. But we happened to know the dates."

Forester was still a little puzzled. "But what about the story he had already told about the other approaches? What did he say about those?"

"He said he had invented it."

Forester tried to piece all the elements together in his mind. It didn't quite make sense.

"Anyway," Forester said finally, "now he has admitted that his first story was a lie."

Gregg shook his head.

"You don't get it. These two—Block and Ampter—are *friends*. Very close friends. Now you may not have a very high opinion of Bloch's veracity or integrity after reading his record. But even so, is it reasonable to believe that he would deliberately invent a story that would show that his friend was involved in a criminal espionage conspiracy, when the truth would show that he was perfectly innocent?"

"I find that hard to believe," Forester admitted.

"So do I," said Gregg. "And we're forced to conclude that the story he told to our officers in Valhalla four years ago about Ampter's approaches to various scientists for purposes of sabotage and espionage was the truth, and that his recent story to the effect that Ampter simply communicated a suggestion which he had no intention of following up is a lie."

"I get it now," said Forester. "And that also brings the matter right up to date, doesn't it?"

"Yes," said Gregg. "There is also that advantage."

Chapter 43

SEBASTIAN'S hand went limp, and the letter it was holding fell to the floor.

"Mark," his lips whispered. "Mark!"

It was a long letter. A letter of farewell. Passages of it ran through his mind . . . *You taught me that man deepens his humanity through communion with his fellow man . . . You*

*taught me that the isolated individual is sterile, and that true
fertility resides in the people. You taught me . . .* All this was
so long ago! And now Mark had found out about his fabrication. He was sorry about that. But then Mark had been a special agent, and had probably been responsible for a lot of the
trouble that had come to *him.* They had loved each other, and
in loving each other had hurt each other. And that, perhaps,
was the law of human life.

Was it his recent illness—or was it something deeper, more
fundamental—that made everything seem to stand out in fearful sharpness these days? Had his mind grown more percep-
tive? His eyes keener? Every blade of grass, every twig, every
detail of masonry, seemed to have an intensity all its own.
Looking up from his work with his reading glasses still on, he
would watch a fly on the pane of glass for minutes on end, marveling at the details of the veining on its transparent wings, at
the articulations of its tiny legs.

It was not only the physical things, perceptible to the senses,
that had this hallucinatory clarity, but also the things that
were hidden, that eluded the senses. It was as though the veils
that concealed or obscured the blinding light of reality from
men were gradually, progressively, lifting for him. And he was
able to see that this reality was both fixed and evolving, was
both one and many, both absolute and relative.

The fact that nothing was final had come as a revelation.
The world was both an instrument and an end, and society too,
and the individuals that composed it, were both instrument
and end. The two hundred thousand men, women and children who had been destroyed by the Monster were but a part
of a larger pattern. And it was necessary to see the whole pattern, in which they would appear not as the unfortunate victims of a historic accident but as the predestined agents of a
higher plan.

Yet this morning, as he read in the paper of the death of
three more belated victims of the Monster in a hospital, he was
able to participate, with all his organs, in all the atrocity of

their suffering. His own ailing, aching body could thus be the repository of all earthly suffering.

Ever more vividly he was conscious of the fatality that was carrying him, and the world, as on a current, toward a solution. Fatality—current—the world—himself: all separate and yet one, each a part of the others and each at the same time all, and all participating in the solution. And he would be alone, yet in being alone he would embody all mankind.

Visions of cataclysm and terror, the heavens splitting, the earth opening, oceans sinking into the yawning crevasses left by the convulsive shudders created by a new race of super-Monsters run rampant. Mountains toppling, skyscrapers pulverized, cities bursting like giant hand grenades, avalanches of bodies incinerated, the earth scorched, lakes and rivers parched. Desolation, a lunar desert, the sterile emptiness of interstellar spaces. A harvest of death, measured no longer in tens or hundreds of thousands, but in millions, tens of millions, hundreds of millions: cosmic annihilation.

Yet if he had been the instrument of inexorable necessity, he had also been moved by a great love. And this love would bear fruit.

He was familiar with death. But what he envisioned now, in the new light that illuminated all things for him, was another dimension of being beyond the span of his life's mission.

He would vanish. But he would be present still. He would forever be a part of this life and of this earth that he had loved. He would be present in the cool winds that blew over the desert sands, and in the life-bringing rains. He would be present in the brightness of the sun and in the dancing waves of the sea. He would be present in the budding leaves of spring and in the deepening red of autumn. He would be the white heron poised on outspread wings above the marsh in the rosy dawn, he would be the antelope leaping in the mountain, he would be the trout in the icy stream, he would be the many-voiced song that rose from field and forest. He would be the night that fell like a benediction over the tired earth after the heat of a long day.

He would be present among men. Wherever men existed, in solitude or in community, his spirit would hover over them. Wherever men labored, struggled, suffered, his presence would lighten the weight of their days. He would be the gesture to ease the movement of a task, he would be the symbol that would illuminate the formulation of a theorem, he would be the lightning flash of insight that would open new vistas for the mind. And wherever men gathered, in meditation, in worship, in council, in fear or in jubilation, he would be the faith, the inspiration, the hope, the love that would bind them together.

He would be nothing, and he would be all.

He went through the rooms of the house. Only the furniture and objects that had belonged to the original owner were left. All their own things had been put in storage. The suitcases— Tanya's and Gino's and his—were all in the front entrance. Tom would come and fetch them in the car in twenty minutes.

He had started his courses. For a short while he had thought he could do it—devote most of his time to teaching and research, go back to the old life. But it hadn't worked out. There were too many demands on him. The pressures were becoming too great. An ever more appalling menace hung over the world. Now they were all flying back to Washington.

Gino came running out of his room and threw himself headlong against his legs, nearly knocking him over.

"For heaven's sake, stop acting like a four-year-old!" To Gino the whole business of moving, of pulling up roots, of starting a new life, was one huge lark. He was seven years old, and probably fairly mature for his age. But he still lived only in the moment. Now he was off in the direction of the kitchen, probably to say good-by to Peradventure the cat, who was being adopted by a neighbor.

Tanya came into the living room wearing her green tailored suit; and as she approached, it suddenly reminded him of the suit she had worn that time—it was eight years ago—when she had come to him and he had given her the grand piano. And she had the same troubled look now. Her face was pinched and a little pale as though she had been weeping.

She fished in her bag and pulled out an envelope and handed it to him.

"Here, you'd better take this now," she said. "It's your ticket."

He looked at her.

"What about yours—and Gino's?"

She parted her lips, but no sound came immediately. Then he heard her say:

"We're not going."

"What do you mean?"

He had heard the words, but they conveyed no meaning to him.

"Gino and I aren't going with you to Washington," she said, more composed. "We're going to my parents'."

"And then what?" Sebastian was bewildered.

"I haven't any definite plans. Just that—" She had started to say something, but the words didn't come. Her eyes looked strange.

"What is it?" he said. "What's wrong?"

"I—I'm leaving you, Sebastian." She swallowed and tried to smile, but it didn't work.

Sebastian looked at her and let the import of her words slowly penetrate him. This too, he recognized, fitted into the pattern. In what lay ahead there was no room for Tanya, no room for Gino. And this was surely the easiest way. But what exactly was it that had brought her to this decision? And why was she making it just now? He asked himself these questions, yet they did not seem too pressing.

"I haven't been very good for you, darling," he said, shaking his head.

He looked at her, studying her features, deriving something of the aesthetic thrill that it always had given him to contemplate her sheer beauty. Yet even as he did so he was aware of a certain unreality. Tanya was already out of his life. She had been out of it for a long time.

"It isn't that," Tanya said. "You've been very kind, very considerate . . ."

She was finding it difficult to speak.

"It's—it's—I don't know how to say it. But I can't live with you any more. You—you've changed so. I don't recognize you . . ."

Her face suddenly turned even paler.

"You frighten me. You've become—you've become . . ."

Something welled up in her that congested her face, that she tried to control, to keep down.

"You've become *inhuman!*" she managed to burst out.

And then she broke into uncontrollable sobs.

He was going to Washington. What awaited him there? He had enemies. Would they let him do what he had to do?

Tanya and Gino had driven out to the airport with him and he had said good-by to them. His wife. His son. He would probably not see them again. There was a sadness in the parting. But he did not feel too great emotion. All this belonged to a minor order of reality.

As the plane reached its cruising altitude and his ears grew accustomed to the roar of the motors, he remembered Tanya's face—the face of a hurt, angry child. "You've become inhuman!" she had cried.

He nodded his head slowly as he sat, unnoticed, alone, in the cabin of the airliner flying over fields and woods and rivers. He remembered Mark. He remembered Tanya; her beauty, her grace, her love. He remembered other women. He remembered students, colleagues, friends, comrades; many discussions, many gatherings; convictions, passions, hopes . . .

"Yes," he whispered to himself. "Yes."

San Francisco, 1948–Paris, 1958